She Wants Her

She Wants Her

A NOVEL BY
TASHA C. MILLER

CREATIVE AFFLICTIONS PRESS

ISBN-10:0985477806
ISBN-13:978-0-9854778-0-6

Author photograph: © Tasha C. Miller
Editing: Jill Bailin
Jacket design: Tasha C. Miller
Jacket photography: Javier Sánchez

FOR MOMMY

YOU'RE GONNA HEAR THE PAGES TURN
--JILL SCOTT,
CIRCA 2012

SHE WANTS HER

"Can I ask you a personal question?" Jacqueline sat with the leggy, brown-haired receptionist and pointed to Cleopatra in the courtyard. "You dated her? The tall, cocoa dread?"

"Oh. Cleopatra?" Nikki rolled her eyes. "Uhmm hmmm. Insatiable. She had me speaking in tongues, all night, every night. I would cry." She pretended to wipe tears from her face.

"So, what is Cleopatra like? What's she into?"

"Sex." Nikki massaged the back of her own neck while she rotated her head from left to right and smiled.

"Ok, when you managed to control yourself, what else did you do?" Jacqueline asked.

"I couldn't restrain myself. We had sex *nonstop*." She shook her finger in the air. "Always. I couldn't get enough."

Jacqueline exhaled. This was exasperating. "So, what happened between you two, then?"

"Why all the questions? Are you interested in her? She obviously hasn't seen *your* pretty ass yet. You are just her type, full breasts, plump ass. Get in front of her, and she'll handle the rest."

"Good to know. Why'd you break up, though?"

"I fell in love with her." Nikki gazed over at Cleopatra. "She doesn't do relationships."

◘ ◘ ◘

Jacqueline Angel Tripp was almost beautiful enough to be able to hide her inner torment. She was a gentle soul from a loving family, who as a little girl realized she was gay. She remembers as a seven-year-old being attracted to females, but she didn't know what it was or that there was a name for it until she kissed her best friend, and the girls' parent's forbade her to play with Jacqueline ever again. The attraction to women never went away and persisted into high school and beyond. In her early teens she admitted to herself that she was gay but shared that declaration with no one. She suppressed her desires to be with women, and she lived an invisible existence with no one seeing who she really was. She'd lived her life never once giving in to temptation – until she laid eyes on Cleopatra Giovanni.

Most of Cleopatra's ex-girlfriends were all too willing to reminisce. And they told Jacqueline much more than she ever wanted to learn, but at the same time not enough – none of them could tell her who Cleopatra was *as a person*. Jacqueline didn't want to believe that a woman so young and accomplished was as one-dimensional as her exes made her out to be. There had to be more to her, and Jacqueline wanted to know what it was.

Jacqueline had lunch with Paulina, a slinky Jamaican woman from accounting, who also opened up to her about Cleopatra.

"Cleopatra has a sensitive heart, but she never lets anyone see the soft side of her. To be honest, you don't care when she's fucking the perm right out of your head, you know?" She laughed as she stuck the fingers of her left hand in her wild afro and practically inhaled a forkful of yellow plantains with her right.

"What's her personality like? What is she like, really?"

"She's dominating. She'll fling you around the bedroom, girl, if you let her."

"Interesting, ok. But I meant, what is she like to be around?" Jacqueline took a bite of her salad and covered her mouth with a napkin. "Is she nice? Funny? Sweet? What?"

Paulina's eyes glazed over. "We didn't talk much, never seemed to be enough time. Hours passed like seconds, weekends like minutes."

"How long did you date?"

"Two months. I confessed my love for her, and she bailed on me. She said I didn't know what love was." Recalling that moment, she looked annoyed. "The problem is not falling in love with Cleopatra, the problem is getting her to fall in love with you. She won't allow it. And the crazy part is, she decides what she's going to do with you the first time she meets you. Determines your destiny right on the spot."

"What do you mean?"

"Come at her like a ho and she'll treat you like one. Come at her like you can't control yourself, give it up too soon, or do something like tell her you aren't wearing panties on the first date and you'll be a jump-off, nothing more. Good luck, girl, you're going to need it."

No woman had ever had an effect on Jacqueline like Cleopatra, and they hadn't even met. Jacqueline thought at the least Cleopatra would be the one to turn her out; she would give herself to her. The fantasy occurred to her after she caught a glimpse of Cleopatra while she was leaving the company gym one early morning before work. Muscles towered up Cleopatra's six-foot, dreadlocked chocolate frame.

Jacqueline practically melted when she thought Cleopatra was smiling in her direction. She fantasized about her full lips making love to her, and dreams of Cleopatra's rippling body invading her kept Jacqueline up most nights.

She set out on a mission to get Cleopatra. It started with getting to know her, as much as she could from a distance. Jacqueline went to the company website, and memorized Cleopatra's bio, which was extremely impressive. At only twenty-five years of age, just a few months out of the Stern School of Business at NYU, Cleopatra had landed the position of Executive Vice President of Asset Management at Midtown Properties.

Jacqueline Googled her, but didn't find much of personal interest, just a few social media accounts with sparse activity. No doubt she was too busy doing other things. Jacqueline wondered who and what those other things might be. This research was nothing other women hadn't done before to get close to Cleopatra, but Jacqueline took it one step further. She befriended every woman at work who had dated her – women who had labeled themselves as being *Cleopatra'd*.

Jacqueline had a conversation over lunch with Carmen, a straight, buxom Haitian woman from human resources who had also dated Cleopatra.

"But you're straight, right?"

"I am. At least, I used to be." The large-breasted woman leaned forward, her chest comfortably resting on the table. "Cleopatra did it to me." Carmen sighed as she leaned back in her chair. She released her hair from its bun and let her black curls fall to her shoulders. "I was in this same cafeteria having lunch with my then-fiancé right over there." She pointed to the row of tables lined up against the wall of windows. "Cleopatra sat at the next table, and something drew me to her. She's obviously gay, but she's pretty, and so fucking masculine, but she doesn't look like a man. You know what I mean?"

"Yeah, I do." Jacqueline smiled and squeezed her thighs together. "So what happened?"

"I got up, and walked over to her table. Some woman was with her, but I ignored her, and I whispered something in Cleopatra's ear."

Jacqueline pried for an answer. "What? What did you whisper?"

"This is embarrassing." The woman looked down at her plate. "I said I wanted her to fuck me."

When Jacqueline realized her mouth was open, she tried to compose herself. "Let me get this straight. You left your fiancé at the table, walked over to Cleopatra, and said *that*? What did she do?"

"She smiled, and she nodded, and she didn't let on to her date what I said. She was unfazed. As if women tell her every day they want to fuck her. I don't know. Maybe they do." The woman palmed her breasts to adjust her cleavage. "Such a turn-on. After that, I pursued the hell out of her. But she knew I was engaged and she told me to stay away from her. So I lied, and I said I called off my engagement. I even stopped wearing my ring whenever I was around her. Eventually I wore her down, and then, you know she wore me *out*." She slapped the table. "Let's just say Cleopatra loves the female body. She will leave no part of it neglected." Carmen exhaled. "I'm sorry, I went there for a minute." She involuntarily caressed her own breasts. "Ask her to stick her tongue out."

"Why? Is it pierced or something?"

"No. Trust me. It's the gift that keeps on giving. Just try to get her to stick it out."

"You're serious?" Jacqueline shook her head. "So why did you break up?"

"My fiancé caught her throwing my back out, I mean my ankles were literally in the air. He gave me an ultimatum, him or her. I chose her, but she didn't choose me for long, she was done with me a couple of months later."

"That didn't piss you off?" Jacqueline asked. "You broke up with your fiancé for her."

"I couldn't be mad. I lied because I wanted to fuck her, I mean, who does that? The fault is with me. Anyway, I got a lifetime of memories."

"Are you friends now, at least?"

"No, I can't be her friend. Every time I see her I get flashes of the fits she put my body through. Who wants a friend like that? But she did send my mother a beautiful basket for

Mother's Day. My mom absolutely loved her. Do you want some advice? If you want more than two months of amazing sex, Cleopatra is not your woman. You're going to end up being her jump-off if you give in too soon, which is damn near impossible not to do. Don't say I didn't warn you when she breaks your heart, girl."

The warnings that Cleopatra would crush her fell on deaf ears. It had been weeks since she'd first laid eyes on her and now Jacqueline was all in, and she had wasted enough time. Something had to be done. Cleopatra liked voluptuous, feminine women and they all seemed obsessed with her sex. And she didn't keep them around long. That's pretty much all Jacqueline had learned. The vivid dramatizations of Cleopatra's tongue-flick and hip-pop left Jacqueline dizzy. She tried not to let her fantasies distract her. Jacqueline couldn't figure out what exactly drew her so strongly to Cleopatra, made her act irrationally, and made her ready do things she had never done before. But Jacqueline was ready to explore her sexuality and wanted Cleopatra to be her first, Cleopatra intrigued her, but there had to be more to her, Jacqueline was certain of it, more than any of those other women had been able to unearth. For the first time in Jacqueline's life, she refused to let fear or anything else keep her from her deepest desire: to be with a woman and maybe even fall in love. She longed for Cleopatra, and she was going to have her.

Time for some action.

IN THE BEGINNING: YOU LOVED HOW I FUCKED YOU

"Come here." Cleopatra said. "I want to whisper something to you."

Trina, the Dominican woman whose dark brown eyes lit up whenever she looked at Cleopatra, danced across her small Washington Heights apartment and sat down on the rickety black futon. She positioned her ear in front of Cleopatra's lips.

"I want you." Her breath tickled Trina's ear, and her long locs brushed against Trina's breasts, causing her to jerk away.

Cleopatra pulled her back to her mouth and kissed her. She tasted the chicharrones de pollo and maduros that Trina had eaten on her tongue. She kissed down her neck making a path to her chest; Trina smelled of the various oils she soaked her body in whenever she was going to see Cleopatra. Her chiseled face slid on the oil down to Trina's breasts while her strong

7

hands slipped up her back. Her fingertips massaged Trina into submission as she climbed on top of Cleopatra and straddled her. Her short, cotton skirt abandoned her bare ass, rolled up around her waist and now served only as a belt. She leaned back and rested her hands on Cleopatra's knees, giving her a full view of her shaved pussy.

Cleopatra nodded her head, and the corners of her mouth turned up as she thought about everything she was about to do to Trina. She kissed Trina hard as she slid her thumb inside of her. Trina moaned as she grinded on top of Cleopatra, hoping that she had packed a surprise for her underneath her baggy jeans. "Got something for me, papi?" Her breasts hit Cleopatra in the face, and when she bounced hard on her hand, she caught herself.

"Stop." She tried to climb off Cleopatra, but her thighs quivered and her body refused to release Cleopatra's thumb.

"You don't look like you want me to stop." Cleopatra circled her hard nipples through her thin pink camisole.

She kissed Cleopatra again, and sucked her thumb into her mouth.

"No, I gotta stop." Trina's legs finally relaxed enough to allow her to slide off of Cleopatra's lap. She fixed her skirt and paced around the tiny living room. The apartment was neat, but nowhere near clean – the only things she bothered to keep clean were the sheets. Trina stumbled over to the end table and lit a Nag Champa incense stick. Now the living room reeked of fried chicken, incense, her Fordham Road body oils and wet pussy.

"What's wrong with you?" Cleopatra jumped up and opened up a window. Merengue blared from the street below and filled the apartment. Cleopatra stuck her head out the window into the fresh air.

"Nothing. You want to go out somewhere?" Trina sat down on the futon.

"I want to stay here." Cleopatra walked over to her, bent down and kissed her on the neck. The enticing aroma of empanadas and chimichurris that swirled through the open window from the street vendors below made Cleopatra hungry.

"You make this so hard." Trina said.

"That's how you like it, hard."

Trina's chest heaved. She pulled Cleopatra on top of her by her belt buckle. Sprawled across the futon, she threw the oversized rainbow pillows to the floor as Cleopatra put her weight on her. She spread her legs wide as the wetness welled up between them.

"Motherfucker," she whispered in Cleopatra's ear when she realized she was strapped. "You already have it on?" She ripped open Cleopatra's white button-down shirt, sending multiple buttons bouncing to the floor and revealing a black wife beater underneath. She kissed Cleopatra hard, biting her. She frantically unbuckled her belt, and undid the button on her jeans. She mustered up all of her strength.

"Cleopatra, stop." Trina pushed her away again.

"Seriously?" Cleopatra sat up on the futon. "What's wrong?"

"Can we just talk for once? I mean we are always, always butt naked and sweaty in the bed." Trina's breath was heavy as she squeezed her thighs tight together.

"True. But that probably has something to do with you pulling my clothes off the moment you see me and never wearing panties." Cleopatra defended herself. "So, what's on your mind?" Cleopatra stared at her as she waited for a response. The noise from St. Nicholas Avenue below filtered through the open window, filling the apartment. "What do you want to talk about? Current events, war, politics, the stock market? Read any good books recently?"

Trina twirled her curly black hair around her index finger as she thought about everything she wanted Cleopatra to do to her. The imprint of her dick hung low in her jeans, and Trina needed it. She looked at the muscles in Cleopatra's arms, the same strong arms that held her up and allowed her to pound at her body for hours at a time.

"Uhm…what do you like to do in your free time?" Cleopatra persisted.

Trina flicked her tongue, and smirked at her.

"Besides that."

"I like to shop a lot. I can shop all day and never get tired."

Wow. That's all you got, huh? Cleopatra wondered why someone with no conversation wanted to have one. "Ok, that's cool. What else? What are you passionate about in life? What's your calling?"

"Shopping," she said confidently. "I love to shop. Did I say that already?" She moved closer to Cleopatra on the futon.

"So have you read anything interesting lately?" Cleopatra tried again, ignoring her comment about shopping, and zipping up her jeans.

"No, I don't really read."

"You don't really read?" Cleopatra mouthed the words in slow motion, she put her shirt back on and buttoned up the few buttons she had left. Cleopatra thought about all of the other places she could be on a rainy Friday night in late May. All the other sheets she could be in between if she left right now.

Trina stared at Cleopatra's lips. She moved in closer and kissed her.

Cleopatra broke away from her. "I should go." She lunged for her coat.

Trina followed her and blocked the door.

"What are you doing?" Cleopatra put on her black leather jacket and tightened her belt.

"How bad do you want me?" Trina grabbed Cleopatra by her coat, massaging the butter-soft material between her fingers before pulling Cleopatra by her locs.

Cleopatra pushed her up against the door. "I love when you pull my hair. Are you done playing games?"

"What are you going to do to me, if I am?" Trina moaned and tore off her coat. She scratched at her belt buckle like a cat.

Cleopatra lifted up her camisole. "Whatever you want." She growled as she took Trina's breast into her mouth.

"It's happening, I said I wouldn't fall for you." Trina gasped as she pulled her top off and tossed it to the floor.

"Just let it happen." Cleopatra said, not processing what Trina had just confessed to her. Cleopatra pulled down her skirt and let it puddle around her feet, leaving nothing but the reflection of the street lights on Trina's naked body.

"I swore I wouldn't fall in love with you. I tried so hard. So hard." Cleopatra stood back and watched a tongue-tied Trina ramble with a tongue she usually had masterful control over. "I, I can't help it." She tried to explain herself and looked much younger than her twenty-three years now. More like a child caught with her daddy's tittie magazines.

"You can't help what exactly?"

"Te amo. I'm in love with you, papi." Trina pulled Cleopatra to her and kissed her hard. "Say you love me. Fuck me, papi. It's so good." She moaned.

Cleopatra sucked on the crook of her neck and palmed her ass.

"Tell me you love me," Trina demanded.

"Are you serious?" Cleopatra picked her coat up off of the floor and walked over to the futon.

"I want you to say it. Tell me." Trina walked up to Cleopatra. She looked up into Cleopatra's eyes, waiting for her to say those three little words.

But Cleopatra had some other words in mind. "I can tell you the truth and leave, or I can lie, fuck you, and then leave. Either way this evening is not going to end the way you want." Cleopatra paused. "I don't love you."

"But I love you." Trina wrapped her arms around Cleopatra's waist.

"You don't even know me." She peeled away from her embrace.

"We've only been together for a couple months, but I know what I need to know." Trina pulled her skirt up. "I'm pouring my heart out to you. How come you're not taking me seriously?"

Cleopatra was momentarily mesmerized by her naked breasts jiggling as she fixed her skirt. "How would I do that? You gave up the panties on our first date, within the first hour.

Oh, wait, I'm sorry, you weren't wearing panties. I've never seen you in panties actually. Do you own any?"

"I was trying to get your attention. I would have done anything."

"You had my attention, all night. Remember? You're confused because I fuck you like I love you."

"I understand the difference between love and sex."

"Not between my love and my sex, you don't."

"I want to be with you." Trina said raising her voice.

"Why are you yelling?" Cleopatra whispered. "I told you from the start. I don't want a relationship."

"I know that's what you said. But I can make you happy if you give me a chance," Trina pleaded.

"You've known me almost two months. In all that time we've never even sat down and talked over a meal. You eat before you see me. Today was the first time you wanted to talk. The idea to have a conversation was yours, and yet you can't even hold up your end."

"I was nervous, I can do better. I know about your reputation. I can change you."

"I don't need changing." Cleopatra's cell phone rang. "Excuse me." She searched for her phone. "This is Cleopatra. How are you, sweetheart? Nothing, why? All right, I'm on my way." She hung up. "So, yeah, I gotta go now," Cleopatra said to Trina.

"Who the fuck was that?" She reached for Cleopatra's phone. Her bare breasts rubbed against her.

"That's the second time you've screamed on me. You need to relax." Cleopatra held the phone up in the air out of Trina's reach.

"I'm sorry. Don't leave. This isn't what I want." She pulled on Cleopatra's arm. "Maybe it *is* the way you fuck me."

Cleopatra smiled. "I never wanted to hurt you. That's why I was honest with you from the start. That's all I've ever been with you."

"I can change the way you feel. I can make you love me."

"You haven't understood anything I've said to you at all. I've had all that you're offering, you gave me your body immediately. And even though it's good, it's not life-changing."

"You can be such a bitch."

Cleopatra moved toward the door. Trina jumped in front of her again.

"You're not leaving until I'm ready for you to leave."

Cleopatra laughed out loud. She scooped Trina up into her arms, kissed her and carried her into the bedroom. She softened as Cleopatra laid her down on the bed.

"This is what you want, right? All of this?" Cleopatra grabbed her dick through her jeans.

"Yes." Trina rolled over on her stomach and squirmed around the bed like a caterpillar. "Yes, give it to me. Give it to me."

Cleopatra made a beeline for the door, undid the multiple deadbolts, and flew down all three flights of the fifth floor walkup. As she exited the building onto St. Nicholas and 171st, Cleopatra – along with everyone else on the block – heard the girl scream from her window.

"Fuck you, Cleopatra!" Trina hollered when Cleopatra stopped at a food cart in front of her building.

"No hard feelings, sweetheart," Cleopatra yelled as she hoisted up her bag of chulitos and a Malta beer. Nearly nine p.m. The rain had subsided, and the street was again packed with people. The darkness was littered with bursts of light sparked by nocturnal vendors and buses. Cleopatra took a bite of the hot cheese-filled roll into her mouth and washed it down with the icy Malta as she headed toward the A train.

"I love you Cleopatra. We can still hook up, right?"

TASHA C. MILLER

THE JUMP OFF?

Cleopatra had moved on from the drama of the previous week with the help of several other willing women. On this sweltering June day, the after-work rush hour crowd flooded Sixth Avenue in midtown in anticipation of the weekend beginning. As soon as Cleopatra left her office she took off her suit jacket, undid a few buttons on her shirt and put her locs up in a bun to cool off. She was a block from the F train at Rockefeller Center when, from behind, she spotted the body of a particularly beautiful woman.

"Damn, baby." A bearded man cat called the same woman as he honked his truck horn and dangled out of the driver's side window. Cleopatra laughed to herself, knowing the man had a slim chance of the woman acknowledging him. An athletic bike messenger refused to quit staring at the woman's legs, and so slammed into the back of a black sedan and landed on his face, but he quickly sprang back onto his feet and gathered his scattered envelopes. Cleopatra was several paces behind her when they walked past the hotdog and popcorn vendors who were packing up for the day. The crowds had forsaken them for Italian ices and the Mister Softee truck that had lines stretching down 51st Street between Sixth and Seventh avenues. Yellow cabs snaked down Sixth Avenue advertising their air conditioning.

The woman's ass had Cleopatra mesmerized but something else intrigued her, and she hadn't seen her face yet. Her black business suit fell in love with every inch of her curvaceous, caramel body. Wavy, black hair hit her in the middle of her back, and her long, shapely legs made Cleopatra's eyes water as they held up her perfect ass. Cleopatra wanted to bite it; she was going to, she had decided. And those stiletto heels – she already pictured them perched underneath her bed.

The woman carried herself with confidence. She walked like a dancer, with long seductive strides, almost in slow motion compared to the manic horde on the street. Men ogled her and women twisted their lips in envy. She stopped just short of the subway entrance and handed a homeless woman a small wad of bills. Cleopatra saw the woman mouth *God bless you, too* as she pulled the cash from her hand and tossed it into a tattered coffee cup. Cleopatra was determined to get a glimpse at the face that belonged to this vision from behind.

They entered the train station, which on this day doubled as an oven. The industrial fans placed every dozen feet only circulated hot air. Everyone wore a thin layer of moisture on their faces, and clothes were committed to sticking to their owners. The woman removed her suit jacket, giving Cleopatra and everyone else full view of her hourglass shape. Cleopatra positioned herself to get a glance at her face as they approached the turnstiles.

They swiped their MetroCards in unison. Cleopatra looked up at her and gazed into the eyes of the most gorgeous woman she'd ever seen. The woman opened her red blouse as much as she could without a breast falling out – much to Cleopatra's dismay.

"Damn," slipped from her lips. *I think she heard me.* Cleopatra smiled.

16

Her hair flowed freely away from her face, revealing big, beautiful brown eyes, full lips on the sexiest pre-orgasmic smile ever directed at Cleopatra. Her dimpled face wore hardly any makeup; she had an innocence about her that made Cleopatra want her even more. They made eye contact for what seemed like forever and in an awkward moment, the beauty licked her lips slowly.

Lust flooded Cleopatra's body, and compelled her to tell the woman what she was thinking. "I appreciate you, sweetheart."

"I'm sorry, what?"

"You are the most stunningly sensual woman ever to gaze into my eyes. I appreciate how beautiful you are." Cleopatra flashed a smile, winked at her and walked away.

The woman stood motionless for a moment, not sure what to do or how to respond. "Wait!" She ran up to Cleopatra with her hand extended.

A rush of excitement surged through Cleopatra as the woman grabbed her arm. Cleopatra flexed instinctively as the woman pressed her fingertips into her bicep. People scurried around them running to their trains, some even curious as to what was about to happen.

She pulled Cleopatra to the side of the turnstiles out of the way of the other commuters.

"Thank you, you're sweet. Uhm… can I walk with you?"

"Of course." Cleopatra noticed the woman hadn't let go of her arm. She used it to lead her to the train.

But they were immediately interrupted by one of the beauty's colleagues. A fragile lady with tan skin and a delicate face began to bombard her with work questions. Cleopatra excused herself and walked away from them and over to the newsstand where she bought two bottled waters. The beauty moved closer to her, ignoring her older colleague who was still in tow. Their eyes met again and locked in on each other. She was not paying attention to her friend who had yet to stop talking or take a breath.

"Here you go." Cleopatra placed the ice cold water in her hand.

"Thank you. So thoughtful of you." She rolled the bottle across her chest.

Cleopatra was consumed with the sight of her moving the bottle back and forth between her breasts. She was jolted back to reality when she felt someone's tongue licking the side of her face.

"Cleopatra. How've you been? I've missed you." A tall, slender woman with reddish brown hair was in her ear. The woman had come out of nowhere and nearly tackled Cleopatra, forcing the beauty and her friend to fall back.

Annoyed, Cleopatra managed to say, "I'm good." Without taking her eyes off the beauty, she wiped her cheek. "I'm sorry, I forgot your name." Cleopatra lied, hoping to turn the woman off so she'd go away. She never forgot an ex. Especially not a double-jointed one.

"Redd. You remember me. Stop playing." She grabbed Cleopatra around the waist.

Cleopatra looked at the beauty, who shot Redd a harsh glare. She unclenched Redd's hands from her body. "I'm sorry. It was good running into you, but I have to go." Cleopatra left the woman standing alone, and nodded toward the beauty before she headed for the stairs to the downtown platform. She put the cold water bottle to her forehead as she weaved through the other rush hour commuters.

As Cleopatra walked away, she overheard the beauty abruptly end her conversation with her coworker. She descended the stairs to the train, and the woman followed close behind her. Cleopatra maneuvered her way through the packed platform and found an open spot to stand. She turned around and found the beauty invading her personal space. She stood close as Cleopatra leaned on a column, so close she could smell the peppermint on her breath and the Jean Paul Gaultier perfume wafting up from between her moist breasts.

"I'm Jacqueline." She smiled and held out her hand.

"Cleopatra, but my friends call me Cleo." She took hold of her soft hand.

"I'll stick with Cleopatra. I have no intentions of being your friend." She squeezed her hand. Cleopatra was turned on immediately. She loved aggressive women who spoke their minds. "Your hands are huge." Jacqueline traced the inside of Cleopatra's palm with her fingers.

The downtown and Brooklyn bound F train pulled into the station packed with commuters.

"After you." Cleopatra stood behind Jacqueline, letting her get on the train first. Cleopatra took the opportunity to examine her body up close as they squeezed on and stood in the middle of the car.

"That looks heavy, would you like me to hold that for you?" Cleopatra pointed to her large handbag. "I promise not to run off with it." She teased her.

Jacqueline hesitated, then smiled. "Sure. Thank you." She dropped the bag from her shoulder. Cleopatra took hold of it with one hand. "Oh, my God. What's in here? Wait, are you one of those women that carries bricks for protection?"

"No." Jacqueline laughed. "I have mace."

"On your key chain?"

"Yes."

"Very good." Cleopatra winked at her. "So what's in here that's so heavy?"

"I can't tell you that. It's girl stuff. Stuff I need to maintain myself. Our purses are always heavy." Jacqueline touched Cleopatra's chest and traced a line from her neck to the top of her wife beater. "You're not sweating anymore. I mean you had sweat right here before." She caught herself, embarrassed. "I'm sorry."

"Don't ever apologize for touching me." Cleopatra realized that Jacqueline was struggling to keep her hands off of her, and she liked it.

"Sorry about my colleague, too. I didn't think she would ever leave us alone."

"Good things come to those who wait." Cleopatra took a gulp of water.

"I hope that's true, now more than ever." Jacqueline licked her lips and stared and Cleopatra didn't do anything to stop her. Jacqueline took a delicate swig from her bottle. "Can I tell you something?" Jacqueline stared down at the floor.

Cleopatra was struck by how beautiful she was, even in the cheap fluorescent lights of the subway car, and framed against the backdrop of the metallic walls and orange and beige seats. "You can tell me anything." Cleopatra imagined her confessing how she liked it from behind, how she liked it in her mouth and that she wanted to be dominated. "Don't be shy."

Jacqueline gazed up at her, nervously biting her lip. "I think you are unnecessarily sexy."

Cleopatra smiled, caught off guard. She couldn't remember the last time a woman threw her off of her game to this extent. She stared at her. "I'm sorry, you have really beautiful eyes." Cleopatra said to her. "Unnecessarily? What does that mean?"

"Thank you. You are very sweet." Jacqueline smiled wide. "Unnecessarily sexy means you are sexier than what's reasonable, doesn't make any sense really. I'm sure you cause the ladies a lot of trouble." She fixed her eyes again on Cleopatra's wife beater peeking out from underneath her button-down shirt.

"Well, I didn't hear anyone honking at me. And no bike messenger ever risked his life to look at my butt."

"Well, I've never had someone grind on me at a subway station newsstand."

"That wasn't a grind." Cleopatra shook her head.

"And she licked your face. If that wasn't grinding, I'd love to see what you think grinding is."

"That could be arranged." Cleopatra winked at her.

Jacqueline giggled and licked her lips. "So, you were watching me?"

"Maybe."

"You like to watch?"

"Are we really going to have this conversation?" Cleopatra asked. "Ok, I'm in. I much rather do than watch."

"So, you rather do me?"

I'll do the hell out of you, if you let me. Cleopatra's neck was burning, and Jacqueline wouldn't take her eyes off of her. "Are you always so forward?"

"No, I'm so sorry." She stepped back. "I'm actually a little shy, and I'm really nervous right now, but I don't want this opportunity to slip away."

"You don't have to be nervous or shy around me." Cleopatra assured her. "What opportunity are you talking about?"

"I have a confession." She paused. "I've been watching you. I work at Midtown Properties too, on the top floor in the VP's office. I catch sight of you in the building a lot. You're usually with someone. Other times I've just been too fearful to approach you."

"That's cute. But I'm nothing to fear." Cleopatra said.

"Do you have a girlfriend or anything? Kids?" Jacqueline asked before she lost her nerve again.

"You've been watching me, and you don't know the answers? I don't have either."

"You don't have a woman?"

"That's what I said."

"So, you're a player?" She bit her lip again. "Your reputation is true?"

"What reputation?" Cleopatra was not happy Jacqueline knew so much about her and she'd never even seen her before.

"You'll make me fall madly in love with you, have me climbing the walls, and then break my heart and wonder why I'm stalking your ass." She laughed.

Cleopatra looked at her suspiciously. She'd obviously been doing some research. "I'm not sure where you got your information, but you shouldn't believe everything you hear."

"So, I won't be climbing the walls?"

"Oh no. You definitely would be." Cleopatra tried to steer the conversation away from sex. The pressure between her legs was starting to annoy her. "What about you? You must have a girlfriend. Do you have kids?"

Jacqueline answered her quickly. "No," she said.

"How come you don't have a girlfriend?"

"Because I've been waiting for you." She gazed into

Cleopatra's eyes. Cleopatra saw something that drew her in. A pain or a deep sadness in her eyes that for some reason Cleopatra wanted to help her heal.

The crowded car had demanded that they touch slightly, but the vigorous motion of the train forced their bodies to thrash against each other harder and Cleopatra was getting turned on. She struggled not to get lost in Jacqueline's eyes as she held on tight to the hand rail.

"So, what do you do in your spare time besides break hearts?"

"A little of this, a lot of that."

"Uh huh? You write poetry, don't you?"

"Every black lesbian in New York City writes poetry." Cleopatra laughed.

"Can you recite some for me?"

"I do have something in my head since I've been looking into your eyes, but it's not a poem. I don't want you to think I'm running a line on you."

"I won't. You don't need to run a line on me at this point."

Cleopatra scanned the crowded subway car and motioned for her to lean in even closer. She whispered in her ear.

I'm not going to recite a poem for you, but you should know that I see you.

Your beauty is not hiding your pain, at least not from me.

You should let me dry your tears. Let my mouth silence all the voices in your head.

I can lead you into a love like you've never seen.

Again, this is not a poem. I just want you to know that I see you.

Jacqueline's eyes widened. She wouldn't look at Cleopatra. "You think I have pain?" She looked down at the floor.

"I see it. I feel it." Cleopatra trailed her fingers across the back of Jacqueline's hand.

"And you want to help me with it?" She stunned Cleopatra by interlocking her fingers into hers.

"If you want me to."

"Oh, I want you to." She squeezed Cleopatra's hand as she exhaled. "So, why don't you have a woman again?"

"You must have talked to some women at work about me, that's fine. But let me ask you this. When they were reenacting my relationships with them and I know they did because they are all extra animated, did anyone mention anything about my personality? Or my sense of humor? Did anyone know what my favorite color is, or my favorite food? Anyone know I can't sleep through the night without the TV on?"

Jacqueline was a bit stunned by Cleopatra's defensiveness, but she understood. She shook her head. "No, they didn't speak of anything remotely close to those topics. I tried to ask those types of questions, but I didn't get any answers. They were more preoccupied with another aspect of your relationship."

Cleopatra shook her head. "There's a lot more to me, but those women were not interested in my other assets. I date a lot, because I'm yet to find what I'm looking for. When I do, things will be different, and I will act accordingly."

"Don't tell me, you want a lady in the streets and a freak in the sheets?" Jacqueline grinned.

"And what's wrong with that?" Cleopatra laughed. "Seriously," she wiped the smile from her face. "I'm looking for the woman who can make me believe in forever, because right now I don't. When *the one* comes along I'll know it almost immediately. I will give her my full attention, and I'll love every minute of giving it to her. Trust me." Cleopatra ran her eyes slowly up and down her body taking her all in and making sure Jacqueline knew it.

"How will you know when you have met *the one*?"

"I'll see it in her eyes when she looks at me." Cleopatra stared into Jacqueline's eyes, and she stared back. The jostling of the train shook them out of their gaze.

"Understood." Jacqueline bit her lip.

Cleopatra wished she was that lip. "My stop is coming up next." She said. "Would you like to have lunch with me on Monday?"

"I would love to have you. Lunch with you. Sorry, you still make me a little nervous." She took Cleopatra's wrist and looked at her watch.

"What are you doing?" Cleopatra asked as Jacqueline stared at the massive timepiece.

"Nice watch." She ran her fingers around the diamond encrusted dial. "I'm just counting down the hours until I lay my eyes on you again."

They exchanged phone numbers as the train pulled into Cleopatra's station and she handed Jacqueline her handbag back.

"Until we meet again. Have a great weekend, beautiful." Cleopatra caressed her hand.

"You too." Jacqueline said, but wouldn't release her hand. Cleopatra's other hand was wrapped around the train pole, and Jacqueline leaned in close and pressed her breasts against it.

"Uhm." Cleopatra fought the urge to grab at her chest and mush her face between Jacqueline's dewy titties. She watched the doors open, and the people scurry off and onto the train. Jacqueline stared in her eyes, still holding one hand and teasing the other with her hard nipples. "What's on your mind?" Cleopatra stared at the closing train doors. The train pulled out of the station and away from where Cleopatra needed to be.

"I have to be honest with you. This is my first time doing anything like this." Jacqueline said shyly.

"Like what?"

"I've never been out on a date with a woman before."

"You are gay, aren't you?"

"Definitely, but I'm kind of in the closet."

"Kind of? Being seen with me outs you immediately. Just so you know."

"I can see that from the attention we've gotten on this train ride so far. It's fine with me."

"Good." Cleopatra said. "How is 'kind of' being in the closet working for you? That's the sadness that I see behind your smile?"

"I need you to not do that." Jacqueline snapped at her.

"I'm sorry. What did I do?"

"I need you to not see through me." Jacqueline averted her

eyes.

"Maybe that's exactly what you need." Cleopatra knew she had upset her. "I'm sorry if I made you uncomfortable." She studied Jacqueline. "But there must be a good reason, right?"

"Is fear a good enough reason?"

"Can't say I understand. I've been out since I was like twelve." Cleopatra smiled.

"Are you serious?" Jacqueline laughed. "You must feel free."

"I'm pretty comfortable in my skin."

"That's just part of what makes you so sexy."

"How does this feel right now?" Cleopatra took her hand into hers again. "Being here with me. Are you comfortable?"

"Yeah. I feel safe. No place I'd rather be."

Cleopatra couldn't shake thoughts of Jacqueline for the rest of the night. Her mind was filled with the smell of her perfume, her eyes, her lips, her soft little hands and her legs wrapped around her neck. Never mind that she left Jacqueline on the train to make a dinner date with another woman. Cleopatra didn't want her, she wanted Jacqueline.

TASHA C. MILLER

NOW SHE REALLY WANTS HER

Shortly after meeting Cleopatra for the first time, Jacqueline arrived home alone to an empty apartment. The small one-bedroom on the first floor of a multifamily house on Coney Island's Surf Avenue was not far from the water. But the vast openness of the bay did not extend to the rental that was too tight to even be considered cozy. But it was all Jacqueline needed, and she was happy there. The house was dark on this summer Friday night, and she flipped through her mail as she went from room to room turning on the lights. The house with its stark white walls was made warmer by the addition of bold orange, red and purple accents and framed African-American figurative prints.

Jacqueline had carefully decorated her home and kept it spotlessly clean. Her bedroom smelled faintly of the fragrant oils and the caramel vanilla candles she loved to burn. She stripped down to her heather gray bra and panties and slipped on a short black silk robe. The robe was cool and slick against her skin, making her shiver the moment it touched her bare arms, much like Cleopatra had caused her to tremble not too long ago in the subway.

She went into the living room where she sat down on her favorite piece of furniture, a flared arm crimson microfiber sofa. She sat down on the sofa in front of the bay window, and then got up on her knees and peeked through the bronze colored drapes to the street out front. It was eerily silent for a hot Friday night, no street party, no cars racing up and down the street, no music blasting, no neighborhood kids bouncing basketballs or chasing each other around. She longed for the usual noise to distract her from her thoughts, but her neighbors would not oblige her. It was past dinner time, and usually by this point in the evening she'd be starving and in the midst of one of her favorite hobbies, cooking, but she had no appetite. She stared across the room at her parents' wedding picture on the wall – they'd be celebrating their thirtieth wedding anniversary soon. She desperately wanted and needed a love like her mother and father shared.

Stretched out across the couch she popped open a bottle of Louis Jadot Pouilly-Fuisse chardonnay and surrendered to her thoughts and fantasies about Cleopatra. Her body felt heavy against the soft microfiber and she was finally comfortable allowing herself to feel all the emotions and desires that she had kept contained for so many years. Jacqueline moved her fingers inside of her panties as she imagined being with Cleopatra, imagining ordinary everyday activities like watching TV and cooking together, as well as the extraordinary – making love to her.

Could it be possible she was missing Cleopatra already? They hadn't even spent a half hour together, but in that time Cleopatra made her feel so many emotions, safe, sexy, desired, cared for, and she made her feel heard. Cleopatra felt her and was possibly the first person to get a glimpse of the real Jacqueline. Jacqueline wanted her, but now her desire was stronger. It had taken all her strength not to ask Cleopatra to come home with her, but somehow she managed. Somehow.

She wanted to call Cleopatra, but Jacqueline knew she was probably on a date. No way she was alone on a Friday evening. She should have done something to keep her from going, she thought. Jacqueline realized that the idea of Cleopatra with another woman upset her now. Cleopatra was hers. She wondered if Cleopatra was thinking about her. Jacqueline even thought of what she'd say to her or her voicemail, if she'd had the nerve to call just then. But she didn't. She just took a sip of chardonnay, closed her eyes and threw her head back. She swished the fruity, smooth wine around her mouth before letting it slide down her throat and allowing herself to continue her fantasizing.

Cleopatra's hands were soft and strong, and she smelled delicious. *How does someone covered in sweat smell that good?* At times she smelled like lavender, then vanilla. Or she'd turn her head and Jacqueline smelled sandalwood and jasmine. And the way Cleopatra looked into her eyes put her in a trance. Her energy overwhelmed and enveloped her. Just thinking about Cleopatra gave her butterflies, and it seemed like no amount of wine would ever make them go away.

Cleopatra was not what she had expected, not the shallow person her ex-girlfriends had portrayed her as. Jacqueline thought that Cleopatra was going to be arrogant and full of herself. But she wasn't any of that. She knew Cleopatra was right when she'd said that those women hadn't been interested in getting to know her; that was obvious from her own conversations with them. That was fine, because Jacqueline was going to get to know her well enough for all of them. Jacqueline thought about their meeting again. Cleopatra was kind of shy. Extremely sweet and sensitive toward her. She made her feel beautiful, the way she looked at her. She held her bag for her, she bought her water to cool her off. The way she touched her was sensual. All those emotions and events, just in a few minutes on the subway. How was all of that even possible?

Jacqueline had been waiting for the one who'd make her feel the way she needed, the way her mother described the relationship with her father. "Pay attention to how a person makes you feel. What they say is important but how do they make you *feel?*"

Finding her own version of her parents' loving relationship was one of the most important things in her life. Lots of girls had dreams of growing up, falling in love, getting married and living happily ever after, but it was even more important to Jacqueline than most little girls. After all, she'd grown up with a front row seat to what that looked like every day. Cleopatra reminded her of her father in some ways. The strong, silent type, not big on a lot of unnecessary words – but what he did say was usually impactful or profound. Her father was a person of action, and she wondered if Cleopatra shared that same trait. Jacqueline had made mistakes that weren't in line with her dream of the perfect romance, but now that she was trying to rectify those errors she was particularly picky. So it was way out of her character when she set her sights so narrowly and aggressively on Cleopatra without knowing her, seemingly based on pure physical attraction. The prospect of what lay ahead of Jacqueline both scared and excited her, because now she had an up-close peek at what she was about to get herself into.

RIDE OR DIE

Saturday morning Cleopatra and her best friend Shawn were hanging out in Soho as they often did on weekends, catching up on each other's conquests over the previous week. Shawn worked at Midtown Properties too, but she didn't get up to visit Cleopatra on the executive floors too often, and Cleopatra rarely visited the mail center that Shawn managed like a military academy. The close friends had a lot in common – they both dated a lot of women, and they both got into a lot of trouble because of it. Physically, though, they were total opposites, so one of them was sure to attract any given woman. Shawn, short for Shawnette, was often mistaken for a guy, with her shaved head and heavier build. She had no discernible feminine characteristics at all until she spoke, and she didn't mind a bit. It was a plus, in that she figured her masculine looks gave her the opportunity to live without incident in rougher areas at cheap rent.

Cleopatra and Shawn had grown up together in the same

East New York, Brooklyn neighborhood. Cleopatra moved to the Village the first chance she got, but Shawn never left. Even though she had the means to live next door to Cleopatra if she wanted, she chose to stay put. Living in the hood kept her close to her first love, hoodrats. Shawn's taste in women was a bit less discriminating than Cleopatra's, so she was a regular fixture in the police station, caught up in some domestic dispute for which Cleopatra had to come to her rescue. While they both dated lively women who were prone to show up at their houses long after they were done with them, Cleopatra's exes would bring sleeping bags and camp out until she surfaced. Shawn's would just throw a Molotov cocktail through the window to get her to come outside.

The lifelong friends often joked that they didn't need to settle down and find good women because they had each other, the only one each of them could always trust and depend on.

The sun was out that Saturday and so were the people. Sidewalks overflowed with crowds, and fascinated tourists gawked from their double-decker buses. Cleopatra and Shawn wandered through a street fair on Spring Street where Cleopatra bought some ginger beer and a bag of coco bread.

"How long have we known each other? Forever, right? I just enjoy the company of ladies." Cleopatra winked. "I'm not a player, you're the player. You love them and leave them before the wet spot dries," she said, as she tried on a pair of aviator sunglasses.

"Uh uh. You aren't a player. I know deep inside you want to settle down with one girl. But you aren't acting like it right now. You run through women just like I do. How do you expect the right one to get to you if all of these other women are in the way?"

"I do want a relationship with one woman, I always have." Cleopatra's thoughts briefly drifted off to Jacqueline. "One woman that's really down for me, and wants nothing but to love me. If she's 'the one,' she'll knock all the other women out of her way." Cleopatra smiled at the prospect. "And I don't run through women. I treat them with the utmost respect. That is,

until I'm done with them. And even then I'm gentle."
Cleopatra smirked.

"You are smoother with yours, because you have to be. We deal with a different type of chick. My girls are more passionate. Not so subtle like yours."

"You call sticking you with a stun gun passionate?" Cleopatra laughed.

"That happened one time!" Shawn held up her index finger. "One time. So Ms. I'm-not-a-player, how many dates did you go on last week?"

"None."

Shawn sighed. "How many women did you have sex with last week?"

Cleopatra hesitated. "Uhm...three, four."

"See what I mean?"

"No. I'm in a relationship with every one of those women. They may be sexual relationships, but they're relationships. You, on the other hand, just have sex and leave. When was the last time you went out with a woman after she gave you some? I'll wait," Cleopatra said, as Shawn rolled her eyes. "I'm not mad at the quantity, but can you work on the quality of these women? Ease up on the crazy, maybe? If I'm called down to the Seventy-fifth Precinct again...the desk sergeant sent me a Christmas card *and* a Kwanzaa card last year."

"I tried being upfront with these chicks. I told this girl last night, 'I just really want to fuck you and once you give it up I'll probably never call you again, so you can't be mad.'"

"How did that work out for you?" Cleopatra smirked.

"She gave it up like she was daring me, like she was going to be different. I hit it and left." Shawn pulled her phone from her pocket. "Thirty-five missed calls." She held her phone up. "Now my battery is dying."

Cleopatra shook her head. "See. Crazy. That's what I'm talking about."

"All right, what about you? You went out with fine-ass Michelle last night, right?"

"Yeah, picked her up right after work." She handed the

vendor a twenty-dollar bill for the shades. "Thank you." They weaved their way out of the street fair and back down Broadway.

"So how was she?" Shawn asked.

"Pissed off. I took her out for a nice dinner and a Broadway show. She got heated when we went back to her place and I didn't want to fuck."

"You didn't want to hit that?"

"I did. And you know after some good food and some orchestra seats she was ready to work me out, but two things happened. First, on the way to meet her I met this woman in the train station, and she just blew me away. I thought about her pretty ass all night. But I still could have fucked Michelle. Only Michelle's house was so nasty that I didn't want to sit down in that motherfucker. No way I was getting naked and catch something up in my crawl. I would have fucked her in the hallway first."

Shawn hollered laughing. "Hey, come on." She pulled Cleopatra into a tiny underground store where she learned they could buy real designer jeans for fifty bucks. Jeans were stacked up to the ceiling on card tables. There were no windows, and the only light came from floor lamps connected to industrial-strength orange extension cords leading out the door and up the stairs. The two box fans did nothing to cool off the damp, stuffy hole in the ground. Biggie Smalls blasted from the speakers near the makeshift register, a ragged shoe box overflowing with cash was guarded by a short woman with oily light-brown hair, dark brown eyes and a pierced nose. She wore a royal blue tank top, tight blue jeans and some white Adidas shell-toe sneakers. Cleopatra pulled Shawn away from the woman because her wearing a thick blue knit scarf tied tight around her neck in June looked sketchy to her. "Don't mess with that." Cleopatra warned her. "She's got something going on right here." Cleopatra rubbed her own neck up and down.

Cleopatra and Shawn picked out as many jeans as they could carry and lugged them into the back of the store to an impromptu fitting room with no stalls. Separated from the rest of the establishment by a red flannel sheet, it was a large dark area, a tad bigger than the average bedroom, with dirty gray carpet, mirrored walls and a drop ceiling with water-damaged acoustic tiles. Only a few torchiere floor lamps lined the walls giving off more heat than adequate lighting.

Several half-naked customers tried on jeans in the humid back room. Cleopatra was wriggling into a pair that looked promising when Shawn gave her a nudge and asked, "Yo, you know that Puerto Rican girl? She keeps staring at your ass, she looks young, but she's pretty though."

"I hate these open fitting rooms," Cleopatra said as the girl approached them. "Can I help you with something sweetheart?" she asked the girl who wore only a t-shirt and panties, and was holding a pair of jeans in her hand.

"Hi, Cleopatra," she said, as Cleopatra zipped up her jeans.

"Do I know you?" Cleopatra tried to remember where she knew the cute girl from.

"You probably don't remember me, I guess. It's been a while. Paola Gomez. You used to date my sister, Christina."

"Oh, yeah. You are all grown up now."

"Exactly what I'm saying." She tilted her head to the right and popped her tongue on the inside of her mouth.

"Oh shit, I'm going to holler at that cashier." Shawn laughed and walked toward the front of the store, leaving Cleopatra to fend for herself.

"Uhm, so how's your sister doing?" Cleopatra looked in the mirror at the fit of her jeans.

"She's all right. She still talks about you."

"Well, tell her hello for me. And it was good seeing you." Cleopatra hoped the girl would go away.

"I read about you in her journal." The girl paused for a moment. "How all she thought about was your tongue. She compared your dick to a crack pipe." She hooked her thumb into the side of her panties.

"Ok. Wow." Cleopatra fumbled around with another pair of jeans.

"I didn't need to read her journal to know that. I saw you."

35

"What are you talking about?" Cleopatra noticed that they were the only two left in the back room now. It made no difference to her but it seemed to give Paola the courage to say what was on her mind.

"One night you thought you had the house to yourselves, but I was there. I heard her screams from my room. I watched you from the door, and the things you did to her." The girl slid her hand down into her panties and wiggled her fingers. "I masturbated to you fucking her."

"Why do I have the feeling that you have been waiting forever to tell me this? I hope you enjoyed it, because that was the last time you'll see me fucking." Cleopatra put her own jeans back on.

The girl pulled her hand out from between her legs, her fingers glistened. She waved her sticky fingers in front of Cleopatra's lips. Cleopatra matrixed, bending her body back to avoid the girl's hand. "You wanna hook up sometime?" she asked Cleopatra.

"What would your sister say?"

"I don't care."

Cleopatra laughed. "How old are you anyway? You can put your pants on now."

"Nineteen." Paola slipped into some skinny jeans.

"You're too young for me. Most importantly, I don't want to cause problems in your family. Your sister's temper is insane."

Paola took out a piece of paper and a pen from her purse and scribbled on it. "Playing hard to get? Cool. I'm patient. And I can handle my sister." She walked up to Cleopatra, pulled on the waist of her jeans and put her phone number inside of her briefs. She wiped her hand down the front of Cleopatra's black t-shirt and left the fitting room.

Shawn brushed past Paola as she walked back in. "Did you get the cashier's number?" Cleopatra asked.

"No, she gave me her address."

"Who does that?" Cleopatra laughed.

"Why do I smell pussy?" Shawn sniffed the air. "I asked for

her info and that's what she gave me."

"What are you gonna do with it?"

"I'm gonna deliver."

"Get away from me." Cleopatra laughed. "And do me a favor don't call me when you find out what she is hiding under that scarf."

"What is that on your shirt?" Shawn asked.

"That's what you smell."

As they stood in line to pay for their jeans, Cleopatra told Shawn about Jacqueline. "So, I was saying before, I met this queen on the train last night. My future wife, mother of my children," Cleopatra joked.

"Uh huh. So how was it?"

"It's not even like that. We just shared the train ride, and she's got my stomach all in knots. She's got this sultry voice, this hourglass shape like bam, bam." Cleopatra grabbed her chest and smacked her own ass. "And she's so sweet." Her cell phone began to vibrate in her pocket.

"Hold on a second. It's her. She sent me a picture." Cleopatra smiled. "Ooh."

"Is she naked?" Shawn tried to grab her phone.

"No." Cleopatra yanked her hand away. "She sent me a picture with her lip poked out. The message says 'Why haven't you called me yet?'"

Cleopatra began to text her back when Jacqueline called her. "Hi, Jacqueline."

"Hi, Cleopatra. What are you doing?"

"Buying some jeans."

"How do I know you're not on a date?"

"I wouldn't have picked up my phone."

"Good answer." She laughed. "Why don't you call me when you get home, and you can give me your undivided attention? I'm hoping that won't be too long from right now. Can you handle that?"

"Oh, I'll handle it. I'll call you back in a bit." Cleopatra hung up. She hugged Shawn. "She told me to get my ass home and call her, and that's what I'm about to do."

"Wait. You aren't going to hook up with her; you're going home so you can talk to her on the phone?"

"Yeah. I guess I am." Cleopatra smiled.

"Like that, huh?" Shawn asked, surprised.

"Yeah. I can't put my finger on what it is about her, but I want to."

"I'm sure you will on the first date, as usual."

"No, I don't think I will. I've already decided. She's not a jump off – they announce themselves immediately. I want to touch her, but I'm going to control myself. Hopefully she won't make it hard. There is something special about this one."

◙ ◙ ◙

"So you really went home and called me, just like that?" Jacqueline asked Cleopatra over the phone.

"Yes." Cleopatra was putting the key in her door and punching in the code on her alarm system. "Why are you so surprised?"

"I know there are probably a million other things you could be doing or people you could be spending time with."

"Perhaps, but I would rather spend this time talking to you. Is that all right?" Cleopatra plopped down on her living room couch.

"Yes." A huge smile spread across Jacqueline's lips.

They talked on the phone for hours. All Saturday night and early into Sunday morning. They connected.

Cleopatra didn't try to invite herself over to Jacqueline's house, or try to force some two a.m. booty call. Jacqueline wasn't sure she would be able to resist or deny her if she asked, but she didn't. Frankly, Cleopatra was happy when Jacqueline asked her to call her back on the phone instead of asking her to come over strapped; she'd heard that so many times before. During all those hours on the phone they watched bad reality TV together, shows that were so bad they were embarrassed to admit to anyone else that they watched them religiously. They bonded over their love of Blaxploitation films. Cleopatra joked that Jacqueline could possibly steal her heart when she quoted, verbatim, scenes from "Car Wash" and "Willie Dynamite." Cleopatra couldn't remember having that much fun with a female without being naked. Jacqueline had wanted her undivided attention, and Cleopatra gave it to her. Cleopatra asked Jacqueline all types of questions, about her life, her family, her hopes and dreams. A news junkie, Cleopatra could watch CNN all day and never get enough. She asked Jacqueline questions about war, politics, art, music and books. She wanted to know her thoughts and opinions on everything. And to Cleopatra's delight, Jacqueline had a firm stance on every subject she threw at her. Cleopatra loved a smart woman; that made Jacqueline even sexier than she already was. Cleopatra had never asked so many questions of anyone before. No one really took the time to have conversations with her, but then again, she never really wanted to get to know someone like she did Jacqueline.

Jacqueline usually spent her Sundays with her family in New Jersey starting with church in the morning and ending with dinner in the evening. Even so, she found time to miss Cleopatra and wonder what she was doing. Jacqueline fought not to look at her cell phone during the service, but when she thought she couldn't take it anymore she peeked at it. She had a text message from Cleopatra. "I can't stop thinking about you." That made her year. Consumed with thoughts of Cleopatra, she counted the hours until their lunch date the next day. On Sunday night, they spoke only briefly, when Cleopatra called just to hear her voice. Jacqueline spent hours picking out the right outfit, like a fourteen-year-old girl picking out her clothes for the first day of high school. When she couldn't get to sleep that night, she got out of bed and started cooking up a surprise for Cleopatra.

TASHA C. MILLER

LOVE JONES

Cleopatra's first impulse when she arrived at work on Monday morning was to call Jacqueline at her desk, even though they had spent most of the weekend on the phone. But she decided to wait. Instead, she met with her assistant to touch base on her ongoing projects. In any other setting, Racquel would stick out like a sore thumb. A forty-something Ethiopian immigrant, she had a love of vibrant reds, oranges and blues that translated to her wardrobe daily and proudly. Racquel served as Cleopatra's gatekeeper, and worked hard to keep her focused and out of trouble.

Cleopatra didn't appear to be a hard-edged business executive, but she'd graduated at the top of her B-school class. At graduation she walked across the stage with a dozen job offers in her pocket. She chose Midtown Properties for its commitment to diversity, the corner office, and the ridiculous salary. It would never occur to strangers on the street that she was a businesswoman, and she preferred it that way.

She constantly tested security, and during her first few days at Midtown, her colleagues mistook her for a messenger at first glance. She carried a North Face backpack, and most days wore a hoodie, baggy jeans and Timberland boots to the office, changing into business attire in her bathroom and changing back again before leaving. Cleopatra was most comfortable blending in. She was shy at times, and introverted. She didn't crave the spotlight and only wanted to be a face in the crowd. On the street she got far less attention in her jeans and hoodie than she would in her Armani pantsuits and Mark Nason boots. Her presence was already commanding, and she did not want or need any extra attention. Even though her body was near perfect, she was more relaxed in clothes that hid her form, and her designer and tailored work clothes did nothing but accentuate her curves. Cleopatra worked to find a balance between her business life and her true identity. She was comfortable in her masculinity and expressed it to the fullest extent and as much as possible.

Even when she was all business, her style stood out in the straight-laced, good old boys club. Her shirts were whiter, platinum cufflinks shinier, creases sharper, and her watches more exotic.

Cleopatra was younger than most of her staff, and they returned the love and respect she gave them. She hired the best, paid them the most and gave them the freedom to do their jobs. She was approachable, although that required getting past Racquel, who let people through only if she liked them or if they were a higher-up.

The asset management division took up the entire fifty-first floor, and Cleopatra's corner office was larger than the apartment she grew up in. The modern space was decorated in black and white with red accents sprinkled throughout. Equipped with a flat screen TV, a large black leather sectional for long nights, a kitchenette and a full bath, her office possessed all the luxuries she needed for work and play. The floor to ceiling windows along the two exterior walls gave her office a sweeping view of midtown, but she always felt exposed, so most of the time she had the black privacy shades pulled half way down. Walls not covered in glass were adorned with vibrant abstract paintings, which were bracketed by built-in shelves where Cleopatra kept some of her numerous business texts. Cleopatra sat at a massive triple-bevel-edged glass desk facing the couch and windows. In front of her desk were two black leather modular chairs with horn-shaped headrests. Tossed onto the chairs were white and red accent pillows. Cleopatra was particularly fond of those chairs, their form and most notably their strength. She had entertained on them several times.

Cleopatra kept her office temperature in stark contrast to the weather outside. In the winter, it was sweltering, and on this summer day the office was freezing.

"Why do you keep looking at the phone?" Racquel asked as she sat across from Cleopatra's desk. "Are you expecting a call?" She adjusted her fluorescent orange shawl across her shoulders.

"No, I'm trying not to make one. I met this woman, Jacqueline. She works upstairs. She's the VP's new assistant."

"You're scared to call a female?" Racquel leaned back in the chair, surprised.

"I'm not scared. We talked all weekend. It's no big deal."

"Then call her. I'll wait." Racquel folded her arms. Cleopatra didn't move. "Oh, my God. Who is this woman?"

Cleopatra rolled her eyes at Racquel, picked up the phone, and got Jacqueline's voicemail.

"Don't worry." Racquel got up from her chair and tucked her yellow notepad under her arm. She slid her pen between her ear and her short curly fro. "If she's like the rest of these women around here I'm sure she'll call you back in a minute, if she isn't on her way to see you already."

"Do me a favor, please?" Cleopatra asked. "Order a dozen long-stemmed red roses and have them delivered to her desk by one o'clock today."

Racquel did a double take.

Cleopatra smiled. "What? Should I send two dozen? Or should I just send candy?"

Racquel walked around behind Cleopatra's desk and felt her forehead with the back of her hand. "What's wrong with you, child?"

"Stop teasing me." Cleopatra laughed.

"One dozen roses coming right up. Do I have a budget?"

"No budget. Find the biggest, reddest roses in the city. And the card should read, *My actions speak louder than my words.*"

"I'm all over it." Racquel grinned. "I'll be at my desk if you need me."

"Thanks, Ma," Cleopatra said. Racquel was about as much of a mother as she had now. She was the personification of a watchdog. She took her job of looking out for Cleopatra seriously, convinced that someone needed to. She had years and life experience on Cleopatra and didn't hesitate to call her on her bullshit. Cleopatra needed and appreciated Racquel more than either of them realized.

Cleopatra was going through her emails when she heard a knock at her door. "Yes?" she said without looking up from her monitor.

"Good morning. Your assistant said it was ok to come in." Jacqueline stood in the doorway.

"Good morning, beautiful." Cleopatra tried to contain her excitement as she stood up.

"Your office is sexy. I love it." Jacqueline smiled.

"Please come in." Cleopatra walked toward her. She fought the urge to grab her, peel her out of that gray business suit and tongue her down.

"Your assistant is very protective of you. Did you two ever date?" She walked around Cleopatra's office, checking out the decor.

"That's gross." Cleopatra pretended to throw up in her mouth. "Absolutely never." She leaned on the end of her desk.

"Just wanted to make sure. She's pretty. I didn't want to roll into enemy territory not knowing what I was up against."

"You have nothing to be worried about." Cleopatra looked at her legs. She wondered if they were as soft as they looked.

"Racquel is like family. We've known each other for years.

We met when I was in high school. She's super-straight, and married." She reassured Jacqueline. "I'm the godmother to her twins." She pointed to a picture on her desk of her holding two newborns. "They are almost twelve months old now." She smiled.

"Twins? They are so adorable." Jacqueline stared at the picture.

Cleopatra snapped her out of her trance. "What's in the bag?"

"Almost forgot. I brought you a peppermint tea, and an egg and cheese on an everything bagel." She handed Cleopatra a brown paper bag.

"Thank you. How do you know what I like for breakfast?" Cleopatra asked with a curious smile on her face.

"This crush I have on you makes it mandatory that I know what you like."

"Is that all? A little crush?" Cleopatra took a sip of tea.

"A crush is an understatement. I couldn't sleep this weekend thinking about you."

"So, I kept you up?"

"You did." Jacqueline stopped in front of Cleopatra's framed degree certificates. A bachelor's from Columbia and a master's from NYU. "I'll earn mine one day." She stroked the seal on Cleopatra's grad school diploma.

"You will. I know how important it is to you to go back. You seem like you get what you want."

Jacqueline had told Cleopatra during their phone conversation how she recently had to leave NYU's Stern School of Business just after her first semester and go to work because she couldn't make tuition. She was afraid it would take her forever to be able to go back to school full-time. If she ever made it back all.

"So you like Scooby-Doo?" She saw a framed animation cel autographed by the animator Iwao Takamoto on her shelf. "That's quite a collector's item."

"I used to have a huge stuffed Scooby when I was a kid. I would hug him whenever I was scared and he made me feel safe."

"That's sweet." Jacqueline sat down in the chair in front of Cleopatra's desk, and crossed her legs. She caught Cleopatra staring at the thigh that was peeking out from under her skirt. Instead of covering herself she gave her more, and Cleopatra enjoyed it.

Cleopatra tried hard to stop staring at her legs again but was failing. She decided she was obsessed with them. She wanted to lick the fullness of Jacqueline's thighs, the curves of her calf muscles all the way down to her heels. Pictures of the two of them fucking flashed before her eyes.

"Do you like kids?"

"What?" Cleopatra shook her head. "I love kids, but I'm nowhere near ready for any right now. Are we still on for lunch today?"

"Yes. I can't wait." She stood up from the chair. "I'm going to surprise you." Jacqueline smiled.

"I hope you do." Cleopatra stared at her ass as she walked out of her office. "Lord help me." She slammed her hand down on her desk.

◎ ◎ ◎

A few hours later Cleopatra was leaving to meet Jacqueline for lunch when Jacqueline knocked on her door.

"I was just going to meet you downstairs."

"This is my surprise. I made you lunch." She presented Cleopatra with a huge insulated lunch bag.

"This is serious, like a cooler you take to a family reunion." Cleopatra laughed as she took the basket out of her arms. "When did you do this?"

Racquel peeked around the corner as she closed the door, and gave Cleopatra the thumbs-up sign.

"Last night." Jacqueline said.

"Thank you so much. No one has ever done anything like this for me before."

"Get used to it." She winked at her.

Cleopatra headed over to the table in the corner of her office as Jacqueline opened up her shades to let in some sunlight.

"Cute. You even packed a tablecloth." Cleopatra spread the red and white checkered cloth over the table. "Am I sensing a theme here? Is that Italian I smell?"

"You said you loved manicotti, and I promised to make it for you. I just decided to do it sooner than later."

"I didn't think you were serious. Where did you learn to cook manicotti?" Cleopatra wanted a woman who would cook for her, and the women she dated couldn't or wouldn't cook. If she didn't cook herself they starved or ordered in, and she had made a decision not to settle down with anyone who couldn't feed her outside of the bedroom. That small requirement eliminated most of the women she met from serious consideration.

"So you know my mom is from down south. She taught me how to cook everything," Jacqueline said as she helped Cleopatra unpack the pasta and put it in the microwave. "My father is a very happy man."

"I bet he is." Cleopatra nodded her head. "Peach cobbler too? My favorite." She shrieked with joy.

"Did you just jump?" Jacqueline teased her.

"I did not."

"No. You definitely got air under your feet. That was really cute."

"You listen to me, huh?" Cleopatra asked her.

"Of course I do. Sit, I'll fix your plate." She took the manicotti out of the microwave. She loaded Cleopatra's plate with the cheesy pasta and some spinach salad. She laid a small serving of peach cobbler on the side.

Cleopatra waited for Jacqueline to fix her own plate before she dug into the manicotti. She pulled the fork toward her mouth and unearthed the ricotta, mozzarella and parmesan cheeses intermingled with large chunks of stewed tomatoes and marinara sauce. She was embarrassed when she opened her eyes and found Jacqueline watching her eat.

"Do you want to be alone?" Jacqueline laughed. "Is it good to you?"

"Oh yeah." Cleopatra leaned back and picked up the plate of manicotti and examined it. "This may be the best thing I've ever had in my mouth."

"Is that right?" Jacqueline sucked her index finger into her mouth and bit it. "We'll have to see if we can change that."

"What else did you have in mind?"

"Something sweet."

She had the full attention of Cleopatra's clit. "I'm listening." She put her fork down on the table.

"Peaches."

Cleopatra watched Jacqueline's nipples harden through her white silk blouse as her chest heaved and her breaths got shorter. Cleopatra imagined Jacqueline calling her name as she sat on her face, her pussy spread and pouring into her mouth.

"The peaches in my cobbler." She pointed to the pan of cobbler in the middle of the table and smiled.

Cleopatra sat back and squirmed in her chair trying to separate herself from the dampness in her boxers. "Of course. Thank you so much for doing this for me."

"You're welcome."

As the afternoon sunlight shone into the office, they sat and ate in silence, except for Cleopatra's inadvertent moans and Jacqueline's giggling at her reactions. The manicotti wasn't the only reason Cleopatra was quiet. Over the weekend, they'd talked about almost everything over the phone. They shared a lot of the same interests and hobbies. Jacqueline had already fulfilled two of Cleopatra's requirements to be taken seriously. She loved to cook, and she read voraciously. She hadn't met a woman like Jacqueline in a long time, and she wasn't sure what to do with her. It was really early, but she was revealing herself to be the type of woman that Cleopatra had been waiting for. She wasn't sure what Jacqueline wanted from her, but she appreciated her using a different approach in order to get it.

"This is a small manicotti and cobbler for you to take home

tonight. Don't forget about it." She put it in the mini-fridge as Cleopatra helped her clean up.

"Look at you still taking care of me. Thank you." Cleopatra sat down on the couch.

"That's what a good woman is supposed to do." Jacqueline sat down next to her and crossed her legs.

"Anyone who would bake manicotti and peach cobbler for me in the middle of the night, in the summertime, and lug it into to work in that trunk of a cooler is not just a good woman – you are like Superwoman."

"Keep it up." She smiled. "Flattery will get you whatever you want." She rubbed Cleopatra's knee. "But I have to confess this is selfish on my part. I didn't want to share you today. I wanted to be alone with you."

"Do you always get what you want?"

"That remains to be seen. I don't remember when I've wanted something this much." She stroked Cleopatra's long fingers between her hands. "Have you ever been in love?"

Stunned by the question and the sharp turn in the conversation, Cleopatra answered, "No. You?"

"Never, but I'm ready. Are you?"

"Wanting it and being ready are two separate things. I don't know."

"I think you're ready."

Cleopatra momentarily had second thoughts. Did she want to do this? Deal with all of the ramifications of being someone's first lover? The sexual tension between her and Jacqueline was so thick that it was almost uncomfortable.

"I'm ready," Jacqueline said. "I've never met a woman before that I wanted to give myself to, before now."

"You seem pretty sure of yourself."

"I am. I want a committed relationship. Someone I can totally give every part of my mind, body and soul to." She interrupted her. "If I was just out for sex, I could have had that a long time ago, and until recently I thought I would have to settle for that. But I realize now I don't have to. You made me realize that I need more than that and I can have more than that. I want to be in love."

This was about to turn into the typical, deep and accelerated lesbian conversation that Cleopatra usually wanted no part of. And why she didn't get up and run out of her office yelling "Fire!" when Jacqueline said the word "committed" was beyond her. But, she didn't want to leave. There was nowhere else she wanted to be other than right where she was.

"So how do you know that I'm not just out for sex?" Cleopatra asked.

"You are." She laughed. "But only until you find someone who can give you everything you need. I understand that and I don't fault you for it. You may want sex but you are going to want more from me, and you're going to get it." She leaned forward.

"Is that right?" Cleopatra was seriously attracted to her confidence.

"Yes. The same way you see pain in my eyes, I see your need to be loved in yours. And after all that heat I was giving you on the train you could have taken me home and had your way with me, but you didn't."

"You're serious?" Cleopatra leaned back on the couch.

"Very serious. You are sincere, and I'm at ease with you already, like I've always known you. I like you, a whole lot, way more than I should for having known you less than seventy-two hours. This weekend was the most enjoyable time I've had in a while."

"What did you do?"

"I was on the phone with you, silly!" She pinched Cleopatra's arm. "I love talking to you. I want to get to know you better, everything about you. What makes you happy, what makes you sad, what gets you excited..."

"You do." Cleopatra stopped her. "You excite me. You are so sweet, and you can cook and you're sitting this close to me, giving me those thighs in my office with the door locked. You don't know what you do to me."

Jacqueline exhaled. "You have no idea what you do to me." She caressed Cleopatra's hands and tugged on her long fingers.

"I can't put it into words. I'd have to show you."

Jacqueline's eyes, her body, everything she was doing told Cleopatra she wanted her. But Cleopatra knew enough about her already to know she would never want her first time with a woman to be on her first date, at work or on a couch. But Cleopatra wanted Jacqueline, and she would leave it up to her. Cleopatra put her hand on her thigh, then surrendered control. "Show me."

Jacqueline leaned back on the couch and parted her legs a bit. She took Cleopatra's hand and slid it between her thighs. The heat from her pussy enveloped Cleopatra's hand. She looked in her eyes, their lips nearly touching. "Please."

The phone startled them and broke the spell. They leaned back on the couch for a moment, chests heaving, mouths wet, among other spots. Cleopatra ran to her desk and picked up her phone.

"Yes, Racquel? We are fully dressed." She laughed. "All right, thanks."

"We should get back to work. I have to get ready for a meeting this afternoon." Cleopatra said to Jacqueline.

"Yeah, I need to get back upstairs." She straightened her clothes.

Jacqueline stood by the door, picnic basket in hand. "What almost happened here, can't happen yet. I'm not ready. And I refuse to let you make love to me and leave me. I'm not in this for a one night stand."

"Understood." Cleopatra nodded her head.

"But that doesn't mean I won't have a hard time resisting you, because I am already."

"Good." Cleopatra said softly.

"I have to ask you. Is there room in your life for me? The way I want to be in it? Before you answer, I can't do this if I don't have your focus. Just you and me. I want exclusivity."

Cleopatra growled softly in the back of her throat. "There is plenty of room. However you want it." Cleopatra moved in to kiss her.

Jacqueline grabbed her face with both hands right before

their lips touched. "I have to leave you wanting more." Jacqueline blew her a kiss instead and walked away. Cleopatra leaned on her door as she watched Jacqueline strut down the hall and get on the elevator. *Damn, she got me.* Not three days since she first laid eyes on Jacqueline and already she was tugging on Cleopatra's heart.

A few minutes later Racquel knocked on Cleopatra's door. "Jacqueline asked me to give this to you after she left." She winked at Cleopatra as she sat the gift bag on her desk.

Cleopatra pulled out a small Scooby Doo keychain with a note.

For your Scooby fetish. Now you can carry him with you. Always, Jacqueline.

Cleopatra smiled as Racquel watched her add him to her keys. She wondered if Jacqueline had seen her gift yet, when the desk phone rang.

"Hi, Jac."

"You are so unbelievably sweet to me! I've never seen roses this beautiful before. They must be three feet tall."

"I'm glad you like them." Cleopatra gave Racquel the thumbs up. "I'll talk to you later, sweetheart. Have a good afternoon." Cleopatra hung up.

"I think I could actually hear her smiling over the phone." Cleopatra grinned.

"You like her a lot." Racquel said.

"What are you talking about?"

"I've never seen you respond to a woman like this one. Today was your first date, and you sent her flowers, from a florist and not the bodega. And those flowers were not cheap. Watch out now!" She slicked her hair back and did a two-step.

"Are you done teasing me?" Cleopatra twisted her lips.

"Actually, no. Look at your face."

"How am I going to look at my face?"

"I mean you look happy, that's all I'm saying. She cooked for you! That's major points in my book."

"I know. And she can cook something besides breakfast."

"Well, if it makes a difference, I like her. She's not like these other crazy bitches around here."

"Yeah. She's not like them at all."

"Maybe it's because I'm straight, but sometimes I'm like, *what is it about you?* I mean you have a pretty smile, you dress immaculately, your locs are shiny, you're smart, you have lucrative employment and you're a sweetheart, but..."

"Are you building a case for or against me?" Cleopatra laughed. "You mean you never heard about the tongue flick and the hip pop?"

"What are those, exactly?" Racquel placed her hand on her hip.

"You have to be there, and since you are the best assistant in the world, that's never going to happen. Your husband would whip my ass, and I'm just way too delicate."

"Speaking of ass, Susan from accounting and Jennifer from legal both came by, wanting to know what you were doing this weekend."

"That's so inappropriate." Cleopatra shook her head. "What did you tell them?"

"I told Susan you had joined the National Guard, and this was your weekend away. I told Jennifer that you were straight now and only dating white men with pierced penises."

"Remind me to give you a raise."

TASHA C. MILLER

LOVE

Shawn called Cleopatra early Saturday morning to curse her out. They hadn't hung out in weeks. Shawn had been busy with her stable of women and Cleopatra had been busy with her one woman, Jacqueline.

"You're about to go where?" Shawn laughed.

"The Museum of Modern Art."

"Stop bullshitting, they got a hotel in the back of that motherfucker now?"

"You know we haven't gotten to that point yet." Cleopatra sighed. "My right hand and I have become real tight recently."

"Damn. Let me find out, she got you."

"She can get it. All of it, and she will."

"Speaking of opening wide, I ran into Trina at the club last night, she kept asking about you."

"Dominicana Trina? What did you tell her?"

"That you had a woman now. She asked me to give you her new number anyway. You want it?"

"Throw it out."

"Damn."

◉ ◉ ◉

After the museum, Jacqueline and Cleopatra went for lunch in Union Square. The Italian eatery was cozy and movie theatre dark. Wine bottles plastered the walls, and white tablecloths and the orange and red glow from the strategically placed wall sconces broke up the dark monotony. The only other light peeked in from the outdoor patio. The few customers made the noise of a much larger crowd, so Cleopatra requested a booth in the back. The smell of garlic, parmesan and fresh bread overtook them as they were seated by their redheaded waitress.

"So, did you enjoy the museum?" Cleopatra slid in on her side of the booth.

"I loved it. Thank you for taking me, baby. But I must admit I had a hard time taking my eyes off of you to look at the exhibits. You look especially sexy in all white. That shirt is hitting you everywhere I need it to."

"That's funny, because I can never keep my eyes off of *you*. I've been meaning to thank you for all of that cleavage." Cleopatra's eyes locked in on Jacqueline's form in the red low-cut t-shirt. "And those heels you got on? It's not right." Cleopatra shook her head.

"You love them, don't you? I spotted you checking them out a few times."

Cleopatra bit her bottom lip and took a deep breath. "They make me want to lick your whole leg." She fingered the heavy silverware. "I want to see you out of those heels actually." Cleopatra caught herself. "I mean, I want to see how tall you are without them."

"You would tower over me." Jacqueline said. "Somebody has a shoe fetish. I'm so going to take advantage of that. Speaking of getting checked out, I know we've talked about this before but you command a lot of attention from women – gay, straight, doesn't matter, huh?"

"You noticed? Maybe a little bit." Cleopatra took a sip of water. "Does it bother you?"

"It can be annoying. It's going to take some getting used to."

"I understand. I don't want you to be uncomfortable. I know this is all new to you. If you ever want to leave somewhere or you want me to have a word with someone who's bothering you, please tell me."

"You're sweet. But I like being on your arm. Knowing you can have anyone you want and that you want to be with me makes me feel special."

"You are special." Cleopatra winked at her. "I plan on showing you how special."

The pudgy redhead took their order without paper and pen, and they were convinced she would screw it up. Cleopatra ordered a hearty scampi oreganata for herself, jumbo shrimp sautéed in white wine over a bed of angel hair pasta, and for Jacqueline she ordered fettuccine Alfredo with sweet peas and black truffle sauce and a bottle of Bergstrom Sigrid chardonnay for the table. Cleopatra firmly but politely corrected the waitress and suggested she write down the order when she came to the table with two orders of spaghetti and meatballs. After the second attempt with a notepad and pencil their food arrived flawless.

"What's the itinerary for the rest of the day?" Jacqueline asked, taking a sip of wine. "Ooh. That's delicious." She looked at the wine as she swirled it around her glass. "You remembered chardonnay is my favorite."

"I remember everything you tell me." Cleopatra winked at her. "I don't have anything big planned for today. The movies, hang in the park or maybe the bookstore. And then to my house so I can cook dinner for you."

"Or we could go to your house right now." She leaned across the table and dared Cleopatra to accept her offer.

"What's at my house that you need to see right now?" Cleopatra prodded. She could smell Jacqueline's perfume; the sweet smell made her tingle and moist.

"I want to be alone with you." She rubbed Cleopatra's calf muscle with her foot. "How come you haven't kissed me yet?" Jacqueline asked.

"I'm afraid I won't be able to stop."

Jacqueline had taken Cleopatra's restraint as a good sign, given some of the stories she'd heard. She was definitely treating her differently from the other women she'd dated, as far as Jacqueline could discern.

They talked while they ate, but fell silent from time to time. Jacqueline would stare down at Cleopatra's hands as she caressed her fingers. She was obsessed with how big and how strong Cleopatra's hands were. Cleopatra imagined Jacqueline was daydreaming about how they would feel massaging her naked body or how they would feel inside of her, because that's what Cleopatra was thinking too. As far as Cleopatra was concerned, the day was going perfectly. Then the dreaded question came, the one she rarely answered, at least not honestly.

"So, tell me about your family? You never talk about them."

Cleopatra didn't answer, and she pretended not to hear Jacqueline. She twirled some angel hair pasta around her fork, shoveled it into her mouth, and took a gulp of wine. Her body was rigid, and she appeared to be holding her breath.

"Are you not going to answer me?"

Cleopatra played with her water glass, wet with condensation.

"If there is a problem we can end this date right now." Cleopatra got up and stood next to the table.

Stunned by Cleopatra's reaction, Jacqueline calmly grabbed Cleopatra's hand. "Sit down, please."

Jacqueline had the softest hands she ever held. Cleopatra wanted them all over her body, but she was not using them to seduce her. Jacqueline was trying to crack her protective shell. Cleopatra surrendered and sat back down.

"I'm sorry. This is a sensitive subject for you. Forgive me?"

Cleopatra was silent. She began to eat again. Her eyes watered as she prayed her tears would not betray her, and they didn't. Jacqueline picked at her food and kept her eyes on Cleopatra.

"Look at me," Jacqueline said. Cleopatra strained her eyes in her direction.

"You are obviously in a lot of pain. I can't force you to talk, but it feels like you need to." She caressed Cleopatra's hand. "You can talk to me about anything. I want you to know that."

Cleopatra saw a twinge of pain on Jacqueline's face, like she shared in her hurt. She was conflicted. Should she hide this part of herself with the woman she was trying to have a relationship with? Or did she need to open up and tell her the truth and allow herself be vulnerable?

"I don't really have any family," Cleopatra said as she took a sip of wine.

Sadness crossed Jacqueline's face. She sat motionless, waiting for Cleopatra to explain.

Cleopatra couldn't bring herself to look Jacqueline in the eye. She took a deep breath before she continued. "I was fourteen when my father left after my mother had a massive stroke." She swirled the pasta around her plate. "That's when I started taking care of her and I had to work to support us. She died eighteen months ago." She gripped her fork tighter. "Sorry, I still count the months. She was my only family." She looked at Jacqueline, whose eyes were watering. Tears pooled in Cleopatra's eyes, but she still refused to cry. She couldn't show Jacqueline her heart. Not yet. "I'm sorry. I can just now think back without totally breaking down. So, I must be healing, I guess." Cleopatra took a sip of water. "She loved me. Unconditionally. I think I've been looking for that type of love."

Jacqueline got up and sat on Cleopatra's side of the booth. She didn't say a word, she just held her. In Jacqueline's embrace, a lone tear slid down Cleopatra's cheek.

"I'm sorry for falling apart." She sniffed. "Don't be scared. This is not a common occurrence."

"You don't have to be strong all the time. Don't apologize for showing me who you are." Jacqueline took Cleopatra's hand and pressed it against her heart.

Cleopatra thought better of torturing herself by trying to sit in a dark movie theatre with Jacqueline for two hours, so they roamed around the "eighteen miles of books" at the Strand bookstore on Broadway and East 12th for a while. They separated almost immediately upon entering. Both of them searched in the ugly fluorescent lighting of the decades-old bookstore for treasures among the new, used and rare books that were jam-packed into every available shelf, table and spot on the floor. Cleopatra had picked up *Wench, Cutting for Stone, Flash of the Spirit* and *The China Study,* four books she had been meaning to read for quite some time. They separately weaved their way in and out of the people crammed into the store, walking up and down the stacks on opposite ends of the building. Jacqueline carefully took books off the tops of piles that were taller than she was. Cleopatra spotted her at the Best of the Best table. *Damn, she is fine.* Jacqueline looked up and caught Cleopatra watching her, and winked at her before Cleopatra disappeared to the rare book room upstairs. Next she found herself in the literary fiction stacks and self-help sections while Jacqueline went through the memoirs and the African-American history shelves. When Cleopatra saw Jacqueline again she had a stack of books in her arms and was holding them in place with her chin. Cleopatra took them from her and sat them down on a free corner of a display table.

"You didn't see any books you wanted?" Jacqueline asked, shaking her arms out.

"No." Cleopatra spotted an empty basket under the table and grabbed it. "I saw like fifteen books that I wanted so I just looked them up and bought them on my Kindle." Cleopatra smiled as she patted the messenger bag where she stashed her tablet. She loaded Jacqueline's books into the basket. She looked through Jacqueline selections and was impressed. "This was an amazing book." Cleopatra pulled out Harry Belafonte's memoir *My Song* from the pile. "He's a remarkable man. Well written. It was long as hell, but a great book."

"You've read that already?" Jacqueline was surprised. "It just came out like yesterday or the day before."

"It came out electronically a week ago. We have to get you some type of e-reader." She winked at Jacqueline.

"Never. You do realize you are single handedly killing this bookstore right?"

"Really? Single handedly? Just me? Strand is going to be just fine." Cleopatra smiled. "I do own a few books, you know, I buy hard copies too." She picked up Jacqueline's basket and went to the register.

"What are you doing?" Jacqueline asked Cleopatra as she put down her ATM card to pay for the books.

"I'm paying for your books."

"But you don't have to."

"I know that. I want to. No expectations, if that's what you're worried about."

"Really?" Jacqueline asked, a bit surprised. "That's too bad." She smiled. "You are going to spoil me. Thank you, baby," she said as she went to grab the bag from the cashier.

Cleopatra took the bag away from her. "Sweetheart. I carry the bag for you too."

Afterward they walked through Union Square Park. To Cleopatra's surprise Jacqueline laced her fingers in between hers as they walked through the greenmarket and past the countless vendors selling their wares. The summer sun beamed down on them as they watched a group doing capoeira. The all-male group of around twenty or so Brazilian capoeiristas danced two at a time inside the circle formed by the crowd of nearly one hundred people. Shirtless, barefoot and wearing white abadas, they danced as the live musicians dictated their speed, style and aggressiveness.

"Come on." Jacqueline pulled Cleopatra away from the performers and the crowd, and they moved into the shade. She took it upon herself to wipe Cleopatra down when she saw sweat on her forehead.

"You just want to rub on me, don't you?" Cleopatra teased her as she slipped her arm around Jacqueline's waist.

"I do," she said, as she dabbed her face with a tissue. "I wish I was making you sweat like this. Do you sweat when you make love?"

"No, but when I'm fucking it drips off of me." Cleopatra winked at her.

That caught Jacqueline off guard. Cleopatra enjoyed shocking Jacqueline with her responses. She knew that, as good as Jacqueline was trying to be, she wanted her, and Cleopatra liked teasing her. Before Jacqueline could respond, a man called out Cleopatra's name. He wore a green hooded sweatshirt and white capoeira training pants. He was running toward them down East 14th Street.

"Hey, Raymond, good to see you." Cleopatra hugged a tall, cinnamon man with deep set eyes. "This is Jacqueline. Jacqueline, this is Raymond."

"It's a pleasure to meet you." He shook her hand, not taking his eyes off of Cleopatra.

"So you're in the group?" Cleopatra asked pointing at the green cord that held up his pants.

"Yeah. But I'm a beginner so they don't let me dance in public or on the concrete yet. Plus I've knocked a couple of dudes out by mistake."

"I'm sure you'll be kicking guys in the head on concrete in public in no time. How's your mom doing?" Cleopatra asked him.

"She's good. She misses you," he said, lightly rubbing her arm.

"I'm going to visit her soon. Promise."

"She'll love that. All right, I gotta get back."

"Tell Moms I said hello." Cleopatra said.

"You know I will. Great meeting you," he said to Jacqueline as he kissed Cleopatra's cheek. Then he took off running back toward the still growing crowd watching the performers.

"He was nice. He likes you a lot." Jacqueline said. "How do you know him?"

"I volunteer at a women's shelter, and we deliver meals to seniors. I deliver to his mom, and she likes to talk, so I sit and listen."

"That's the sweetest thing I've ever heard. You never mentioned that before."

"It's not something I talk about, just something I do." Cleopatra was embarrassed. "Let's go." She grabbed Jacqueline's hand. They crossed 14th Street and walked in the direction of Whole Foods when Cleopatra heard her name again. She turned around and saw a little boy scurrying toward her through the crowd. She bent down and caught him as he ran into her arms.

"Hi sweetie. Where's your mommy?" she asked the dimple-faced boy as she picked him up and gave him a hug.

"She's coming." He pointed to his mother who was a few feet away and walking up to Cleopatra and Jacqueline.

A milk chocolate woman with a large untamed afro came up to Cleopatra and kissed her on the cheek and acknowledged Jacqueline with an exuberant "Good afternoon."

"Jacqueline, this is Xavier, and this is his mother Bonita."

"What are you doing running down the block without your mama?" Cleopatra asked the little boy who had his hands tangled in her locs.

"I got excited when I saw you. I won't do it again, I promise."

"I haven't seen you since you left the shelter," Cleopatra said to his mother. "How's everything?"

"I know, I been busy with my new job."

"Congratulations." Cleopatra beamed. "I knew you could do it."

"It's not brain surgery but they have tuition reimbursement, so I can go back to school soon. How's Racquel?"

"She's thriving. She's so good now. I'll tell her hello for you."

"Please do. Is this your lady?" She looked at Jacqueline.

"Yes. That's me."

Bonita put her arm around Cleopatra. "She's the best," she said to Jacqueline. "I wouldn't be here without her."

"Stop." Cleopatra grew uncomfortable.

"Seriously. Treat her well and you won't have any problems. If you don't, she has a lot of seedy friends that will come looking for you. I'm one of them." She winked. "Don't be scared. I'm only serious."

"I understand." Jacqueline said, with a nervous smile on her face.

"Bonita, no one is going to come looking for anyone. Still hood, I see." Cleopatra laughed.

"All day, ev'ry day."

"I'll see you soon. Ok?" Cleopatra said to Xavier, as she put him in his mother's arms.

"You promise?"

"I promise. How's the apartment?" Cleopatra asked his mother.

"Quiet. It's safe. So, yeah, it's perfect."

"You be good for your mama." Cleopatra accepted a kiss from the little boy and kissed Bonita on the cheek. "Keep me updated on school and let me know if you need anything." Cleopatra watched them walk away.

Cleopatra started to walk into Whole Foods.

"Hold on. What just happened?" Jacqueline yanked Cleopatra away from the door and off to the side.

"I guess you want me to explain how I know them, too?"

"Yes. And your seedy associates that are going to come for me?"

"Bonita and her son lived at the shelter for a while. That's all."

"She said if it wasn't for you that she wouldn't be here."

"She can be dramatic sometimes."

"I think you are being modest. Wait. So, was Racquel in the shelter?"

Cleopatra hesitated a bit. She was tentative when talking about her own business so she wasn't one to blab about others, either. "Let's just say life hasn't always been so good for

Racquel. She was born and grew up in extreme poverty in Ethiopia and she was able to find her way to New York. She got caught up in some unfortunate people and circumstances while she was trying to survive here. That's how she ended up in the shelter. She's kind of a big deal and after my mother, probably the strongest woman I've ever met."

"You've known her forever. So, you've been involved with the shelter a long time?"

"Since I was fourteen."

"The same year your mother got sick and your father left?" Cleopatra was silent. "All that happened in your life, and you found the time to volunteer?"

"Not exactly." Jacqueline waited for her to explain.

"The state found out my mother couldn't take care of me, or herself for that matter. They put her in a home up in the Bronx, and they put me in a foster home in Queens. I ran away and ended up at the shelter. They helped bring me and my mother back together. They saved my life. So, I kind of never left them."

"You're amazing." Jacqueline took both of Cleopatra's hands in to hers. "When do you have time?"

"I make the time. What do you want for dinner?" Cleopatra tried to change the subject.

"Thank you for confiding in me. I know it's not easy for you to share with me the way you have today. Why don't I cook you dinner instead?"

"You've already cooked for me."

"I know, but it's not a one-time thing. I'm trying to take care of you. Will you let me?"

"A beautiful woman, in those heels, cook a meal made with love for me? Yeah, I would let you do that."

● ● ●

After dropping a small fortune on groceries, they took a cab downtown to Cleopatra's house on Waverly Place in the West Village. Cleopatra gathered the four paper bags full of food and

Jacqueline's books from the trunk. Jacqueline was seduced by the quiet stretch of row houses. The tree lined street with its nearly identical brownstones was calm for a Saturday afternoon in July. As she wondered how anyone could find their house among the uniform boxes, one stuck out to her, its exterior a little different from the rest, a bit more manicured, its front door more ornate and imposing. That's where Cleopatra stood on the steps looking back at her.

"Are you coming?" she asked as she put the key in the door and punched in her security alarm code.

Jacqueline walked up the steps and entered the foyer. "Is this whole brownstone yours?"

"All mine," Cleopatra said as she brought the bags in from the steps.

"Wow. How many floors? How many bedrooms?"

"Five floors. Five bedrooms, five baths."

"Incredible. Renting?"

"No. I own it." Cleopatra smiled.

"Can I ask how you can afford your own house in the West Village? This is prime Manhattan real estate."

"Of course you can ask." She winked at her, but didn't answer. Another question Cleopatra never answered. And Jacqueline didn't press her on it.

"Make yourself at home. Look around if you like. This is the parlor floor. That's the living room, next to it is the library, then the terrace. On the third floor is the movie and game room and on the fourth and fifth floors are the bedrooms and there's a roof deck. Downstairs is the garden level, the dining room is down there, the kitchen and…"

"Let me guess, you have a garden, don't you?"

"Yup." Cleopatra smiled cunningly at her.

Jacqueline watched Cleopatra walk down the stairs with the groceries before she ventured into the living room. It was long and narrow with high ceilings. Two windows draped by long white sheer panels that faced on to Waverly let in only delicate patches of light. The room was minimalist with every item in an orderly fashion. She could see straight through to the library and to the glass doors of the terrace. The sunlight from the terrace flooded the entire floor and warmed the room up. The living room walls were a milk chocolate brown set against white crown molding and looked like velvet, forcing Jacqueline to touch them to find out for herself. The dark chocolate living room furniture with it straight lines added a masculine feel to the interior. Jacqueline's eyes were drawn to the large black marble fireplace mantel where she saw a picture of Cleopatra as a child with her mother. Cleopatra was most certainly her child. She was a beautiful woman, tall, lean and statuesque like her daughter. Similar to Cleopatra's office, there was no clutter or excessive details. The only burst of color was the abstract art on the walls, and scattered burgundy and violet accessories.

Jacqueline walked from the living room into the large library. Books lined the wall from floor to ceiling. She ran her hands along the cherry wood built-in shelves, taking note of Cleopatra's eclectic and extensive book collection; the fact that Cleopatra was so well read turned her on. Cleopatra was sexy as hell, sensitive and sweet to Jacqueline. She was also intelligent and accomplished – how would Jacqueline ever get through this night without ripping Cleopatra's clothes off, she thought. Jacqueline looked out the glass doors on to the terrace at the immaculately manicured landscape and the white-cushioned and bronze-framed lawn furniture. These rooms were seducing her; they were dark, quiet and peaceful like Cleopatra. She went back into the living room and sunk down into the leather couch. It too was like Cleopatra, she thought as she fingered the Moroccan leather. Brown, soft and strong.

"You like the couch?" Cleopatra stood in the doorway.

"I love this entire floor, it's erotic. Makes me want to get naked or something." Jacqueline laughed. "Don't tell me, heard that before, haven't you?"

"No comment." Cleopatra smirked.

"The energy in here is overwhelming."

"Are you going to be ok if I let you roam free?"

"I rather you take me on a tour, I might get lost." She grabbed her hand. "At least show me your bedroom. You can show me the rest later."

Cleopatra took her up two flights of stairs.

"This is my bedroom."

Jacqueline hesitated. She had fantasized about being in Cleopatra's bedroom many times, but now it was happening. She peeked into the room.

"Oh, ok, I was expecting something else," she walked around the bedroom. It was a softer version of the living room. The huge bed dominated the mocha space and was covered with a merlot Natori duvet and what Jacqueline estimated to be a dozen pillows of all shapes and sizes. Long vanilla velvet panels hung from the ceiling down to the floor and puddled in front of the windows. Perched in the corner and facing the 70" flat panel TV in front of the bed was a futuristic recliner that doubled as a massage chair. Sepia toned photographs of naked women making love graced the caramel colored walls The more Jacqueline stood there, the more she warmed up to the room. Cleopatra was not what she expected and she was pleasantly surprised, and turned on. Everything Cleopatra did turned her on. "It's peaceful. Very soothing. Warm."

"But not what you were expecting?" Cleopatra asked. Jacqueline shrugged her shoulders. "You requested to see my bedroom. You didn't ask to see something else."

"This is where it goes down right?"

Cleopatra smiled slyly. "This is my bedroom where I sleep, watch TV and read. If you meant something else, you should have said *something else.*"

Jacqueline put her lips near Cleopatra's ears. "Show me something else." She extended her hand.

Cleopatra led her down the hall, opened the door to a dark room and went in. "This is the room you wanted to see."

Jacqueline stood in the doorway. She could barely make out Cleopatra's white clothing in the darkness.

"This is the sex room," Cleopatra said.

"Where's the light switch?" Jacqueline's hand grazed the wall by the door. She was stunned when she realized she was fondling velvet for real this time, and not plaster.

"Only I know where the lights are," Cleopatra answered. "You can come in. I won't attack you."

"Too bad." Jacqueline walked in, taking careful steps.

Cleopatra was on the other side of the room and switched on a small Tiffany styled glass and antique bronze lamp, giving Jacqueline just enough light to move about.

"What do I keep kicking? Are those pillows?"

"Yes, in case you fall off the bed, the pillows would cushion your fall."

"How could someone fall off of that bed? Do you think it's big enough?" She teased, looking at the California king canopy bed.

"Oh, it can happen." Cleopatra assured her with a smile.

Jacqueline stepped gingerly through all of the pillows and embraced Cleopatra.

"I'm a big girl, I need a big bed, I need room." Cleopatra looked down into her eyes. Jacqueline loved how she had to look up at her and how safe she felt wrapped in her arms.

"Room to what? And I don't see anything in here but that bed."

"There are other things in here." Cleopatra said. Jacqueline walked toward the closet door. "I don't suggest you open that door."

Jacqueline stopped in her tracks. She looked around the room as her eyes adjusted to the darkness.

"Is this room soundproof?"

"Yes." Cleopatra smiled.

"So you could lock me in here and no one would ever find me?"

"I would never lock you in here, if you didn't want me to."

"And there's a camera in here somewhere, isn't there?"

"That's also in the category of things I would never do without your permission."

"And I still can't open that closet?"

"I would prefer that you didn't."

"What's in there?"

"Do you really want to know?"

"I do."

"Your next seventy-two hours, if you open that door."

"What does that mean?" Jacqueline chuckled nervously.

"It's going to take me three days to use everything behind that door on you. "Factoring in a little recovery time, of course."

"Can I sit on it?"

"What?"

"Your bed, can I lie on it?"

"Oh. Yeah, go ahead."

Jacqueline pressed her hands down on the duvet and hopped up on the bed.

"Oh, my God. This is so good." She moaned as she sunk into Cleopatra's bed, almost disappearing into the darkness of the purple bedding. She looked up at the ceiling.

"What are you looking for?" Cleopatra asked her.

"I was expecting to see a mirror."

Cleopatra laughed and walked over to the bed, she pulled the pillows away from the headboard.

"In the headboard?" Jacqueline turned over on her stomach.

"That's there because I want you to look at yourself while I'm making love to you." Cleopatra watched Jacqueline as she stared at her reflection in the mirror. Besides her clit throbbing, Cleopatra didn't move. Jacqueline raised herself up on her hands and knees and looked back at Cleopatra standing at the foot of the bed.

"So, you don't make love in the other bed."

"No. I've never been with anyone I wanted to have all over my space like that."

"So, never in that bed?" Jacqueline asked again and rolled over on to her back.

"Only to myself." Cleopatra smiled.

"Do you make love to yourself often?"

"More recently. But not that often. no."

"You don't have to, right? Have you since you met me? Made love to anyone?" Jacqueline braced herself for the answer.

"No. I'm dating you."

"Have you made love to yourself?"

"Hell, yeah." Cleopatra laughed. "Sorry. I may have popped off a few times. Keeps me from doing something stupid when I'm around you."

"Is that how you control yourself? I'm going to have to try that."

"So, are you just going to stand there?" She patted a spot on the bed beside her. They hadn't even had their first kiss yet, and Jacqueline was lying on Cleopatra's bed. Cleopatra had many first kisses in that bed, and that's not how she wanted this to go down. As bad as she wanted Jacqueline, she knew she wouldn't want to stop. Most importantly, she knew Jacqueline still wasn't ready.

"Why don't you get off of my bed before something happens to you?"

Jacqueline sat up and looked back at the bed like she didn't want to leave it. "Are you scared of me?"

"I want you."

"And I want you. So, what are you afraid of?"

"You're the one that should be afraid. You're not ready for me, but you insisted on seeing where it goes down and you insist on lying on my bed, with all that cleavage, in those jeans and with those heels on."

"What am I not ready for?" She rested her chin in her hands.

"You are not ready for me to tongue down every inch of your body. You are not ready for me to fuck you with my fingers, my tongue, or any of my dicks. You are not ready to suck honey off of my cock or for me to walk up to you bend you over and ease my dick inside of you and fuck you slow. You are not ready to ride me, or take it like a good girl from behind and push it back on me. Not ready to sixty-nine with my entire face in your pussy while you suck my dick. Not ready

71

to scream my name, scratch my back up, or beat me in my chest. Not ready for me to fuck you in every room in this house. You're not ready for me to take it."

Jacqueline stared at Cleopatra, her chest heaved as she closed her legs tight together. Her nipples had hardened through her t-shirt. She licked her lips and conceded defeat as she peeled herself off of the bed. She walked up to Cleopatra, grabbed her hand and whispered in her ear.

"I think we need to get out of this room now." She pulled Cleopatra toward the door.

"Hold on." Cleopatra pulled Jacqueline back to her lips. "Are you wet right now?"

"It's raining."

"You're right. We need to get out of this room."

◙ ◙ ◙

Jacqueline prepared dinner while Cleopatra kept her company in the kitchen. She cooked grilled lobster tails, rosemary mashed potatoes, and broccoli with carrots. Cleopatra chipped in by making dessert, baked apples with rum and brown sugar. They enjoyed spending time in the kitchen talking, laughing and flirting with each other. A day like this was something Cleopatra had never experienced before. She had honestly never enjoyed herself so much with a woman that she had yet to touch. After dessert, they moved to the couch in the living room. Cleopatra lit some candles and put some slow jams on.

"Are you trying to mack me or something?" Jacqueline asked, as she lay down on the couch.

"I didn't think I had to." Cleopatra sat down next to her.

"Thank you for cooking, sweetheart. Dinner was so good." She rubbed her stomach.

"My pleasure. I love your kitchen, top of the line everything. I can see myself cooking in there all the time." She swung her body around and put her legs in Cleopatra's lap.

"I was thinking the same thing."

"You liked seeing me in the kitchen cooking for you, didn't you?"

"It's one the sexiest things I've seen you do so far."

"Is that the way to your heart?" She poked Cleopatra's stomach.

"It might be one of them. Especially if you keep cooking meals like that."

"Tell me what else I do that's sexy."

"The way you call my name." Jacqueline waited for Cleopatra to explain. "It's sensual, that's all. It's how your lips move when you say it, it's almost breathless." Cleopatra looked away from Jacqueline. "It makes me wonder how you'll sound when we make love and you call my name."

"You're going to find out soon." Jacqueline said.

"These feet were in those stilettos all day?" She grabbed Jacqueline's toes.

"I take care of them." She threw her head back as Cleopatra massaged her feet.

"Your hands are so strong. What are you trying to do to me?"

"I'm just rubbing your pretty little toes."

"That's so good." She moaned. "Can I ask you to do something? And you don't have to if you don't want to. Can you stick out your tongue?"

Cleopatra stopped mid-massage. "Who have you been talking to?"

"I was just curious." Jacqueline immediately regretted asking.

"Curious what my tongue looks like? It's a tongue just like everyone else has."

"I'm sorry. Don't be mad at me." She sat up and put her head on Cleopatra's shoulder.

"I will show you when it's time for you to see it. Ok?"

"Ok, I'll be good. I have a hard time behaving around you." She said – and immediately followed up her apology with another proposition. "You want to play True Confessions?" She got up and grabbed a bottle of tequila from the bar.

Jacqueline had the bottle to her lips even before she made the first confession.

"I've never thought about what your locs would feel like on my naked back as you take me from behind." She took a swig.

Cleopatra grabbed the bottle. She usually avoided playing True Confessions. The game always ended up with someone naked so she tried to play it safe with Jacqueline.

"I've never thought about the faces you make when you make love."

"That was G-rated and sweet." Jacqueline took the bottle back.

"I've never had an orgasm that wasn't by my own hand." She took another swig.

"Game over." Cleopatra took the bottle from Jacqueline and sat it down on the coffee table. "Seriously? That's just wrong."

"There are so many things we could do, right? That aren't necessarily sex?" she asked.

"You mean like dry hump you till you come or something?"

"It wouldn't be dry. I know we are trying to take it slow and you are respecting my wishes and I know it must be hard for you, but you can at least touch me. If I said it was ok to do whatever you wanted to do to me right now what would it be?"

"Kiss you." Cleopatra answered.

"I love your lips. Are they as soft as they look?" She pulled Cleopatra on top of her. "Please kiss me."

For the first time Cleopatra took her mouth into hers. She licked her bottom lip with her tongue and Jacqueline's body tensed up. Her lips were sweet and wet. She moaned and her body went limp under Cleopatra's weight. Cleopatra sucked and licked on Jacqueline's lips hungrily as she moved on top of her. Jacqueline pulled Cleopatra harder against her as she clawed at her back. She gave Cleopatra her tongue and she surrounded it with hers as Cleopatra pushed her pelvis into Jacqueline's. Cleopatra started to pull away and Jacqueline locked her legs around Cleopatra's waist pulling her back into her.

"Don't stop." She slipped her tongue inside Cleopatra's

mouth.

Cleopatra was in a trance as she slid her hands up Jacqueline's shirt and caressed her back. Jacqueline pushed her body up against hers. Cleopatra pulled away again.

"We are going to end up in bed if we don't stop."

"You promise?" Jacqueline let out a deep breath. "So soft and warm."

Cleopatra kissed her again gently on the lips. Jacqueline wrapped her arms tight around her. Cleopatra was struck by how right her body felt against hers.

"Ok, we have to stop now." Jacqueline pulled away from her lips.

Hours later after they had talked, laughed, kissed and rolled around trying to refrain from going up to the sex room, the clock struck three a.m. Jacqueline composed herself and prepared to go home.

"I guess I should probably go." She felt like she was asking Cleopatra, more than telling her.

"Ok, I'll call you a car service."

"Oh. Ok." Jacqueline was disappointed that she didn't ask her to stay.

"I don't want my woman on the train at this time of the night."

"You called me your woman. That's the first time I've heard you say those words. Did you mean it?" A huge smile spread across her lips.

"Is that what you want?" Cleopatra asked.

"You know the answer to that already. Is that what you want?"

"It is." Cleopatra kissed her. "You know you don't have to go home if you don't want to."

"I don't want to."

TASHA C. MILLER

CHEATING

"Nothing happened. I swear, Shawn."

"So, you spent almost two days together, there was wine and tequila, she cooked for you a few times, slept next to you in your real bed – and you didn't?"

"It was one of the hardest things I've ever done. You ever want to fuck so bad that the throbbing between your legs starts to hurt?"

Shawn laughed. "Naw, man. That's never happened to me, but good to know."

"I told Jacqueline about my family. She got the short version."

"You never do that. What did she say?" Shawn asked, surprised.

"Not much. I was trying not to cry, she was trying not to cry, and she just held me. I felt exposed as hell, but I trust her with my feelings."

Jacqueline and Cleopatra spent much of their free time together. There were constant emails back and forth about how

77

they missed each other, although only two floors separated them at work. The days Cleopatra worked late, Jacqueline brought her dinner, napped on her sofa and went home with her later that evening. Nights when Jacqueline worked late she'd come and spend the night at Cleopatra's instead of going home to Brooklyn. The nights she slept over were torture, and Cleopatra yearned for her body.

Cleopatra went out to Jacqueline's place a few times. She met her upstairs neighbor, a mean looking football player type that Cleopatra swore had a crush on Jacqueline. But Jacqueline was at home at Cleopatra's house, and that's where they spent the majority of their time. As their relationship grew closer they decided never to spend more than two nights apart; more than that was too hard on them. Jacqueline usually stayed with Cleopatra on Mondays, Wednesdays, Fridays and Saturdays. The confirmation that they were in an all-out relationship came when Cleopatra gave Jacqueline an entire closet to herself. But Cleopatra had yet to let the relationship get sexual.

"I love being with you." Jacqueline hugged Cleopatra, her head on Cleopatra's chest. "You make me feel like the only woman in the world. I always feel that when I'm with you. And I've never been kissed the way you kiss me. I've never felt anything like this before. You melt my heart and I want you to know it."

"I'm a little afraid, but you are the one I want to be with. I've never had such strong feelings for anyone before," Cleopatra confessed.

"You're not just playing with me? I'm scared, too."

"I'm not playing. I would never do anything to hurt you."

"When are we going to make love?" Jacqueline caressed Cleopatra's cheek.

"When we're both ready," Cleopatra said.

"I'm ready. I want to show you how I feel about you. I want to try and make you understand."

"I feel the same way, but I'm not ready."

"Of course you are."

"I'm not talking about physically. I know what to do. I'm not ready emotionally. For all that it's going to mean. I'm trying to protect my heart."

"I understand, whatever you need."

◻ ◻ ◻

"Sweetheart. I think we should chill for a while," Cleopatra told Jacqueline over the phone. "I don't feel in control. I need some time to sort my feelings out."

"What the hell? Are you breaking up with me? Are you upset because I couldn't come over tonight? You're just missing me."

"I'm not breaking up with you. Not really."

"Not really? Why are you doing this? You're scared. That's all it is. Scared of what you're feeling?"

"I don't know."

"I've felt you trying to pull away from me for the last week or so. Baby, there is no reason to be scared anymore. What we are building is beautiful. Why are you fighting it? I love what I'm feeling for you."

"I feel like the walls are closing in on me."

"You expect me to go away? To stop seeing you? No."

"You should respect what I want," Cleopatra said.

"You should respect what I want," Jacqueline replied.

"What are you going to do? Force me to see you when I'm telling you that I don't want to see you anymore?" Cleopatra cringed as soon as she heard the words come out of her mouth. She didn't mean a word of it.

"All right, if that's what you need." Jacqueline slammed the phone down, hanging up on her.

It had been three days with no Jacqueline; she was giving Cleopatra the space she asked for that Cleopatra now no longer wanted. Cleopatra had just gotten home from work when her cell phone rang. She was hoping it was Jacqueline calling to tell her how stupid she was and that she was coming over. It wasn't.

"What's up, sexy?"

"Who is this?"

"Noel. Remember, last year at D.C. Pride? You nicknamed me Deep Cock, and said Pride was named after me. Remember now?"

"Ooh, yeah. How are you?"

"I'm good. I'm in town for a few days and that platinum tongue has been on mind since I set foot in the city."

"Sorry, I'm in a situation. I have a girlfriend."

"Oh, a girlfriend? Well, is she there now?"

"No."

"Good." Noel hung up.

Cleopatra's doorbell rang. *No. She doesn't have the nerve to be outside of my house.* Cleopatra ran down the steps to the first floor and looked out of the peephole. Sure enough, it was Noel standing on her steps in a trench coat. A trench coat in July could only mean trouble.

"Are you crazy?" Cleopatra yelled as she opened the door.

She unbuttoned her coat and flashed Cleopatra. Totally naked, Noel wasn't even wearing panties. She started singing, "Put it in my mouth." Cleopatra pulled her off her steps before anyone on the street saw her.

"You don't take *no* for an answer, do you?"

"Never," she whispered, and stuck her tongue in Cleopatra's ear. That shook Cleopatra. It had been a while since she'd gotten any, because she'd been faithful to Jacqueline. But this couldn't hurt. Just one quick fuck, and she'd kick her out.

"Come on." She grabbed Noel's hand.

There was banging on the front door.

"Who the hell is that?" Cleopatra heard Jacqueline yell through the door. Then Jacqueline started to kick the door.

"Shit." Cleopatra opened the door, Jacqueline blew past her.

"Who is this bitch?" Jacqueline demanded. She reached for Noel's coat. She saw her nipple ring and Brazilian bikini wax underneath her trench. "Oh my God. You're fucking naked."

"Bitch? This must be the girlfriend you told me about." Noel laughed.

"Leave. Now." Jacqueline pointed toward the door.

"I'm not going anywhere." Noel stood her ground.

"If you don't leave now, I'm going to choke you out right here," Jacqueline said as she backed her up against the wall.

"Noel. Please leave right now." Cleopatra stepped between the two women.

"All right, damn. Call me, Cleopatra." The girl stood in the doorway and buttoned her coat.

"Get out now!" Jacqueline was getting angrier.

"Do you have any idea how close I am to strangling you right now? What the hell is your problem?"

"I don't have an explanation." Cleopatra hung her head low.

"You were about to fuck her?"

"Yeah. I was gonna try."

"I'm out of here. You don't want to be with me." She walked to the door.

"Baby, yes I do want to be with you. I don't know what I'm doing." Cleopatra grabbed her hand to stop her from leaving.

Jacqueline yanked her hand away. "You were going to have sex with her, and I'm supposed to be your woman. We haven't even made love yet. How's that supposed to make me feel?"

"I'm sorry. I don't want to hurt you."

"That's what you're doing. You're scared, I understand. How do you think I feel? You are my first love, and my first woman. You think this is easy for me? I don't know what to do or how to be. I want to be with you, that's all I know. I'm not running from you. And I'm not going to do shit to push you away."

"I am scared, but I know I want to be with you."

"You are all I think about every minute of the day. Do you understand that? I hear what you are saying, but your actions say something totally different. You really have to figure out what you want."

"I want you. I've missed you so much these last few days. I got overwhelmed and confused. I got scared of my feelings. I didn't mean what I said on the phone that I didn't want to see you anymore." She tried to hug Jacqueline. "I'm sorry I hurt you."

"Don't touch me Cleopatra, please." She pushed her away. "I'm so angry with you right now. I can't be around you."

◉ ◉ ◉

Cleopatra was convinced she fucked up the best thing to ever happen to her. She thought Jacqueline was never going to forgive her. She didn't see or speak with Jacqueline for another week, not even at work, and everyone noticed.

"So, you and Jacqueline aren't together anymore?" Carmen, Cleopatra's ex beamed when she caught Cleopatra outside of her office door talking to Racquel. "I tried to tell her this would happen, that you would throw her away when you got tired of her."

"How's your fiancé doing?" Cleopatra shot back. "Oh, I forgot, he left your ass when he caught me sliding my dick between those fat titties of yours."

"Racquel, can you make sure Carmen finds her way back to her desk?"

Cleopatra walked back into her office and shut the door. She didn't like how it felt not having Jacqueline in her life. She was miserable.

"Have you showered at all this weekend?" Shawn asked when she dropped in on Cleopatra early on Sunday morning.

"Why?"

"Jacqueline is eventually going to come back, so you might want to clean yourself up, maybe twist a loc or two."

"I don't think she's coming back. I really fucked up and hurt her."

"You realize this is around the two-month mark, right?" Shawn asked. "You've been breaking up with girls at two months for so long it's like you have an internal clock that is set to implode your relationships sixty days in. I saw Jacqueline at work Friday. She misses you. I think she's just giving you time to figure out what you want."

"I want her."

"Then tell her until she believes you. I've seen how happy she makes you and you aren't even fucking her yet! I mean come on! Don't run off the woman you've been waiting for because you're scared. Have you two said the L word yet?"

"Not yet." Cleopatra smiled.

"You both love each other. You need to say that shit and start acting like it. So please, I'm begging you, take a shower, no, take a bath, a long one, and call your woman."

Cleopatra cleaned herself up and called Jacqueline over to her house.

"You asked to see me, so talk." Jacqueline sat on the couch in Cleopatra's living room.

"I've missed you."

"I've missed you too," she said, not looking at Cleopatra.

"I'm not good at expressing my feelings."

"Say what's on your heart." Jacqueline said.

"I'm sorry for hurting you. I didn't know what I was doing. You are the only one I want to be with. I don't want that other girl, I never did. She just showed up uninvited."

"I know," Jacqueline said.

"How did you find out she was here?"

"I was coming to tell you how stupid you were acting and to try to work it out. She was a few yards in front of me when I saw her walk up your steps. I stopped and watched her. She was on her phone, then you opened the door and yelled at her, but I saw you pull her inside when she opened her coat."

"Can you forgive me?"

"I remember her saying something like this must be the girlfriend you told me about. So, she knew about me and she didn't care. I'm learning quickly how trifling some women can be, so I need to be able to trust you. You didn't invite her, but you *were* going to sleep with her. You have to take responsibility for that."

"I take responsibility for being stupid. I promise you another pussy could be right here." She put her index finger to her nose. "And I'll run from it. I never want to be responsible again for the hurt I saw on your face."

"I forgive you baby." Jacqueline kissed her softly on the lips. "I've missed you. I need you." She tugged on Cleopatra's black t-shirt. "Please, make me ready," she said as she pulled Cleopatra on top of her and slipped her tongue inside of her mouth.

Cleopatra caressed her thighs. "Sweetheart, not like this. Soon. Then you're really going to get it." She kissed her on the lips again.

"You know I'm not seeing anyone but you. I'm asking you again, to only be with me. I want to be your only woman. Give me a chance to be that. I want you to be all mine."

"I am all yours." She kissed her as Jacqueline grinded down on her crotch.

"I have to admit something to you, but I'm a little embarrassed." Jacqueline whispered in her ear.

Cleopatra braced herself. "What? Do you have like three nipples or something? That would be entertaining, actually."

"No, freak." She punched Cleopatra in the arm. "Be serious. I'm not all that experienced with sex."

"I know." Cleopatra said. "You told me."

"No. You don't understand." Jacqueline bit her lip.

"Are you a virgin?"

"Almost. Close."

"What does close mean?" Cleopatra laughed. "Once?"

"Yes."

"Seriously? You ooze sex. When I look at you, that's what I think of, what I want to do. You're that fuckable." She buried her face in Cleopatra's neck. "Baby, I'm sorry. It's nothing to be embarrassed about. It's very sweet that you respect your body. I know I respect it." Cleopatra trailed her fingers down Jacqueline's back.

"I want to be able to please you. Do whatever I need to do to keep you happy and satisfied."

"That's the last thing I'm worried about." Cleopatra kissed her on the forehead.

"You're right when you say we should wait, but not too much longer. I can't take feeling what I'm feeling for you and not being able to take it to the next level. In the meantime, you need to stay away from other women."

Cleopatra had an innocent look on her face. "Who, me?"

"Listen to me, because I want us to be clear on this. I'm only going to say this one time and this is real."

"I love how when you get mad Brooklyn comes out of you. That's so sexy." Cleopatra interrupted.

Jacqueline grabbed Cleopatra by her shirt and pulled her to her lips. She looked in her eyes. "If I ever catch you with another woman they will find pieces of her body in Brooklyn, the Bronx, Queens and uptown, and I will cut out your tongue and keep it in a jar by my bed. Do you understand me?"

Cleopatra looked in Jacqueline's eyes. "Yes." She swallowed hard. "I understand."

TASHA C. MILLER

CLIMAX

Cleopatra and Jacqueline were celebrating their three-month anniversary. They had almost made it to the restaurant in time for their reservations, but Cleopatra could not keep her hands off of Jacqueline. It was approaching eight o'clock on a chilly summer evening, and they were on 51st off of 7th outside of the brass revolving doors of Le Bernardin. Jacqueline's little red dress confirmed for Cleopatra that tonight was going to be the night.

"You know I love you in all black. What are you trying to do to me?" Jacqueline fingered the titanium cufflinks on Cleopatra's buttondown.

"Same thing you are trying to do to me with that little piece of a dress you have on. Seduce you." Cleopatra pulled Jacqueline to the side of the restaurant doors and backed her up against the frosted privacy glass of the building.

"You don't need to seduce me. It's already yours." Jacqueline kissed her. Cleopatra devoured her mouth. She felt herself losing control.

"You can have as much as you want later, baby." Jacqueline slid from between Cleopatra and the building. She bit Cleopatra on the ear and whispered, "I want you to make love to me. Then I want you to fuck me. I want you to teach me the difference."

"Oooh." Cleopatra's body twitched.

"You want me?" She slipped her hands around Cleopatra's waist.

"More than anything, you know that. Are you sure?" Cleopatra asked.

"It's our anniversary. Three long, wet months. Yeah, I'm sure. Do you want me to beg? Because I will." She licked Cleopatra's bottom lip.

"Maybe I do want you to beg. Maybe I want you to tell me what you want," Cleopatra said.

"I want it in my mouth." She stuck her tongue out and sucked her finger.

"I want to taste you." Cleopatra unraveled her freakishly long tongue from her mouth.

Jacqueline's eyes bulged out. "Are you serious right now with that tongue?"

"It's very serious." Cleopatra flicked and twirled her tongue at her again. "How hungry are you?"

Jacqueline stared hard at Cleopatra's mouth in the hopes that her tongue would reemerge. "Uhm, for food? I'm not."

"Taxi!" Cleopatra grabbed Jacqueline's hand and hailed a cab.

Jacqueline was quiet in the taxi, and by the time they got in the house Cleopatra wondered if she was having second thoughts.

"Wait. I have to tell you something." Jacqueline paused as soon as they walked into the dark living room.

"Are you changing your mind?"

"No. I've felt this way for a long time, I've wanted to say this for a while, but I've been too scared." Cleopatra caressed her face as she waited for Jacqueline to speak and held her hand.

"I'm in love with you."

Cleopatra's heart fluttered in her chest. She stared into Jacqueline's eyes as she held her breath and waited for a response. "I'm in love with you too, baby. I love you so much."

Jacqueline's eyes lit up. Cleopatra kissed her softly.

"I have something for you. Don't be mad, I know we agreed not to exchange gifts, but I saw this and thought it would be beautiful on you." Cleopatra grabbed a long jewelry box off of the fireplace mantel.

"What did you go and do?" Jacqueline smiled at Cleopatra when she handed her the blue Fortunoff's box. "Oh, my God." She covered her mouth when she saw the diamond eternity bracelet.

"Do you like it?" Cleopatra asked, when nothing else came out of Jacqueline's mouth.

"It's beautiful. I love it." She stared at the bracelet.

"Let me put it on you." Cleopatra snapped it around her left wrist. "Perfect." She kissed her hand.

"You're perfect, baby. Thank you so much. You are so good to me." She kissed Cleopatra.

Cleopatra pushed her up against the wall as she sucked Jacqueline's tongue into her mouth.

"I'm ready for you to take it." Jacqueline moaned. She took Cleopatra's hand and led her upstairs to the sex room.

"We have plenty of time for that." Cleopatra said. Instead, she led her into her bedroom. Jacqueline came out of her heels as she watched Cleopatra light scented vanilla candles all around the bedroom. It wasn't long before the chocolate room glowed with tiny flames.

"You have on way too many clothes," Cleopatra said to Jacqueline. She unbuttoned her shirt and tossed it to the floor. She stood before Jacqueline in just her pants and bra. Jacqueline couldn't take her eyes off of the muscles in Cleopatra's stomach or the curve of her cleavage. She traced her fingers over the ripples of Cleopatra's six-pack leading down to her belt and unbuckled it.

Cleopatra caressed the silk of Jacqueline's dress with her fingers. She watched her as she played with the material. "I've fantasized about your hands all over me and what I wanted them to do."

"What do you want them to do first?"

"Undress me."

Cleopatra slid the spaghetti straps off of her shoulders. Jacqueline pulled her arms out of the dress, and held it up with one hand before letting it fall to the floor.

Cleopatra studied her lover's body. "You are perfect." Jacqueline stood in a black G-string with her breasts exposed. Cleopatra made her feel beautiful every time she looked at her, but her eyes were different tonight. "Come here." She held out her hand. "I'm going to take my time. You should know that before we start." Cleopatra kissed Jacqueline. The first kiss was different from any other they had before, because no restraint was needed as this night didn't have to end. Cleopatra couldn't remember the last time she wanted anything as much as she wanted Jacqueline. At that moment, she couldn't recall why she had waited so long. She drew Jacqueline's mouth into hers as she pulled her harder into her body. Jacqueline gasped when she felt the thickness between Cleopatra's legs. She stroked the length of the shaft through her pants before pulling them down to the floor. In an instant, she felt a rush of wetness between her thighs.

Jacqueline pushed Cleopatra down to the bed, parted her legs and stood between them. She struggled to maintain control when the head of the long cock peeked out from Cleopatra's briefs. The dildo matched Cleopatra's complexion perfectly and was so realistic that Jacqueline caught herself licking her lips. She turned her back to Cleopatra and stuck her ass out.

"Take my string off."

Cleopatra palmed her behind. She licked and bit her cheeks as she slid her fingers between her thighs. Her hand was quickly covered in wetness. Jacqueline whimpered as Cleopatra pulled her panties down to the floor.

Cleopatra stood up and turned Jacqueline around. She pulled

her close, rubbing her dick against her bare pussy as she caressed her ass and tongued the side of her neck. Jacqueline moved away from Cleopatra and pulled the covers back on the bed, and slipped between the sheets. She purred at the coolness of the Egyptian cotton against her skin. Cleopatra stood looking at her body on display in the chocolate sheets. The candles on her mocha skin provoked a violent throbbing between her legs. Her body had been aching for months, and she was finally going to have her deepest wish.

Jacqueline reached out for her. She pulled off Cleopatra's bra and caressed her breasts, loving how they felt pressed against hers. Cleopatra covered her flesh with her tongue, overcome by the softness of every inch of Jacqueline's body. Every part smelled as sweet as her favorite spot behind Jacqueline's left ear. They kissed softer, slower and more passionately than they'd ever kissed before. Cleopatra slid her hands down Jacqueline's arms, the light touch of her fingertips sending a shiver through Jacqueline's body. Cleopatra knew what they were about to do was going to change the rest of their lives. She was willingly surrendering everything to Jacqueline – first her heart, and now her body.

"Promise me something," Cleopatra asked her.

"Anything, baby."

"Crave me, every minute you aren't with me, think about me. I need for you to need me."

A sultry smile spread across Jacqueline's lips. "I already do. Every minute."

"After tonight everything will be different. I promise you," Cleopatra said. She was going to show Jacqueline exactly what she felt for her, emotionally and physically.

"I'm a little scared," Jacqueline whispered.

"I'll be gentle, until you tell me not to be. Trust me."

"I do."

She grinded her wetness into Cleopatra's thigh. Every time Cleopatra's cock rubbed against her leg she quivered with anticipation of Cleopatra invading her. Cleopatra sucked her breast and flicked her nipples with her tongue. The way

Jacqueline moved her ass underneath Cleopatra threatened her self-control. Jacqueline slapped Cleopatra's shoulders, pushing her lower. She squirmed as Cleopatra's face slid between her thighs.

"Please." Jacqueline pulled at the sheets.

Heat rushed from Jacqueline's pussy as Cleopatra kissed her inner thighs. Her body tensed, begging Cleopatra to explore her further, but she took her time. Jacqueline slammed her hand down on the bed in frustration.

"Don't tease me." She moaned. Cleopatra laughed to herself as she inhaled Jacqueline's sweet scent, before giving in. She licked her clit in one long stroke from the bottom to the top of her before slowly sucking it into her mouth.

"Oh God." Jacqueline sprung up and gasped for air.

Cleopatra moved up her body, put her weight on Jacqueline, and pinned her hands down.

"You want to taste how sweet you are?" She stuck her tongue out. Jacqueline took most of it into her mouth. "Do you see how good that is? Are you going to let me have some more?"

"Yes."

"Ask me for it."

"I need it. Please."

Cleopatra slithered back down Jacqueline's body and took her now swollen clit back into her mouth. She fell in love with her pussy as she buried her face in her wetness and licked her over and over. Jacqueline grabbed Cleopatra's locs and pulled her harder into her as she opened her legs wider. Cleopatra growled as Jacqueline dug her nails into her shoulders, bucking into her face as she terrorized her clit with gentle fury.

Jacqueline's moans filled the room as she shook. She gushed as her body spasmed and Cleopatra took in every drop of her. Jacqueline locked her thighs around Cleopatra's neck and wouldn't let her go.

"Don't move," Jacqueline whispered.

"I kind of can't breathe, baby." Cleopatra tried to wiggle free. Jacqueline loosened her grip slightly. She lay between her legs, her cheek on her pussy. She lay still for a few moments, listening to Jacqueline breathe and riding out occasional quivers.

The room was stuffy with the sweet smell of vanilla and sex intermingled.

"I thought your first one would calm me down" Cleopatra said. "But it hasn't." That first taste had set it off. She needed more of her.

Cleopatra raised up on her arms, lifted her head to look at Jacqueline. Their eyes met and no words were necessary. Jacqueline lay back and allowed her body to open up again. Cleopatra slowly worked her finger across her slit and inside of her, one long finger. Her body rocked back and forth, then spread open for one more and met the thrust of Cleopatra's hand.

"Don't stop."

Cleopatra slid her fingers deep, flicking them inside of her, working her tight pussy gently. She rotated her hips fucking Cleopatra's hand as the feeling overtook her. Cleopatra took out her fingers and pushed her tongue deep inside of Jacqueline until her back arched.

"What?" she gasped.

Cleopatra felt her pussy clamp down and pull on her tongue.

Jacqueline closed her thighs on Cleopatra's head as a wave erupted inside of her and spilled out into Cleopatra's mouth.

She was still trembling when she reached into Cleopatra's briefs to stroke her. The large dildo tented Cleopatra's underwear and Jacqueline was fixated on the thickness. She rolled on top of her and kissed her from her lips to her breasts; she eased her way down Cleopatra's body and pulled her briefs off, freeing the giant dick that sprang up to meet her. She kissed around her navel, her hips and inner thighs as she stroked its length with her hand. She was turned on by Cleopatra's reaction to getting her dick jacked. Jacqueline licked the underside of the shaft, and rose up on her hands and knees and took Cleopatra's dick into her mouth.

"Damn. Take all of it." Cleopatra watched Jacqueline as she

swallowed all of her. Cleopatra moved her hair away from her face in order to see her woman devouring her cock. Jacqueline was turned on by Cleopatra's moans and the power she had over her. The more excited Cleopatra got, the more excited Jacqueline got. She started fucking her mouth, pulling out to the head and pushing it back into Jacqueline's throat as she held the back of her neck and Jacqueline took every stroke until Cleopatra could take no more.

"I want to taste you, baby." She moaned as she leaned back and spread Cleopatra's legs.

Cleopatra loosened the strap and pulled it to the side. "Take your time," she said, knowing it was her first experience. "I just want your lips on mine."

Jacqueline's hand was drenched when she ran her fingers along Cleopatra's pussy. She spread her lips apart and ran her thumb back and forth over her clit.

"Is all of this for me?" Jacqueline licked her fingers.

"All yours." Cleopatra squirmed in anticipation of her woman's lips on her as she played with her clit. Jacqueline crawled up Cleopatra wanting her mouth on hers. She kissed her hungrily. Cleopatra noticed something in her eyes she had never seen before.

"Tell me what you want," Jacqueline said.

"Make me come."

Jacqueline dove between Cleopatra's legs. She inhaled her sweet scent as she played with Cleopatra's engorged clit. Then she took her into her mouth licking her long and slow.

Her tongue was like fire to Cleopatra. "Just like that."

Being between her legs was intoxicating and she wanted more, Jacqueline wanted that feeling all the time because Cleopatra's whimpers alone were getting her off. It wasn't long before Cleopatra was ready to explode when Jacqueline's finger slipped inside her, with her tongue still on her clit. She never let anyone penetrate her, but Jacqueline felt good, and she reached for her hand to let her know she wanted more. Jacqueline went deeper. Cleopatra grabbed her head to ride out the pure bliss of her lover sucking on her pussy, her first time, with her fingers doing things inside of her that she never allowed. Ecstasy built up in Cleopatra as Jacqueline feasted on her like she'd been waiting all of her life for this moment. Her body flexed and Jacqueline hungrily lapped up the explosion.

"I want you inside of me," Jacqueline said as Cleopatra teased her clit with the head of her cock.

"Close your eyes," Cleopatra said in her ear.

"Take it." She looked up at Cleopatra and then shut her eyes. She grabbed a hold of Cleopatra's waist as she lowered her body onto hers. Cleopatra rubbed her clit with the length of her shaft until Jacqueline screamed for it. Cleopatra pushed inside of Jacqueline, so tight that her pussy put up a fight at first. Jacqueline scratched Cleopatra's hips asking for more. Cleopatra on her hands and tiptoes slid all the way inside of her in one slow and long stroke. Jacqueline yelped and pounded on Cleopatra's back.

"You want me to stop?" she asked. Breathless, Jacqueline shook her head *no*. Her nails dug so deep into Cleopatra's back that she ripped her skin. Cleopatra growled and slid deeper into her with slow expertise.

"Cleopatra." Each time she called out her name, Cleopatra would thrust deeper inside of her in a slow circular motion. "I love how you move your ass," she gasped.

Jacqueline wrapped her legs around her waist and opened up for her. Cleopatra slipped in deeper, tapping her g-spot.

"That's so sexy." Cleopatra gazed down at Jacqueline's pussy full of her dick. Cleopatra wrapped her arms around Jacqueline and stood up holding Jacqueline by her thighs and still inside of her. She lifted Jacqueline higher and lowered her down slowly, sliding into her in controlled thrusts.

"Oh my God." Jacqueline threw her head back as she held on to Cleopatra's shoulders. She saw their reflection in the mirror, mesmerized as she studied the muscles in Cleopatra's ass as she pumped inside of her.

"Mirror." Jacqueline pointed. Cleopatra looked in the mirror. A dirty smile graced her face.

"You like that?" Jacqueline kissed her as she bounced on

Cleopatra's dick.

"I love that."

"You ready to fuck me now?" Jacqueline licked the side of her neck.

She sensed Cleopatra had been holding back and was about to lose control. She looked into her eyes. "Fuck me."

Cleopatra carried Jacqueline over to the bed. They fell on the mattress with Cleopatra still inside of her. Cleopatra pinned her hands down over her head and pumped her strong. Jacqueline transformed into an animal underneath Cleopatra. She pulled on her tongue with her teeth. She begged her to fuck her harder, desperately wanting every inch, and Cleopatra gave it to her.

Cleopatra had long abandoned the idea of being able to walk the next day. Pumping Jacqueline's pussy made her see stars when she closed her eyes. She could have stroked her for days. She knew that, because it had already been hours.

"I need you to come inside of me."

Cleopatra fucked her hard, from every angle. She felt the effects of her own orgasm rising but tried to fight it and concentrate on Jacqueline. She felt things that she had never felt with any other woman and it was taking control of her body.

She called out Jacqueline's name. "Look at me when you come," Cleopatra said as she watched her. She lowered herself down on Jacqueline's wet body. Their flesh slid together in rhythm as Cleopatra moved inside of her. Nipples, stomach, and thighs slippery with sweat as they moved toward climax. Jacqueline called Cleopatra's name as she grabbed her face and stared into her eyes. Their bodies shuddered as Cleopatra moved furiously inside of her.

Cleopatra awoke the next morning to the smell of food coming from the kitchen. She threw on some blue mesh New York Knicks basketball shorts and a black wife beater. She went down stairs where she found Jacqueline making biscuits and frying catfish in her t-shirt and panties.

"Good morning sweetie. Uhm…where did you get the

catfish from?"

"Morning, baby." Jacqueline hugged Cleopatra tight, burying her head in her neck.

"I ran out to the market. And I'm making my grandmama's biscuits. Smell that?"

"It smells delicious." Cleopatra kissed her woman softly on the lips. "You realize you are never going to live this down, right?" She sat down on a stool at the center island.

"What are you talking about?" Jacqueline checked the biscuits in the oven and pulled the fish out of the deep fryer.

"Last night we made love for the first time, and you wake up the next morning and cook catfish and biscuits?" Cleopatra smiled.

"You're right." Jacqueline stopped and thought for a moment. "Something happened to me last night."

"What? Are you ok with everything we did?"

"Am I ok?" Jacqueline walked up to Cleopatra. "I mean. What did you do to me? I swear at one point it felt like eight of you were on me, and I couldn't get right. I didn't know what I was saying or anything. And I couldn't stop coming."

Cleopatra sat with her hand over her mouth to camouflage her smile. "So what are you saying exactly?"

"I may seriously be addicted to making love to you." Jacqueline stood between Cleopatra's legs. "I hope that won't be a problem."

"I don't see how it could be." She traced her finger down between Jacqueline's breasts.

"You taste so good. Did you know that?" She kissed Cleopatra. "You get so wet. It's making me wet just thinking about it." She pulled the waistband of Cleopatra's shorts and caught a glimpse of the strap-on dangling loose between her legs. She grabbed it and stroked the thickness in her hand.

"Show me the snake," she said to Cleopatra. She stuck out her tongue and Jacqueline licked it before sucking it into her mouth. She pressed her pussy against Cleopatra's dick.

"You know you can have whatever you want from me," she said to Cleopatra. "Did I please you, baby? Was it good to you?"

"You couldn't tell?" Cleopatra smiled. "You pleased me all night, baby. I love making love to you." She kissed Jacqueline. "Your body is a blessing. You make me lose control."

"Oh no. You had control. I never felt so loved until you made love to me. You were so gentle with me when you needed to be and rough when you didn't. I love the way you feel inside of me." Jacqueline took off her t-shirt. Cleopatra took her breasts into her mouth. "I need you. Again." Jacqueline moaned as she pulled off Cleopatra's wife beater, and pulled down her shorts, leaving them on the floor around her ankles.

"I'm afraid I'm not going to be able to get enough of you." She pulled Cleopatra down to the kitchen floor, and on top of her.

"Leave them on." Cleopatra said when Jacqueline started to pull down her panties. She spread Jacqueline's legs wide, pulled her panties to the side and slid inside of her hard. That weekend Cleopatra created a monster, and she loved it. They called in sick and spent three days fucking in every room in the house, including the sex room.

◼ ◼ ◼

"Are you teasing me?" Jacqueline lay across Cleopatra's stomach in bed.

"No, baby. Being multi-orgasmic is a beautiful thing. I want to make you come all the time." She grabbed her and kissed her softly. "I live to make you come."

"I can't help what you do to me, so you better get used to it." Jacqueline slid her naked body across Cleopatra's. "You think you got me, don't you? You can admit it." She smiled at Cleopatra.

"Maybe. Just a little bit." She pressed her thumb and index finger tightly together.

"You do. I have no problem admitting it. You got me, all of

me. I would do absolutely anything for you." She kissed Cleopatra. "But you know what? I got you too."

TASHA C. MILLER

FAMILY

Jacqueline set four place settings on the patio table in the garden of Cleopatra's townhouse. The open area overflowing with trees and red roses was one of Jacqueline's favorite spots in the house, especially when she and Cleopatra made love at night under the stars. The garden was serene with the sound of chirping birds mixed with the muffled sounds of the city. The fresh garden air was wiped away by the barbeque coals when Cleopatra opened the hood on her colossal outdoor grille. The aroma of the Cajun shrimp and barbeque chicken swirled in the air aggravating her hunger. All of this was in preparation for their dinner guest, Jacqueline's younger sister Robin. She wanted to introduce two of the most important women in her life to each other.

Moments before Robin and her date were to arrive, Cleopatra and Jacqueline were in the garden, sprawled across a chaise longue. Their tongues and fingers invaded each other in the shade of a large lilac tree. Months had gone by since they first made love and they still couldn't keep their hands and mouths off of each other, and couldn't be counted on to show up anywhere. They had already missed two previous meetings with Robin. Without fail, as soon as Jacqueline put on any type of high heels, tight jeans or showed the slightest peek of leg, it set Cleopatra off. And since Jacqueline could never resist her, a marathon fucking session soon followed. Jacqueline thought she solved that problem by inviting her sister over to Cleopatra's for dinner.

"We have to stop," Jacqueline said, out of breath. She got up and gathered her clothes.

"You started it." Cleopatra pulled up her pants.

"Keep it up and we're going to miss dinner again. Don't you want to meet my sister?" She slipped her dress on over her head.

"Of course. She's your family, and your best friend." Cleopatra followed Jacqueline inside to the kitchen. "But she's not here yet." She hugged her from behind.

"Be serious, baby. She's still pissed at me for not coming out to her sooner." She dumped a blob of hand soap into Cleopatra's hands. "Does it bother you that I haven't told my parents yet?"

"Nope." Cleopatra washed her hands and face. "Everything happened so quickly. It'll be all right." She tucked her shirt into her pants.

The doorbell rang. "Ooh, I forgot. She's bringing her boyfriend, not her girlfriend." Jacqueline ran upstairs to the front door.

"I thought she was dating women?"

"She does, but she's on men right now."

"This should be fun." Cleopatra walked behind Jacqueline to the door. On the steps stood a twenty-year old version of Jacqueline and a pretty Latino man dressed in a hoodie, baggy jeans and construction boots.

B-Boy Blues, Cleopatra thought when she shook his hand. "Nice to meet you, Javier." She wondered where she'd seen him before.

Robin hugged Cleopatra longer than she was comfortable

with, but she shook it off. Her uneasiness returned quickly when Robin inhaled the side of her neck and commented on how delicious she smelled. They all went down to the garden where they sat and talked for a bit while they waited for dinner to finish. Cleopatra was tending to the chicken and shrimp on the grill when she realized where she'd seen Javier before. She took the food off of the grill and she excused herself.

Jacqueline followed her into the kitchen. "So, what do you think of my sister?"

"She's cool, very friendly. But Javier does gay porn, and he's a bottom. Does she know that? Does she care?"

"Are you serious?" Jacqueline's jaw dropped open and she covered her mouth with her hand.

"Yeah. Like gang-bang gay porn."

"I'm going to go talk to him." Jacqueline ran out to the garden passing Robin on the way. Robin walked into the kitchen.

"This is a beautiful home. It's all dark and masculine, kind of like you. What type of wood is this?" Robin stroked her hand across the cabinets.

"It's mahogany."

"Like the movie?"

"Yeah, almost exactly." Cleopatra laughed.

"So, you've got money, huh?"

"I'm comfortable." Cleopatra was uneasy when it came to talking about her money, so she didn't.

"You need help with anything?" Robin lifted herself up onto the black granite countertop, crossed her legs and pulled up her skirt, blatantly exposing her thighs for Cleopatra's benefit.

"I can handle it. Thanks." Cleopatra noticed Robin's bare ass cheek on her counter and made a mental note to wipe it down later.

"I'm sure you can." Robin stared at Cleopatra. "We should probably talk and get everything out in the open, don't you think?"

Cleopatra was a bit taken aback by her approach. "Sure. You first."

"So, I was shocked when my sister came out to me. Then she told me all about this amazing woman that she fell in love with. She went on and on about you." Robin jumped down from the counter, and backed Cleopatra up against the stainless steel refrigerator. The cool metal made Cleopatra shiver when it touched her arm. "She didn't lie, you are sexy as fuck."

"You are not really doing this to your sister, are you?" Cleopatra pushed past Robin.

Robin started to follow Cleopatra around the long center island. Jacqueline came back into the kitchen. She put her arms around Cleopatra and kissed her. "She's not being too rough on you, is she, baby?"

"Uh yeah. A little." Cleopatra laughed nervously.

"Be good to her." Jacqueline smirked at her sister. She kissed Cleopatra long and slow on her mouth as her sister watched.

"I'm trying to be." She licked her lips.

"I got it covered in here, Robin." Jacqueline said. "We'll bring the mojitos and the rest of the food out in a minute." Cleopatra hesitated as she watched Robin walk out. Jacqueline pulled the corn bread and barbequed beans out of the oven and the potato salad and deviled eggs from the refrigerator.

"What's wrong?" Jacqueline slipped her arms around Cleopatra from behind.

"Nothing baby. Nothing." Cleopatra picked up the pitcher of mojitos and placed it on a tray with the potato salad and deviled eggs and followed Jacqueline back out into the garden. Maybe it was nothing. She didn't want to blow anything out of proportion and ruin dinner. All Robin said was that she thought she was sexy. No harm done. She prayed that was the end of that.

Besides Robin not being able to take her eyes off Cleopatra throughout dinner and Jacqueline asking Javier leading questions about everything from his childhood to how his fledgling acting career was going, it was uneventful. Cleopatra offered to do all the cleanup so the sisters could spend some time together and she could get away from Robin. She wasn't alone in the kitchen long before Robin appeared.

"You know, my sister has told me a lot about you." She sat across the island from Cleopatra as she loaded the dishwasher.

"She's told me a lot about you too."

"You don't understand. I mean she's told me about you and her. She never gives me any details. But she did say you drive her crazy."

"She told you that?" Cleopatra stopped to take a sip of her mojito. It was confirmed: the evening was a bust, Jacqueline's sister was trying to get to know her in a different way, and it was about to get even worse.

"You must be amazing." She unbuttoned her blouse two buttons exposing her bra. Cleopatra almost choked on her mojito and spilled some on her shirt. Robin hopped off the stool and walked toward her.

Cleopatra was shocked, and she thought that she ought to tell Jacqueline. But what if Jacqueline didn't believe her, or what if she did and it ruined her relationship with Robin? Cleopatra started laughing hysterically. "Ok, ok. I got it. This is a joke, right? This is some kind of trick to see if I could be trusted? That's fucked up."

"What's fucked up?" Jacqueline walked into the kitchen and caught Robin with her blouse open and Cleopatra across the room with a drink on her shirt.

"What the hell is going on?"

"You don't trust me? You got her to come on to me?" Cleopatra pointed to Robin who was frantically buttoning her shirt.

"What?" Jacqueline asked. "You came on to her?" She swooped over to Robin and hemmed her up against the wall.

Cleopatra realized it wasn't a game when she saw the fear in Robin's eyes.

"You weren't in on this?" Cleopatra walked up to Jacqueline and grabbed her arm.

"No, I don't play around like that." She held her sister by her shirt collar. "What the fuck were you thinking?"

Javier came in from the garden and stood in the doorway of

the kitchen. "You might want to step back," Cleopatra said, waving him off.

"I'm sorry," Robin stuttered.

"That's all you have to say?" Jacqueline waited for something that made sense to leave Robin's mouth.

"I wanted to see for myself, what she was like." Javier sucked his teeth, switched past them and walked out of the house.

"There are a lot of sharp objects in this kitchen that I could hurt you with. Get out of my woman's house before I pick one up." Jacqueline pushed Robin away from her. Robin ran out of the kitchen, and out of the house.

Jacqueline looked at Cleopatra. "Come here."

"Baby. I'm sorry." Cleopatra reached out and took her hands into hers.

"No, I'm sorry. I saw how she looked at you. I just didn't want to think she would go there. I should have handled it immediately. I'm not through with her, but that won't happen again."

"Can you blame her for not being able to resist me?" Cleopatra joked, trying to lift her woman's mood.

Jacqueline smiled slightly. "Can I stay over baby? I don't want to sleep without you tonight."

"Of course you can, you never have to ask." Cleopatra hugged her tight. "So you told your sister that I drive you crazy, out of your mind?"

Her smile widened. "I may have said something like that. I'm not foolish enough to give any woman the exact details on what you do to me."

She kissed Jacqueline. "Why don't you tell me?"

"The thought of you excites me. When I see you, I want to touch you. When you are touching me, I want to kiss you and when you are kissing me I want your tongue working across my body and when you are tonguing me down I want you inside of me. When you are inside of me I don't ever want you to pull out."

"Let's go upstairs." Cleopatra groaned and pulled Jacqueline out of the kitchen.

"Wait." Jacqueline stopped her. "I need to say this. No one is going to come between us. I don't care who it is. You're mine. I love you more than I love myself."

◻ ◯ ◻

"Where is my phone?" Cleopatra asked. About four in the morning, in the middle of making love to Jacqueline, Cleopatra suddenly stopped and pulled out of her. She emerged from under the sheets butt naked and covered in sweat. The strap-on that was buckled tight around her waist drenched in Jacqueline's wetness glistened in the candlelight.

"What? Are you serious?" Jacqueline tried to catch her breath.

"Something's not right." Cleopatra ran around the dim bedroom looking for her cell phone.

"Look in your pants, they're on the floor." Jacqueline sat up in bed and turned on the lamp.

When Cleopatra pulled her phone from her pocket it was vibrating. "Hello." As Cleopatra slumped down on the edge of the bed, Jacqueline scooted down behind her. She rubbed her shoulders, and rested her head on her back. Cleopatra hung up.

"That was Shawn's mother. There was a fire, and Shawn's apartment building burned down. She's at Brookdale Hospital."

"Is she ok?"

"I don't know. There was screaming in the background, then the phone cut off." She tried to redial the number, but got voicemail. She sat on the bed, frozen in fear.

Jacqueline hopped up, blew out the candles, and started putting on her clothes, but Cleopatra didn't move.

"Baby, get dressed. What are you doing?"

"I can't."

"Can't what?" She sat down on the bed next to her. "Look at me." She turned Cleopatra's face toward hers. "What is it?"

"I can't go. I can't lose her."

"You're not going to lose her. And you're going. I'll go with you. It's going to be all right." She picked Cleopatra's jeans up off of the floor and handed them to her. "You have to be there for her." She extended her hand and Cleopatra took it.

Cleopatra stopped outside the hospital doors before going in. "I really hate hospitals. I haven't been in one since my mom passed away."

Jacqueline hugged her tight. "It's going to be fine. I'll stay with you as long as you need me." She took her by the hand. Brookdale was usually a zoo and a Sunday morning in early fall would be no different. The weather outside was still warm enough for people to run the streets and the more people out, the higher the chances for stupid shit to go down. The repercussions always ended up right there on Linden Boulevard. Brawls in the waiting room were a common occurrence. One might consider it convenient to get their ass whipped at the hospital, but it was common to leave Brookdale more fucked up than when you came. If you ever left.

Before they arrived at the information desk, Cleopatra spotted Shawn's mother who grabbed her and hugged her hard. Shawn's mother was in her fifties. She was the spitting image of her daughter, and wore a salt and pepper bowl-cut wig. Her face was covered in tears.

"Where is she?" Cleopatra asked her.

She pointed down the long hallway. "In the far corner to the left. *One time!*" She waved Cleopatra down the hall in her thick Trinidadian accent, telling her to go *right now*.

While most hospitals were bright white with fluorescent lighting and a sterile vibe, everything at Brookdale was dirty yellow, and carried the smell of sick piss in the air.

"I mean, do they spray the piss? Is there like an aerosol can of piss that they use?" Jacqueline asked, making Cleopatra laugh.

They found the corner where Shawn was supposed to be. Cleopatra called her name, but she didn't answer. She hesitated, then pulled the curtain back. Shawn was sitting up in her street clothes sucking on oxygen.

"Hey, Cleo, 'sup." She lifted the oxygen mask off of her face. Her voice was raspy.

"You're ok." Cleopatra tackled Shawn for a mighty hug.

"Yeah." She took a drag of oxygen and hugged Cleopatra back. "I got some smoke in my lungs. I'm gonna have a nasty cough for a while, but I'm ok. The women are going to love my deep voice."

"Hey, Jac."

"Hey, Shawn. So glad you are ok." She hugged Shawn. "I'm going to leave you guys, and sit with your mom." She kissed Cleopatra softly on the lips. "You want anything, baby? You ok now?"

"I'm ok, thank you." She watched Jacqueline leave the room as she sat on the bed next to Shawn.

"You got a good woman."

"You have no idea. I was mid-stroke just so you know, and I will be making an appointment to beat your ass later. So, tell me what happened?"

"You know Kameelah? Bitch burned down the whole building."

"Kameelah? What did you do to her?"

"We hooked up a few times. You know she's crazy."

"Yeah, but she was functioning crazy. What did you do to set her off?"

"She lost her job and she got evicted. She came crying to me about she didn't have a place to stay."

"You didn't." Cleopatra interrupted. "Wait. She got fired? Didn't she work at the Popeye's on Empire Boulevard? How do you get fired from Popeye's?" Cleopatra covered her mouth and tried not to laugh. "What do you know about that, Shawn?"

"She might have gotten caught hooking me up with a two-piece."

"She lost her job because your cheap ass wouldn't pay for a two-piece?"

"Can I finish the story, Cleo? Damn."

"I'm sorry, go ahead." Cleopatra shook her head, knowing

once again Shawn's poor choices had landed her there.

"I let her know she could stay with me, but only for a couple of days." She inhaled more oxygen. "She took my generosity like we were shacked up together in a relationship and shit. She cooked dinner, put on some lingerie, and she was waiting for me last night. But I didn't get home until – " Shawn looked at her watch, "like, three this morning. And we start arguing. She's like, *Let me smell your fingers, pull your pants down, you better not have your dick on you cause I searched for it and I couldn't find it. Let me see what's in your backpack?* Luckily I put my dick in the mailbox before I went into the apartment. Stop laughing." Shawn took in some more oxygen. Cleopatra was shaking with laughter.

"Next thing I know I'm running through motherfucking flames." She took a drag of the oxygen.

"Did they catch her?"

"She's in jail. I gotta stop messing with these crazy chicks. I'm getting too old, for real."

"So, what are you going to do now?"

"Can I stay with you until I find a new place? Please don't make me stay with my mama. She still thinks I'm going through a phase, and she'll make me go to church."

"You need church!" Cleopatra laughed. "Of course you can stay with me, but there's one condition. No women, especially not the fire-starters you hang with."

"Damn, I won't be living with your ass long then." She laughed.

"Seriously, whatever you need, I got you." Cleopatra said.

Shawn left the hospital a few hours later and went home with Cleopatra and Jacqueline. Jacqueline cooked them a breakfast complete with pancakes, eggs and turkey sausage before heading back to bed.

"Come to bed soon. If I'm sleeping, wake me up." She kissed Cleopatra. "And Shawn, your mama told me to make sure you rest. Eat and go to bed." Jacqueline walked out of the kitchen.

"Yes, ma'am." Shawn sat up straight in her chair. "Can I tell you something? That woman loves the shit out of you. I've never seen anything like it."

"I love the shit out of her too. I must have done something right in a past life."

"It's a beautiful thing. I'm glad you finally got your woman. I want a love like that. And it's not just this whole fire, almost-dying thing. I'm tired of running the streets. I'm ready to settle down with, like, two women. Yeah, I don't need more than two."

"You're almost there, Shawn. Almost." Cleopatra laughed.

After breakfast Cleopatra slipped into bed. Jacqueline rolled over and kissed her.

"How you doing, baby?"

"I'm good. Thank you for being there for me tonight."

"You don't have to thank me." Jacqueline covered Cleopatra's neck with light kisses and crawled on top of her, straddling her. "I love you."

Cleopatra caressed her hips. "I love you, too. Just how much scares me. Something strange is happening to me."

Jacqueline lowered her body down and kissed her. "Don't be scared."

"I love you more than I thought I was capable of. I need you to take care of my heart." Cleopatra ran her fingers through her hair.

Jacqueline traced her fingers over Cleopatra's chest and rested her hand on her heart. "I will, always."

TASHA C. MILLER

ADDICTED

The impossible happened. The sex got even better. Jacqueline was down for just about anything and everything, anytime and anywhere. Her desire for Cleopatra was as uncontrollable as Cleopatra's was for her. She longed for the feelings she got that first night with Cleopatra and she wanted it over and over. But it wasn't just physical. She lived and breathed Cleopatra. Jacqueline was consumed with thoughts of her when they were apart and as Cleopatra had asked her to promise the first time they made love, she craved her every minute.

One of their favorite quickie spots was at work, in the women's bathroom in the basement near the loading dock. After Cleopatra's first business trip since they got together, and two whole days of being apart, they reunited there. Cleopatra had been gone for four days at a conference in California – the longest they had ever been separated. When she landed in New York early in the a.m. she went straight from the airport to work thinking she and Jacqueline would meet up in the basement again before her day started, but Jacqueline was nowhere to be found. And the phone tag began.

Cleopatra sat at her desk missing her woman and checked her email when her office phone rang.

"What up? Cleo, welcome back," Shawn yelled into the phone.

"What's good with you? How's the apartment?" Cleopatra asked. Shawn had been in her new home over a month. She had moved to a "less enticing" neighborhood in Inwood, as she called it.

"It's beautiful, man, it's quiet. I haven't heard a helicopter once since I been there." She laughed. "But we gotta catch up. I met a girl."

"You meet girls in your sleep."

"I'm trying to say I like her."

"What? All right, you have to tell me all about her."

"I need you to tell me how not to screw this up."

"You haven't slept with her yet, have you?"

"Nope."

"That's a good start. I'll holler at you later and I'll tell you how not to ruin her."

Racquel came in with a bunch of action items that needed Cleopatra's immediate attention before getting tied up in a big negotiations meeting all day and possibly into the evening. Midtown was in the midst of brokering a deal for a group of buildings on the Upper East Side and Cleopatra was second in command in the negotiations, just under the CEO.

After Racquel was done with her, she met briefly with her team in the conference room and did a quick run-through of the meeting agenda. When she went back to her office Jacqueline had called her cell, her desk, and Racquel. Cleopatra quickly tried to hit her back before the meeting started but only got her voicemail. Right before Cleopatra was set to go into her meeting she got a "Good luck baby! I love you! See you tonight!" text message from Jacqueline that made her smile.

Before these big meetings Cleopatra always chanted her mantra "no concessions without reciprocity" over and over again in her head. She was an uncompromising business woman, and a hard-nosed negotiator. She saw Racquel sprinting down the hall with Meredith, the CEO's assistant, both racing toward her with their arms flailing as she was about to enter the conference room.

"What's going on?" Cleopatra asked, concerned.

Meredith was heavy, with pale skin and a round, chubby face. "Cleopatra," she huffed, as she tried to catch her breath. "Mr. Kelly isn't coming. He said you can handle the meeting."

Cleopatra's eyes widened. She looked at Racquel whose chest was poked out with pride. "What are you talking about he's not coming?" Cleopatra asked Meredith to explain.

"He just said you can handle it." Meredith smiled. "And to give you this." She extended her index finger revealing a Post-it note that was stuck to it.

Cleopatra, still caught off guard, pulled the note from her finger and read its two words. *Full authority.*

The smile spread wider across Cleopatra's lips. "Oh yeah." She pumped her fist at her side. The CEO had granted her full authority to make or break this deal. She had final say and didn't need to run anything past anyone.

"You a boss." Racquel beamed. "Now. Get in there." Both Racquel and Meredith pushed Cleopatra into the meeting. As she entered the conference room Cleopatra revised her chant, to "full authority, I'm going to be home by dinner."

Nine hours later the clock struck six-thirty, and all the contracts were signed. Cleopatra and her staff were celebrating with champagne in her office when she got a call from Jacqueline on her cell.

"I did something. I've been bad." Jacqueline spoke low over the phone.

"What? Where are you?"

"You told me not to touch myself. I disobeyed you."

"You did?" Cleopatra walked over to a quiet corner of her office.

"I missed you, so I stayed at your house last night. I slept alone in your bed. Just smelling your pillow made me wet.

What was I supposed to do?" She started to moan.

"So, you touched yourself. What do you need me for?" Cleopatra teased.

"I need you to punish me." She breathed heavily into the phone. "Please come home and teach me a lesson."

"Racquel? Anything you need me to look at before tomorrow morning? I might be a little late." Cleopatra said, as she straightened up her desk and packed up her bag. Racquel looked up in the air as if the ceiling tiles would help her focus.

"Nope. You're good."

"Excellent. Use my vouchers to take a car service home so you can get to those babies quicker. Good night." She hugged Racquel goodbye.

Thirty minutes later Cleopatra walked into the sex room. It was dark, lit only by a few candles. She saw Jacqueline by the window and from the looks of her silhouette, she was naked.

Damn. Those four days felt like forever, Cleopatra thought, as she stepped gingerly over the floor pillows and tried to control the throbbing between her legs. Jacqueline met her halfway in the middle of the room. Cleopatra slipped her arms around her and kissed her.

"Full authority? Huh?" Jacqueline whispered in her ear. "Congratulations baby. I'm so proud of you."

"Where were you, baby? I was looking all over for you."

"Oh. I was running around, I had some errands to run."

"So you heard?"

"It was all over the building. So sexy. You know I love it when you use your authority. I hope you don't think you are done for the day. I haven't been able to get you fucking me off of my mind." Jacqueline led her to the bed where she had restraints, a suede whip and a blindfold laid out. "What are you gonna do to me?"

"Why do I smell my cologne?" Cleopatra scolded her.

"I missed you, so I put it here." Jacqueline circled her nipples with her fingers. "Stop talking." She placed her hand over Jacqueline's mouth.

Jacqueline's black body suit was so tight that from a distance

Cleopatra couldn't distinguish between it and her skin. She grabbed Jacqueline by the neck and pushed her down on the bed. Jacqueline rose up to kiss her. Cleopatra denied her before letting her mouth play with hers, softly licking her lips and sucking on her tongue. Cleopatra's hands slid over her body, and then palmed her breasts. She picked Jacqueline up and wrapped her legs around her and pinned her back down on the bed.

"Why should I reward your disobeying me by fucking you?"

"You said I had the sweetest pussy you ever tasted and the tightest one you ever fucked. Because you fucked me so good that we both cried. You remember that?" She asked. "Make me cry."

"Get out of the bed." Cleopatra ordered her. "Now." She watched Jacqueline wiggle off of the canopy bed in the tight cat suit.

"Strip." Cleopatra walked around her, stalking her body while she peeled herself naked. Her nipples were rock hard, saluting Cleopatra and begging to be sucked.

"Lie down and open up for me."

Cleopatra stood at the foot of the bed for a moment and looked at her. She watched Jacqueline slide a finger into her pussy and fondle her breasts.

"You just can't help yourself, can you?" Cleopatra walked up to the front of the bed. She put the restraints around her wrists and chained her to the headboard.

"I'm sorry." Jacqueline squirmed, and she gasped when Cleopatra covered her eyes with the blindfold.

Cleopatra took her time and undressed while she watched the torture of waiting get to Jacqueline. She heard her exhale hard and watched as she bucked her body up into the air in anticipation. Cleopatra walked over to the bed and rubbed Jacqueline's pussy, so wet that Cleopatra could see her juices glistening and thick on her hand in the candlelight. Jacqueline howled at the first touch.

"What did you use?"

"My fingers." Jacqueline said breathlessly.

117

"How many? Did you come?"

"Two." Her body jerked; her legs were moving all over the bed crashing into Cleopatra. "No."

"You lying to me?"

"No, baby, I couldn't make myself come."

"Is this how you did it?" Cleopatra flicked two fingers quickly back and forth across her clit.

"Fuck." She screamed, her legs flailed in the air, her thighs closed on Cleopatra's hand. "It didn't feel like that."

Cleopatra spread her legs and pinned her thighs to the bed.

"Do that one more time and I'm tying your ankles down."

"Please, no, daddy. I'll be good. Lick me."

"Stop talking. You must think disobeying me is conducive to your getting what you want." Cleopatra draped the suede whip over her pussy.

"Oooh." Jacqueline pulled at her restraints.

She spanked the inside of her thighs with the whip. "I'll decide when, and if you get what you want." She teased her clit, then unleashed three lashes across her mound.

"Uhhh…" Jacqueline bucked her legs again and moved up the bed.

Cleopatra lowered her body over Jacqueline, whose heavy breathing tickled her cheek. "I warned you not to do that."

"No, daddy. I'll be good." Cleopatra got off the bed and grabbed her ankle.

"I don't like repeating myself, and it seems you can't listen." Cleopatra tied her ankles to the bedposts.

"I need some discipline." Jacqueline said. Cleopatra was silent. "Where are you?" She asked. She couldn't feel or hear Cleopatra anywhere. "Daddy? Please." She tried to move but the restraints were tight and wouldn't let her. "I'll be good." She pleaded. She felt Cleopatra's weight on the bed, her hand slipping behind her neck and her dick sliding across her lips.

"Take it." Cleopatra pushed into her mouth. She started off shallow teasing Jacqueline before going deeper with each stroke. Knowing the other side of the dildo was inside of her Jacqueline sucked Cleopatra fast and hard until she came in her mouth.

"Good girl." She kissed Jacqueline, sucking her tongue into her mouth. "You missed that dick, didn't you?"

"Every inch."

Cleopatra unbuckled the restraints on her ankles. "If you're good, I'll set your wrists free.

"I'll do whatever you want."

Cleopatra buried her face in her pussy, pushing her tongue deep inside of her.

Jacqueline made a noise she had never heard before as Cleopatra glided her tongue in and out of her.

Cleopatra could feel Jacqueline's clit pulsate in her mouth as it swelled. Her body squirmed as she devoured her.

"That feels so...ummm I'm gonna come." She thrust her pussy into Cleopatra's face. Cleopatra sucked on her clit, bobbing her head, all the while drinking the sweetness that poured from Jacqueline. When she started to shake, Cleopatra licked a trail up her body, over her breasts, lingering at her nipples, then to her lips.

"No, you're not coming yet." Cleopatra covered her mouth and couldn't hear Jacqueline's muffled curses. She undid one of her wrist restraints.

"Take off the other restraint and get your pretty ass in that swing." Cleopatra whispered in her ear. "I need to fuck you."

Cleopatra stood to the side of the bed stroking her dick while she watched Jacqueline take off her blindfold and undo her wrist restraint. Her stroking got faster as she watched Jacqueline tangle her body up in the swing, legs spread at 180 degrees, pussy wet, clit swollen and pulsing, inviting Cleopatra in. Without a word, kiss or caress, she walked over to Jacqueline and slid inside her. Her breath was heavy with Cleopatra's crotch slamming into her.

"That's so deep." Their moans grew louder. Jacqueline held on to Cleopatra's neck, squeezing her. Cleopatra was soaked with sweat and her body ached as she yearned to explode.

Jacqueline closed her eyes. "Uhhh..." Cleopatra pulled out and dropped to her knees between Jacqueline's legs. She flicked her tongue over her clit, she stood up and pushed into her again and stroked her pussy momentarily before bowing down between her legs and invading her with her tongue again. Two more cycles of that and Jacqueline couldn't take it.

"Make me come. Damn."

Cleopatra laughed as she slid back into Jacqueline and worked her body with a painstakingly slow stroke until Jacqueline's body erupted.

That night Jacqueline told Cleopatra. "I don't ever want to be separated from you again. Those were the four longest days of my life. I don't like life without you."

On mornings after Jacqueline had spent the night, she was often awakened by Cleopatra's tongue licking delicately between her legs. Usually she thought she was dreaming until the pleasure became too intense and she woke up to find Cleopatra waiting to full-on devour her. Jacqueline woke Cleopatra up that last morning, not able to wait for her lover to wake on her own. Jacqueline scaled her naked body along Cleopatra's and waited for her eyes to open before sitting on her face. Cleopatra woke up that last morning in heaven.

I WISH I NEVER MET HER AT ALL

Jacqueline and Cleopatra were walking into the office together as they did most mornings when Jacqueline had spent the night. The weather was unseasonably cold even for early November.

"Yo, what's up with you? Let me holler at you for a second." Shawn was upset. She clutched Cleopatra's arm and pulled her away from Jacqueline.

"Hey, this leather leaves fingerprints," Cleopatra teased Shawn. But Shawn wasn't laughing.

"Baby, I'll catch up with you later." She kissed Jacqueline goodbye and watched her walk into the building.

"What's wrong? You look pissed."

"I am. Do you know what you're doing?" Shawn bundled her red scarf around her mouth.

"What are you talking about?"

"I'm talking about your girl? You can't possibly know." She

shook her head. "You don't get down like that." She got increasingly agitated.

"Know what? Why are you so hot right now?"

"She's married!"

"Stop playing." Cleopatra rolled her eyes.

"She's married to a man. You really didn't know?"

"I don't believe you." Cleopatra shook her head. "She's mine."

"She's married, Cleo."

"How do you know?" Cleopatra folded her arms.

"I found out last night. I just realized that the Robin I'm dating is her sister. I was at her apartment and I saw this picture. I swore it was Jacqueline. I asked her who it was, and she said it was her sister Jacqueline and her husband."

"No. No." Cleopatra kept shaking her head.

"You have to believe me." Shawn pleaded with her as she watched her eyes fill with tears.

Cleopatra wiped her face with her sleeve. "Did she say her ex-husband?"

"No, they are still married, Cleo, she said *husband*, they live in Coney Island."

"This can't be happening. She's always with me. She stays over like every other night and when we aren't together we talk on the phone before we go to sleep. How could she do that with a husband? Those late night conversations were not tame." Cleopatra still refused to believe Shawn. "What did the man in the picture look like?"

"This huge dude, built like a football player or a wrestler or something."

Cleopatra paused before she spoke. "I think I met that motherfucker, no wonder he kept giving me the side eye." She laughed nervously. "She introduced him as her neighbor, but he didn't say anything different." She put her hands over her face. "Maybe they are separated." She was digging for answers.

"Cleopatra. Stop fucking making excuses for her. She's married. For like two years or something. Not divorced. What if she is separated? Whatever it is, she lied to you."

"All right, all right. I believe you."

"You going to be ok?" She put her arm around Cleopatra.

"No." Cleopatra shifted her body weight onto Shawn.

"Think. Were there ever any clues?" Shawn rubbed her shoulder.

"Not that I can think of right now. She's a fucking pro, she's good." Cleopatra was starting to get angry now.

"What are you going to do?"

"I'm not sure yet, I need time to think." Cleopatra said. She took deep breaths to try and calm herself down.

"You coming in to work?"

"Yeah. I got to figure this out."

Racquel played gatekeeper and blocked Jacqueline's calls and visits while Cleopatra worked with her door locked. Because she knew Racquel's temper, Cleopatra didn't fill her in on the details. She only asked Racquel to shield her like her first-born, and Racquel didn't question her. Jacqueline caught her at the end of the day when she was leaving the building on her way home.

"Where've you been all day? Why didn't you call me or email me?"

"I've been in meetings all day, sorry."

"You've been busy before, but you always still manage to give me some attention. And what's wrong with Racquel? She was in a bad mood today – she gave me this hateful look."

"She seemed fine to me. You must have caught her at a bad time."

"I missed you, baby, I'm used to seeing you." She put her arms around her.

"I know." Cleopatra's body softened in her embrace. Cleopatra couldn't just turn off her desire for her. "Why don't you let me make it up to you? I'll come home with you tonight and make you dinner." Cleopatra wanted to know what Jacqueline's reaction would be when she invited herself over to her apartment.

Jacqueline hesitated. "That's not necessary baby, I forgive you." She looked down at her watch. Something was very wrong with Cleopatra and she knew it. Jacqueline saw the pain in her eyes. *Just hold on baby, I'm going to fix this.* She would be late for her meeting with her divorce attorney if she didn't leave now.

"I know I don't have to, but I want to," Cleopatra insisted as she studied Jacqueline's body language.

Jacqueline couldn't look her in the eyes. She looked at the ground as she stuttered. "But it's so far. Why don't I hang with you? I can come over later for a little while," she said.

"A little while? Naw, we always hang at my house. What's wrong? You have somewhere to be? Or is someone at your house that you don't want me to know about?" She looked dead into her eyes.

"No." She stuttered. "Of course not, Cleopatra, what are you talking about? I got something to do tonight."

"Wow. Was that another stutter?" Cleopatra sighed. "Why are you being so secretive?"

"I'm not being secretive. Why are you grilling me?"

"Is that what I'm doing?"

"We don't keep tabs on each other like that."

"You know, you're right. Because we have trust in our relationship."

"You are being real cryptic."

Cleopatra wanted to blast her right on the street, but her energy was low and all she wanted to do was go home. Could she ignore what she learned today, and continue to be with a married woman? What was the situation at home? She wanted to know, but she didn't want to know.

"I'm tired, I'm going home. Peace." Cleopatra said.

"Peace? It's like that?"

"Just like that." Cleopatra sucked her teeth as she walked away. Something told her that no matter what the situation was, Jacqueline loved her, and she had never doubted that, ever. She was hurting, devastated to the point that her heart was broken. She was numb, still in shock, she had to go home and think. All she knew for sure was that this had to end soon. There was no way Jacqueline was going to have her cake and get eaten too.

That night she didn't answer any calls and Jacqueline blew her voicemail up. *She loved her, she missed her, and she needed her,* Jacqueline said, and *whatever was wrong she could fix it.*

You can't fix this.

◉ ◉ ◉

"Shawn, I need to talk to you." Jacqueline burst into her office. "Have you heard from Cleopatra? She was avoiding me yesterday, and today Racquel said she's not coming to work. I need to see her."

Shawn had promised Cleopatra that she wouldn't say anything to Jacqueline. "I don't know anything. She probably didn't feel like coming in. She used to do that before when she was laid up with a li'l...nevermind." She couldn't resist. She wanted Jacqueline to hurt.

"What are you talking about? Is she with someone? All I know is she's avoiding me and I don't know what to do." Jacqueline paced back and forth.

"You really don't have any idea what's wrong?" Shawn looked at Jacqueline with raised eyebrows.

"She hasn't said a thing. Does she have someone else? Please tell me."

"I know how much Cleopatra loves you. She's not cheating on you. If something is wrong, she would have told me. Leave her alone and let her come to you in her own time. It's the anniversary of her mom's death this weekend. She may just want to be alone. Every anniversary, or holiday or birthday she handles differently. She may be fine and she may not. Stay out of her way."

"I'm her woman. I'm supposed to be with her while she's going through this. What am I supposed to do in the meantime?" Jacqueline asked.

"I don't know."

"I should go to her house to see how she is." Jacqueline said. "I have the keys."

"I don't suggest you do that. If she wanted to see you, she would tell you. Give her some space. She'll come to you when she's ready."

"Fine. I'll wait."

"Good. Going over there would just make it worse."

"Why do you sound like you know something?"

"I don't know what Cleopatra is doing, but if I did I wouldn't tell you."

◎ ◎ ◎

"It's been three days and I still haven't heard from her. Racquel said she's working from home. Have you talked to her?" Jacqueline stood on one side of the desk, opposite where Shawn was sitting. Shawn was texting on her cell phone. Unbeknownst to Jacqueline, Shawn was giving her answers that Cleopatra was dictating to her by text message.

"I don't know what else to tell you, Jacqueline." Shawn replied. "You should probably prepare yourself for whatever is about to happen."

"What does that even mean? What are you not telling me?"

"She hasn't contacted you in like four days. What do you think that means? That's all I'm saying."

Jacqueline's face sunk. The separation from Cleopatra had been wearing on her. She looked as if she hadn't slept in days.

"She'll be back on Monday. I'm sure you'll see her then." Shawn walked out of her office. And left Jacqueline standing there alone.

Cleopatra needed time away, and time to pack up all of Jacqueline's things. She couldn't go back to work, and sit at the same desk and couch where she and Jacqueline had made love dozens of times. That first night she was angry. So angry and hurt that she cried like a baby. Then she was mad again for allowing herself to cry. How could the woman that she was so deeply in love with be such a liar, such a cheat? They'd talked about a future together, about making a real commitment to each other. All lies.

The whole situation reminded Cleopatra of her first relationship with a woman. The wealthy older woman turned a nowhere-near-legal-Cleopatra out. They lasted six turbulent, sex-filled weeks that ended with a confession in the middle of their lovemaking.

"I had no idea what I was getting into when I started messing with you. There's something I've been keeping from you." The brown haired, hazel eyed woman paused. "I have a partner. We've been together about five years now. She has a son and we ..."

"So, what are you doing with me?" Cleopatra blurted out. She moved away from the woman to the other side of the bed, using the sheets to cover her naked body.

"I love you. I don't love her."

"Does she know about me?"

"I'm going to tell her tonight. I'm leaving her to be with you." She scooted across the bed and up close to Cleopatra.

"Tonight?" Cleopatra stared at her. "Where do they live? I spend a lot of time in this penthouse. You gave me the keys."

"Connecticut. This is only one of my apartments."

"Of course it is." Cleopatra nodded her head. "My first woman and you do this to me." Cleopatra said. "You've probably been sleeping with both of us." She started to get out of the bed.

"I have not. And honestly baby, you wear me out. I couldn't sleep with her even if I wanted to, and trust me, I don't." She pulled Cleopatra back into the bed. "Let me prove it to you." She kissed down Cleopatra's body and stopped between her legs.

Cleopatra looked down at her. She was a beautiful woman, and her first. She had a weakness for her and couldn't get enough. That night they had sex into the wee hours of the morning, to the point of exhaustion. Cleopatra gave her a fucking she would never forget, all over that penthouse. Afterward the woman rolled over in bed, picked up the phone and broke up with her girlfriend of five years right in front of her. Cleopatra took a long, hot shower and got dressed. She had remained calm until the woman asked her to move in with her, and offered to take care of Cleopatra and her mother.

"I'll get her round the clock care, the best money can buy."

Cleopatra sucked her teeth. "Uh, yeah, no. Who said we were going to be together?" Cleopatra interrupted.

"Stop it. Don't play like that."

"I never told you to leave your woman, did I? Or that I would even continue to see you. Rewind the conversation back in your mind." Cleopatra stuffed her few belongings into her backpack.

"What are you saying?" The woman sighed.

"Be certain of a new home before you wreck your old one."

◎ ◎ ◎

Now, all these years later, she was in a similar position again, caught up with a liar. Her first experience had ruined her ability to trust women, but it didn't destroy her lust for them. She had sworn she would never give any woman the opportunity to hurt her again. But that's exactly what she had done. She didn't love her first girlfriend, not even close. But Jacqueline was the air she breathed. The pain was only intensified by the second anniversary of her mother's death. She had been so consumed with Jacqueline, and anger, that she hadn't honored her mother's memory appropriately. She would mourn the loss of her two loves in her house, by herself.

A few days later Cleopatra had an idea, a plan for revenge.

Cleopatra called Shawn in the middle of the night to run it by her. "So what do you think? You cool with this?"

"I don't know. That's evil, kind of low down, don't you think?" Shawn asked.

They were both silent for a moment.

"Yeah, go ahead." Shawn laughed. "You sure it's going to work?"

"Positive. I told you what happened the first time I met her sister. Money in the bank."

"It's on, then. Hopefully she has no idea what's going on yet." Shawn said.

"I'll holla, and tell you what happens."

"You better!"

○ ○ ○

"So, you couldn't do it, huh?" Shawn asked.

"Naw. Couldn't make myself go through with it. I didn't even call Robin, much less sleep with her." Cleopatra admitted.

"You still love Jac, don't you?"

"If you had asked me a few days ago, I would have said I hated her. But I've calmed down. Yeah, it's crazy, but I still love her."

"What are you going to do?"

"Break up with her."

"And you are sure about this?"

"There is no working this out. There are no compromises to be made."

"You went missing for days. She's been an absolute mess without you, you should see her. She loves you, Cleopatra, in spite of everything she's done, and whatever is going on at home, that woman is deeply in love with you. It will probably destroy her if you break up with her."

"So what am I supposed to do? Ignore her lying to me every day for the last six months? Ignore that she has a husband? I can't compete with that."

"You have been competing with that, and you've been winning. You're obviously blowing him out of the water. I'm just saying, I don't think you should kick her completely out of your life. When I first found out I really wanted to whip her ass for you, but now I feel sorry for her."

"Why all of a sudden? Do you feel sorry for her husband?"

"I don't know exactly what's going on with her situation, she's leading a double life, yeah, but she can't be happy."

"Probably true, but guess what? That's her problem, not mine."

IN THE END: YOU LOVED HOW I FUCKED YOU, DIDN'T YOU?

Cleopatra was certain that it had to end. No need to put off the inevitable. She would break up with Jacqueline and move on with her life. She had no other choice. She sat in her office early that Monday morning, wearing all black. She felt dark, and she wanted to look dark. She had pulled the last of her window shades down, blocking out all of the morning sun. She had just turned the thermostat up to eighty-six, blasting hot air into her office in an attempt to compensate for the frigid winter weather, when she heard a knock at her door.

"Hi." Even though she'd told Racquel it was ok to let her in, Cleopatra was still startled when she saw Jacqueline standing in her doorway.

"That's all you have to say?" Jacqueline locked the door behind her.

Cleopatra shook her head and couldn't look at her. One week apart and she'd forgotten how beautiful Jacqueline was and the effect she had on her. Cleopatra's need for her had not weakened. Jacqueline wrapped her arms around Cleopatra, and she in turn held Jacqueline tight as her fingers caressed the small of her back.

"I've missed you. Why did you disappear and not say a word?"

Cleopatra freed herself from her embrace. "I needed some time away. Sorry if I worried you." She sat down at her desk and opened her email.

"That's it? Sorry if you worried me?" She raised her voice. Jacqueline walked behind the desk and turned off the monitor, significantly decreasing the already sparse light in the room.

Cleopatra was silent. She could tell her cavalier attitude was making Jacqueline angry by the grimace on her face.

"What did you need time away from? Me? Work? How did you handle the anniversary? I wanted to be there for you so badly."

"I got all of your voicemails. They were sweet, thank you." Cleopatra's eyes began to water. "I handled it just like I do everything, I survived it. I never thought anything could hurt anywhere close to losing my mother." Her voice cracked.

"What are you talking about?"

Cleopatra got up and stood by the window. She raised the blackout shades so she would have something to do with her hands.

"The last few months I've just been very caught up and sometimes I get sidetracked and I lose focus and forget what's really important. I needed to clear my head, so I could plan for my future."

Jacqueline glared at Cleopatra. "That's a bullshit answer. But I'm not going to push, I don't know what this is really about, your mom or something else so I'm not going to come at you all crazy. Answer one question for me please and we'll squash this, because I don't want to fight baby. While you were getting your head straight, were you alone?"

"Are you seriously asking me if I was with another woman?"

"That's precisely what I'm asking."

Cleopatra rolled her eyes, and shook her head as she looked out the window. "No, I wasn't with another woman, damn."

Jacqueline's shoulders relaxed. "Good. Then nothing else matters. I'm just glad you're back and you're ok, I've missed you like crazy." She walked up behind Cleopatra and slid her arms around her waist and held her tight against her body. "These few days apart have been miserable, I can't function without you."

Cleopatra turned around and faced her. She gazed into her eyes and looked for a reason to stop loving her, and couldn't come up with one. Jacqueline cracked a smile for the first time since she came into her office. Cleopatra still loved this woman without question or hesitation. But she knew she couldn't have her. She wasn't for her to have; she belonged to someone else and there was no way around it.

"Come here, baby." She pulled Cleopatra by the hand over to the couch.

Cleopatra sat down beside her and Jacqueline quickly slid over and sat in her lap.

"I've realized this over the last few days that I don't know what I would do if I didn't have you in my life. You are my world." She was making this hard for Cleopatra, not enough time apart had passed to make her strong enough to push her away.

She kissed Cleopatra softly. She put all of her weight on her as she straddled her, her thighs clinched tight around her. Cleopatra was overwhelmed by the power she still possessed over her. One taste of her lips and she was ready to make love to her and forgive everything.

"I've missed your touch so much." Jacqueline pulled her sweater off over her head. She kissed Cleopatra again and pressed her breasts hard into her face. Cleopatra resisted her at first before melting into the couch and accepting her mouth into hers.

"You know you want me." Jacqueline watched Cleopatra

trace the outline of her bra before unhooking it in the back. Jacqueline untied Cleopatra's locs and let them fall spread out across her body. She grabbed handfuls of her dreads and rubbed them against her breasts. "You know how I get when I haven't seen you. We have days of lovemaking to catch up on. I want to see the snake."

Cleopatra stuck out her tongue and Jacqueline took all of it into her mouth and sucked it like a cock. "I need you to come inside of me. Can you handle that?"

Cleopatra took a nipple into her mouth and flicked it lightly with her tongue.

"I can handle whatever you want to do."

◎ ◎ ◎

"Hey, Cleo. I came to check on you. How you doing?" Shawn peeked her head into Cleopatra's office.

"Hanging in there." She got up to hug her.

"I just saw Jacqueline at the elevator. She had a big-ass smile on her face."

"I haven't done anything yet, if you're wondering. We were too busy fucking." Cleopatra sighed. "I can't believe I let it happen. But, why is it so amazing?"

"Yeah. You made it harder on yourself. So, you still gonna break up with her?"

"I still love her, and that scares me. I'm going to end it peacefully. I don't have the energy for some elaborate plan anymore."

"Do what you got to do, let me know if you need me," she said, heading out the door. "And remember, no more fucking." Shawn shook her finger at her friend.

Later that day Cleopatra found herself face to face with Jacqueline again.

"I got your message to be here at five." She closed Cleopatra's office door behind her and locked it, as she always did.

"Come in." Cleopatra got up from her desk. She walked over to her, slipped her hand behind her neck and pulled her ear to her mouth.

"Take your clothes off." The smell of her perfume behind her left ear sent twinges of desire through her body. Without hesitation, Jacqueline stripped.

She's so fucking hot, Cleopatra thought. *Why does this have to end?* In seconds Jacqueline was naked, with only her heels on.

"What are you going to do to me?" Jacqueline asked softly, passion building up in her eyes. She was pinned between Cleopatra and the door.

"I need you to do what I tell you to do from now on." Cleopatra said. "Spread your legs." She watched Jacqueline part her legs as she leaned her body against the office door. Cleopatra pressed her body into hers. Jacqueline yelped when she felt Cleopatra's strap confined in her trousers. Cleopatra stood back from Jacqueline and pulled her dick through her zipper, letting it stand erect to Jacqueline's delight. Cleopatra started jacking the dildo as she stared at Jacqueline's body.

Jacqueline's nipples hardened, her legs shook and she slapped the door as she watched Cleopatra stroke her dick. Cleopatra walked up to her still rubbing her thickness, only now she was much closer. Her cock touched Jacqueline's thigh and Cleopatra dared her to move, even after she began whispering in her ear.

"You know, from the first moment I saw you there was something about you that I couldn't explain." She kissed the side of Jacqueline's face, and she sped up her stroke. "And it's not even about how beautiful you are, or the sex. I've been with hot women before, but I didn't love them. I love you and that just intensified everything we did a hundred times. Who knew?" Cleopatra said breathlessly as she pulled hard on her dick. "You know how you always say you belong to me?"

"I do belong to you. Forever."

"I guess it's probably selfish of me to hope that after tonight you will still be in search of me, or to hope for a moment that will likely never come."

"Baby, what are you talking about?"

"Please, just let me get this out."

"You know how sometimes in the morning you wake me up by kissing my neck? That drives me crazy."

"I know, that's why I do it." She kissed Cleopatra's neck as she pressed her naked body up against the door.

"I love how our bodies are connected. Every curve fits together perfectly. You were what I needed, and I didn't even know it. How good it was amazed me, and scared me. But, I never questioned that we belonged together. There was no question we were meant to be."

"We are perfect for each other, baby."

Cleopatra kissed her again as she palmed Jacqueline's ass in her hands and let her dick poke her in the stomach. "Lay down on the couch." Cleopatra stuffed her dick back in her pants and zipped up. Still fully dressed she sat in the black leather armchair as she watched Jacqueline's naked body slither onto the couch.

"I want to play a game."

"You're too far away from me baby, come closer." She held out her arms.

Cleopatra went over to Jacqueline and pinned her down on the couch.

"Is that better?"

"Uh hmm." She grinded underneath Cleopatra. "I love it when you take control of me."

"So you ready to play?"

"I'm ready. I need you."

"Good." Cleopatra lowered her body down onto Jacqueline's pelvis, making sure she could feel the length of her thickness still contained in her pants. "First question."

Jacqueline wrapped her legs around her waist thrusting her body upwards, their lips almost touching. Cleopatra tightened her grip on her hands and looked deep into her eyes.

"Tell me about your wedding day. Was it the fairytale that all little girls dream of?"

Jacqueline's body froze. She closed her eyes, not able to face

Cleopatra's glare.

"Was that question too hard? Ok, I got an easier one. Why didn't you tell me?"

Jacqueline squirmed and tried to break free from under Cleopatra, but she wasn't strong enough.

"Were you ever going to tell me? Answer me." Cleopatra yelled in Jacqueline's face as she kept her pinned down. Jacqueline begged Cleopatra to stop screaming at her.

"Who are you when I'm not looking?"

"Please stop." Jacqueline pleaded. Cleopatra got up and threw Jacqueline's clothes at her. She stood watching as Jacqueline sobbed.

"I don't ever want to see you again, don't call me here at work, on my cell or at home, don't email me, don't come by my office and don't come by my house. If you see me in the street forget you even know me."

Cleopatra rifled through Jacqueline's purse and found her keys. She pulled her house key off of the key chain and put it in her pocket.

"Please, give me a chance to explain," she pleaded.

"Now you want to talk?"

"I wanted to tell you from the start, but I fell in love with you so quickly, I knew if I told you, you wouldn't want anything to do with me. I don't love him, I don't want him, I'm leaving him to be with you. Please just give me the chance to make everything right. Don't leave me. I'll die without you." She grabbed Cleopatra's arm. Her body tensed at her touch.

"Jacqueline, it's been more than six months. You were living a lie, I was living a lie. Every day you lied to me. You said you loved me."

"I do love you. That's not a lie."

"I would have done absolutely anything for you. All you say may be true, that you don't love him. You may even be leaving him. I don't know and I honestly don't care. How could I ever believe anything you say? All I know for sure is that you're a liar."

Cleopatra reached to unlock the door. Jacqueline tightened

her grip on Cleopatra's arm and pulled her to her lips. "You knew this morning, didn't you? But you still made love to me. It was real and passionate just like every other time we've been together."

"We've never had a problem making love. My only problem is resisting you. I'll have to work on that. I've been a fool, but that's over. This is over. Because this is wrong." She snatched her arm away. Jacqueline sank down to the floor and cried as Cleopatra walked out of her office.

◎ ◎ ◎

The next day Jacqueline cornered Shawn in her office again.

"What can I do to get her back?"

"First, let me say that this is the last time I'm talking to you about Cleopatra. This is the last time we need to speak at all actually." Shawn said to Jacqueline. "Let her go."

"I can't do that."

"You are so selfish. Can't you do this one thing for her, and it not be about you? You're not available, that's a fact."

"I need her."

"You need to straighten your shit out, that's what you need to do. Cleopatra wants unconditional love."

"That's what I have for her. And you know that."

"I consider having a husband a condition." Shawn said. "You know as well as I do how hard it is for her to feel something for somebody. It's because of people like you that she's learned not to depend on anyone who claimed to love her. Don't worry your pretty little head. She will hurt for a while, then she will shut down and stop feeling altogether and eventually, replace you with the bodies of numerous other women."

GOODBYE LOVE

"Please, I'm begging you at least let me talk to you." Jacqueline pleaded with her through Cleopatra's chained front door.

For a whole week, Cleopatra had dodged her visits and rejected her calls. But she grew tired and Jacqueline had worn her down. Exasperated, Cleopatra opened her door.

"Can I come in? It's freezing out here and it's starting to snow."

"I don't have anything to say to you, and I can't imagine what you have to say to me. I don't know what you want from me."

"I want the chance to explain. That's all I want right now. Please. I need you to listen to what I have to say."

"Come in." Cleopatra pointed toward the living room.

"I can't take being away from you." She hugged Cleopatra. "You've lost weight." She stood back and looked at her body.

"Please, don't touch me. You're just making this harder." She pushed Jacqueline away.

"Are you eating? I can make you some dinner."

"I don't have an appetite, but that's not your concern. Have a seat."

Jacqueline sat down and took off her coat. "I don't know where to start."

"The beginning, maybe?" Cleopatra said, as she sat down on the other end of the couch.

"Ok. I've struggled with my sexuality all of my life, I've always been attracted to women as long as I could remember, but I was always too scared to come out of the closet and to live my life as a lesbian."

"You told me this." Cleopatra interrupted her as she leaned back on the couch and stared up at the ceiling.

"I know. I just needed to start at the beginning. Growing up, my parents had the perfect marriage, and I wanted what they had. I was young and thought I needed to be with a man to experience that. Plus, I was scared and I didn't want to hurt my family. So, I did what I thought I was supposed to do, I married a man. I didn't go with my heart."

Cleopatra turned her entire body toward Jacqueline and looked in her eyes. "Do you love him?"

"No, I don't. I never have. We're only married on paper. It's a marriage of convenience, for show."

"Do you have sex with him?" Cleopatra's face winced with pain. "Of course you do. I don't know why I'm asking." She shook her head.

"You're asking because you care. We only had sex one time. I didn't lie to you when I said I only had sex once before you."

"I'm supposed to believe that?" Cleopatra laughed out loud and slapped her own knee.

"I understand if you don't. I know I've lied to you, but I'm not now. I was a virgin when I met him. We only had sex once, and I haven't let him touch me since. When I say I don't want him, and I don't love him, I mean it."

"I'm not buying it. The way we used to fuck?"

"It's the truth, but if you must know, I watched a lot of porn and I took some workshops at Babeland."

"Really?" Cleopatra burst in to laughter. "Rookie of the year, they taught you so well."

"You taught me well. I would do anything to please you. That's what it is." Jacqueline leaned across the couch and caressed Cleopatra's fingers.

Cleopatra looked down at Jacqueline's hand on hers before snatching it away. "Why did you stay married, if there was no love?"

"It was easier than shaking everything up – or so I thought. I accepted that I was going to just always be unhappy. Then one day I saw you and something happened, I wanted you so bad, I fell so deeply in love with you and I realized that I didn't have to live my life unfulfilled anymore."

"Does he know about this other life of yours? About me?" Cleopatra studied Jacqueline's eyes hoping she would know if she was lying or not.

Jacqueline looked her in her eyes. "He knew who you were when you came to the house. I told him about you the same day that we met. A couple of weeks before our three-month anniversary I told him that I was in love with you and that I was going to file for divorce."

She's not lying. "Before we made love?" Cleopatra asked.

"Yes baby. Before you made love to me. He was angry, but he was aware of my desires before we were married. I got an attorney and I filed the paperwork. Then he threatened to out me to my family. That scared me and stopped me in my tracks. I wasn't ready to come out to them. Then you and I made love for the first time and I've been so consumed with you that I got complacent. Everything happened so fast. I wasn't working on getting out of this marriage or building up the courage to tell you or my parents the truth. But now I'm not scared anymore. I'm ready to tell everyone that I'm gay and that I'm in love with you."

"You can lop off the last part." Cleopatra turned away from Jacqueline again and stared back up at the ceiling. "I don't have anything to do with what you do in the future."

Jacqueline slid down the length of the couch and held on to

Cleopatra's bicep. "You have everything to do with it."

Cleopatra shot Jacqueline a look that caused her to catch herself. "I'm sorry. I've never been able to not touch you." Jacqueline released her arm and backed up from her a bit but still sat close and Cleopatra didn't push her away.

"Why didn't you tell me all of this in the beginning?" Cleopatra turned to Jacqueline, wanting desperately to hear an explanation that she could understand.

"Tell you that I'm married? That I'm a closeted lesbian married to a man?" Jacqueline turned her head away from her. "Would you have even talked to me?"

Cleopatra turned Jacqueline's face back toward her with her hand. Jacqueline took Cleopatra's hand into hers as it caressed her cheek. She kissed her fingers as Cleopatra pulled her hand away.

"I would have talked to you, but I would have never touched you." Cleopatra admitted. "I sure as hell would not have fallen in love with you. But I at least should have been given a choice. Since I found out I've been trying to rationalize staying with you, trying to come up with a reason not to end this."

"Don't end this, because you love me and I love you. We don't have to end. I don't want to lose you." Jacqueline placed her hand on Cleopatra's thigh and squeezed it.

"The same way you didn't give me a choice in the beginning you don't have a say in how this ends. Were you ever going to tell me, Jacqueline?"

"I wanted to so many times. I chickened out when I imagined your reaction. I didn't want to give you up. I still don't."

"You need to understand that I don't trust you. I don't trust myself right now." She moved Jacqueline's hand off of her thigh. "I don't know what's real anymore. How can I ever believe another word that comes out of your mouth?"

"I understand, but can you imagine what I felt, what I had to go through?" Jacqueline asked.

"No. I can't, actually. But you are responsible for your

decisions. I'm sorry he threatened to out you, but, I didn't ask to be brought into your life."

"And I didn't ask to fall in love with you. But it happened."

Cleopatra didn't like her response. She got up and walked across the room. "What do you want from me? I can't be in a relationship with someone I don't trust, and I don't trust you. Never mind your being somebody's wife. Maybe if I had learned the truth from you I would feel differently, but that wasn't the case – you were busted. Go home and take care of your business and forget about me. I can send your things to your house if you like."

Jacqueline sprung up from the couch and walked over to Cleopatra. "How the hell do you expect me to forget about you?" Her voice cracked. "I don't care about those things. Do whatever you want with them, burn them."

"I know you're not serious. I'll send them to your house. You probably want to take these too, or I can destroy them. I don't care." Cleopatra handed Jacqueline a flash drive with all of their sex tapes on them, knowing Jacqueline would never destroy it.

Jacqueline took it from Cleopatra and tossed it in her purse. "Look in my eyes." She said. "Cleopatra, look at me." She pulled her by her t-shirt. Cleopatra looked at her. "Are you still in love with me?"

"Yes."

Jacqueline exhaled hard. "Then you'll wait for me to straighten this out. Whatever your version of waiting is, please do it. I'm going to fix this. Because I can't be without you. I hope in time you'll forgive me. For now, know that I love you. That will never change."

"You'll always have my heart." Cleopatra said.

"I don't deserve you. I know that. I knew this day would come. I guess this is what it feels like to have a broken heart and want to die." Her eyes filled with tears. Cleopatra wiped Jacqueline's cheek with her hand and brought her lips to meet hers, and kissed her gently.

Jacqueline squeezed Cleopatra tight around her waist. "You

still want me." She ran her finger across her lips. "I can feel it. Kisses don't lie."

"I never once said I didn't want you, now, did I?"

"I'm so sorry, baby."

"Don't apologize for showing me who you are."

After she left, Cleopatra tried to convince herself that she did the right thing. She had to let her go, she needed to handle her business and then maybe somewhere down the road, if it was meant to be, it would. For now, Cleopatra called herself setting Jacqueline free. But apart, neither one of them would ever be free.

Jacqueline didn't let go of her easily. The next day Cleopatra found a pan of manicotti and a pan of peach cobbler on her steps with a note: "please eat." Jacqueline wrote long emails and left voicemails in the middle of the night apologizing and professing her love. She kept that kind of contact up for a couple of weeks. Cleopatra believed her non-responses were louder than anything she could have put into words. Before this, there wasn't anything Cleopatra wouldn't have done to make Jacqueline happy. They had become dependent on the other's nurturing ability to keep them safe from all those who could hurt them. It made them inseparable, or so Cleopatra had thought. But all along, Jacqueline was the one she needed protection against.

◎ ◎ ◎

Cleopatra spent weeks walking around in a daze. She went to work and rushed home in the afternoon only to sit in the dark and watch TV until she fell asleep. She didn't answer her phone or her door and rarely returned personal emails. She shunned the sun more than usual and refused to let it into her house. Her appetite was nonexistent and she worked out like a madwoman. She slept mostly in her theatre room on the recliners. Watching hours and hours of television made her focus on other people's lives, keeping her from thinking too much about her own. She turned the volume up high and fell asleep; the noise of the TV soothed her and lulled her into a sound sleep as it did every night. This was a habit she formed after moving to Manhattan, growing up in East New York she was more often than not rocked to sleep with the sounds of fighting, sirens, gun shots and helicopters. Now she couldn't sleep without noise, listening to the crickets in her garden was maddening. Her only saving grace was to sleep with the television on.

Shawn came over often to check on her; she was worried about her lifelong friend whom she'd never seen brokenhearted before. She didn't know what to say to Cleopatra. She just hoped that time would heal her pain.

It had been over a month since the day Cleopatra's heart crumbled into a million little pieces and still the everyday activities were hard, from riding the train to eating meals without Jacqueline, but it had gotten better. When they first split Cleopatra told Racquel that Jacqueline had no reason to be on the floor, and to keep her away from her office. Seeing the pain in Cleopatra's eyes, Racquel asked for no explanation. She made it her mission to protect Cleopatra from Jacqueline.

"I miss you so much. I love you. I'm going to make this right. We will be together again. That's all I have to hold on to," Jacqueline said on Cleopatra's voicemail. Whenever a moment or an hour passed when Cleopatra didn't think about her, Jacqueline would inevitably call, email or text her.

Jacqueline showed up at the year-end board meeting in place of her boss, who was out of the country. She sat directly across from Cleopatra. They couldn't keep their eyes off of each other. Jacqueline mouthed, "I love you" and "I miss you" across the table numerous times. Cleopatra responded with "You're beautiful" and "I miss you too."

Jacqueline cornered Cleopatra at the end of the meeting. "Can I speak with you for a minute?"

"What's on your mind?" Cleopatra inhaled the perfume that she missed so much.

"You remember the first night we made love?"

"Of course I do. Why are we talking about this?"

"You asked me to promise you something. That I would crave you. I thought I knew what you were talking about then."

"I don't understand."

"I haven't broken that promise. I still crave you. I think about you every minute, ever since the first time we made love. You said it would be different. I understand what you mean now. I hunger for you. I hurt. I feel physical pain. My heart is still breaking. I just wanted you to know, I'm keeping my promise to you."

Christmas crept up fast and everyone was in the holiday spirit except for Cleopatra, who couldn't wait till the holidays were done. Instead, she looked forward to the New Year and starting over. With the New Year came a new title. She'd been promoted to VP of Acquisitions and Asset Management at the Times Square office. She'd be moving eleven blocks downtown to the headquarters on 42nd Street, and she was taking all her staff, including Racquel, with her.

Even though they hadn't spoken or run into each other in weeks, Cleopatra felt obligated to tell Jacqueline she was leaving, before she found out from someone else.

"Hi, Jacqueline."

"Cleopatra, baby, how are you? It's so good to hear your voice."

"I'm ok, and you?" Cleopatra asked.

"I'm dealing."

"Can I see you sometime today for a few minutes? I need to talk to you."

"I'm on my way down now." She quickly hung up.

A few minutes later she was sitting in front of Cleopatra's desk.

"You look lovely. Your scent still puts me in a trance," Cleopatra admitted.

"I miss you. It's so hard being away from you."

"I asked to see you because I wanted you to hear this from me. It hasn't been formally announced yet, but I've been promoted. I'll be taking on some new duties in Acquisitions.

146

I'm moving to the 42nd Street office after the holidays."

"You're leaving? So I won't see you anymore at all now? Not even from a distance?" Her eyes fell to the floor.

"It's a ten minute walk." Cleopatra explained.

"I'm sorry. Congratulations. I'm proud of you. I really am."

"Thank you. That means a lot to me."

"Thank you for being the one to tell me. I wouldn't want to hear this from anyone but you. I have to get back upstairs now." Water pooled in her eyes. "I love you, baby."

"I love you, too." Cleopatra watched Jacqueline run out of her office and her life, breaking what was left of her heart again.

"You ok?" Racquel stuck her head in.

"No."

During the department's Christmas party on their last day before the move, Jacqueline came down and asked to see Cleopatra in her office. She looked around at all of the boxes stacked up in every available spot.

"I know you understand why I can't celebrate your moving, but I wanted to wish you luck and give you my love. I know you'll be amazing, you are at everything you do. I wanted to give you this." She handed Cleopatra a Tiffany's box, robin's egg blue with a white satin ribbon around it.

"You didn't have to get me anything."

"I wanted to."

She pulled out a sterling silver necklace with a half of a heart pendant.

"It's beautiful," she said as Jacqueline walked behind her, lifted Cleopatra's locs as Cleopatra hooked the necklace. Jacqueline pulled her necklace from around her neck to show her the other half of the heart.

"Promise me, you'll never take it off."

"I won't." Cleopatra said. "I'm not leaving the country, I'm going a few blocks downtown."

"I know."

"Listen to me." Cleopatra took her by the hand. "I'm proud of you too. I know the divorce is in motion finally. Robin told

147

Shawn, and she knew Shawn would tell me. I know you're going through a lot right now. If you need me for anything, you let me know. I mean it, all right?"

"Ok," she said. Cleopatra kissed her, the first time they'd kissed in weeks. The same feelings jolted through her body as if nothing had changed, no distance separated them and as if this whole situation had been a ridiculous nightmare. Jacqueline's body went limp in Cleopatra's arms. She moved back and sat on the desk and pulled Cleopatra between her legs.

"Don't you miss making love to me?"

"You know I do." Cleopatra placed light kisses down Jacqueline's neck.

"Baby, take me. Please." Jacqueline kissed Cleopatra and wrapped her legs around her waist.

"We can't. You know that." Cleopatra pushed herself back from her. "It won't change anything. It will just make all of this harder."

"Ok." Jacqueline hopped down from the desk and straightened her clothes. She kissed Cleopatra softly on the lips. "I still love you. But I know that won't change anything either."

I'M FUCKING YOU TONIGHT

"Me pum pum tighter than tight," the girl said, spitting on the side of Cleopatra's face.

She was officially in hell, in the musty basement of a South Jamaica, Queens, house party. She'd done some stupid shit since she had broken up with Jacqueline and Shawn was usually by her side, just as much of a ho as she was. The night was a blur – she only remembered seeing Shawn get tazed and thinking, *Damn, she just got tazed.* The next thing she remembered was waking up on the floor with Ms. Tight Pum Pum and another girl sprawled across her, and on the other side of the room Shawn lay face down on top of two Puerto Rican girls. Both Cleopatra and Shawn had the taste of spoiled fish in their mouths.

"We should go get tested. It's been a while anyway." Cleopatra zipped up her coat and threw her hood over her head. She hunched over as the winter wind whistled and beat down on them.

"Yeah, it's been six months." Shawn agreed. They always went together to take their STD/HIV tests. They offered each other moral support and breathed a collective sigh of relief when they dodged the bullets again. "My foot is freezing," Shawn complained. She had only found one of her Timberland boots in the pile of drunken bodies and tossed clothes. She hopped alongside Cleopatra as they hobbled down Baisley Boulevard in the freshly fallen snow. One would think waking up with two women draped across your body with no recollection of the night before would cause Cleopatra to second guess her judgment, but now with a broken heart she had no such ability.

Barring the South Jamaica incident, Cleopatra was in desperate need of some quivering thighs wrapped around her neck. She'd been out of circulation for over a month, healing her heart and working long hours. She hadn't had any real action since Jacqueline. It was long overdue. She needed to slap some ass or she would explode.

◉ ◉ ◉

Rhonda held the top spot on Cleopatra's comeback list. They'd seen each other before on crowded subway cars and they'd been watching each other across the packed tables at Europa Cafe during the lunchtime rush. But Cleopatra was always with another woman. Rhonda had grown tired of waiting. She grabbed Cleopatra's arm as she passed her on the street on her way back to work.

"Excuse me, sweetheart, I've waited too long for you to be alone." She slipped her business card in between Cleopatra's fingers. "I'd like the opportunity to get to know you."

"Is that so?" Cleopatra smiled and looked at her long legs disappear up into her short red skirt. She sipped on her mango pineapple smoothie. "I know what you want and I'm going to give it to you," Cleopatra said. Rhonda caressed the back of

Cleopatra's hand with her thumb.

"I don't like to wait, so why don't you call me when you get back to work. You can tell me how you want me to cook your eggs in the morning."

The next morning Rhonda served Cleopatra scrambled eggs and bacon in bed. Rhonda was dismissed from Cleopatra's life a week later. The aggressiveness that initially attracted Cleopatra to her came across in everything Rhonda did. She had proclaimed herself as "bossy," and ruler of Cleopatra in a few short days. Cleopatra finally had to tell her as she kicked her out of her house during a nor'easter, "I had a mother, she raised me already and she did a hell of a job. I'm a grown ass woman."

In February Cleopatra celebrated her birthday at the club with her latest girl, Kiana. When Kiana had gone to the restroom, her two friends, Alana and Nicola asked Cleopatra to dance. Kiana returned to discover her BFFs grinding hard on Cleopatra. Kiana intervened in the middle of the dance floor and kissed Cleopatra full on the mouth and said, "Do you think you can handle all three of us tonight?" Cleopatra looked at Kiana in disbelief. "Happy Birthday, Cleopatra."

◎ ◎ ◎

A few days later Shawn came over to Cleopatra's house early on a Sunday morning. She was concerned because she had called Cleopatra a dozen times and she hadn't answered her phone or returned any of her voicemails or text messages in the last day. Cleopatra only appeared after Shawn kicked the door for a minute straight and her security alarm went off.

Cleopatra was annoyed with Shawn. "You do realize I gave you the key to my house and the alarm code right?" She looked down at her door to make sure there were no dents or scuff marks on the door's kick plate.

"Oh shit. I totally forgot." Shawn covered her mouth. "Sorry. I got worried."

Cleopatra's house phone rang at the same time two private and unmarked security cars screeched down the street and stopped in front of the house. Cleopatra assured the dispatcher on the phone and the four security officers who could have doubled for the secret service that everything was cool and Shawn was not there trying to rob her.

"I'm gonna take a quick shower." Cleopatra said. "Why don't you make yourself something to eat. I'll be right back." She ran up the stairs.

They ate breakfast in the kitchen while Shawn learned what dirt Cleopatra had been up to.

"Weren't you supposed to go on a date last night? What happened? What was her name, Kyren?"

"Yeah. She ordered three appetizers, a lobster, two sides, and a bottle of wine all for herself. Every time she spoke to the waiter I swear I heard a cash register. So I said, 'We are fucking tonight just so you know.' And she said, 'Cool.'"

"Sounds like a quality female." Shawn laughed.

"It gets better! The girl at the next table was studying me. But Kyren didn't see our flirting because her face was so deep in her plate. When Kyren went to the ladies room, the girl came over to me, asked for my cell phone, and proceeded to call herself so we would have each other's number. That would have been fine, but after Kyren got back from the ladies room, ole girl starts texting me from her table!" Shawn laughed as she shook her head. "My phone is flashing and vibrating like crazy. Kyren was annoyed, she grabbed it and read the text messages. She was so hot with me that she left the restaurant. But not before she got a doggy bag for the lobster and the baked potato." Cleopatra laughed. "So, I'm cracking up, because now I'm sitting there by my damn self. I finished my dinner and left, and waiting outside of the restaurant is the chick from the other table. So she came home with me and guess who is on the steps waiting for me?" Cleopatra paused.

Shawn drew a blank. "Uhm…I don't know, who?"

"Kyren."

"What the…so what happened?" Shawn was distracted by

footsteps coming down the stairs.

"Who the fuck is that?"

"That's Kyren."

"She's still here?"

"She likes to keep a dick up inside her."

"How you doing?" She acknowledged Shawn. She came over and stuck her tongue in Cleopatra's mouth. "You lucky I gotta go to work today. Shit. You better call me later, Cleopatra." She grabbed an energy drink out of the refrigerator and left.

"You need to calm down. Find yourself one good woman and chill with her." Shawn said.

"Look who's talking." Cleopatra twisted her lips at Shawn. "I'm a player, I accept that now. I'm just rotten."

"No, you're not. I've watched you do this shit for months, and you aren't happy because I've been there most of the time and I know I'm not happy. You can't keep up this pace, and do the shit you are doing. You know that."

"My pace was fine last night." Cleopatra looked at the clock on the kitchen wall.

Shawn heard more footsteps and realized someone else was coming down the stairs. "Really, Cleo?" She said.

"Cleopatra. I'm starving, baby." A tall, voluptuous woman came into the kitchen wearing only a towel that barely covered anything.

"There's some breakfast left on the stove." Cleopatra said, without diverting her eyes from Shawn.

"I'm not talking about the food." The woman tried to get Cleopatra's attention.

"Hi, I'm Eva." The girl extended her hand to Shawn.

"Hi." Shawn couldn't keep from staring at the woman. *Damn*, she mouthed to Cleopatra.

"I'll come back up in a little while." Cleopatra slapped the girl on the ass and sent her back to bed.

"She fine, ain't she? See those enormous titties? She can make them and her ass clap at the same time. Oh my God. It never got old."

"Who the hell was that?"

"Eva, the other girl from the restaurant last night. Now where were we?"

Shawn stared at Cleopatra in disbelief. "You need pussy rehab or something. That," she pointed upstairs, "is not going to help you get over Jacqueline."

"Don't mention her to me please."

"How long has it been? Three months, four months?"

"I know exactly how long it's been. Right down to the day, the hour and minute."

"You need to meet a decent woman. You've been messing with ho's."

"You got something against ho's?"

SHAKE WHAT YOUR
MAMA GAVE YA

"The Pink Houses? You know I don't go to parties in the projects. But the Pink Houses?" Cleopatra gritted her teeth at Shawn. "Let something jump off, and I'm whipping your ass."

They walked into the Pink Houses in East New York, Brooklyn. "You need to spend some more time in the hood," Shawn said.

"Don't even try it, Ms. Burning Down the House. We grew up not too far from here. Your ass moved out of the hood too, are you forgetting that? You live on a safer block than I do now. If I want to get beat up, shot in the head, duct-taped and thrown off the roof, or set on fire, I'd come to the Pink. Otherwise I'm good."

"Come on, we need to go in." Shawn said. "It's starting to snow." Shawn was determined to get her around some grown women.

Cleopatra didn't understand how that translated to a house

party in the projects, but she knew it was time for her to calm down. Juggling so many women had tired her out mentally. Settling down with one girl wouldn't be so bad, but finding a girl who could compete with Jacqueline was a different problem.

"It's going to be good. I promise." Shawn said.

"Ok, let's go and find my woman then." They stepped off the piss infused elevator, and into a tiny apartment where every wall was painted red, and the only relief was the stark white ceilings. The only thing more aggravating was the lack of ceiling fixtures. All of the floor lamps illuminated the apartment with red light bulbs.

"I seriously may go blind before the night is over, you do realize this, right?" Cleopatra asked Shawn.

Not ten minutes had passed before they realized they were probably the only single women out of what appeared to be about fifty lesbians crammed into that apartment.

"Good looking out," Cleopatra bitched to Shawn.

Shawn guided Cleopatra to the hostess of the party, a short, portly older woman who wore a red spandex dress at least two sizes too small. She introduced herself as Rose.

"You're kidding, right?" Cleopatra laughed. "Oh. Nice to meet you Rose. So you like red or what?"

"Is it cold in here or is it me?" Shawn asked Cleopatra. "I'm freezing." She put on the coat that she'd been holding in her arms.

Cleopatra hadn't taken off her coat and noticed that most of the other women were still wearing theirs, too. She wondered if it was a security issue or a space issue, but when she entered the kitchen and saw women gathered around an open oven heated to 500 degrees she realized it was neither: there was no heat in the apartment. The kitchen table was filled with buckets of Kennedy Fried Chicken and boxes of french fries whose grease had penetrated the cardboard and was seeping into the white tablecloth.

"You want a margarita?" Shawn asked.

"Hell, yeah," Cleopatra said. A couple of minutes later

Shawn appeared with two red cups and handed one to Cleopatra. "Did you make these?"

"No, but I know the girl, and I watched her make them. I've learned my lesson." Shawn winked at her.

Cleopatra looked at the drink harder, holding it up in the red light. What is that on the rim? She touched it with her finger. "Is that table salt? She salted the rim with table salt?" Cleopatra cried. "I'll drink to that."

Back in the living room a petite girl drinking from a bottle of red Alizé came over and struck up a conversation with Cleopatra, and proceeded to place her hand at the small of Cleopatra's back. Cleopatra was immediately attracted to the woman, and didn't question her single status because she came at her so hard. It wasn't until a five foot five, three hundred pound butch stepped between them and dragged the woman away that she realized she should have inquired.

"You sure pick some good ones. Drink this." Shawn handed Cleopatra another plastic cup wrapped in a pink floral napkin.

"She picked me." Cleopatra gulped down the drink. "Oh God. You made this one didn't you?" Cleopatra looked down into the cup. She swirled the ice cubes around with her finger and attempted to dilute the drink.

"Enjoy." Shawn said. "I'm gonna go talk to somebody's woman."

Cleopatra sat down in an armchair in the corner of the living room. She listened to the nineties R&B music blare from the house speakers while she babysat her drink. A woman sat across from her with her legs parted wide enough for Cleopatra to see her panties. She stared much longer than what was polite, mostly due to not being able to tell what color the panties were against the red lights. Definitely not girlfriend material, but she didn't see her come in with anyone. Cleopatra went over and sat with her. The woman was attractive but had an enormous gap between her two front teeth that Cleopatra was fixated on. She estimated she could probably slip a pencil and maybe even a ballpoint pen through the gap and she went back and forth between visualizing what else she could do with the gap and thinking she should probably get it fixed. She was enjoying the conversation and the woman had put her hand on Cleopatra's knee. Her hand had found its way to Cleopatra's thigh when she noticed a giant diamond ring on the woman's ring finger.

"Um. I'm sorry. Are you married?" Cleopatra asked.

"I am. But my husband doesn't mind."

"Doesn't mind what?" Cleopatra leaned in so she could hear the woman.

"That I sleep with women."

"You don't say? Lucky you." Cleopatra got up and walked away.

The party had spilled out into the hallway. Cleopatra assumed the women couldn't take the constant and oppressive red tint that flooded the apartment. A few minutes later Cleopatra saw Shawn talking to Miss My-Husband-Doesn't-Mind and she pointed to her ring finger. Shawn faked an upset stomach and ran into the bathroom.

Cleopatra laughed as she chalked the evening up as a loss. She wouldn't find her woman tonight, if at all. The drinks she was throwing back made her ok with it. She cared less and less with each sip. She posted back up in the corner with a full view of the red-tinged party. She spotted a short but voluptuous brown-skinned beauty with long, light brown locs, and big almond eyes, coming in late, and alone. She made eye contact with Cleopatra as she weaved through some women dancing, but then she disappeared.

Cleopatra didn't know where she went and wasn't interested enough to get up and look for her. She sat and enjoyed the music, the booze and the ass groove she had cultivated in the armchair. The music stopped and the ladies posted up against the wall and sat down on every available surface. Moments later a slow jam boomed from the speakers and in the doorway appeared the cute girl with the locs.

She's the freaking stripper, Cleopatra said to herself. The girl moved seductively to the middle of the floor as she danced, slowly shedding her clothes down to some gold pasties and a

G-string. She danced for a few women in the group before making her way to Cleopatra, who would keep her attention for the duration of her performance. She straddled her in the chair and put Cleopatra's hands on her ass as she ran her fingers through Cleopatra's locs. It wasn't long before they forgot about everyone else in the room. Cleopatra was hot. She wasn't sure if the girl or the alcohol turned her on, or both. The throbbing between her legs intensified when the girl moaned in her ear. She kissed Cleopatra on her neck and bounced hard on her lap. Cleopatra popped her pelvis back to the girl's delight. Cleopatra buried her face in her breasts and slid her hands up and down her thighs.

"I want to make you cum," Cleopatra said to her as she sang the words to the song.

At the end of the song, the stripper whispered in Cleopatra's ear. "Meet me in the back bedroom in ten minutes."

Fifteen minutes later, Cleopatra stood at the makeshift bar with Shawn sipping on a toxic Long Island Iced Tea. The drink was working its way through her system nicely, affecting her speech, vision and concept of time, when someone caressed her hand.

"Hey. Stripper lady," Cleopatra teased the girl. "Has it been ten minutes already?"

"Yes. Come with me." She took her hand. Cleopatra looked at Shawn who mouthed, "She wants it."

"So, what's your name?" The girl closed the bedroom door behind them.

"Cleopatra." She sipped on her drink. The girl's locs fell forward covering her face. She used her hand to pull them from her eyes. Cleopatra decided then that she could definitely get it. "But you can call me Cleo."

"Nice to meet you. I'm Kenya. Your hands are so soft," she said, as she shook Cleopatra's hand. "Do you like my body?"

"Excuse me?" Cleopatra asked.

"Did you like the show?" she asked her again.

Cleopatra would have sworn that she asked if she liked her body. She realized she needed to put her drink down. She got flashbacks of tazing and South Jamaica, Queens.

"Oh. I liked it a lot." She put her cup down on the dresser. "Thank you for the lap dance."

"That you can have whenever you want," she said with a naughty look on her face, and sat on the bed. "So….do you have a girlfriend?"

"If I did, I wouldn't be alone with you in a dark room. No, I don't have a girl. I'm a lot to handle," Cleopatra confessed, as she leaned against the bedroom door.

"I'm attracted to things that aren't good for me."

"You should probably work on that." Cleopatra had thought she was going to hit it in the bedroom, but the girl's energy wasn't as sexual anymore. "What island are you from? Your accent comes and goes."

"Trinidad," she said proudly, and stuck out her tongue.

"A Trini? Yeah, you need to get away from me now." Cleopatra reminisced on all the trouble she'd gotten into with Trinidadian women. The sexier they were, the crazier they were. "Trinis and my loving don't mesh well." Her body shook from the flashbacks. "You should go back into the party and forget you met me."

"That's not nice. What are you saying about Trinis?"

"You're not listening. I said, my love and Trinidadians I've dated don't go well together. It just doesn't work. I love Trinis. My best friend is Trinidadian. She's my family, I love her to death, but she's crazy and she knows it. She takes pride in that shit."

Kenya laughed at Cleopatra, unmoved by her plea. Cleopatra noticed that she didn't look like a stripper anymore. She was actually dressed conservatively, completely covered up in a cream cashmere turtleneck and black slacks.

"So what do you do for a living, if you don't mind my asking?" Kenya ignored Cleopatra's warning to save herself.

"I work for a commercial real estate company."

She looked impressed. "So you went to college?"

"Yup. Something like that."

"Sexy. Any kids?"

"Do I look like I have kids?" Cleopatra smirked.

"I had to ask." She laughed.

I'm getting grilled by a stripper, Cleopatra thought. This was getting entertaining. "So do you have a girlfriend?" she asked Kenya.

"No. It takes a special type of person to handle my dancing."

"You wouldn't happen to be secretly married to a man or anything?" Cleopatra asked, only half joking. "Sorry. So, what do you really do? I sense there is much more to you than your G-string, no disrespect."

"None taken. I'm a law student at Columbia, studying criminal law. I shake my ass to pay what my financial aid doesn't cover. I'm doing what I have to do."

"I respect your position."

"Very observant of you, and you've been drinking that concoction." She said. "You picked up that this is what I do, not who I am. Most people can't see past my dancing and I get pigeonholed."

"I went to Columbia for undergrad. I did what I had to do to pay that high ass tuition too. And I can't recall any dancer I've ever met using the word 'pigeonhole.'" Cleopatra laughed.

Kenya got off of the bed and stood in front of her. She looked up at her. "You're dangerous, aren't you?"

Cleopatra nodded her head. "I'm nothing but trouble."

Kenya wrapped her arms around her waist. Cleopatra wanted to push her away, but she felt good. Any decision she made now could possibly dictate future events. "So, would you consider going out on a date with me?"

"I would consider it." Cleopatra broke her own rule.

"Good. Because you aren't going to make me come tonight." She smiled. "What type of girl do you think I am?"

"I'm not sure actually. But I like it," Cleopatra said.

"One thing you should know. I'm not trying to do anything serious like be committed or anything," Kenya said.

"Cool with me."

◉ ◉ ◉

Cleopatra was surprised when she arrived at Kenya's door and she was startled and unprepared for their date. Kenya apologized. She said her studying hadn't gone well, and she wouldn't be able to go out. Unfazed, Cleopatra offered to go get her some dinner. She returned with some Indian food and flowers, and arrived at her door smelling like curry and roses. Kenya appreciated her gesture, and the kiss she laid on her proved it.

Kenya had a small studio apartment uptown on 112th Street, not far from campus. They sat down on the floor, ate and talked for a while, with Kenya apologizing profusely.

"You sure you aren't upset that we can't go out on a real date and that I look like this?" she said, referring to her t-shirt and shorts.

"Not at all. But I will be upset if you apologize one more time. And there is no reason for me to be mad about those little panties you have on. Are those supposed to be shorts?" She winked at Kenya. She thumbed through Kenya's textbooks.

"Federal criminal law, evidence and international and comparative criminal law. Ugh. This looks really hard." Cleopatra closed the books and pushed them back toward Kenya.

"You look hard." Kenya crawled over to Cleopatra on her hands and knees, Cleopatra licked her lips as she could see the full exposure of Kenya's cleavage. Kenya climbed on top of Cleopatra and massaged her neck. Cleopatra kept her hands by her sides, struggling not to touch her. Kenya kissed her slow and long and Cleopatra felt emotions she hadn't felt in a long time. Cleopatra wrapped her arms around her and Kenya melted as she grinded on Cleopatra.

"You didn't come prepared?" she asked after she realized Cleopatra wasn't strapped.

"I'm prepared." She gestured to her backpack. "It's better if I don't wear it on the subway. You can get into trouble doing that."

"How so?"

"How can I put this? I need to use it soon after I put it on."

"Put it on now."

"No. I should go so you can get back to your studying. This was supposed to be a short dinner break." Cleopatra picked Kenya up off of her and began to clean up their plates. Kenya reached out to her.

"You don't have to go yet."

"Yes, I do. You need to get back to work."

"Why are you so sweet to me? How come you don't have a girlfriend?" She said as she wrapped Cleopatra's arms around her waist and placed her hands on her ass.

"Are you cross-examining me?"

"Do you know how attracted I am to you? You don't even realize how sexy you are. That makes you even hotter," she said.

"Last week at the party, I didn't see anyone in that room but you. I only wanted to dance for you." She worked her fingers into Cleopatra's locs.

"Ok, stop. That feels too good."

"There's no such thing as feeling too good."

Cleopatra threw her head back. She decided to resist temptation and got her coat. "Studying is more important than anything. I won't be a distraction."

"You're different from the other women I've dated."

"I could've told you that." Cleopatra smirked. "I figure I have two options. I can be totally selfish and fuck you until tomorrow afternoon sometime, or I can be unselfish and leave and let you handle your business. So, I'm going to go."

"How am I supposed to focus after kissing you?"

"You'll be fine." Cleopatra threw her backpack over her shoulder. She opened the door and stepped out into the hallway.

"So, it's Friday night and still early." Kenya said. "You smell good, you look fine, and you have a dick in your bag. How do I know you're not going to go and get some loving from some other chick?"

"You don't." Cleopatra walked away.

Shocked by her response, Kenya ran into the hall and grabbed Cleopatra's arm. "I don't believe you just said that to me."

"I think your exact words were you weren't trying to do anything committed or serious. Call me when you have some time. I'll be around." She kissed Kenya goodbye.

Kenya was erotic and one of the most intelligent women Cleopatra had met in a while. They became close quickly and although they weren't doing anything serious, Cleopatra was dating her exclusively. Their relationship was straightforward, no drama, just how she liked it. The sexual attraction was thick primarily because Cleopatra hadn't slept with her yet. They double-dated with Shawn and her latest conquest. Shawn's only comment on the relationship was: "You need to fuck that girl."

"Make up your mind. First I'm fucking too much, fuck, don't fuck, damn." Cleopatra said.

"I know what I said. But the way she looks at you is crazy. She really wants it."

But Cleopatra wasn't really trying to have a relationship with Kenya. She knew deep down what it was, but she wasn't willing to admit it to herself. She knew Kenya wanted her, she could see it in her eyes anytime they were close.

Kenya had tired of Cleopatra shutting her down. Late one evening at Cleopatra's house she confronted her. "I need to make love to you." She sat down on Cleopatra's lap.

"I can't give you what you want right now." She tried to move Kenya to the couch.

"Don't you want me? It's been two months. Why do you put up this wall? Every time I think you may be falling for me, you shut me out. Is there something you need that I'm not giving you? Tell me so I can fix it."

"It might be your dancing," Cleopatra lied.

"Out of the blue? It wasn't a problem the night we met." Kenya stood up. It didn't take much to set her off.

"Everything was different then. I wasn't thinking about the

future."

"So, I would have been good enough for you to fuck. But not good enough to have a relationship with?"

"You are the one who said you didn't want anything serious. And I was fine with that. I mean who wants their girlfriend to be a stripper?" Cleopatra looked up at her.

"I'm not doing this forever. You know this. You're my girl, regardless of what I said I wanted in the beginning. I know you are not insecure about my customers. I belong to you."

"I'm not your girlfriend. I just think we need to go our separate ways."

"You're breaking up with me because I strip, and you met me stripping?"

"There's nothing to break up."

"This is not right. I love you."

Cleopatra made up excuses not to become attached. She was beginning to fall for Kenya, but she was relieved that it was over.

"You broke up with her? Why?" Shawn asked.

"She really wanted to make love. I haven't made love since Jacqueline, I wasn't willing to give that to her. All I can give right now is a whole lot of unemotional fucking."

It had been over a month and Cleopatra had run through more women. She grew tired of the games and decided to be celibate. She didn't want any more drama, so she just stopped dating altogether. Every day she'd go to work, spend a few hours at the shelter volunteering, then come home and lock herself in the house until the next day.

Who the hell is calling me? It was two a.m. on a Saturday. She looked at the caller ID on her house phone. *Unavailable.*

Then her cell phone rang. Also *unavailable*. But they didn't leave a message. She thought whoever it was, it must not have been that serious. Then the doorbell rang. Cleopatra immediately thought *stalker*.

"Who the hell?" she yelled. Mad now, she went down the stairs, grabbed her bat and looked out of the peephole.

"Damn." She put down the slugger, turned off the house

alarm and opened the door.

"Hi," Kenya said shyly, as she stood in the doorway in a long black coat.

"What are you doing here?"

"I tried calling you, but you weren't picking up."

"It's late."

"Do you have company or something? Is someone here?" She looked around the living room and sniffed for sex in the air.

"No. Is something wrong that couldn't wait until daylight?"

"I have to tell you something." She sat down on the couch.

Cleopatra could tell Kenya didn't have on much under her coat. The leg that peeked out wasn't helping her new vow of celibacy. She decided she wanted Kenya to leave before she uttered a word; she didn't need the temptation. She wasn't that strong yet.

"I didn't realize how much you meant to me until you broke up with me. So, I did something tonight, and I wanted to share it with you. I did my last show. I don't have to dance anymore."

"That's great. You must be excited." Cleopatra yawned and covered her mouth.

"I am. I'm here because we can be together now since my dancing was holding you back from me. We had a great relationship." Kenya got up and stood in front of Cleopatra. "Now I can focus on school, getting ready for the bar exam, and you."

"There will be no me when you are studying for the bar exam. Even I know that." Cleopatra smirked.

"We can worry about that later. I need you to help me with something." She loosened the belt on her coat and put her stiletto boot right in her crotch. "Take off my costume."

"I'm celibate."

"Bullshit, since when?"

"Three days ago."

"I'm done with your resisting me. I'm going to have you tonight." She dropped her coat to the floor and revealed a red lace bra and G-string. She licked Cleopatra's earlobe as she climbed on top of her.

"Tear my panties off, just rip it. I don't need them anymore."

Cleopatra knew if she put her hand between Kenya's legs it would be all over. Kenya had already professed to love Cleopatra months ago and they hadn't even taken it to this level yet. Cleopatra rubbed her pussy until she found the soaked G-string. She pulled it with both hands until she heard it rip.

"I can't take it anymore." Kenya grabbed her hand and pulled her upstairs to the sex room. She laid Cleopatra on the bed, crawled on top of her and kissed her all over her body.

"I've wanted you for such a long time," she moaned. "What's this? Kenya pulled on Cleopatra's half-heart pendant that hung low down in her t-shirt. "I've never seen this before."

"Never mind it." Cleopatra pulled it out of her hand.

They made love well into the next day. And for the first time Cleopatra didn't picture Jacqueline. Was she finally getting over her and falling for Kenya?

◉ ◉ ◉

"Are you waiting for Jacqueline?" Shawn asked Cleopatra.

"Why would you say something like that?"

"You refuse to fall in love with Kenya, still." Shawn was in Cleopatra's bedroom with her as she put on her half heart.

"You are putting the necklace on. You still have it?"

"Of course I do. I wear it when I'm not with Kenya."

"And you don't see anything wrong with that? So, the necklace, and the fact that Kenya thinks that the sex room is your actual bedroom and your bedroom is a desolate guest room. You don't see a problem?"

"I'm not sharing that bed with anyone."

"Anyone but Jacqueline, you mean? You are still hanging on to her."

"I'm not."

"Then why the necklace?"

"I promised never to take it off."

"Wow. Not cool, man."

"So, can we change subjects? You've never said what you really think about Kenya."

"She's insecure, jealous, a bit needy, obsessive, analyzes the shit out of things and has abandonment issues, but besides that, she's cool."

"You're harsh." Cleopatra scowled at her.

"You asked. She's no Jacqueline."

"That's low. Are you done?" She glared at Shawn.

"Seriously, if you don't love her, you need to end it. What's wrong with admitting you're still in love with Jacqueline? She was your first real love. It's not supposed to be easy to get over."

"Go in my closet and grab the Timberland boot box all the way in the back on the top shelf."

"This one?" Shawn came out of the closet with an old, tattered shoe box.

"Yeah. Open it." Shawn opened the box full of handwritten letters. Some were opened, some were not. "Those are all from Jacqueline. She's written me at least twice a week since we broke up."

"Have you written her back?"

"No reason to. Nothing to say."

"What do you mean *nothing*? You still love her, tell her. Is she still married?"

"I don't know. I haven't opened a letter in months. She wrote that the process of writing me made her feel closer to me. They were mostly how much she loves and misses me."

"All this time neither one of you has let go. That means something, don't you think?"

Cleopatra and Kenya had been back together for two months, but the wall was still up. Kenya tried to be her superwoman, unaware that Cleopatra already had one and was still in love with her. It bothered Kenya that she wouldn't discuss her previous relationships, especially her last one. Kenya asked Shawn about Cleopatra's past.

"So, what went down with Cleopatra's last girl? Who was she and why did it end?"

"Why are you asking me?" Shawn asked, annoyed.

"Cleopatra doesn't want to talk about it."

"Well, she must not want you to know, so it's not my place to say."

After that Kenya was even more insecure than before. She was determined to break through to Cleopatra. Even though she had her physically, Kenya knew her heart didn't belong to her. She wanted it and would do anything to get it. She craved an intimacy with Cleopatra that she seemed unwilling or maybe just incapable of giving her. She wanted Cleopatra to open up to her, to express her true feelings about everything from the most trivial of subjects to how she truly felt about her. Kenya wanted her to show some vulnerability. She was attracted initially to Cleopatra's strength but at times she wanted Cleopatra to allow her to take care of her, Cleopatra fought Kenya every step of the way, insisting she could take care of herself. But Kenya didn't help her case with her actions. Cleopatra's unwillingness to be transparent and one hundred percent present with Kenya raised her suspicions. She didn't trust Cleopatra, even though she gave her no reason not to. Kenya would pop up at her house unannounced expecting to find another woman there. She would wait at her job after work, and if she saw Cleopatra talking to a female coworker, Kenya concocted a fictitious affair in her head. Cleopatra and Shawn had both had enough when Kenya showed up at a New York Liberty game after party looking for her. It became clear to Cleopatra that Kenya had some deep-seated issues that had started way before they met.

Kenya showed up at Cleopatra's office in the middle of the day. "What's up, baby? Who is that at Racquel's desk?"

"A temp. Remember Racquel is out on maternity leave?" Cleopatra said, annoyed with Kenya's surprise visit. Racquel was due to give birth any day to Cleopatra's third godchild. *Great timing!* Cleopatra thought, half-joking. She could have used Racquel's help with Kenya. She needed her gatekeeper back desperately.

"What are you doing here?" Cleopatra looked at her watch.

"I brought you lunch."

Cleopatra looked in the bag and peeled the foil from the plastic plate. "Chicken roti?"

She smiled. "Made it fresh this morning."

"Aren't you supposed to be at your internship? What are you doing here?"

"I didn't feel like going. I cooked for you instead."

"How many times have I said school is more important than anything else? All of those scholarships and opportunities you have and you aren't doing your part. How many students applied for that internship and you were the one they awarded it to and you don't show up? And to make me roti? What's that about?"

"I want to take care of you. That's what's important to me right now."

"I appreciate your wanting to do things for me, but you don't have to try this hard. It's not sexy." She packed the food back in the bag. "Last weekend you cooked my dinner for the whole week, and I know you should have been in the library. If you don't cook, I'm still going to eat. If you don't do my laundry I'm still going to have clean underwear. It's sweet that you want to do these things, but it's not necessary. And it shouldn't be your priority. Handling your business is sexy." She handed the bag back to Kenya. "This right here is not."

"Why don't you want me take care of you?"

"Everything I say doesn't have to have a hidden agenda. I hate that shit. I know how to cook and clean and do laundry. It's not necessary that you screw up in school trying to do it for me."

"I just want to make you happy."

"I'm starting to think maybe you shouldn't be in a relationship. If you can't get your priorities straight, I'm going to have to step out of the picture. I don't want anything to do with your screwing up your life."

"You're serious? You'd break up with me over this."

"Dead serious."

Cleopatra cut Kenya off for a few weeks, hoping it would force her to get back on track. Going forward they would stick to a strict schedule of date nights.

During their hiatus Cleopatra spent most of her free time split between volunteering at the woman's shelter and bonding with her newest god child Gabriela. Cleopatra was a proud and doting godmother who took her duties seriously. Just like with her first two god children Amare and Ayana, she set up a trust fund for Gabriela. Upon acceptance to college their tuition and monthly living expenses would be paid. Cleopatra set up extra bonuses for high GPAs, and graduate degrees. The further they went in school and the more successful they were in their studies the larger the financial reward. Just how large was a secret, between Cleopatra and her attorney. Not even Racquel or her husband knew the details. Cleopatra simply said she started a savings account for the children and gave them her usual present, an engraved three-piece cup, fork and spoon baby set in sterling silver, and five thousand dollars toward whatever the new parents needed for the baby, and to supplement Racquel's decreased income while she was on maternity leave. She took the term "being born with a silver spoon in your mouth" very seriously when it came to her godchildren.

For that short span of time that Cleopatra and Kenya were apart. Cleopatra liked the solitude with no one having any expectations of her. She felt conflicted about not missing Kenya, and the more days that passed the further she was from Cleopatra's mind. Cleopatra missed having sex but the drama that came with good sex kept her from entertaining any thoughts of making a booty call or having a one night stand with anyone. Cleopatra instead caught up on her reading, sometimes staying up all night to finish a good book.

At the end of their trial separation period, Cleopatra liked the changes she saw in Kenya. The confident and secure woman she met dancing in the projects was back. She was more secure in their relationship and appeared to trust Cleopatra now. But things weren't as secure as Kenya wanted to believe. Cleopatra still wore the necklace Jacqueline gave her, and made sure she didn't wear it when Kenya was around. But Cleopatra knew she was bound to forget, sooner or later.

MEN'S
MEETING IN THE~~LADIES~~
ROOM / GIRLFIGHT

Jacqueline and Robin had been working on repairing their relationship for some time. Robin's propositioning Cleopatra right under her sisters' nose nearly tore the sisters apart, but over the course of the last several months Jacqueline needed to lean on Robin more than ever before. They had made up and were nearly back to normal. On this night Robin talked her big sister into getting out of the house and going to dinner uptown.

It was the first time in months that Jacqueline had gone anywhere but work or the gym. Even with the restaurant's wall of windows facing 116th Street, she thought she would suffocate – the low ceiling and the large number of people dining on that Saturday night were overwhelming to her. White-hot track lighting completed the cafeteria theme and the orange cream walls were a harsh contrast against the white countertops and the long row of ferns that hung behind it. People of all colors, a rainbow of brown hues with natural hair,

173

dreadlocks, bantu knots and box braids were speaking loudly, their voices blended into a melodious tone. As Jacqueline looked around the restaurant, she felt exposed and vulnerable. She had decided that she wanted to go home, but the smell of honey-dipped fried chicken, smothered pork chops and barbecue ribs emanating from the kitchen made her mouth water. She would eat and then go straight home, she decided.

"So how do you feel?" Robin asked.

"Good, I guess. I don't know."

"This is supposed to be a celebration. The divorce is final, and you are free to do what and whom you please."

"I know. But I can't stop thinking about Cleopatra. I wrote her about the divorce and she hasn't responded. As if I mean nothing to her. I want her back so bad, you can't understand." Jacqueline shook her head.

"You're going to have to start all over with her to regain her trust," Robin advised her.

"I got her before. I just have to do it again. When I first saw her, I wanted her, and it took weeks before I had the nerve to do anything about it." Jacqueline exhaled. "But I knew we were going to be together. I didn't care what I had to do, and I don't care what I have to do to get her back."

They were interrupted by the five-foot-two butch waitress who took their order while flirting unsuccessfully with Jacqueline.

"So, it's obvious you aren't open to other possibilities." Robin laughed.

"Never. And that," she tilted her head back toward the waitress, "would never be a possibility."

"Still feening for Cleopatra after – what has it been – ten months? You need to go after her. Go get her."

"I'm going to." Something changed in Jacqueline's eyes in that moment. She had made the decision to take some real action. "Forget writing letters, calls and emails. I'm just going to go get my woman back." Jacqueline rocked back and forth in her chair, getting increasingly excited about the prospect of reuniting with Cleopatra.

"Do whatever you have to do. Just go to her house, go to her job." Robin said, continuing to hype her sister up.

"When was the last time you saw Shawn?" Jacqueline asked her.

"I haven't talked to her in a long time. She won't mess with me because I don't eat." Robin averted her eyes.

"Cause you don't eat what?" Jacqueline stared at her. "Ooh. You don't eat pussy?"

"Shut the hell up! I don't want the whole restaurant to know." Robin kicked Jacqueline hard under the table.

"No wonder you can't keep a woman." Jacqueline looked exasperated. "All this time I thought you were just a ho. What kind of lesbian are you?"

Robin rolled her eyes and stuck her middle finger up. "I'm bisexual, and you know this."

"Bi, lesbian, whatever. Wait – so have you ever gone down on a woman – or you just don't?"

"I've never done it."

"Damn, what do you do when you're having sex?" Jacqueline asked, curious and trying to run a scenario in her head.

"They do me."

"So you're a pillow bitch?" Jacqueline rolled her eyes. "Cleopatra had the most perfect pussy, and she used to get so..." Jacqueline stared at the ceiling.

Robin snapped her fingers. "Would you like to join us in reality?"

The waitress was back, and had been placing platters of food on their table. "Oh. Thank you," Jacqueline said to the excited butch.

"Did she hear me?" She whispered to Robin.

"Yes!" Robin covered her face with her hand and dug her fork into her macaroni and cheese.

"Whatever. If you ain't eating pussy you ain't fucking. It's an equalizer," Jacqueline said. "How are you going to get them where you want them? Cleopatra, built like an Amazon, to the outside world she has this tough exterior, people think she's all hard, but as soon as I have her in my mouth, she's mine. You better learn to eat some pussy, like your life depends on it. I'm sure you can find someone to practice on." Jacqueline laughed.

"Fuck you," Robin said, annoyed.

"You ain't fucking nobody, obviously." Jacqueline laughed as she took a mouthful of collard greens.

◎ ◎ ◎

Cleopatra was almost ready to commit to Kenya. They had a good time together and the sex was good. Kenya had told Cleopatra she loved her, many times, but Cleopatra had yet to say it in return. She wasn't there yet and Kenya didn't push.

They went out for soul food on 116th right outside of the number 2 train. The hostess led them through the packed main dining room and as they maneuvered through the tables, Cleopatra could've sworn she saw Jacqueline by the front window. Her heart sank to her stomach and she couldn't bring herself to look back. She tried to shake off the waves of feelings of loving and missing her, and followed the hostess and Kenya up the stairs. The upstairs dining room was quiet, with only a few couples scattered about. The room was small with a low ceiling, sparsely decorated, with nothing adorning the super white walls, none of the color or liveliness of downstairs. Light and oppressive heat emanated from the low dangling track lighting. It was quiet, almost solemn. Couples spoke in low tones, with the hum from the diners below almost inaudible.

Soon after they were seated a waitress came and took their order. Cleopatra ordered catfish, mac and cheese and yams and Kenya ordered ribs, collard greens and potato salad. They sat at the table in an awkward silence, because Cleopatra had Jacqueline on her brain.

◼ ◻ ◻

"Oh my God." Jacqueline was frantic. Her body got hot and she fanned her face with her hand. "I can't believe she's here." She went to take a sip of water when the red plastic tumbler slipped out of her hand and spilled across the table. Water flooded the table, surrounded their plates and utensils and dripped down to the floor.

"First, you need to calm down," Robin moved quickly to wipe up the spill with the paper towels that the waitress had left for them to wipe their barbecue sauce-covered fingers.

Jacqueline took a deep breath and leaned back in her chair.

"You should go for it. Go get your woman!" Robin pointed toward the stairs.

"I'm about to." Jacqueline nodded her head.

"She came in with some chick."

"I'm not going to let that stop me." Jacqueline took a gulp of her Corona.

"I got your back."

"She's mine. I'm not waiting. How do I look?" she asked Robin, and stood up. Robin examined her in her white halter top, blue jeans and red high heels.

"I'd fuck you." Robin winked.

"Yeah, but you wouldn't eat me so it would just never work out between us." Jacqueline laughed as she headed to the upstairs dining room.

◼ ◻ ◻

"Baby, what's up with you?" Kenya rubbed Cleopatra's hand. "You don't seem like you're all here."

"Everything is cool." Cleopatra wondered why Kenya had averted her eyes.

"Cleopatra." Jacqueline rested her hand on her shoulder.

She immediately recognized that sultry voice and the electricity that shot through her body whenever they touched.

She looked behind her and Jacqueline was standing there, as beautiful as ever.

"Jacqueline. How are you?" Cleopatra rose from her chair and hugged her tight. She struggled not to float outside of her body.

"I can't believe it's you." She caressed Cleopatra's cheek.

"Jacqueline, this is Kenya. Kenya, this is Jacqueline."

Jacqueline's eyes stayed focused on Cleopatra. Kenya grinded her teeth as she watched Jacqueline.

Cleopatra couldn't resist looking at her body. "How are you? You look amazing."

"I'm doing ok." Jacqueline locked eyes with Kenya. "Actually, I need to speak with Cleopatra in private, just for a moment. I'll return her soon," she said to Kenya as she took Cleopatra by the hand and led her out of the dining room.

Cleopatra glanced back at Kenya. "I'll be right back."

Jacqueline took her to the ladies room. "She's going to come looking for you in here." Jacqueline changed her mind and pulled her into the men's room. Cleopatra nodded her head, distracted by her focus of trying to resist whatever Jacqueline was about to do. As long as she didn't admit her real feelings for Jacqueline she could get back to the table without anything jumping off.

They entered the small bathroom, the exposed light bulbs brightening the dark brown stucco walls. Two urinals and two sinks lined the wall opposite two private stalls. The room reeked of Strawberry House Blessing air freshener and Cool Water cologne. Jacqueline pulled Cleopatra into the last stall and hugged her hard.

"You have no idea how much I've missed you. My divorce is final. It's all over." Jacqueline rested her head on Cleopatra's chest.

Cleopatra's nose grazed the side of Jacqueline's face. "I'm happy for you." She pulled away and leaned on the other side of the stall. Her heart threatened to jump out of her chest. In the dingy light of the men's bathroom Jacqueline looked even more beautiful than Cleopatra had remembered. "I know it must have been a hard time for you."

The bathroom door opened. They stood still as they stared at each other and waited for the man to do his business and leave.

"Losing you was the only hard part." Jacqueline caressed the side of Cleopatra's neck. "You didn't read my letters? Never mind. Doesn't matter now. All that matters is you're here and I'm here. I'll do whatever it takes to get you back, anything."

"So, are you really ok?" Cleopatra asked.

"I'm ok, just need you."

"And your ex?"

"He moved out to California right after I filed for divorce."

"Do you need anything? Are you ok financially?"

"I'm ok, really. What I need is you Cleopatra. Do you hear me?"

"Regardless of what feelings I have, it doesn't matter because I have a girlfriend. And I can't disrespect her or the relationship."

"She's your girlfriend? I was your woman, Cleopatra. I'm still your woman. Do you even love her?"

"What?" Cleopatra asked, stunned at the question.

"You heard me. If you are in love with her, I might consider respecting your relationship. I might."

There was an eerie silence and Cleopatra didn't say a word. She wasn't going to lie; she didn't love Kenya. She cared for her, but *love*? That wasn't a word she used a lot, especially since Jacqueline.

Another man came in and used the urinal.

Jacqueline grabbed Cleopatra by her belt and pulled her across the stall. "You can't answer a simple question?" she whispered softly in her ear.

"I don't love her," Cleopatra whispered back.

They heard the man leave and the door close again.

"After everything that's happened, did you ever doubt my love for you? Never mind after all this time I still fall asleep clutching my pillow wishing it were you. I touch myself to videos of our lovemaking."

179

"Don't tell me that," Cleopatra said.

"Sometimes I swear I can feel you and taste you." She caressed Cleopatra's face. "You still have that effect on me. I don't want any other woman because they aren't you. Do you understand that?" She came closer and pressed her body against Cleopatra's exactly as she had done the day they met. It seemed so long ago.

"I never once doubted your love," Cleopatra confessed.

"I still love you. Are you still in love with me? I need to know. Can you forgive me?"

"I understand you made some bad decisions because you wanted me so much. And you got caught up because you were in love with me. I forgave you a long time ago." Cleopatra looked her in the eyes. "I've been trying to move on, but it's pointless. You are always with me, no matter who I'm with or what I'm doing. I'm still in love with you. You are a part of me. That will never go away." Cleopatra lifted her head and her eyes met Jacqueline's. Jacqueline pulled her close, their lips nearly touching.

"I need you. I stopped living when you left me."

"I can't."

"You can't what? Resist me?" Jacqueline stuck her tongue out.

Cleopatra had only seconds to react. She could push her away or succumb to the feelings she had suppressed for months. Cleopatra took her into her mouth. She couldn't protest, or stop kissing her even if she wanted to, and she didn't want to. She pulled Jacqueline closer, held her tighter, and kissed her hard holding her face in her hands. Jacqueline caressed her tongue with hers. After the kiss, they held each other, listening to each other breathe.

"Make love to me." Jacqueline kissed the side of Cleopatra's neck. "Right here."

Cleopatra caressed her way up and inside her top, then down to the button of her jeans. She grabbed her waist and kissed her neck. Jacqueline moved backward so Cleopatra could get to her zipper.

The bathroom door opened again. Cleopatra held her breath and didn't move until she heard someone peeing at the urinal. Jacqueline hadn't stopped; she didn't care anymore about who might walk through the doors. Jacqueline kissed Cleopatra again. Eventually the man left and Cleopatra wanted to pull away, trying half-heartedly to resist her but she couldn't. She surrendered and undid Jacqueline's jeans. Jacqueline gasped and buried her face in Cleopatra's neck as she cupped Jacqueline's pussy with her hand. When Cleopatra's hands hit the top of her panties she pleaded. "I need your fingers."

Cleopatra stopped herself and leaned back against the stall door.

"Don't stop," Jacqueline pleaded. Cleopatra saw the half-heart necklace hanging around Jacqueline's neck.

"You're still wearing it," Cleopatra said.

"Of course. I never take it off."

Jacqueline slid her hand inside of Cleopatra's shirt collar. Cleopatra froze as she waited for Jacqueline's response when she didn't find her necklace. But then Jacqueline pulled it out of her shirt and held it in her hand.

"You still have it. You didn't break your promise." Cleopatra was a bit surprised she had forgotten to take off the low-hanging chain; removing it around Kenya never really slipped her mind before tonight. There would be no good way to explain wearing an engraved half-heart pendant from your ex.

"You never let go?" Jacqueline asked her.

"I couldn't." Cleopatra kissed her. Jacqueline could always turn Cleopatra on in an instant and that hadn't changed. The warmth of her body made her weak. Kenya had to be looking for her by now, and if she found them, she would be devastated, but at this point Cleopatra didn't care. She had to have Jacqueline and the excitement of the risk was overwhelming. She had to do it.

But Cleopatra stopped herself. She was still in a relationship with Kenya. She had already disrespected her by going as far as she had and she wasn't going to cheat on her, even with Jacqueline, no matter how bad she wanted to make love to her again.

"I can't do this. I really, really want you but I can't. I'm going to get out of here before I do something terrible. Ok?" Cleopatra unlatched the stall door and stood at the sink, straightening her clothes.

"Baby, wait." Jacqueline followed her out of the stall. "We need to talk, I have to see you." Jacqueline fixed her own clothes.

The bathroom door flew open and Kenya stood in the doorway. Cleopatra's face scrunched up as she mouthed the word *fuck*.

"What the hell is going on, Cleopatra? Why are you hiding in here?"

"Nothing is going on," Cleopatra said. She knew she didn't sound convincing.

Kenya walked up to Cleopatra and turned and folded her arms as she looked at Jacqueline. "I don't know who you are, but she's mine now. Whatever you had is over."

"She's not yours," Jacqueline said confidently, leaning up against the stall door with her arms folded and one leg crossed over the other, mocking Kenya.

"Jacqueline, you aren't making this better." Cleopatra said.

"No, baby, she addressed me." She looked at Kenya.

"Don't call her 'baby.' She is not your baby," Kenya proclaimed.

"If she was yours, her tongue wouldn't have been snaking down my throat a minute ago. She wanted to taste the familiar," Jacqueline said with a huge smile across her lips.

"Really, Cleopatra? Really?" Kenya yelled at her and backed her up against the wall.

Kenya removed her earrings and tied her locs back away from her face. "You think this is a game?" She walked up to Jacqueline. "I'll snatch that weave clean out of your head." Jacqueline was eerily relaxed, not fazed that Kenya was an inch from her nose and fuming.

"That's her real hair." Cleopatra regretted her comment as soon as the words left her lips. Kenya glared at her.

"Tell her, baby." Jacqueline laughed. "She would know, she used to pull it when she was fucking me."

"What's going on?" Kenya backed Cleopatra up against the wall.

"Kenya, you need to calm down and fall back a bit. I'm only going to let you back me into this wall so many times. Jacqueline is my ex-girlfriend and we were catching up."

"In the men's room? You weren't just talking. Did you have sex with her?" She grabbed Cleopatra's hands, attempting to smell her fingers.

"Are you serious?" Cleopatra snatched her hand away.

"No, we didn't fuck." Jacqueline answered. "Only because you were here. Wait till I get you alone." She winked at Cleopatra. Cleopatra was turned on by Jacqueline's confidence. She was cocky and Cleopatra loved it.

"You're an arrogant bitch." Kenya shook her head.

"No, I'm not. I just know how much this woman loved me and how much she still does." She waved her finger back and forth at Kenya and Cleopatra. "You two are over."

Kenya walked up to Jacqueline. "Fuck you, you want her, you got to go through me."

"I was planning on it," Jacqueline retorted.

"All right, enough. Kenya, let's go." Cleopatra took Kenya's arm. Kenya jerked away from Cleopatra and swung a slow right hook at Jacqueline. Jacqueline ducked under the punch and dug both fists into Kenya's stomach. Kenya doubled over in pain and Jacqueline mushed her in the face and pushed her down to the floor.

"Damn, Jacqueline!" Cleopatra yelled, as she helped Kenya to her feet.

"She came at me first. You saw her."

Cleopatra had Kenya halfway out of the door when Jacqueline said, "Remember, she's mine," and blew Cleopatra a kiss.

Robin walked into the bathroom and a distracted Cleopatra loosened her grip on Kenya, who took the opportunity and ran toward Jacqueline again fist flying, fist missing. Jacqueline swung on Kenya and hooked a right hand to her face. She fell back into Cleopatra's arms. Robin pulled Jacqueline off of Kenya.

"Get her out of here," Cleopatra yelled to Robin.

"I'll be waiting for you, Cleopatra," Jacqueline said as Robin pushed her out the door. "Don't be mad when she calls my name," she yelled to Kenya. "I know what she likes for dinner." Cleopatra wanted to go with Jacqueline, but there was no way she could live with herself if she did.

Instead, she put cold paper towels on Kenya's face and cleaned up her busted and bloodied lip. The manager came in and kicked them out of the restaurant. The fact that Cleopatra was more upset about not getting her catfish and macaroni and cheese than Kenya getting beat down made her feel guilty. She took Kenya home, and Kenya only spoke when she said, "I want to be alone," and slammed the door. Cleopatra went and got her some Chinese food and a bag of ice and came back to a chained door. She left it outside and through the closed door, she apologized for bringing her drama.

"I won't bother you, Kenya. Call me when you're ready."

Kenya was ready four a.m. the next morning.

"Where are you?" She grilled Cleopatra over the phone.

"I'm at home, it's four in the morning. Why?"

"Are you alone?"

"Yeah, why?" Cleopatra rolled over in bed and turned on her lamp.

"I'm sorry about tonight," Kenya said.

"I was wrong. I should have never left the table," Cleopatra admitted.

"You're right, you shouldn't have, but I let her get to me. That's what she wanted."

"You forgive me?" Cleopatra asked.

"I'll think about it if you come over right now and make it up to me."

Kenya answered the door naked. She pulled Cleopatra inside and clawed desperately at her pants.

"Give it to me hard." She begged Cleopatra. "Fuck me like

this is the only pussy you want. Prove it to me."

For the rest of the night and well into the morning, Cleopatra fucked Kenya until she convinced her she was the one she wanted. But deep down Cleopatra knew their days and nights together were numbered by Jacqueline's return, and she was totally fine with that. She needed to find her way back to where she belonged, with Jacqueline.

○ ○ ○

Cleopatra called Shawn the next day and told her what happened.

"I told you that bitch was crazy," Shawn said. "So, Jacqueline whipped her ass and the same night you got a booty call? She's crazy. So, come on, how did you feel when you saw Jacqueline?"

"Nothing has changed. If I wasn't worried Kenya was going to catch us we would have gone at it right there on the toilet. She makes me that weak, still."

"You know what you have to do, right?" Shawn said. "You've been fucking around. Now she's free, stop bullshitting and get back together."

"What about Kenya?"

"What about her. You love Jacqueline. You do realize you set her free and she came back to you? She is yours forever."

○ ○ ○

A few days had passed and Kenya and Cleopatra had gotten back to normal. Cleopatra hadn't contacted Jacqueline since that night, and she struggled with the longing for her. The only decision she made was not to make one. Her plan seemed to work until she and Kenya ran into Jacqueline at Cleopatra's favorite bakery in the East Village.

"How are you?" Cleopatra asked Jacqueline as she looked ahead at Kenya, who had yet to notice she was walking by herself.

"I've been waiting for you to call me, but I've been trying to give you time to wrap that up." She motioned to Kenya. "Now that I know you still love me, I can't take being apart."

"I know. I can see your heart." Cleopatra pointed to the other half of the necklace dangling in her cleavage.

"Always. You?"

Cleopatra moved her shirt collar and showed her the chain. "I better go. I don't want anything to pop off here."

"She can't love you, like I love you. You know that," Jacqueline said as she watched her walk away.

Cleopatra joined Kenya at the counter. "What the fuck was that?"

"Just let it go. I don't want any more drama, no fighting. I want peace."

"I did let it go. I let her walk out of here, didn't I?"

Cleopatra laughed to herself. *Yeah right, you let her leave. Do you not recall the ass whipping she gave you?*

"But she's going to do whatever she has to do to get to you?" She was yelling at Cleopatra, attracting attention.

Cleopatra placed her order at the register. "Hi. How are you? Give me a blueberry, a chocolate covered, a plain and a small coconut milk, please."

"Do you want anything?" she asked Kenya.

"No!"

"I haven't called her, I haven't seen her since that night. Doesn't that mean anything?"

"No, it doesn't. Because you aren't supposed to, so you don't get points for that shit."

"I understand you're upset, but if you want to get all loud up in a donut shop you'll be doing it by your damn self. If you want to discuss your feelings calmly, rationally, without the cursing and the eye and neck rolling, then let's go and talk."

Cleopatra paid for the donuts and walked to the door. She glimpsed back and Kenya hadn't moved. Cleopatra threw up her hand, her index and middle fingers forming the peace sign, and she walked out of the door. A homeless man approached her asking for change. She handed him a twenty dollar bill and he handed her a slip of paper.

"A pretty young lady asked me to give this to you."

Cleopatra smiled and nodded, and took the paper. "Thank you, sir."

It was a note from Jacqueline.

"Baby, wait!" Cleopatra was halfway in a cab when she heard Kenya yell after her. She slipped the note in her pocket as Kenya ran up to her. "Let's go back to your house and talk."

The entire ride Kenya was silent. Cleopatra could tell she was trying to calm herself down. But all she could think about was Jacqueline. When they got to Cleopatra's house, without asking, Kenya poured Cleopatra's milk into a glass and put her donuts on a plate at the kitchen counter. Knowing that Cleopatra liked eating her donuts from the bag and the milk from the carton.

"Thank you," Cleopatra said, annoyed at the blatant disregard for how she liked to eat her favorite treats. "So tell me what's going on in your head." Cleopatra put the plate of donuts in the microwave uncovered, knowing it bugged the hell out of Kenya when she did that.

"She wants you back and that makes me insecure as hell. You are still yet to tell me about her or why you two broke up. And look at her, she can have anyone she wants and she is after you and she knows she can get you. It's just a matter of time. I refuse to apologize for being pissed."

"I'm with you, you know that." Cleopatra took her donuts out of the microwave and sat at the island.

"For how long?" Kenya interrupted. "I don't have your heart, she still has it. She's the one who's had it all along, isn't she?"

"That's not important, it ended, that was months ago. What do I need to do, for you to feel secure?" She took a bite of the warm blueberry donut and a gulp of milk.

"Fucking talk about her, that's what you need to do. I don't even know what I'm up against. Who is this woman?" Cleopatra didn't respond. Didn't look her in the eye. She bit into the donut again. "I saw the pendant around her neck, I saw it the first night but I tried to ignore it. It's the other half of yours. You both wear that shit like a fucking badge of honor. It's been how long and you're still wearing that shit? I should rip it off your fucking neck."

"Don't touch my necklace."

"Really? Well, there it is." Kenya threw her hands up in the air.

She pushed Cleopatra off the stool and Cleopatra landed on her feet. Kenya tried to grab at her necklace. Cleopatra held her by her wrists, wanting to restrain Kenya without hurting her.

"What is it with you and this pushing shit? You know I would never hurt you, but I will protect myself. Don't come at me like that again," Cleopatra warned Kenya, and released her grip on her. "I can guarantee I hit harder than Jacqueline and let's face it, you didn't take those punches so well."

Kenya massaged her sore wrists. "Are you threatening me?"

"Take it in whatever context you need, to not do it again." She sat back down on the stool and bit into another donut.

Cleopatra hadn't raised her voice. She was calm. She wasn't even breathing hard. But Kenya knew she was serious.

"I'm in love with you. Can you tell me you love me? And you don't love her?" Kenya asked her.

Cleopatra took a sip of milk and a deep breath. "I've always been straight with you about my feelings. In my own way, I care for you. I think you know that, but I'm not going to lie to spare your feelings. I'm not in love with you. Understand, I don't take that word lightly, and I don't want to hurt you."

"Are you still in love with her?"

Without hesitating, Cleopatra said, "Yes." She was tired of lying to herself and to everyone else.

Kenya's face went cold. "Wow, you didn't even have to think about it." She sat down as the air escaped her body. "What am I supposed to do?"

"I'm sorry for putting you in this situation. You deserve better than this."

"You're sorry?"

"I can't shake her. I've tried. I still belong to her. I can't continue to fool myself, and I can't do this to you anymore. I don't want to hold you back from being happy. I can't give you what you want. You should do what's best for you."

"I will." Kenya walked out of the house and slammed the door behind her.

REUNITED

Cleopatra's heart was far from broken. She was sad that she hurt Kenya. Even though she didn't do it deliberately, she still did it. She knew their relationship could never survive Jacqueline's reappearance. Jacqueline was the real reason she couldn't love Kenya or anyone else. Cleopatra hoped that maybe one day Kenya would forgive her.

After Kenya walked out on her that night, all she wanted to do was sleep. She took off her clothes and emptied her pockets and found the note Jacqueline wrote.

Cleopatra,
I miss you so much,
You know in your heart that we belong together.
I love you, please come back to me.
I'll do anything.
Jacqueline

She listed her contact info, as if Cleopatra had ever deleted her numbers from her phone or her memory. She resisted the urge to throw her clothes back on and go to her. She placed the note on the dresser and went to bed. She slept till late the next evening, when her cell phone woke her up.

"Yes God." Shawn rejoiced when Cleopatra told her Kenya was gone.

"I'm on my way. We're going out tonight, start getting ready."

Cleopatra staggered into the shower. By the time she got out Shawn was ringing her doorbell.

"Come on, I'm trying to get my party and bullshit on."

"I still have to find something to wear." Cleopatra ran up the stairs. "Come with me."

"Yo, what's this?" Shawn picked up Jacqueline's note off the dresser.

"It's from Jac."

"Forget the club. Why don't you go to her?"

"No, if I do that you know what's going to happen."

"You'll fuck each other's brains out and get back together?"

"Exactly." Cleopatra laughed. "We're going to the club. I need some alcohol in my system."

"Why do you want alcohol when you can have Jacqueline? You are tripping." Shawn put the back of her hand up against Cleopatra's forehead. "You don't feel cray cray," she teased.

Cleopatra put on a white button-down shirt, a pair of dirty black jeans and some black Timberlands. When she went to look for her keys, Shawn slipped into the bathroom.

"Shawn, I'm ready. What are you doing? You better not be shitting in my bathroom. All the bathrooms in this house, you better not be blowing up my master."

"Damn, I'm coming." Shawn yelled from the bathroom.

"When the hell did you get this!" Cleopatra yelled, when they walked up to a black Range Rover parked on the street.

"This baby is more than my rent, cell phone, electric, cable *and* my student loans combined. That's why I didn't tell you. You would have talked me out of it. But women love it." She jangled the keys in the air.

"Good to see you have your priorities straight. More than your rent? How is that even possible? Why didn't you just pay cash?"

"Oh, it's possible when your credit is as fucked up as mine is. And you know I don't touch my money, even if you do."

"We worked hard for that money," Cleopatra said as she circled the truck. "At least buy some real estate with it or invest it. And why do you still have loans? You can't take it with you. You are going to fuck around and lose all that money."

Shawn leaned across the hood and buffed off a spot with her elbow. "Everyone didn't have a wealthy sugar mama named Alexis writing them blank checks. You worked real hard, all right." Shawn stuck out her tongue. "She was fine as hell though. Have you heard from her?"

"Hell no. She was fine, but her level of crazy was tremendous. Being that wild and that wealthy made her dangerous as shit. I heard she splits her time between L.A. and Dubai now."

"She still paying you?"

"Goes into my account every month like clockwork." Cleopatra tapped her pocket. "As long as I don't out her to the entire world."

"Must be nice. I could barely get my clients to pay me for the sex. And you got them paying you to keep your mouth shut."

"You make it sound like I'm blackmailing Alexis. The payments were her idea. I would never out any of those women, I have no interest in ruining anyone's life if they choose to keep what we did in the dark a secret. You know that. Alexis felt better with a nondisclosure agreement with some money attached. After Alexis came up with the contract idea it kind of caught on."

"What do you mean caught on? You have agreements with other clients? Who?"

"The boss heard about the contract with Alexis. She knew I was trying to get out of the life and focus on grad school, so let's say she mediated this whole pay-for-my-silence thing with the rest of my clients."

"Of course she did." Shawn shook her head. "That's why

you were able to up and quit so easily. You had the boss wrapped around that long ass tongue of yours. She would have done anything for your ass."

"That's because I never turned down an assignment. You were too picky; she got tired of fucking with you."

"She had me eating bitches out in the back of bulletproof limousines in Hoboken. I was doing tequila and tongue jobs, and you were giving the girlfriend experience in mansions in San Tropez." Shawn twisted her lips. "So who else?"

"Ask me one more time! I can't talk about them. You only know about Alexis because you caught her giving me a job that time."

"Oh yeah. I remember that. She had skills. She sucked your dick like she was hungry, like she missed lunch or something." Shawn laughed. "So all of these women are paying you? I can't believe you didn't tell me. So that means Jacqueline doesn't know you used to be a ho?"

"Oh she knows. She just doesn't know I got paid for it. Same way Robin doesn't know you pumped your ass for cash either." Cleopatra raised her eyebrows.

"Point taken. So, what's keeping me from going to Alexis and asking for a little supplemental income for myself?"

"Don't do that." Cleopatra's face turned serious. "Promise me. Don't fuck with her. She doesn't negotiate with people she has no use for. She has this crazy obsession with me that has never gone away. I can get away with things, you can't. I'm serious, don't cross her."

"Ok. Ok. I won't. I promise." Shawn knew she was serious.

"That part of our lives is over, that's the past. I'm not 'Taylor Du Bois, Lover Extraordinaire' anymore. I fuck for love now. Anyway, what were we talking about? Oh, why do you need a truck?"

"Why else? To have sex in."

"Oh God. Uhm…that's why you have an apartment."

"You must be crazy, you think I want the ho's I deal with to know where I live? I'm not trying to have all my shit burnt up again."

"Did you really just say that? Seek help. You were just bitching about eating somebody out in the back of a car. You aren't evolving."

"Yes I am. That wasn't my ride back then, but this is."

"Uh no it's not your ride, you're leasing it, it belongs to the finance company. You need a higher power or something. You should pick one. Jesus, Allah, Buddha." Cleopatra joked.

"Look who's talking!"

"I'm driving." Cleopatra snatched the keys from Shawn's hand.

A crowd of women were gathered outside the club when they pulled up. At the door the bouncer took Cleopatra's I.D. and proceeded to fondle her all over.

"If I'm hiding anything between my legs, sweetheart, believe me, it's not meant to hurt anyone," Cleopatra said, as security cupped her crotch and winked at her.

The three-story club was dark even by nightclub standards. Strobe lights in gay pride colors flashed chaotically to the beat of the music. The DJ spun old skool tunes that had mostly everyone on the dance floor sweating through their clothes, like back in the day when dancers wore track suits and headbands to the club because they were there for a workout. The bar reeked of beer that had spilled in transit to slightly (or very) inebriated lips. Overpriced eau de toilette and cheap weed from the VIP section mixed to create an aroma that could only be thoroughly ignored with the help of a salted lime and a whole lot of Patron.

Shawn and Cleopatra did tequila shots at the first floor bar as they studied the crowd. After Cleopatra turned down the second girl who approached her, Shawn knew something was wrong.

"I've made a decision. The tequila cleared my head," Cleopatra said. "I'm tired of all of this drama. I'm going to get a bunch of cats and just be by myself."

"You hate cats! You need to ease up on the alcohol. I have a feeling you'll be changing your mind soon." Shawn headed to the dance floor with a girl who wore a pink wig, red sequined hoodie and a white bodysuit.

"Good luck with that!" Cleopatra raised her glass to Shawn. She sipped her third Long Island Iced Tea and started to feel the effects. She leaned on the bar when she felt someone come up behind her and press her breasts against her back. The woman pulled her locs from her ear and Cleopatra felt her breath on her neck.

"I've been waiting for you."

Cleopatra started to turn around.

"No, not yet." The woman stopped her.

Cleopatra couldn't place the voice over the loud music.

The woman grabbed her by the waist with both hands. She breathed heavily in her ear and on her neck as she continued to press her body against Cleopatra's.

Oh my God.

From her touch and her energy she knew it was Jacqueline, but she played along with the "mystery."

"There's no competition here," Jacqueline whispered in her ear. "You need a thorough woman who can make you happy. Fulfill all of your desires."

Cleopatra turned around and stood face to face with Jacqueline.

"What are you doing here?" She was smiling from one ear to the other.

"Shawn called and said I should come and get my woman. That's what I'm doing. Let's get out of here." She grabbed Cleopatra's hand and led her through the crowd and out the front door.

"How many drinks have you had?" Jacqueline asked as they walked down Sixth Avenue.

"Just a couple of shots of Patron and three L.I.T.'s." Cleopatra smirked.

"Interesting. I've never seen you drink more than one Long Island Iced Tea, and Patron makes you black out. Maybe I should get you home now and take advantage of you."

"It's not taking advantage if I want you to."

Jacqueline hailed a cab and fifteen minutes later they arrived at Cleopatra's house.

"You need some food in your system." Jacqueline handed Cleopatra a soda as she inspected the contents of her refrigerator. "What do you want to eat?"

Cleopatra began to laugh uncontrollably, and she only stopped when she saw Jacqueline staring at her. "Oh, I thought you were being *nasty*." She cleared her throat. "Your Belgian waffles please." She sat up straight on a stool at the island.

"Whatever you desire." Jacqueline searched the cabinets for the ingredients.

"So where is your uhm…girl?" Jacqueline asked in a condescending tone, as she washed her hands in the sink.

Cleopatra studied Jacqueline's form while she had her back to her. Her body seemed even tighter than before. She wanted to peel those jeans off of her and do her with her high heeled boots on. While Cleopatra was deciding that she wanted to bite Jacqueline's ass like she used to, Jacqueline must have felt her eyes on her body. She didn't turn around; instead, she let Cleopatra look as long as she needed to.

"She broke up with me." Cleopatra snapped out of her trance and took a sip of the cherry Coke. "I told her that I was still in love with you."

"You actually told her that? It's really over?" She bit her bottom lip. She walked over to Cleopatra and stood between her legs. "So now what?"

"You're going to pop those tight ass jeans you got on if you eat waffles." Cleopatra said. "What do you suggest I do?" She licked her lips.

"I plan on coming out of these jeans in a little while, for your information." She winked at her and rubbed her hand across her behind as she walked back to the counter. "This is what we should do. Make love for a few days nonstop. You meet my parents, we get married and we live happily ever after."

"How many drinks did you have?" Cleopatra laughed.

"You asked what I thought." She growled as she stirred the waffle batter.

"Did you come out to your parents? You'd get married again?" Cleopatra sobered up.

"I wrote you letters all about it," she said as she stopped and glared at her. "Yes, I came out to anyone who would listen. Mother said she knew all along and was just waiting for me to tell her. My father was mad for a while. But he eventually came around. We are closer now than before."

"That's beautiful." Cleopatra smiled. "And I got all of your letters, I still have them. It was just too hard for me to read them."

"I hope one day you will."

"There must be fifty of them."

"Eighty-nine. I didn't ever want you to think for a minute that I wasn't thinking about you, or that I was giving up on us. And to answer your other question. I'd marry you right now, just like that." She snapped her fingers.

"I don't want my heart broken again."

"I understand, we can go as slow as you want." Jacqueline exhaled. "But there is something that I need." She walked up to Cleopatra and took her hands in hers. Cleopatra put them to her lips, kissing them softly before grabbing Jacqueline around her waist. Jacqueline moaned as Cleopatra moved her hands to her ass. "I've missed those hands more than I realized." She took a deep breath and whispered in Cleopatra's ear. "I need you to touch every part of me. We don't have to talk if you don't want to." She caressed Cleopatra's face. "I need to taste you and feel you inside of me."

Cleopatra brought Jacqueline's face to hers and took her lips into her mouth, her heart racing as she kissed her.

"What about my waffles?" Cleopatra looked at the batter.

"You can have them for breakfast. I'm ready for you to take it back." She grabbed Cleopatra's hand and led her upstairs to the bedroom. "You have no idea how much I've missed you," Jacqueline said to Cleopatra as they stood in the middle of the dark bedroom.

"Yes I do." Cleopatra kissed Jacqueline hard. It had been ten long months since they had made love. She watched Jacqueline as she came out of her clothes and let them drop to the floor. "I don't understand how you can be more beautiful than you were the first time we made love." Cleopatra licked her lips.

"It's the alcohol," Jacqueline teased her. She walked over to Cleopatra in her purple silk bra and panties.

"It's not the alcohol." Cleopatra said. "It's you. It's always been you."

"And it's always been you, baby. And it always will be." Jacqueline kissed Cleopatra as she undressed her. She scratched Cleopatra's stomach with her nails, "I've missed those abs." She kneeled down and ran her tongue across Cleopatra's stomach. She ran her hands up Cleopatra's thighs to her ass. "Did I ever tell you how much I loved the way you moved your ass?"

"No, I don't think I ever heard you say that." Cleopatra smiled, cupping Jacqueline's breasts. "Take all of this off." Cleopatra pointed to her bra and panties. "And put your boots back on."

Jacqueline stripped naked and put her knee-high boots back on. She watched Cleopatra as she put on her strap and tucked the massive thickness into her briefs.

"Do you realize your tongue is hanging out?" she asked Jacqueline, when she saw her eyes fixated on her bulge.

"That's how bad I want you."

Cleopatra laid Jacqueline on the bed. She kissed her way down her body and bit the insides of her thighs. Even in the dimly candlelit room, Cleopatra noticed something between her legs that she had never seen before.

"Is that real?" Cleopatra traced her fingers across the body art. She read the text of the tattoo. "This and my heart belong to Cleopatra."

"Of course it is, silly." Jacqueline smiled.

"How long have you had it?" Cleopatra said, amazed that Jacqueline would get a tattoo with her name, especially when they weren't even together.

"I got it the day after you broke up with me. I had to make being apart not an option." She threw the chocolate sheets off of them and pulled Cleopatra up to face her. Their bodies glided against each other. The strap that bulged out from Cleopatra's briefs made Jacqueline squirm. "It's always been yours." She moaned as Cleopatra moved on top of her.

"I've been messed up without you. I've done some stupid shit," Cleopatra said.

"I know, I couldn't get right being away from you either. I should have never lied and put you in the position that I did. I wasn't being fair to you." She trailed her nails down Cleopatra's back as she pressed into her.

"I don't want to think about that anymore."

"If you give me another chance I promise to spend every moment making you happy."

"I need to take my time." Cleopatra laced her fingers into Jacqueline's, pinning her hands under the plush pillows.

"As slow as you need." She wrapped her legs around Cleopatra's waist.

"We don't have to talk about it now. There's something else on my mind." Cleopatra rubbed her dick against Jacqueline.

"Wait." Jacqueline gasped. "Wait. I think I know the answer, but I'm going to ask anyway. Has anyone else been in this bed since I was in it last?"

"Not in my bed. You know how I feel about that. That hasn't changed," Cleopatra admitted.

"Good. I haven't been with anyone else," Jacqueline said. "But I know you have." Cleopatra started trying to explain her behavior. Jacqueline shushed her. "I don't want to know. One is too many for me. All I want to know is can you go back to it being just me and you? Will I be enough for you?"

"I don't want or need anyone but you. You know that."

"Those girls you were fucking with aren't me." She grinded her pussy up into Cleopatra. "I know you've missed me. So don't hold back."

Cleopatra trailed light kisses on her neck as Jacqueline scratched her back with her nails. She could hear Jacqueline's breath get heavier.

"Please." Jacqueline pulled on Cleopatra's earlobe with her

teeth.

She loved it when Jacqueline begged for it, but she wasn't going to make her wait tonight. This was not a game. Cleopatra pulled her dick out and kissed Jacqueline's clit with the tip of her cock. Jacqueline squirmed and bucked her body in the air. Cleopatra pushed into Jacqueline as gently as her excitement allowed. She screamed when Cleopatra slid inside of her and began to move her ass just the way she liked it. Cleopatra felt how tight she was as she pushed deeper inside of her. She pushed Jacqueline's legs up in the air, rested them on her shoulders and licked her boots as she slowed her stroke.

Cleopatra was back to her old self. She wasn't using another woman to get over the pain of missing Jacqueline or pretending she didn't care. Jacqueline was right there, underneath her, loving her and wanting her even more than before. That night Cleopatra admitted to her what she had never confessed to anyone. That she needed her and her life could never be complete without her. They made up for the ten months they were apart. No calls, no emails, no texts interrupting their lovemaking. Only breaking for food in between devouring each other.

◻ ◻ ◻

Two days later the sunlight peeked through the bedroom curtains and forced Cleopatra out of a deep sleep. She awoke on her back with Jacqueline laid out across her stomach. Cleopatra tried to ease out of the bed without waking her up.

"Where you going, baby?"

"I'm starving."

"Bring me something back, please," she said, half asleep. Cleopatra grabbed some black basketball shorts and a white t-shirt out of her dresser and went to the bathroom to wash up. Before heading to the kitchen to get something to eat, she went to check the mail. She opened the door and saw someone coming up her steps.

"What are you doing here?"

"I refuse to give up on us." Kenya backed Cleopatra up into the dark foyer and closed the door behind her. She tried kissing her but Cleopatra pushed her away.

"Are you serious? You need to get out of here."

"I know you're upset with me, just hear me out. We were happy before she came back." Kenya twirled a bunch of Cleopatra's locs around her fingers. "I haven't been able to get you off of my mind these last few days." Cleopatra pulled her hair out of Kenya's grasp. "I was upset, but I was wrong. I don't want to be without you."

"It's too late. It's over between us," Cleopatra said to her.

"No it's not." She argued. "I know you're mad. But we can work this out."

"I don't love you, Kenya."

"I don't believe you. I know you love me in your own way."

"There is nothing left between us." Cleopatra walked toward the front door. "You need to leave."

"Let me make it up to you." Kenya backed Cleopatra up against the mahogany side table in the foyer. Kenya felt the strap that Cleopatra had on dangling loose in her shorts.

"You must have been expecting me." She tugged on it.

Cleopatra smacked her hand away. She thought she heard Jacqueline moving around upstairs and she started to sweat. "You need to get out of here for real."

Jacqueline came down the stairs and stopped on the bottom step. Cleopatra's mouth fell open but nothing would come out other than a loud exhale. Jacqueline stood there in just a pair of black panties, her arms folded over her bare breasts, in silence. Kenya froze. Cleopatra swallowed hard; her throat was dry.

"Seriously, Cleopatra? We just broke up and you fucked her already."

Jacqueline walked over to Cleopatra.

"Baby, I..." Cleopatra mumbled in an attempt to explain. Jacqueline shushed her and put a finger over her mouth.

"Be quiet." Jacqueline kissed Cleopatra, sucking her lips hungrily into her mouth. Jacqueline moaned as she tried to swallow her whole and pressed her hard nipples into her. Cleopatra could not deny her and kissed her back as she slid her hands down into the back of her panties.

"You think she would leave," Jacqueline said as she pulled away from Cleopatra. Cleopatra grabbed Jacqueline around the waist and brought her back to her lips. "No. Get rid of her, then come back to bed." She headed toward the stairs.

"Cleopatra, you need to decide right now!" Kenya exclaimed. "Me or her."

"Enough of the bullshit. She made her decision, is that not obvious?" Jacqueline said, as she stepped between Cleopatra and Kenya. She shooed Kenya away as if she were swatting a fly. Kenya grabbed Jacqueline by her wrist, yanking her away from Cleopatra.

"Are you crazy?" Jacqueline yelled and snatched her hand away. Cleopatra moved between the two women. "I'm tired of playing with you. Get the hell out," Jacqueline screamed and pointed at Kenya as she charged toward her again. Kenya moved backward and Cleopatra picked Jacqueline up and threw her over her shoulder.

"What are you doing?" Jacqueline squirmed as Cleopatra carried her up to the top of the steps, where she gently put her down on her feet.

"Baby." Cleopatra cupped her face in her hands. "Go back to bed, I'll be there in a minute. I promise."

"Ok." Jacqueline took Cleopatra's hand and put it inside of her panties. Cleopatra kissed her and dug her fingers between Jacqueline's legs pushing her back up against the wall. Cleopatra ran her fingers over Jacqueline's clit and slid her fingers inside of her. Jacqueline squirmed as Cleopatra worked her fingers deep; she had to stop her before it went any further. She pulled Cleopatra's hand out of her panties, it was covered in her wetness. "Taste me." Jacqueline pointed toward Cleopatra's hand. Cleopatra lapped up Jacqueline's juices from her fingers. "That's waiting for you in bed." Cleopatra licked her lips and swallowed hard.

"Kiss her and you'll be tasting my pussy," she said to Kenya who was watching them from the bottom of the steps. "Handle it." She looked at Cleopatra and went back to bed. Cleopatra looked at Jacqueline as she walked away. Her own clit was throbbing, she wanted her right then. She licked her lips again.

"Is this really what you want?" Kenya asked as she watched Cleopatra walk down the stairs.

"It is. More than anything."

"I know you have feelings for me," Kenya persisted.

"I care about you. But I'm not in love with you."

"Yes you are."

"I'm telling you *no,* and you aren't hearing me. It's because of that woman up there, I can't love anyone else. You deserve much more than I could ever give you. I'm sorry about all of this. You must know that I never meant to hurt you."

"You're right – I do deserve the best. I still think that's you."

"You should get what you want Kenya, just not from me. Take care of yourself." Cleopatra opened the door.

"This isn't goodbye."

"Don't do this to yourself. You are a beautiful and intelligent woman. You are graduating from law school next year and I know you're going to be successful at all that you do. You have to go on and live your life."

She walked up to Cleopatra and kissed her on the lips. "I can't," she said and walked out the door. Cleopatra thought Kenya didn't really have a choice, it was over and done.

Jacqueline was under the covers waiting for her when she came into the bedroom.

"I'm sorry I lost my temper. You ok, baby?" Jacqueline threw the sheets back as she watched Cleopatra undress and crawl in to bed and on top of her.

"I am now. As long as I have you," Cleopatra looked down at her then kissed her.

"You have all of me." Jacqueline opened up for her spreading her thighs, begging her to come inside of her again.

"I love you so much Cleopatra." She moaned as Cleopatra slid in to her.

FAMILY IS A TRIPP

"What happens now?" Jacqueline asked Cleopatra. "We made love all weekend. We've never had a problem in bed. You know what I want, but what do you want to happen?"

"I want to be with you."

Cleopatra had forgiven her long ago. She wanted to commit to Jacqueline. But she made the decision to go extra slow, to ease back into each other's lives carefully and only see each other a couple times a week. Jacqueline tired of that arrangement quickly.

"It's time, baby, to go all in. The days drip by too slowly. I need to be with you more," Jacqueline said, late one night over the phone.

Cleopatra gave in, and the more time they spent together, the deeper in love they fell all over again. Cleopatra surrendered to the fact that Jacqueline was her soul mate. Jacqueline loved her deeply, unconditionally and obsessively.

"My parents want to meet you. Are you ready?" Jacqueline

asked, excited.

"Uhm...Yeah, I'm ready."

"Why the hesitation? You aren't scared, are you?"

"I'm not scared. It's a big step, that's all. A really big one."

"It sure is, because you've been invited to Thanksgiving, so you'll meet my whole family at one time."

◎ ◎ ◎

Cleopatra and Jacqueline spent Thanksgiving Day at the Tripp family home in the South Orange section of Jersey. As soon as they entered through the front door, they were immersed in the clamor of activity. Kids who weren't watching cartoons ran around the house, men with deep voices could be heard cursing at the football game, and the chatter of women intermingled with Motown music emanated from the kitchen. Jacqueline's family embraced Cleopatra from the moment she walked through the door.

Jacqueline's father, a tall, handsome gray-haired man gave Cleopatra a bear hug while he introduced himself. "Welcome Cleo, Happy Thanksgiving. You can call me Pops."

An older version of Jacqueline and Robin introduced herself. "Happy Thanksgiving, Cleopatra, call me Moms," Jacqueline's mother said while she pinched Cleopatra's cheeks. Moms pulled her into the kitchen where she was overcome by the aroma of candied yams, ham and homemade biscuits and gravy. She draped Cleopatra with a floral apron and promptly put her to work mashing a stockpot of boiled potatoes.

Cleopatra was struck by all the beautiful women in Jacqueline's family and their ridiculously happy significant others. She had not been around that large of a family who actually loved each other in longer than she could remember. She'd spent the last couple of Thanksgivings with Shawn's people, but it was nothing like this. Shawn could attest to that fact since she totally surprised Cleopatra when she walked into the kitchen and saw her sitting with Robin.

"What's up, baby? Happy Thanksgiving." Robin jumped on Cleopatra and gave her a hug.

Cleopatra fell back a bit, but caught her balance. "Hey, sweetie." She smiled and accepted the exuberant welcome.

"It's about time you got her ass in this house," Robin teased Jacqueline as she hugged her big sister.

Shawn came up behind Cleopatra and put her in a choke hold.

"What are you doing here? Why didn't you tell me?" Cleopatra twisted out of Shawn's grasp.

"Recent development, I didn't have time." Shawn said.

"We hung out like two days ago."

"Recent as in last night." Cleopatra stared at Shawn, waiting for further explanation. "Let's just say a certain sister got on the case of another sister for never partaking in a certain sexual activity and then facilitated the acquiring of unsaid skills."

"She went down on you?" Cleopatra covered her mouth and looked around to make sure no one was listening.

"To God be the glory." Shawn threw her head back and rubbed her stomach.

"I think your skin is clearing up already." Cleopatra rubbed the side of Shawn's cheek. "Welcome to the family."

Jacqueline was visibly moved by how quickly her family took to Cleopatra. Not just her aunts, uncles and cousins, but all of the little ones as well.

Cleopatra met all of the eight children who ranged from three to seven years old. Mitchell, Christian, Christina, Akil, Cedric, Tamika, Sophia and Angela. Always good with names, she tried to memorize all of them and who their parents were.

"Cleopatra, they want to know if they can play with your locs?" Jacqueline asked.

"Are everyone's hands clean?" Cleopatra got down on her knees and talked to the children.

"Yes," they replied in unison.

"No boogers or anything?"

"No!" they giggled.

"Wait, everybody didn't answer. I'll ask again. Any

boogers?"

"No!" they all yelled.

"Ok." She pulled out her hair tie and let her locs fall loose around her face and down her back. "One at a time, and if anyone pulls on them too hard I'm going to hang you upside down by your little ankles and shake you until your loose teeth fall out," Cleopatra said, half-kidding. They all converged on her, knocking her over as they played with her hair. Cleopatra sat and watched cartoons with the kids for a while and then sat with the men and Shawn watching the football game until Moms pulled her out to perform another task in the kitchen. Crushing cranberries for the sauce.

Cleopatra joked with Jacqueline. "I'm sensing a pattern with your mom. She thinks I'm strong. I'm crushing and smashing everything."

"You want to smash me in one of the bedrooms upstairs? That floral apron you got on is making me hot. Seriously." Jacqueline was sitting across from her at the kitchen table icing a chocolate cake.

Cleopatra looked around the kitchen crowded with Jacqueline's aunts and cousins. And put her finger to her lips. "Watch your mouth."

"No discretion needed. Look around, have you seen my mother or father since she put you on cranberries?" Cleopatra realized she hadn't seen or heard Moms in a bit. Jacqueline leaned over and whispered to her. "They are in the pantry."

"Who? In the pantry doing…" Cleopatra caught herself and burst into laughter. "Really?!"

"They can't keep their hands off of each other." Jacqueline smiled. "Never could. Reminds me of us." She winked at Cleopatra.

"That's a beautiful thing." Cleopatra smiled.

Moms, Pops, uncles, aunts and cousins, twenty adults in total gathered snugly around the massive wood dining table placed strategically on a red oriental rug. The eight children sat politely on the side at a round table at plastic place settings adorned with cartoon turkeys. The sun that shone through the

French doors leading from the back deck, reflecting off the yellow walls, made the room festive and matched Jacqueline's mother's vibrant personality. A brass chandelier ornate with crystal teardrops hung centered over the dining table, and an antique wood china cabinet stood on the side wall. Cleopatra smiled in appreciation; she hadn't seen furniture that vintage since being in her grandmother's house down south as a little girl.

When it was time to eat, everyone held hands as Pops offered a rousing yet extended prayer that only ended because of a chorus of everyone clearing their throats. When they all said "amen" in unison, food flew everywhere like a starter pistol had gone off, and there wasn't a lot of talking in the beginning. The conversation consisted of, "Damn that's good. Who made this?" and "can you please pass," something or other, and the rest was inaudible grunting. The family dug in to Pops' deep fried turkey and honey glazed ham, and Moms' side dishes, sweet candied yams, macaroni and cheese, collard greens with smoked turkey, stuffing with apples and sausage, potato salad, corn on the cob, and cinnamon cranberry sauce. The three layer chocolate cake, rum cake and peach cobbler sat in the kitchen waiting for everyone's belly to make room. As their stomachs filled, the conversation became lively. Pops was a wise gentlemen, *a cool old dude*, Cleopatra thought, unaffected by the near thirty people who had invaded his home. Moms was nurturing and sweet, obviously very much in love with her husband. She reminded Cleopatra of Jacqueline in her mannerisms and how she took care of Pop's. Pops' brother, Uncle Thomas, was a wisecracking alcoholic reciting limericks in between swigs from the brown paper bag that he hadn't parted with the entire day. Every family had at least one drunk uncle, Cleopatra thought. But he wasn't a mean drunk, he was a hilarious one. The banter between him and his wife Roberta kept the table laughing and struggling not to choke on their food. While they were still eating dinner, two of the kids came over to Cleopatra, food covering their faces.

"We can't eat anymore, Cleo," they complained, "our

clothes are too tight." Cleopatra wondered why they had not gone to their mother, when she glanced across the table and saw her elbow deep with a fried turkey wing. So Cleopatra wiped them clean and loosened their clothes for them.

Then two more kids wanted Cleopatra to clean them up and free their bulging bellies. She didn't hesitate to care for them either, and she took them into the living room where she placed them strategically on the large sectional sofa, like puzzles pieces. They were asleep in minutes. Cleopatra came back to the table and started eating again as if she took care of four kids every day. Jacqueline studied her the entire time.

"What?" Cleopatra asked Jacqueline as she looked down at her shirt, thinking she had spilled something on herself. She wiped her face, thinking maybe she had food on her cheek.

"You are just so good with them, they loved you right away. It's very sweet, that's all." She touched her chest over her heart.

"You got a sweetheart there," Jacqueline's mother said. "Because I wasn't about to get up from the table and I didn't see anybody else making a move." She laughed as she put a piece of honey baked ham wrapped around some stuffing into her mouth.

"So, I see you love kids, Cleopatra," Moms commented.

"Yes ma'am. I do." She smiled and leaned over next to Moms. "I have three godchildren that I adore." She took out her cell phone and showed Moms a picture of Amare, Ayana and Gabriela.

Near the end of the evening Moms and Pops pulled the couple away from the rest of the family and sat them down in the living room to talk.

Moms went first. "When Jacqueline came out, she told us all about you and her, and what happened. I feel the need to apologize for her lack of judgment because we didn't raise her that way, and I apologize for the pain her secrets caused you." Moms shook her head and sucked her teeth at her daughter. She took Cleopatra's hand in hers. She turned her attention back to Jacqueline. "You have to learn from your mistakes and not repeat them Jacqueline. Cleopatra obviously has a forgiving heart but you need not test it." Cleopatra wasn't sure what she was witnessing but it was clear Moms had not been a fan of Jacqueline's behavior. Moms turned, looked at Cleopatra and smiled, "Every parent thinks their daughters are the most beautiful, special people in the world, and she has always been that to her father and I. But there was always an inner struggle we failed to help her with. We didn't know it at the time, but those struggles faded away when you came along. She glowed. She was always happy, smiling and laughing all the time. She exuded a peace like I'd never seen before. We know now that it was because you were loving her. And now with you back in her life, she's even happier than before and it warms my heart. You two make such a beautiful couple. And Jacqueline please heed my words. Take care of her."

"You make my daughter happy and that's all that matters to me," Pops told Cleopatra. "She was sad for the longest time and I'd forgotten what her smile looked like. Do what you need to do, to not mess up this time. And I mean that." He gave Jacqueline a hard look as his face had turned serious. Moms stood up and gave Cleopatra a hug and kiss. "Welcome to the family, Cleopatra," she said. "We'll watch over you like you're our own," Pops said as he joined his wife and Cleopatra in a group hug.

At the end of the evening as the family trickled out of the house, Cleopatra and Shawn stood outside talking. Cleopatra wondered what was taking Jacqueline so long, when she finally surfaced outside the front door with her mother. Instead of a quick hug and kiss, though, she saw what looked to be a heated discussion. Her mom shook her head numerous times, kept her arms folded across her chest and at one point put her finger in Jacqueline's face.

"Everything all right, baby?" Cleopatra asked, concerned.

"Everything is beautiful baby. She likes to fuss, nothing for you to worry about."

◉ ◉ ◉

Later Thanksgiving night Jacqueline lay down in Cleopatra's lap. "So what do you think of my family?"

"I love your family. I had fun, not even considering all the money I made." Cleopatra showed her the knot of cash she won betting on the football game.

"You won that much? What are you going to buy me?" Jacqueline batted her eyelashes coquettishly.

"I got something in mind." Cleopatra winked at her.

"So what do you want for Christmas? It will be here before we know it."

"I have everything I want, right here." Cleopatra kissed Jacqueline on the forehead.

"Yeah, that's sweet, but seriously, what do you want?"

"You always give the best, most thoughtful gifts. I'll love whatever you get me. You know that."

"Good. Because I already know what I'm getting you. Do you know what I want?" Jacqueline asked.

"Yup."

"How do you know?"

"Because I know you."

"You don't know what I want."

"Yes I do. But go ahead – are you going to tell me what you want then?"

"No, you should know."

"I told you I know. You just said I didn't," Cleopatra said.

"Never mind," Jacqueline said, annoyed.

"Baby, I got you. Don't worry." Cleopatra kissed her. She knew what Jacqueline wanted for Christmas or any other time for that matter: an engagement ring. And she had less than a month to figure out what she was going to do.

BOOMERANG, I REALLY NEED YOU TO STOP

Cleopatra had sneaked in some Christmas shopping during lunch and was headed back to her office. Kenya approached her as she took a shortcut through a snow-covered Bryant Park.

"So, are you not even going to return my calls or my emails?"

Kenya had been trying to contact her for a while, but Cleopatra had nothing to say to her. Cleopatra thought, *How do you respond to emails where someone begs you to come back, and you know they were only keeping someone else's spot warm? You don't, you ignore them.* But with each attempted contact that Cleopatra ignored, Kenya seemed to become more and more upset.

"Kenya, I'm with someone, you know that. I thought we had both moved on."

"You moved on. I'm still right here."

"It's been over. You have to let this go."

A few days later Cleopatra was eating lunch alone at a busy bistro on Thirty-ninth Street when Kenya walked in. *Ok, she is definitely stalking me now.*

She stood at the end of Cleopatra's booth. "Tell me what I have to do for you to take me back."

As upset as she was, Cleopatra thought she would try a different approach, because aggression would get her nowhere. "Sit down and have lunch with me." Kenya looked surprised, and her defenses immediately came down. "Sit." Cleopatra pointed to the other side of the booth as she motioned for the waitress.

"Can I get a soy BLT with sweet potato fries and a pomegranate iced tea for her, please? Thank you." Cleopatra winked at the waitress. "So, how have you been?" she asked Kenya. "I hope you don't mind my eating while we wait for your food. I didn't have breakfast this morning."

"It's fine. I'm doing ok." Kenya was a bit unsettled by Cleopatra's hospitality.

"Good. How's your last year of law school coming?"

"Great. I have job offers from firms all over the country. I'm pretty excited about my future." She smiled.

"Congratulations. Have you narrowed it down at all?"

"I'm staying in New York City if that's what you are asking. I wouldn't dare leave you."

Cleopatra changed the subject. "So, how are your parents doing?"

"They're fine. They keep asking when you're coming over for dinner again."

"They think we're still together? It's been months."

"No reason to tell them about a temporary separation." The waitress brought Kenya's food and she started eating. "When's the last time you had sex?" She popped a fry in her mouth.

"That's random and none of your business." Cleopatra replied.

"Probably this morning." She touched Cleopatra's hand. "That's why you didn't have breakfast, isn't it? Had pussy for breakfast, didn't you? You want mine for lunch?"

"Wow. Excuse me." Cleopatra got up from the table. There went any chance of having a civil interaction with Kenya. She went to the restroom to regroup. As soon as Cleopatra entered the bathroom stall and locked it behind her someone on the other side shook the door.

"Occupied," she said. They continued to pull on the door. "Someone's in here."

"Cleopatra, let me in. It's me."

"Go away. This wasn't an invitation, Kenya."

"I'm going to scream if you don't open this door."

"Go ahead," Cleopatra said. Kenya inhaled and just as Cleopatra heard the beginnings of a shriek she opened the door. Kenya pushed her back inside and leaned up against the stall door blocking her way out.

"Are you serious right now? You're going to attack me in the toilet? Why does this feel like I've been here before?" Cleopatra was annoyed now.

"I'm not gonna have to attack you." She unbuttoned her blouse and unsnapped her bra. "I'm not gonna make you do anything you don't want to do."

There was no way out of the stall but through Kenya. So Cleopatra lifted her up and moved her out of the way. She unlocked the stall and walked out just as another woman came into the bathroom. Cleopatra went back to the table and gave the waitress her credit card for the check. While she put her coat and scarf on she heard Kenya's voice come across the restaurant's P.A. system.

"Excuse me everyone." Cleopatra froze in her seat and shut her eyes as she braced herself. She sneaked a peak and saw Kenya standing at the hostess station near the front of the restaurant as she held the audience captive.

"My name is Kenya and I'm trying to get back with my ex-girlfriend Cleopatra. She's sitting in the last booth with the black leather peacoat on."Cleopatra put her hand over her face and sunk down in the booth.

"She's handsome, right? Anyway she doesn't think we should get back together. And I was about to get butt naked for her in the bathroom and she still turned me down. I just want everyone to know how much I love this woman."

This is so embarrassing. Oh my God. Where is the waitress?

The restaurant had stopped. Everyone looked at Cleopatra while listening to Kenya's monologue.

"I don't think you can understand the things this woman has put my mind and my body through."

"Talk about it," a woman yelled. Cleopatra leaned out of the booth to see who was testifying and it was a woman she'd dated years ago. She spotted the waitress and waved her over like air traffic control.

"All right, I got a witness." Kenya continued. "It's some addictive chemicals in this woman's body that seeped into my blood and I need her like food, like water and air."

"What's taking so long?" Cleopatra asked the waitress, who was listening to the Kenya Show.

"Sorry, we're having problems with the credit card machine."

"Great." *I gotta start carrying cash.*

"I would do anything to be with this woman again. But I need help making her understand. I need some support. Will you all tell her to give me another chance? I'm a good catch. I cook, I clean, and I'm smart. I can be submissive or I can dominate."

"Oh my God. She's crazy," one woman said.

"Thank you," Cleopatra said to the lady. Finally, someone empathized with her.

"Come on. Take her back," one guy said.

"Take her back, take her back, take her back," a large group in the corner chanted.

The waitress returned with Cleopatra's credit card, and she'd written her name and phone number on the receipt with a note to call her sometime. Cleopatra signed it and left the contact information behind. She ran out of the front door and didn't look back. Kenya caught up with her on the corner.

"Why did you put my business in the street like that? I probably will never be able to go back in there again."

"I had to say what I felt."

Cleopatra grew tired of being polite and trying to spare Kenya's feelings. "This is not a game." She slid her hands into her gloves.

"No, it's not, Cleopatra. That's what I been trying to tell you."

"What is this about? Is it the sex, Kenya? Is that all it was ever about? 'Cause there are a lot of other butches in the city who can fuck, a whole lot. You should try and hook up with some of them."

"That's not what this is about. I loved you before you ever touched me, you know that. But I can't forget how good it was either."

"How good it *was*. Past tense. What you don't seem to realize is, when I was eating your pussy I was thinking about Jacqueline. When I was fucking you, it was Jacqueline that I was thinking about. That's why it was so good. I was thinking about my ex." Cleopatra covered her mouth with her scarf, and walked away leaving Kenya standing alone on the street. Snowflakes began to fall.

◉ ◉ ◉

"Damn. She went all out, huh?" Shawn said. "You see, it's starting again. This shit happens every time you tell a Trini you don't want her anymore, and she doesn't feel the same. I hope she was worth breaking your rule."

"She was at the time. Not right now, though."

"So, what do you want to do?" Shawn cracked her knuckles.

Cleopatra laughed. "You know we're beyond that, we make phone calls now. I'm just trying to avoid calling in any favors. And don't you do anything either."

"If you say so, but remember that bitch is crazy."

Cleopatra had kept drama to a minimum since moving to headquarters on Forty-second Street nearly a year before, and with Racquel's gatekeeping, she managed to not hook up with anyone who worked in the building. And with the help of her friends in security she had Kenya banned from entering the premises. But that didn't stop Kenya from hanging around outside on the street.

The day after the restaurant fiasco, Kenya caught Cleopatra outside of work on her way home.

"What now? It's getting late and it's freezing out here." Cleopatra watched her breath come out of her mouth in silver clouds as she spoke. "Are you pregnant or something? It's not mine," she said sarcastically.

"You left me with no choice, Cleopatra."

She immediately thought, *This bitch has a gun or something.* She backed up and looked at Kenya's hands which were stuffed in her pockets, and quickly spotted an escape route through the crowd on Broadway.

"What does that mean, Kenya?"

"Either you come back to me, or I'm going to the police and press charges against your girlfriend for assault. Then she'll go to jail and you'll end up with me anyway. The choice is yours."

Cleopatra burst into laughter, further infuriating Kenya. "Wow. Assault? You're talking about the thing in the men's room?"

"It wasn't a thing. She beat me up," Kenya said defiantly.

"You're nuts. That wasn't assault," Cleopatra snickered. "You charged toward her twice. She was protecting herself."

"I'm about to graduate from one of the most prestigious law schools in the country in a few months, the top criminal law firms from all over are trying to recruit me before I even take the bar exam. You don't think I know how to finesse this shit to get your bitch out of the picture?" Kenya placed her hand on her hip in victory.

"You would go that far to keep us apart?" Cleopatra's face turned somber. "You're really serious?"

"Serious as a heart attack."

◎ ◎ ◎

"You coming to bed, baby?" Jacqueline asked Cleopatra as she stood in the doorway to the library.

"In a little bit." Cleopatra turned off her laptop.

Jacqueline came up behind her and rubbed her shoulders. "What's been up with you? You're so tense. You can talk to me about it."

No, I can't. You see red whenever Kenya is in the picture.

"I'm coming, sweetie. Just a lot going on at work. Everything is cool." Cleopatra tried to convince her.

"You never let work come home with you before. We haven't made love in a couple of days."

"I know how long it's been. Can you just leave me alone?" she snapped.

"Yeah. Whatever." She turned around to walk out and stopped short of the doorway. "Just so you know – I know when you're lying."

◎ ◎ ◎

Cleopatra would need some advice from a professional to deal with Kenya's threats to blackmail her into leaving Jacqueline. She called Catherine the Great, the ageless fifty-year-old criminal attorney with the body of a nimble thirty-year-old. They'd dated briefly not too long after Cleopatra and Jacqueline had broken up. Catherine was a former assistant district attorney in Brooklyn, now in private practice. She was a beast of a criminal attorney and if anyone could help Cleopatra deal with Kenya, it would be Catherine.

"I was pleasantly surprised to get your call." Catherine sat down and took her suit jacket off. "It's been too long. I wish we were meeting in a hotel room instead of a restaurant."

"It has been a long time, but it's not about that. I'm in a relationship now." Cleopatra said. "She might be in trouble. I

219

need to retain your services." Cleopatra described the problem to Catherine. "Is what Jacqueline did assault?"

"It was assault. But she can easily plead self-defense. She was protecting herself."

"Good, that's what I thought. Kenya didn't even go to the hospital, and there weren't any serious injuries. She was giving me head a few hours later, and the black eye went away in a couple days,"

"Really, Cleopatra?" Catherine raised an eyebrow at her. "The best thing to do would be to keep her from pressing charges in the first place. You never know what could happen once you go into court. It could just spiral out of control. It's even more risky since she's so hell-bent on getting your woman out of the picture."

"What's the worst-case scenario?"

"If she is convicted of misdemeanor assault she could do anywhere from thirty days to a year, and there could be some financial penalties. Then of course she'd have a record."

"What should I do?"

"Kenya has a while before the statute of limitations is up and she knows it. But the longer she waits, the less credible the allegations will be, both to law enforcement and, subsequently, at the prosecutor's office. Too many intervening things could happen. Any witnesses? Were pictures taken?"

"Only witnesses were me and Jacqueline's sister who came in at the end. I don't think Kenya took pictures. She would have definitely threatened me with them by now. Plus, she was too busy."

"I know, busy giving you head." Catherine laughed. "We need to prevent her from going to the police and then we won't have to worry about prosecution. You could go on and live your life and she can pop up again and again and try and threaten you, so we need to shut her down and deal with her blackmailing you. You need to get something on her. This is what you are going to do. She wants to try and blackmail you, fine, we can show her how it's really done. You are going to get her on tape admitting everything. Get her to say that the altercation wasn't assault, that it was self-defense. That she is only taking this to court to break you two up because she wanted you for herself. Do what you need to do to get her to say it. But that may entail getting her in a position that you don't want to be in with her."

"Are you saying I should sleep with her to get her to confess?"

"You know a better way?"

"Yeah. It might take me some time but I'm just going to get her to come out and say it."

"You think she's that stupid?"

"I know she's that stupid."

A short time later Catherine and Cleopatra emerged from the restaurant. Cleopatra put Catherine in a cab home, but not before Catherine laid a big fat kiss on her.

"You know better than that," Cleopatra admonished her.

"That's my consultation fee. Your first bill will be in the mail."

"I'll pay it as long as you come when I call you," Cleopatra joked.

"I always came." She winked at her before riding off in the cab.

Cleopatra was exhausted when she got home. The stress Kenya had caused her over the last few days and the strain she had put on her relationship and her sex life with Jacqueline had Cleopatra's body twisted in knots. She called Jacqueline at home as soon as she walked in the door, hoping to smooth things over a bit. "Hi, sweetheart. How was your day?"

"Where were you tonight?" Jacqueline's tone told Cleopatra she was pissed.

"I texted you that I was having dinner with a friend, remember?"

"Yeah. I texted you and I called you back. Your phone was turned off. What friend? Your only friend is Shawn, and the rest are exes that want you back. And I happen to know that Shawn is having dinner with Robin right now."

"What's up with the attitude? Why all the questions? Say what's on your mind." Cleopatra got defensive; her exhaustion had lessened her tolerance. Jacqueline was quiet, so there was nothing but silence between them. "I've never cheated on you Jacqueline, and I never will. This mistrust shit you been doing lately is tiring. Just because you are a liar and a cheat doesn't mean that I am too."

Jacqueline slammed the phone down and hung up on her. Days went by, and Jacqueline didn't call her and she didn't call Jacqueline. Cleopatra was stubborn. Jacqueline had hung up on her she should be the one to reach out to her and apologize. But every time her phone rang it was Kenya pressuring her to make a decision. Since she and Jacqueline weren't speaking, it seemed as good a time as any to implement the plan to get Kenya to confess about her blackmail plot. She would get Kenya to admit what she had done on tape, send it to Catherine and make up with Jacqueline as soon as possible.

Cleopatra's timing could not have been worse. The next night Jacqueline beat Cleopatra in the chest when she found Kenya cooking in her kitchen. After the confusion faded from her eyes, there was only pain, and Cleopatra knew she had caused it. She had to scoop Jacqueline up in her arms and carry her up the stairs to keep her from getting to Kenya. Jacqueline squirmed attempting to break free while Cleopatra yelled at her to stop.

"Baby, calm down." Cleopatra put her down on her feet in the foyer.

"You must have fallen and bumped your head. Are you just going to go back and forth between us? Is this what you do when we have an argument? We are supposed to be forever. Do you not love me anymore?" Jacqueline squeezed Cleopatra's face as if trying to extract an answer from her lips. "You don't love her. You love me. I'm so sure about that. I don't understand you."

"Cleopatra." Kenya came up the stairs to the foyer.

"Seriously, if you don't let me talk with Jacqueline privately there are going to be charges against me too. Go." Cleopatra pointed back down to the kitchen. Kenya backed up and walked down the stairs quietly.

"You need to trust me," Cleopatra said to Jacqueline.

"Trust you? How am I supposed to trust you when that bitch is back in your life?"

It was too late. Cleopatra had regretted not telling Jacqueline that Kenya was trying to blackmail her to keep them apart, but the damage was already done, and there was no way she could tell her now with Kenya in the house.

"I have to get out of here." She grabbed Cleopatra's face by her chin. "I'll know if you fuck her, and I will never forgive you." She walked out the front door and with her back to Cleopatra said, "If you want to do that ho a favor, don't let me see her on the street, and don't let her step foot in Brooklyn."

Kenya was angry that Cleopatra wouldn't touch her. She hadn't hugged or kissed Kenya, much less fucked her, and that pissed her off.

"Jacqueline's gone and I'm here with you. You got what you wanted, her away from me. But I'm not having sex with you if I don't want to. And I don't want to."

"That's cool. I know you can only go so long without it. I can wait. I remember a time when you couldn't resist me." Catherine might have been right. Kenya was too on point to just admit guilt. Cleopatra tried several times to goad her into fessing up to the blackmail scheme. She knew if she slept with Kenya she could make her say whatever she wanted, but she wasn't going there. Cleopatra would have to be patient if she wanted to do this right. Kenya stuck to Cleopatra like glue that entire weekend, making sure she had no contact with Jacqueline, but she couldn't watch her forever.

Jacqueline came to Cleopatra's house that Monday evening.

"I don't care if she's here or not. I need to talk to you," Jacqueline said when Cleopatra opened the door.

"It's not a good time." Cleopatra had her three godchildren over. Amare and Ayana were napping and she was holding Gabriela in her arms. Jacqueline looked like she'd seen a ghost when she saw Cleopatra with the newborn.

"Racquel's husband was in a car accident. She had to rush to Harlem Hill. I just picked them up from daycare."

"You need any help?"

"I would love some help. Come here." Jacqueline moved closer. "This is my sweetie Gabriela. I don't think you've ever met her." Cleopatra introduced Jacqueline to the newborn sleeping peacefully in her arms. Jacqueline made a big deal about how good Cleopatra was with the children. Jacqueline cooked dinner and they fed the kids, bathed them and put them to bed. Jacqueline's anger melted away. Seeing how Cleopatra took care of those she loved softened her. She couldn't be mad anymore, even though she wanted to be. Racquel called late that night with an update.

"He has some cracked ribs, a broken arm and a broken leg but he'll make a full recovery." Cleopatra told Jacqueline. "I'm gonna keep the kids for a few days while she gets him home and settled." She flopped down on the couch next to Jacqueline, tired.

"Are you sleeping with her?" Jacqueline blurted out. She couldn't contain the question any longer.

"No, baby. You know I'm not."

"Are you ready to tell me what's going on? What did you mean when you said there would be charges against you, too?"

Cleopatra finally told her the truth about Kenya's threats, her meeting with Catherine, and her plan to make Kenya go away. Jacqueline was furious that she didn't come to her from the start.

"I tried to protect you. But I screwed up and hurt you. I'm sorry."

"We can just go to court and fight it out if it comes to that. We'll deal with it together, baby. Don't keep things like this from me. No one can come between us if we stick together."

Jacqueline picked up Cleopatra's cell phone. "Call her. Tell her the game is over."

Cleopatra left a voicemail. She told Kenya that she was done playing and that she hoped she wouldn't press charges, and that they could all go on with their lives. "I hope you do the right thing," was the last thing she said before she hung up.

Cleopatra never heard back from Kenya. Jacqueline would ask every day if there was any word from her, and every day she would say no. Soon she stopped asking and it faded from both of their minds. This had strengthened their relationship even further. Jacqueline realized just how much Cleopatra loved her and how far she would go to protect her.

◎ ◎ ◎

"Cleo. I'm so glad you picked up." Shawn sighed. "I need you to come get me, and like right now."

Cleopatra looked at the time. Three a.m. "What's up? Where you at?"

"Where would I be, and need you to come and get me? Bring your checkbook."

Jacqueline sat up in bed. "Where you going, baby?"

"I gotta go get Shawn. She's in a situation again."

"Again? You need me to come with?"

"No, baby. Go back to sleep." Cleopatra kissed Jacqueline on the forehead. "Love you."

Shawn had been arrested for statutory rape, along with a slew of child endangerment and pornography charges. A girl she thought was twenty-one was actually only sixteen, a few weeks shy of her seventeenth birthday. The girl's father had seen a video of his daughter and Shawn having sex on the girl's cell phone and went ballistic. Cleopatra called Catherine and met her at the police station in Brooklyn where she posted twenty thousand dollars for her bail. The only thing she said to Shawn that night was, "I really need you to stop doing stupid shit."

TASHA C. MILLER

FOOL ME ONCE, SHAME ON YOU, BUT TWICE?

Cleopatra split Christmas day between the shelter and visiting her godchildren. The evening was dedicated to Jacqueline. Cleopatra had the night planned down to the last detail. She had reserved a suite at the Mandarin Oriental in Columbus Circle.

The large white on white rooms with their walls of windows faced Central Park, and Cleopatra played seductive soft jazz low in the background. Nag Champa incense and vanilla candles teased the nose. Every piece of furniture was plush, and invited the lovers to lose themselves in luxury.

Cleopatra arranged for a seven-course dinner to be served in the room. They sat down at a small candlelit table by the window. Jacqueline dismissed the waiter from his duties when she realized it was his job to stay, watch them eat, clear their plates and serve the next course. Jacqueline would take care of Cleopatra, she decided. She would serve her woman each course; that was the least she could do, after all the trouble Cleopatra had gone through to plan such an intimate evening. Jacqueline wanted to be alone with her, flirt with her and tell her all the nasty things she wanted to do to her. And they needed to be alone for that. First she served Cleopatra the oysters on the half shell, glistening under the ginger mignonette sauce. Then, potato soup, celery, apple and walnut salad with cider honey vinaigrette, lemon sorbet, seared roasted chicken with mushroom truffle ragout and lobster ravioli. For dessert there was chocolate mousse. "Baby, you'll have to wait a little while for dessert," she said to Cleopatra as she took the mousse and carried it into the bedroom. "I want my present now."

They had begun to exchange presents before dinner, when Jacqueline gave Cleopatra a sterling silver and midnight titanium Tiffany link bracelet that she had been eyeing for a while. Cleopatra loved it and put it on right away. But Jacqueline got cold feet when Cleopatra went to go get her gift. It was then that she insisted on saving her present for after dinner. Now she was ready for her Christmas gift.

They sat down in the living room of their suite on the long white couch. Jacqueline kissed Cleopatra's neck as she ran her hand up the back of her shirt.

"You must be trying to start something. Keep it up and you're going to get it," Cleopatra warned her.

"You promise?" Jacqueline pulled Cleopatra on top of her.

Cleopatra kissed Jacqueline as she pressed her body hard against hers. She knew Jacqueline was stalling, and she knew she was nervous. She decided to help her along.

"Merry Christmas, sweetheart." Cleopatra pulled a small black jewelry box tied with a white silk bow from behind one of the sofa cushions. She sat up on the couch as she watched Jacqueline study the box. Then she closed her eyes, took a deep breath and opened it. Her mouth dropped.

"They're beautiful. I wasn't expecting this." She kissed Cleopatra.

Cleopatra knew Jacqueline was not expecting that at all. She was expecting an engagement ring. In the box was a pair of solitaire diamond earrings. She could tell Jacqueline was surprised, and disappointed.

"I love them, baby. Thank you so much." She kissed Cleopatra again.

"See? I knew what you wanted, diamonds." She saw a twinge of sadness cross Jacqueline's face. "Baby? Are you sure you like your present?"

"Yes, and I love you." She hugged Cleopatra tight, as if she was going to pop a ring out of her.

As the evening progressed, she tried to hide her disappointment. Jacqueline failed miserably. Cleopatra saw Jacqueline's eyes start to water, then she excused herself to the bathroom. Cleopatra decided not to torture her anymore.

"Sweetheart, please open the door." Cleopatra jiggled the door knob.

"No," Jacqueline said from the other side.

"What do you mean, no? If you don't open this door right now!" Cleopatra banged on the door.

"You will what?" she yelled back. "What are you going to do?" Jacqueline flung the bathroom door open.

Cleopatra was down on both knees, holding an open jewelry box. Resting inside it lay the largest diamond ring Jacqueline had ever seen. She covered her face with both hands.

"Sweetheart, I think this is the box you were expecting." Cleopatra smiled, looking up at her as she held the box up over her head.

Jacqueline kneeled down to the floor with Cleopatra, her eyes locked on the enormous princess-cut stone.

"Sweetheart. I never thought that I could love someone as much or as hard as I love you. I would do absolutely anything for you. I don't want to live without you. I can't live without you. I want to spend the rest of my life with you by my side. I want to grow old and sexy with you." Jacqueline trembled as Cleopatra took her hand and slid the ring on her finger. "Will you be my wife? Will you marry me?"

"Yes, baby, yes, yes, yes!" Jacqueline jumped into Cleopatra's arms.

"It's beautiful. It's huge. I love you so much baby." Jacqueline cried as she hugged Cleopatra tight. "I've wanted to be your wife since the day I met you." She kissed Cleopatra. "You were right. You got me. Now what are you going to do with me?"

◉ ◉ ◉

It had been two weeks since they announced their engagement. Most people they told were excited. Shawn, who would be Cleopatra's best woman, swore to wear white patent leather shoes no matter the color scheme, assuming she wasn't in prison on their wedding day. But not everyone shared their joy. Racquel displayed what Cleopatra called her "silent fury." Tired of that treatment, Cleopatra confronted Racquel at work.

Cleopatra leaned on the side of Racquel's desk. "So, what is your problem with this exactly?"

Racquel didn't look up from her computer screen. "I don't trust her, simple as that."

"Because of what happened before? Can you face me, please?" Racquel turned toward her. "You're still mad she lied about being married. I understand that. I had to work on my trust issues with her. But we've moved on from that. I love her, and she loves me."

"That, I don't question. I think she would do anything to be with you."

"So, what is the problem then?"

"You trust her now?" Racquel asked.

"If I didn't I wouldn't have asked her to marry me."

"So, you are really going to do this?"

"I am. I wish you would be happy for me."

"I want to be. But you know I'm stubborn and I can't keep my mouth shut. Jacqueline stays away from me now."

"What did you do?"

"After you got back together, I made it clear I didn't trust her. And I may have said something like I was here before her and I would be here after her. She hasn't looked me in the eyes since."

"You shouldn't have done that, Racquel. Not cool. You probably scared her – everyone knows you're a little nuts." Cleopatra smiled slightly.

"This is true," Racquel agreed.

"I don't want to be put in a situation where I have to choose."

"Oh. You won't." Racquel turned back to her computer and continued working.

Jacqueline had filled Cleopatra's house with wedding magazines and product samples. She'd changed into a different woman overnight. She knew Cleopatra loved her, but she was truly going to belong to her now. Being Cleopatra's wife was her dream come true.

"We have a lot to talk about," Jacqueline said to Cleopatra through the shower glass.

"What is it, baby?" Cleopatra turned off the water.

"We need to talk about the wedding, and make some decisions. Where we are going to have it, the guest list, the food, the ceremony, everything."

"We just set the date for June. Do we have to do this right now?" Cleopatra kissed her as Jacqueline wrapped the towel around her wet body.

"I want to, please?" Jacqueline pleaded.

"We can always elope." Cleopatra's suggestion didn't go over well. Subsequent conversations about wedding plans always ended badly. Cleopatra wanted to go to Vegas and do it. And Jacqueline who got married at city hall the first time wanted a fairy tale wedding.

Cleopatra gave in a few days later. "You can have whatever you want on two conditions," Cleopatra said. "You hire a wedding planner, because you aren't driving me crazy. And we have to get married in Hawaii." She handed Jacqueline a black card with her name on it and awaited her answer.

Jacqueline ran her thumb across her stamped name on the exclusive American Express card. "Deal." Jacqueline smiled and took the credit card.

That seemed to do the trick for the most part. Cleopatra was off the hook and Jacqueline was going to get everything she wanted.

Late one evening when Jacqueline and Cleopatra were making love on the living room floor – amidst scattered bridal publications – the doorbell rang.

"They aren't going away, baby. You have to answer it." Jacqueline pushed Cleopatra off of her. Cleopatra put on her clothes and stumbled to look out of the peephole. Kenya stood on the other side of the door. Just as Cleopatra was about to yell at her to go away she was reminded of Catherine's warning that Kenya would keep coming back again and again until she handled her. Cleopatra needed to deal with her. She opened the door.

"Hi. Can I come in?" Kenya pulled the scarf from around her neck.

"No. What do you want?"

"I'm stopping by as a courtesy to let you know that I will be filing a police report on your fiancée first thing in the morning. Yes, I know about the engagement."

"When I hadn't heard from you I thought you had decided to squash this?" Cleopatra asked.

"No, I was tied up with exams and the holidays, you know how it is. You made the wrong choice."

Jacqueline had gotten dressed and came to the door and stood beside Cleopatra.

"You want to take another whack at me? So I can stack my case, and add more prison time?" Kenya asked.

Jacqueline didn't respond. She squeezed Cleopatra's hand hard.

"This wedding is never going to happen. But don't worry. At the most, you'll get a year," Kenya said to Jacqueline. "I'll take good care of Cleopatra while you're gone." She rubbed her palms together. "And your kids will be fine. They won't go to foster care. They'll probably stay with your parents."

"What?" Cleopatra asked, confused. "What are you talking about?" Cleopatra felt Jacqueline's fingers loosen their grip.

"Her kids will be fine. They would place them with family before they'd put them in foster care."

Cleopatra looked at Jacqueline who had turned and walked back into the living room. From the look on Kenya's face she knew Kenya wasn't lying.

"Wait, wait," Kenya said, "Please, tell me you knew she had kids?"

"What the hell are you talking about? How do you know?" Cleopatra exhaled heavily. She was confused and couldn't think straight.

"I ran a background check on her. It's in her divorce records. She has full custody."

Cleopatra stared at the floor for a moment before snapping out of her silence. "Thanks, Kenya. You kept me from making a huge mistake. I have to go." She pushed her out the door.

"Wait. How could you not know? This is good. Maybe I won't need to file charges after all." She yelled into the house for Jacqueline to hear. "There is no way she is going to forgive you for this, you are giving her to me," she called, at the top of her lungs. "You know where to find me, baby." Kenya blew Cleopatra a kiss and left.

Cleopatra leaned against the door. She had lost the strength to hold her own body up. She wanted to yell, but nothing would come out. The wind had been knocked out of her. She went into the living room and stood across from Jacqueline who sat down on the couch. She rubbed her hands together and couldn't stop herself from pacing back and forth. Jacqueline refused to look at her. Cleopatra finally heard herself whisper.

"Look at me and say something."

Jacqueline's head was down between her knees. "Uhm."

Cleopatra watched her stutter as her body trembled. "Uhm? Yeah, uhm… this shit is true, isn't it? Say something!" she screamed at her.

"I've wanted to tell you forever." Jacqueline confessed as she looked up at her. Cleopatra's heart sank. She was up until that last second hoping that Kenya was lying. But Kenya had never lied to her. Jacqueline had. "It was never the right time, and I could never build up the courage. I have twins, a boy and a girl. They're three years old."

Cleopatra stared at her for a moment. Then she began calculating a timeline in her head. "So, they were one when we met?"

"Yeah, about."

Cleopatra snapped. "Who does that shit? Who hides their kids? Get out!" she yelled. "Get the fuck out of my house right now." She picked up Jacqueline's clothes and her bag and threw them outside on the steps. She stood in the doorway and held the door open.

"Cleopatra. Don't. Please just let me explain." Jacqueline reached for her.

"Get out! Don't touch me." Cleopatra barely refrained from balling up her fist, and smacked her hand away. Her voice found the bass she was looking for just a few minutes before. As soon as Jacqueline stepped across the threshold Cleopatra slammed the door hard behind her.

Cleopatra collapsed on the couch with dozens of questions crashing around in her head. How did she have three-year-old twins? Where were they? Who took care of them? Because it sure wasn't Jacqueline. She called her on her cell phone.

"We need to talk."

"Open the door." Jacqueline said.

Cleopatra ran to the door. Jacqueline was on the steps bundled up in her coat and shivering. Cleopatra pulled her inside. They sat back down in the living room.

"You had a fucking entire family the day we met, a husband and two children. When I found out you were married, why didn't you take that opportunity to say *hey, by the way, I got kids too?* Or even better, why didn't you tell me the day we met? Who is the father?"

"My ex-husband."

"Can you explain this to me? Why are they not with you? Where are they? How can you deny your children? For once, can you tell me the truth?"

"I'm not denying my children," she yelled at Cleopatra. "I love them, and I love you more than anything."

"If that were true, how come I didn't know about them? How can you profess to love me, but you still lie to me constantly?"

"Don't do that to me. You know that I love you." She exhaled deeply and fell back on the couch. "It was killing me, keeping this from you."

"Oh yeah, I could tell you were really suffering. Walking around with a forty thousand dollar engagement ring on your finger. Your life is real hard." Cleopatra leaned back on the couch.

"Forty?" Jacqueline looked down at her ring.

"Uhm hmm." Cleopatra nodded. "Go ahead, talk, but only if you are going to speak the truth."

"The truth is I got married because I got pregnant."

"You told me you got married because you thought you were supposed to in order to be happy, and you were trying not to be gay."

"That's the truth, but my babies were a big part of that. They sealed the decision. I wanted them to have a real family. I had them the summer before grad school. My mother had just retired from teaching, and she drove from Jersey to Brooklyn to take care of them every day while I was in class."

"Every day? That's a long commute." Cleopatra said.

"Very long, and later it became a problem. Anyway, something changed in me after I had my babies. Being responsible for their lives when I wasn't living the life that I wanted made me feel like a hypocrite. It tore me up inside. That's when I told my ex I was a lesbian."

"So, tell me the truth about how that really went down."

"My ex and I were friends at first. He liked me even though I had told him about my struggles with my sexuality. He thought that maybe if we had sex that would change my mind."

"And you fell for that? And didn't use a condom?"

"Yeah." She lowered her head. "I hated it immediately. After that, there was no doubt in my mind that I was gay. But I got pregnant."

"So, what happened after you told him you were gay?"

"He moved out and into the apartment upstairs and he had no interest in being a father or helping to support the twins. I had to leave school and go to work almost immediately. I got the job at Midtown, but I wasn't going to be making enough to support the three of us and have two kids in day care all day. My mother had been doing the commute a few months by that time and it was too much of a hassle and wearing her out. So, we decided it would be best if they stayed in Jersey while I got back on my feet and figured out what I was going to do and I would be the one going back and forth to spend time with them. I met you soon after my mom took the kids home with her."

"So that's where they've been, and your parents have been in on this whole secret?"

"Not by choice. My mom has been pissed with me about it ever since she found out I was keeping them from you. We argue about it constantly. Especially since Thanksgiving, and now the engagement. She threatened to tell you herself."

"So, you were going to marry me and not tell me? Were you going to spring the kids on me at the ceremony or after the honeymoon?" Cleopatra asked sarcastically.

"I was going to tell you."

"No you weren't. I don't understand why you lied in the first place. How could you keep this hidden from me for so long?"

"I was being selfish, there is no other explanation. It was the type of lie that there is no rebounding from once I told it. I wanted to confess to you so many times. And when we got back together, everything was so beautiful. It was perfect and I didn't want to ruin it by dropping this bomb on you."

"You call denying your children a bomb?"

"Stop saying that!" she yelled at Cleopatra. "I've never denied them. I'm a good mother and I love my children."

"You know, I don't doubt that you are a good mother, Jacqueline. I always thought you would be. I just hope you haven't wasted too much time chasing me around when you should have been with your kids."

"If I'm not with you, I'm with them, every other day. They are little pieces of my heart, walking around." Jacqueline's face lit up.

"Then why hide them from me?"

"I got scared of losing you."

"Where were they at Thanksgiving?" Cleopatra asked.

"They were with their other grandparents."

"What about on Christmas? Do they ever see their father?"

"No. When he left, he left. I spent all day with them on Christmas before I saw you that evening."

"You have been juggling us all this time? I don't understand how you could lie to me over something this big. You promised never to hurt me again."

"You said you weren't ready for kids."

"Don't blame me for this. I said that on our first date, and I wasn't ready for kids. But they are *your* kids. That's different."

"How is it different?"

"They are yours, and I love you, that automatically means I'd love them. How could you think I wouldn't get over your keeping them from me if you had come and told me yourself?"

"I didn't know you felt that way. But when we met that day on the train, if I had said I'm unhappily married with children, what would you have done?"

"I would have run kicking and screaming down the street mad that I couldn't have you."

"I wanted you to know that you could have me."

"So, you lied thinking that maybe you would just get you some and go back to your unhappy life two months later? That's what everyone told you, wasn't it?"

"They did tell me about your sixty-day rule, but that's not what I wanted from you and you know that. That first day on the train I know I could have had you that night."

Cleopatra raised her eyebrows.

"You know it's true. But I knew if I gave in too quickly you would never take me seriously. If I only wanted sex, if I only wanted two months from your life, I would have fucked you that first night. But how long did we wait?"

"Three months," Cleopatra answered.

"Exactly, on our three-month anniversary you made love to me. I was not after you for sex, you know that. I knew my situation prohibited me from having a chance with you. In a split second I made a bad decision and I lied. I'm sorry I kept this from you. But I would have done anything to have a chance."

"A chance at what? If you didn't want sex."

"A chance to make you fall in love with me, because on the day we met I was already in love with you." Cleopatra shook her head. "What is it?" Jacqueline asked.

"As much as you have lied to me, I believe you. But how am I supposed to get past your deception?"

"I've watched you with my little cousins and with Racquel's kids. They love you so much. Every time I saw you with them, it hurt my heart. I regretted not giving my kids the opportunity to know you and you know them."

"It's not about the kids. Don't you understand? I'm sure I would fall in love the moment I laid eyes on them."

"You will, baby." She interrupted. "I know they are going to love you."

"*If,* I was ever to meet them." Cleopatra continued. "But it's not about them. Like before – it's about your being a liar. I honestly still can't trust you. You know if you had sat me down even as late as tonight and said *Cleopatra I've been keeping something from you, I have two babies,* I would have forgiven you. That's how much I love you. Isn't that crazy? Even after everything that's happened, but that's not what you did, is it? You got busted again. Someone else had to come and tell me about your dirt again. I must really look like a fool to you."

"No, baby."

"Is there anything else that I need to know, anything more you are still keeping from me? This is the last time I'm going to ask you."

"There is nothing else, you know everything now. I swear to God." Jacqueline exhaled and lay back on the couch.

Cleopatra stood up and looked at Jacqueline. "Ok." Cleopatra exhaled. She rubbed her hands over her eyes.

Jacqueline stood up and moved to hug Cleopatra.

"I'm done. I need you to leave," Cleopatra said as she moved away from her.

Jacqueline surprised, stopped in her tracks. She covered her mouth as she burst into tears. Cleopatra walked out of the living to the front door and opened it. Jacqueline followed behind her and didn't protest. "There's one last thing you should know." Cleopatra said as Jacqueline stepped outside. "You and I, we're over."

TASHA C. MILLER

I STILL CAN'T HELP MYSELF/ KEEP SHAKING WHAT YOUR MAMA GAVE YA

"You ever think you have a problem with being alone?" Shawn asked Cleopatra.

"No, I don't think about it. Thank goodness I don't ever have to be alone. You ever think you have a problem fucking underage girls when you have a girlfriend?" Cleopatra was still angry with Shawn for catching a case.

"All right, Cleo. You've barely spoken to me since that night. Say what's on your mind. These little side jabs are getting real tired."

Cleopatra shook her head and took a deep breath. "What the fuck were you thinking? First of all you were cheating on

241

Robin, and you were just at her parents' house for Thanksgiving. And with a little girl? Really?"

"She didn't look sixteen."

"No, she looked seventeen! Still, too young for you to be fucking with. Tell the truth, you didn't really think she was twenty-one, did you?"

Shawn shrugged her shoulders and shook her head.

"Do you realize how serious this shit is? You could go to prison, you understand that? And whose idea was the cellphone video? Don't answer that."

"Given what you are doing, do you think you're being a little hypocritical right now?" Shawn asked.

It had been a few weeks since the breakup and Cleopatra had gone back to plugging the hole in her heart with ho's. It was even worse than the first time her and Jacqueline broke up. With Jacqueline out of the picture, and now the rift between her and Shawn, Cleopatra was becoming reckless.

Shawn went to visit Cleopatra early on a Sunday morning to try and repair their friendship, talk some sense into her, and maybe perform her version of an intervention.

"All the pussy I'm getting is of age. Thanks for your concern," Cleopatra said to Shawn.

"I know you're pissed at me right now. But I'm here anyway. You need to talk about Jacqueline. I hate what she did to you, but I hate how you're dealing with it even more. You're not healing yourself or getting over her. You aren't dealing with this at all."

They sat at the counter in Cleopatra's kitchen downing bowls of sweet and sugary cinnamon cereal. Cleopatra was unmoved by her pleas. Then Shawn heard footsteps in the house.

"Who the hell is that?" Shawn twisted her lips when she realized someone was walking around upstairs.

"Just wait." Cleopatra said, an enormous grin spread across her face.

"Is it Jacqueline?" Shawn smiled.

A tall, mocha woman in one of Cleopatra's white t-shirts came into the kitchen. Shawn recognized her immediately – she was a celebrity, of sorts – and Shawn covered her mouth in amazement.

"Cleopatra, I couldn't find my panties, so I put on your t-shirt, hope that's ok."

"Sure, but you weren't wearing any last night," Cleopatra reminded her. She looked at her erect double D's stab the thin cotton. "But if you rip my shirt with those things, you have to replace it." She joked.

"Oh, those?" She looked down. "They're always like that."

Cleopatra looked at Shawn, who was struggling to retain her composure.

"This is my best friend Shawn. She came over to check on me. Shawn, this is Cassidy."

"Nice to meet you, Shawn." Cassidy smiled, flipped her long black hair and extended her hand.

Cleopatra kicked Shawn in an attempt to get her to return the handshake. Shawn was in disbelief that their favorite porn star was in Cleopatra's kitchen half naked.

"No need to worry. I took real good care of her last night." She moaned in Cleopatra's ear. "Didn't I, baby?" She turned Cleopatra's stool around and stood between her legs and kissed her. Cleopatra slid her hands up her t-shirt and slapped her naked ass. She swallowed her lips as Cassidy grinded her pussy on her. Cassidy started to moan loudly.

"Uh…yeah. Still here." Shawn interrupted them. "Oh my God."

Cleopatra started to pull away but Cassidy pulled her back.

"She can watch if she wants." The porn star licked Cleopatra's neck. "You gonna fuck me again, daddy?"

"I'm gonna fuck the shit out of you." Cleopatra stuck her tongue out at her and looked at Shawn who was shaking her head.

Cleopatra laughed. "Go back to bed, baby. I'll be up in a little while."

"Ok. But I'm starving." Cassidy poured more milk and cereal into Cleopatra's bowl and took it with her. "Nice meeting you," she said to Shawn. "Don't keep her too long. I need her." She kissed Cleopatra. "I'll be upstairs in the bed, baby. Don't make me start without you."

"That's Cassidy! Why didn't you tell me?" Shawn squealed. "I think I wet myself." She rocked back and forth on the kitchen stool.

"You were too busy telling me how fucked up I am. I didn't want to interrupt you." Cleopatra smirked.

"How in the hell did you pull that? What is she doing in New York?" Shawn grinned, looking back to make sure Cassidy was gone.

"She's here on vacation, she's tired of L.A. I ran into her at the club last night. All the butches in there were hovering around her – it was embarrassing. She came over to me, and she asked me why I wasn't trying to get at her, like I had offended her. I said, *I'm your number one fan.* She said I didn't act like it. She was pissed. I told her that I had an incredible amount of self-control."

"Oh my God," Shawn said, excited. "How did you stay calm?"

"I didn't. She didn't know I had a puddle between my legs." Cleopatra laughed.

"So she grabs my hand, and she pulls me through the club, she backs me up into a corner, and tells me she wants to have sex right there."

"What did you say?"

"I said, you may get paid to fuck in public, but I don't. She was hot, like she was going to fight me. She was getting really turned on. Then she asked *what if I go home with you?* I said *I didn't ask you to.* That set it off, she was so heated. She dragged me out the club, and we've been fucking up until you rang the doorbell."

"So, how was it? Amazing? Crazy?"

"I saw the moon and the stars. I think at one point I lost my hearing and feeling in my tongue. She doesn't know the word *no*, or *stop*, or *that hurts*, or *don't*, or *that's too big*. She let me do everything to her. Oh my God. And she did this thing with my hair." Cleopatra grabbed a handful of her locs and showed them to Shawn. "Remind me to wash this section right here."

"What is all of that white shit? Eww...no, she didn't."

"Nasty, right?" Cleopatra beamed. "I could quite possibly be in love."

"You could quite possibly be beyond saving."

◘ ◘ ◘

Six a.m. and Cleopatra had just left Cassidy's hotel after an all-night marathon. She was headed home when her cell rang. She saw Robin's number on the caller I.D.

Ugh...what does she want?

"Hey, what's wrong? You know it's six in the morning, right?"

"I'm sorry to call you so early. Have you talked to Shawn?"

"Not since yesterday."

"I can't find her. We had a fight. She broke up with me, and now she's not answering my calls. Can you please check on her?"

"Yeah, of course. I'll call you when I know something."

Cleopatra jumped on the train and was outside of Shawn's building within the hour.

"What brings you all the way uptown?"

"You got anything to eat? Some juice?" Cleopatra looked in her fridge. "I had a rough night." She rummaged through the expired food. "No wonder you're always eating at my house. Damn. Anyway, your girl called me. She's worried about you."

"She's not my girl anymore, and I'm fine."

"You look like shit."

"She kept Jacqueline's kids a secret from me, too. That's a problem."

"She had no choice. It couldn't have been easy for Robin. There would be no way she could tell you and you not tell me.

245

Don't be so hard on her, you love her. More than you realize. That can't be the only reason you fought. What else happened?"

"I started feeling guilty as hell about this case. So I told her."

"Everything?"

"I told her I cheated. I didn't tell her I'll probably end up in prison. She was really hurt, I mean you should have seen her face. She looked like I kicked her in the stomach, but she forgave me, right there on the spot. That's when it hit me, that this woman really loves me and I fucked up."

Cleopatra shook her head. "Exactly."

"I couldn't take the guilt so I picked a fight with her. I told her that I gave you permission to fuck her, back when you were trying to get back at Jacqueline."

"Oh." Cleopatra leaned against the refrigerator. "Why did you do that? Keep my name out of your mouth. Can you do that?" Cleopatra sighed. "You have to fix this. Where else are you going to find a woman like her to put up with your ass? She never tried to burn your house down. She's never called the cops on you, and you never had to take a restraining order out on her, I mean the woman learned to eat pussy for you. And your mama likes her, and your mama don't like nobody." Cleopatra laughed. "Do you see where I'm going with this? You need to work this shit out."

"We were talking about moving in together," Shawn admitted.

"That's big." Cleopatra said. "You don't like anybody in your space."

"How did we get mixed up with these crazy sisters?"

"Cause they're fine as hell and they put it on us." Cleopatra said. "Get dressed and I'll take you to breakfast 'cause ain't shit to eat in here. I'll call Robin and tell her I found you in Hunts Point doing two-dollar hand jobs." Cleopatra joked. "She's a good woman, you know this. Think before you throw it away."

"Look who's talking," Shawn shot back.

"My situation is so different. Jacqueline lied to me about everything."

"Yeah, but are you going to throw it all away over that? Do you call yourself punishing her because she told mad lies just to be with you? You are not looking so happy yourself right now."

"I'm just tired. I had a long night. Cassidy is literally a fucking machine. I'm so glad she lives on the West Coast. Some food and I'll be good. Go wash your ass, so I can get me some eggs."

"Seriously, Cleopatra. Why are you fucking with these other women trying to get over Jacqueline when it's not humanly possible? You're not chemically equipped to get over that woman. You were about to marry her. She fucked up bad, twice, real bad, but that woman loves the hell out of you. She put you above everything, even her own kids. You seriously need to consider moving past this shit. I mean there is nothing else for her to lie about. Robin swore to me that you know everything now. And their timelines and stories line up." Cleopatra shook her head, not wanting to hear her best friend plead Jacqueline's case. "Go to couples counseling or something. I know you're still angry now, but it's going to wear off, and then what?"

Cleopatra called Robin while Shawn hopped in to the shower.

"Hey, she's ok. I'm going to take her to breakfast. She needs a little time. I'll try to get her to call you later. I just didn't want you to worry."

"Thanks so much, Cleopatra."

"She loves you. She's just mad right now, that's all. I tried to explain your position."

"We can work this out if she'll just talk to me," Robin said. "You know, my sister is so depressed without you. She's walking around half dead."

"We're not talking about Jacqueline."

"No, we aren't. Just as long as you heard me."

A few days later Shawn had still not made up with Robin, and Shawn and Cleopatra each got a phone call from Pops. He wanted to talk to both of them separately about their relationships with his daughters. Shawn punched Cleopatra in the arm when she accepted. "It might be a trick. Get the two women who are making his daughters miserable and chop them up and bury them in his backyard."

"Cleopatra!" Mr. Tripp said as he came in to her office. "Good to see you." He gave her a big hug and kiss and sat down in front of her desk.

"You too, sir." Cleopatra swallowed hard.

"None of that *sir* stuff. I told you to call me Pops. I'll get right down to why I called you."

"Uh oh." Cleopatra leaned back in her desk chair.

"Jacqueline doesn't know about this meeting. She would be mortified if she knew, so let's keep this between us."

"No worries." Cleopatra nodded her head.

"I'm not going to tell you that you should take my daughter back. What she did was unforgivable and it's hard to forgive the unforgivable, but that's what you'll have to do for you two to move on together."

"It is unforgivable, but who said anything about our being together?" Cleopatra asked.

"Do you know how long Jacqueline's mom and I have been together?"

"Thirty years?"

"Married thirty-two years, together for thirty-seven and I've known her for forty years. Take it from me as someone who has been with and married to the same woman forever. When you love someone hard, really hard, forgiveness must come with it. Now that doesn't mean that you are saying what she did was ok, it means you accept it for what was and you are going to move on past it. I want you to think about if her mistakes of hiding those babies was big enough to change the course of your lives, because that's what it comes down to. Both of you are being punished for her mistake. She's hurting, you are hurting. Those babies are hurting because their mother is a shell without you and because they don't know you and they should. Trust me, I've made some mistakes and had to be forgiven. No need to get into details. But when you are in a loving relationship, and you have committed to one another, you just don't leave. You asked me for permission to marry my daughter and I gave you my blessing. And I meant it. Are you happy with the way things are right now? Do you want them to continue this way? Would you be happy with someone else?"

"If I'm honest with myself, no, I'm not happy right now. I can't say I see myself being truly happy with someone else, not like I was with Jac, maybe not ever." Cleopatra admitted.

"Jacqueline feels the same. She has the babies now, if you didn't know. She moved them back to Brooklyn with her. You and those kids are her life, and without you as part of her family, I'm worried about my daughter."

Cleopatra hadn't even begun to clear her head and straighten out her thoughts from her conversation with Jacqueline's dad, when Jacqueline's mother called her at work a few days later.

"Are you available for coffee?" she asked.

"For you? Anything. When and where?" Cleopatra asked.

"How about your office in an hour?"

Racquel buzzed her. "Jacqueline's mom is here. What's going on? First the dad, now the mom."

"They want me back with their daughter. Keep your stun gun out." Cleopatra laughed.

"Hi Moms." Cleopatra gave her a hug and a kiss. "Please, have a seat. What brings you all the way into the city?"

"I just happened to be in the area." She sat down on Cleopatra's leather couch.

Cleopatra didn't look convinced. "Uh huh." She poured her a cup of coffee.

"Ok, I just came from visiting Jacqueline and the children, I miss those babies so much. They are at day care at her job. You remember, just a few blocks that way." She pointed uptown. "But you know that already don't you?"

"Yeah. I'm aware of that." Cleopatra nodded, not sure of how much her mother knew about the details. "I'm happy she is back with them. It's the right thing to do. How is she?" Cleopatra placed the coffee on the table in front of Moms.

"You should go and see for yourself."

"I don't think that would be a good idea."

"She misses you."

"Uhm…yeah. So, what can I do for you? I know you didn't come just to tell me your daughter misses me or for some coffee."

"No, and please don't mention that I came to see you. She'd kill me."

"No worries." Cleopatra assured her.

"I didn't come to tell you to take Jacqueline back, or about the sadness in her eyes now that you two are broken up again. Or even that she is still wearing her engagement ring." She took a sip of coffee.

"She is?"

"Of course. I wouldn't take it off either, that's the most beautiful ring I've ever seen. But there is something else that's troubling me." She hesitated. "She's still planning the wedding."

"What wedding?" Cleopatra did a double take.

"She's waiting for you, Cleopatra. She said you never called the wedding off explicitly, and you never asked for your ring back. That you didn't ask for anything back. She's planning it like she's convinced it's going to happen one day."

"You have to stop her."

"I will keep trying, but she's waiting. She's just waiting. You may be the only one who can convince her not to. She will need to hear the words from you. If it is truly over between you two. Is it?" she asked. "Think about the message you're sending her. You didn't ask for your house key, or the ring back, and you didn't cut off her credit card."

Cleopatra had no intentions of cutting off Jacqueline's credit card after she saw charges for the children's daycare on the account. She knew Jacqueline couldn't afford to take care of the three of them and make the daycare payments without going hungry. Regardless of where they stood now, she refused to have her want for anything. So she let the charges go through, and she paid for their daycare monthly. She wasn't sure if Jacqueline was testing her to get a reaction or what. And

Cleopatra never contacted her about it, she just paid it. Maybe that's why Jacqueline was holding on.

"I guess I'll leave you to think," her mother said. "Anyway I've missed you. I wanted to see how you were doing. You are still family, no matter what."

Later that night Kenya rang Cleopatra's doorbell. She hadn't spoken to her since she dropped the bomb about Jacqueline's kids, but Cleopatra was ready for her.

Kenya walked in to the foyer. "I had been expecting to hear from you long before now."

"Why is that?" Cleopatra played with her cell phone.

"I know you and Jacqueline aren't together anymore, so…"

"You thought I would immediately run back to you?" Cleopatra leaned on the front door, which she had left partially open. The cold air was moving into the house.

"I'm going to the police and pressing charges against her."

"Oh my God. File the damn charges already." Cleopatra threw her hands up in the air. "I don't give a fuck what you do. Just leave me the hell alone."

"You've had a change of heart." Kenya looked confused. "You were begging me not to do it before."

"That was then. I don't care anymore. We aren't together. Send her to prison." Cleopatra paced back and forth.

"Well, then, there's no reason for me to go to the cops. I was trying to break you two up."

"Well, your plot to blackmail me is not necessary anymore. All over a silly spat in a bathroom. You and I both know that wasn't assault."

"I know it wasn't assault. I was charging toward her when she punched me. Any half-witted attorney would have argued self-defense and got her off. Now that you don't want her, I guess there's no need to take this further. You made this so much harder than it needed to be, Cleopatra." She sighed. "You should have just given in when I first threatened you with the charges. But I got what I wanted. Her away from you."

"And I got what I wanted, thanks. You can leave now." Cleopatra showed Kenya to the open door.

251

The next day she emailed the audio of their conversation to Kenya, Catherine and Jacqueline. Catherine assured her that with the audio as insurance and evidence, Jacqueline needn't worry about Kenya trying to send her to prison, and if she tried, the audio would immediately discredit her and ruin her chances of having any type of legal career. Jacqueline called Cleopatra to thank her.

"Your children need you. I did it because it was the right thing to do. That's all."

Cleopatra's mother's birthday arrived. Cleopatra was at home alone and wondering when the pain of losing her would subside. Her doorbell rang several times, but she refused to answer. Moments later, she heard a key in the door.

"What are you doing here?"

"I had a feeling you needed me," Jacqueline said. Cleopatra's eyes were red, and Jacqueline could tell she'd been crying. Jacqueline pulled her into her arms and held her.

"It's ok," she repeated as she rubbed her back and Cleopatra cried in her arms.

"Come on." Jacqueline took her upstairs to the bathroom where she wiped her face. "Whenever I cry I always feel better if I get in the shower and let the water rain over my face. You can cry as hard as you want and it just washes your tears away."

Cleopatra nodded her head and started to undress. Jacqueline started the shower for her. "I'll be here when you get out." Jacqueline walked out of the bathroom and waited for her on the bed.

"I feel a lot better." Cleopatra wrapped a towel around herself as she came out of the bathroom. "Do you do that a lot?"

"Every night now." She tried to avert her eyes from Cleopatra's wet body.

"Thank you. It means a lot to me that you remembered and that you came."

"Have I ever not been here when you needed me?"

"No, never." Cleopatra smiled. "Where are the babies?"

252

"With Grandma and Grandpa." She beamed. "That's the first time you've ever asked about them."

"I'm glad they're home with you. Are you doing ok?"

"No, I'm not. I know that's not what you want to hear." She put her head in her hands.

Cleopatra walked over to her and bent down and tried to kiss her, but Jacqueline moved away. "What is it?"

"That's not why I came, I'm not a booty call, Cleopatra."

"Of course you aren't. But, you said it was mine."

"It is, still. But we aren't together. If you are taking me back, and we are going to work this out, you can have me right now. Can you do that? Because I'm not having a one-night stand." Jacqueline was angry. Cleopatra was silent. "That's what I thought." Jacqueline got up to leave.

"I'm sorry. Please don't leave. I don't want to be alone, not tonight."

Something happened in that moment. Cleopatra had leaned on Jacqueline. She was vulnerable, something Jacqueline had rarely witnessed. She allowed Jacqueline to see her like that even though she was no longer her woman.

Jacqueline immediately regretted turning Cleopatra down. Cleopatra dropped her towel and began to get dressed. Jacqueline saw Cleopatra's necklace dangling between her breasts as she put on a fresh wife beater and some basketball shorts, usually all Jacqueline needed to drive her crazy. That hadn't changed. Jacqueline couldn't get over that despite everything that had happened, Cleopatra still wore her half-heart pendant.

Cleopatra couldn't take her eyes off Jacqueline's engagement ring.

"Along with your house key and the black card. You haven't offered to give it back." Cleopatra pointed to the ring.

"You haven't asked for it back. You haven't cut off the card, and you haven't changed the locks. And the ring? Doesn't matter, you'd have to cut my arm off to get this ring back because we are not over. I'm never taking this ring off."

"That's fine by me," Cleopatra said.

That night, they fell asleep in each other's arms in the bed they used to share. The next morning Cleopatra woke up alone with a note on her pillow.

It has always and will forever be you.

I love you.

FAKE JAC

"They were fucking separated at birth," Cleopatra said when she saw her at the party. "Or have I had too much to drink tonight?" she asked Shawn as she sipped on a glass of merlot.

"You've had too much to drink. But she could be Jac and Robin's sister, though. Like if you squint. I see it," Shawn said. "Stay far away from her. She is bound to be trouble." She took a sip of her Jack Daniels.

Cleopatra spotted Mandisa Lerato Botha at a company event at the Metropolitan Museum of Art, but managed to avoid her the entire night. Mandisa, New York City's newest real estate developer, was born in South Africa, raised in London, and from a wealthy family. She was draped in a red backless gown that hugged the subtle curves of her body.

The party in the Temple of Dendur wing was an elaborate display of excess. Orange spotlights illuminated the ancient Egyptian monument. Hundreds of tea lights at the tables and on nearly every flat surface made the room glow like one giant flame. The band played show tunes and partiers talked loudly as they downed handcrafted hors d'oeuvres that were much too pretty to be eaten.

Cleopatra made numerous rounds through the black tie event, mingling with people she didn't know and people she didn't like. She stayed on the move, slipping away from her newest admirer anytime she came near. Ms. Botha hawked Cleopatra all evening, all but blatantly running after her as she maneuvered through the crowds of people.

"It's the suit." Shawn rubbed Cleopatra's lapel.

"It is a beast, isn't it?" Cleopatra said of her black velvet and satin ensemble.

Every time Cleopatra turned around she found the woman who reminded her of Jacqueline either staring at her or making her way toward her.

Cleopatra and Shawn decided to duck out early. "I feel like I went to the gym," Cleopatra said of all of her running around during the party. She took two steps at a time as they ran out of the front entrance on to Fifth Avenue.

"It's good you dodged that." Shawn slapped her on the back. "She's bad, man."

"Cleopatra Giovanni?" Cleopatra heard someone call her name in a thick British accent. "Cleopatra." She and Shawn turned around and stopped on the steps.

"It's Fake Jac." Shawn nudged her. She walked quickly down the stairs, toward them.

"Don't call her that." Cleopatra laughed. "Actually, she doesn't really look that much like Jacqueline. I guess my mind was playing tricks on me."

"Or maybe Jacqueline is just on your mind." Shawn smirked.

"Take your time," Cleopatra said as she watched the woman take each step thoughtfully in her Alexander McQueens. "How did you know my name?"

"How could I not know your name?" She extended her hand.

"And you are?" Cleopatra shook her hand. She was relieved that the woman looked nothing like Jacqueline up close.

"Mandisa Lerato Botha. *Dit is 'n plesier om uiteindelik maak jou bekendes* Cleopatra."

Cleopatra shook her head. "I'm sorry, what language was that?"

"Sure wasn't Spanish," Shawn laughed.

"It's Afrikaans. I said it's a pleasure to finally make your acquaintance."

"Oh." Cleopatra knew then and there that her accent would eventually drive her wild. "That's a beautiful name, what does it mean?"

"I'd love to tell you, some other time. In private maybe?"

Cleopatra looked at Shawn who was standing shoulder to shoulder with her, and staring at the woman.

"Excuse me." Shawn coughed as she walked down the steps to the sidewalk.

"I haven't been able to keep my eyes off of you all night." Mandisa continued.

"I noticed." Cleopatra smiled. She studied Mandisa, who only vaguely reminded her of Jacqueline now that she was up close and the overpriced wine was wearing off. They were the same height with long black hair but Jacqueline was much more voluptuous and sensual than Mandisa. Cleopatra didn't want to bite Mandisa's ass or bury her face in her breasts nearly as much as she did the first time she met Jacqueline. Mandisa was lean, so Cleopatra decided she probably didn't cook and wouldn't want it rough.

"You noticed my gaze and yet you didn't come to me. *Hoekom is dit?*"

"Ok, the Afrikaan-glish thing you are doing isn't really working for me. It's freezing out here, and you don't have your coat. You should probably head back inside," Cleopatra said.

"I'm a big girl, I'll be fine. Please answer my question."

"What did you ask me?" Cleopatra felt herself losing patience and on the verge of becoming rude.

"I asked why you didn't approach me."

"I'm not sure," Cleopatra lied. "There's no need to be offended."

"I'm far from it, I'm more confused because there is an energy between us and if you find me even half as attractive as I find you, you should have been talking to me hours ago."

A British accent. She's aggressive, impolite, almost bitchy. That's kinda hot.

"You didn't come over to meet me either," Cleopatra fought back.

"It wasn't like I didn't try. Plus I was consumed with figuring out if I could handle the consequences of being with you."

"And what did you come up with?" Cleopatra tried to hide how turned on she was getting and reminded herself to use that line at her next opportunity.

"I can handle you." Mandisa smirked.

"That may or may not be true, but I would have to allow you to handle me and right now you don't have my permission. Enjoy your evening." Cleopatra turned and continued down the steps.

◎ ◎ ◎

A few days later the CEO of Midtown Properties, Maxim Kelly, stopped by to pay Cleopatra a visit in her office. The tall, rail-thin, closeted executive had taken an extra special liking to Cleopatra shortly after he hired her. Cleopatra ran into him late one night as he exited a Village leather bar. Cleopatra never spoke a word to his wife, his associates or even to him about it. And for that, she was particularly untouchable in the company.

"We are courting a potential new client. She's got us by the balls. Literally." Maxim sat down in front of Cleopatra's desk. "Every firm in the Northeast is after her money, I mean, her business."

"No, you mean her money." Cleopatra laughed. "Say what you mean, Maxim."

"If we can sign a deal with her we can expand our international reach. Besides that, she wants to buy up New

York City and that would help us secure the number one spot on the East Coast."

"Where do I come in? This sounds like business development. You know I'm not into ass licking." Cleopatra raised her eyebrows. "Wait. You are trying to pimp me out. Is she African American or gay?"

"She's African and she's gay. But she asked for you specifically. She knows you. And obviously wants to know more." Maxim winked at her.

Cleopatra sat down in her chair and tried not to panic. There were a lot of women in her past with the type of money he was talking about, and a reunion with one of them was the last thing she wanted.

"I thought if you met with her maybe you could sway her business in our direction, if you warmed her up to us."

"So, you want me to supply some heat?" Cleopatra smiled.

"What you do or don't do is your business. She asked for a formal introduction and a meeting with you."

"So, what's her name? Do I get a bio or something?"

"Mandisa Lerato Botha."

Shit. "You are so going to owe me. When is this happening?"

"She'll be at the board meeting this afternoon. I hope you don't have any plans tonight."

Cleopatra and Racquel stood talking in the corner of the boardroom waiting for the call to order when Jacqueline walked in. Racquel's first reaction was to run up on her, and thrash her. Racquel hadn't seen her since Cleopatra found out about her secret children. Luckily, Cleopatra caught Racquel by the arm.

"What is she doing here?" Racquel fumed.

Cleopatra was unaffected and took a swig of water. "That's not her."

"Of course it is."

"I'm serious, it's not." Cleopatra said.

Racquel looked closer. "Oh my God. It's not."

Mandisa walked over to Cleopatra and took both of her hands into hers.

"We meet again, Ms. Giovanni." She was glowing.

Cleopatra scanned her body. She was stunning in a white pants suit and red high heels. Her hair was slicked back into a bun.

"It's Cleopatra, please." She caressed her velvet hands.

"Only if you call me Disa." She winked at Cleopatra. "Your presence brings me light." Disa looked out at the thunderstorms that had kept the sun from making an appearance that day, and Cleopatra heard a crack of thunder as Disa pressed her middle finger hard into her palm.

Maxim swooped over to greet her and introduce her. "Ms. Botha, this is Cleopatra Giovanni."

"I got this. Thanks," Cleopatra whispered to him.

"I'm very much looking forward to our evening together." Disa smiled.

"I can't wait," Cleopatra lied.

"Mandisa barely took her eyes off of you the entire meeting." Racquel beamed. "I like her."

"You like her because she's African." Cleopatra watched Racquel who was studying Disa. "Hey." Cleopatra waved her hand in front of Racquel's face. "If you are thinking that we are going to get together, forget it. She reminds me of Jacqueline. It creeps me out."

Immediately after the meeting, Mandisa swept Cleopatra away in her chauffeured limousine. Cleopatra was determined to end the evening as soon as possible, and without ending up in bed with her.

"I've learned from my sources that you love Indian food, so my assistant made reservations at what is inarguably the best Indian restaurant in the city." Mandisa smiled as she put her hand on Cleopatra's thigh.

In an instant Cleopatra flashed back to old times when limos were her only source of transportation. Back when she was a commodity, a machine used only for pleasure by wealthy women. "Sounds great." Cleopatra looked up through the moon roof at the night sky. The limousine annoyed her. And what was her idea of the best Indian restaurant in the city? No one could beat the NY Dosa food stand in Washington Square Park. Cleopatra had already decided she would hate dinner.

They arrived at the restaurant on West 24th Street, in the Flatiron district. Cleopatra was further aggravated by the blandness of the restaurant's décor. White, cream and tan was not the color palette that came to mind when she thought of her favorite restaurants in Manhattan's Little India neighborhood. Mandisa took her by the hand as they were escorted through the restaurant to a private dining room in the back.

"I didn't want you to have to choose." She locked her arm inside of Cleopatra's. "You can have it all." Mandisa had arranged for the preparation of the entire menu.

The small but intimate back room was in sharp contrast to the main dining room of the restaurant. A gargantuan crystal and gold chandelier hung in the center of the room, but in the windowless room its dozens of bulbs let off just enough light to move about. Cleopatra thought whoever dimmed the lights that low was trying too hard to be sexy, and with no windows she didn't plan on being in there any longer than she needed to. Red and gold silk panels lined the walls and puddled down on the floor. On one side of the room sat a long banquet table draped with a red and gold embroidered silk, the table was covered in gold serving dishes full to the rim with every entrée and appetizer on the restaurant's menu. The dishes were surrounded by dozens of tea lights making the dark room flicker and glow. Along the opposite wall was a long sofa that didn't match anything, Cleopatra thought. The black leather sofa looked more like a daybed and was especially out of place, with several different shaped gold lame pillows thrown indiscriminately across it. It was clear that Disa had arranged for the sofa in the room. What she thought was going to happen back there Cleopatra wasn't entirely clear on yet. Gold place settings were carefully set up on a small round table for two between the sofa and the food. Its white tablecloth was illuminated under the subtle light of the chandelier. Hindustani music began to play softly in the background as they were seated. By this time the smell of curry, turmeric and garam masala had tortured Cleopatra to the point that she didn't care what Disa's intentions were, she was hungry. She loaded up her plate with her favorites, aloo gobi, dal makhani, samosas and pakoras. Cleopatra waited for Disa to sit at the table and begin eating before she dug in to her own plate. The evening's desired outcome was made a bit more obvious when Disa told the wait staff that they required no further assistance, and that they shouldn't be disturbed.

It was obvious Mandisa was trying hard to impress Cleopatra. But Cleopatra was not moved. "Used to the finer things in life, are you?" Mandisa asked.

"I have been a few places and seen a few things. I'm sorry, please don't think I don't appreciate all of the trouble this must have been. I do, very much so."

Mandisa didn't know she had a better chance of turning Cleopatra off with her extravagance than turning her on. Despite her trying so hard, Cleopatra liked Disa and despite her best efforts she was attracted to her. Their conversation was lively. She was funny and smart as hell. She was sexy and seductive and had a dirty mouth that came across a bit more innocently because of her accent. Cleopatra decided that she was fuckable only with some sort of bag or Halloween mask over her face. Only then could she tear that ass up, she thought to herself. Mandisa didn't look like Jacqueline, but she still reminded Cleopatra of her. Or maybe Shawn was right, she just had Jacqueline on her mind.

At just about every opportunity, Mandisa made it clear how into and how attracted she was to Cleopatra. Mandisa was hands on, touching Cleopatra and making sure she was inside her personal space most of the evening. Cleopatra felt conflicted. For the most part, she enjoyed the conversation, even Disa's controlled flirting and gentle innuendo. But as the evening progressed, the tone changed.

"There are two things you should know about me," Disa said. "I don't believe in casual sex. I only have sex within the confines of a committed and monogamous relationship."

Cleopatra nodded her head in acknowledgment of the unsolicited information. "And the second thing I should know?" she asked.

"That I'm willing to break that rule with you if necessary."

"If necessary?" Cleopatra repeated. She rubbed her temples with her fingers and took a sip of her mango lassi. "So, what should I do with this information?"

Mandisa laughed. "Just remember it as you figure out how you want this evening to end."

"Speaking of which, I actually have to rise early tomorrow." Cleopatra looked at her watch. "So, I should really see you home soon."

"I understand." Mandisa said, clearly disappointed. "Whatever you like."

"Do you really mean that? Whatever I like?"

"I do." She licked her lips and moved toward Cleopatra.

"Can we ditch the limo?"

"Really? What do you suggest?" She sat back, examining Cleopatra.

"In the long run, maybe consider a sedan. You were complaining earlier about how long it took to get here. A sedan could get through traffic easier. But right now I'd love to see you on the subway. That would be sexy. Have you ridden the train yet?"

"No. It's filthy. Isn't it?"

"That's a strong word. I prefer grimy. You are getting on the subway," Cleopatra informed her. "No one knows who you are, you'll be fine." She didn't think that Disa would actually go along with it.

Mandisa immediately called her driver and gave him the rest of the night off. She called her assistant and asked her to arrange for a Rolls-Royce Phantom by the next morning.

"It's nine o'clock at night," Cleopatra whispered to her. "You think she might need just a little more time?"

"Of course." Mandisa agreed and asked her assistant to acquire the new car as soon as she could arrange it. Cleopatra smiled as she watched her end her phone call.

263

"I'm not sure how I feel about you telling me what to do and my doing it so easily," Mandisa said, as Cleopatra held the restaurant door open. The cold winter air shocked Mandisa. Cleopatra helped her wrap her scarf.

"Nothing about you appears easy to me," Cleopatra said. "Are you prone to putting up a fight?"

"I can be difficult at times. But I don't seem to be able to tell you *no*, which concerns me."

Cleopatra smiled. "No reason to be scared. So, you'll get on the train with me?"

"I think I'd go anywhere with you." She grabbed Cleopatra's arm as they walked toward the train station.

"Where do you live?" Cleopatra asked.

"The West Village." Disa smiled.

Cleopatra prayed Mandisa, who was very new to the city, had gotten her neighborhoods mixed up, but her heart sank when she realized she knew exactly where she was going. Cleopatra walked Disa up the steps to her townhouse and looked across the street and three doors down at her own front door.

"So, in the morning should I come across the street for breakfast?" Mandisa wrapped her arms around Cleopatra and kissed her. Cleopatra's body shook as she kissed Mandisa back. She wasn't sure how to exit quickly without falling down the steps.

"Would you like to come in?" Mandisa asked, pulling on Cleopatra's coat. "Just for a minute."

"I don't do anything just for a minute," Cleopatra teased. "And what about your rules?"

"You mean the ones that were meant to be broken?"

"It's been a wonderful evening. Thank you so much for dinner. I'm sure I'll see you soon." Cleopatra ran into her house, stripped naked, and jumped into a cold shower. She didn't sleep well at all that night and at five-thirty the next morning her doorbell rang.

"Good morning, Ms. Giovanni. I'm Ms. Botha's chef, Jean Michel. She wanted to ensure that you had a good, hot breakfast before work this morning. May I enter and set this up for you?"

Cleopatra stood with her mouth open. "Uhm...sure, you can set it up in the living room." She stood back and rubbed her eyes. Cleopatra watched as the short, muscular African set up her breakfast of scrambled eggs, waffles, sausage, fruit, granola, freshly squeezed orange juice, coffee, and a mimosa on a crystal plate with sterling silverware.

"Thank you, chef." Cleopatra reached for her wallet and was stopped by his smile as he shook his head.

"No, thank you. I am well taken care of. It was my pleasure. Please enjoy your meal."

Cleopatra saw Disa at work later that day. She smiled from ear to ear when Cleopatra thanked her for the best breakfast she'd ever had. A few days later Disa signed a contract for an undisclosed amount with Midtown. Mandisa Lerato Botha wasn't going away anytime soon.

From the moment she laid eyes on Cleopatra, Mandisa pursued her hard, but Cleopatra refused to lay a hand on her. Weeks passed, and everyone fell in love with Mandisa. Everyone but Cleopatra.

"What's wrong with her besides she reminds you of Jacqueline?" Racquel asked. "Ok, she reminds everyone of Jacqueline."

"Nothing, she's perfect," Cleopatra said. She kept trying to find fault with Disa, but failed every time.

"You are going to have to get over that shit or just go back to Jacqueline," Shawn said.

On a Saturday afternoon Mandisa kidnapped Cleopatra under the guise that she wanted to show off her newly attained subway riding skills. But before Cleopatra knew better, she was standing in the foyer of Mandisa's parent's penthouse, and being introduced as her girlfriend.

Cleopatra was furious but managed to keep calm throughout the entire visit, even when she learned of the surprise dinner.

"We usually dress for dinner so I excused your appearance," Disa told Cleopatra as they walked into her parent's grand dining room.

Cleopatra stopped and looked at Disa, who wore a conservative black dress that cut off right at the knee and then she looked down at her own clothes. Cleopatra had on a dark gray cashmere sweater, black jeans and black Louboutin sneakers. "What are you talking about? I look good," she said annoyed. "Would I have worn this if I knew I was going to meet my girlfriend's parents? No. Because number one," she held up her thumb, "I didn't know I was coming here. And two," she held up her index finger, "you aren't my girlfriend. Let's just get this over with."

Cleopatra held her tongue through the elaborate three-course meal and didn't expose Disa. She was her usual charming self and Disa's parent's seemed to adore her. The succulent filet mignon served as the main course had tempered her anger, but as soon as they left Cleopatra called Disa on her stunt in the middle of the street.

"I wanted to introduce you to my parents because I'm falling for you. I didn't think you would agree if I told you the truth. Are you really upset?"

"You don't blindside people like that. I hate being lied to. I'm not your girlfriend. How do you even think that? I haven't even touched you yet. You need to stop falling. Never mind. I can't do this with you anymore." Cleopatra walked off and left her on the street alone.

Days slipped by, and Cleopatra stayed to herself, no Jacqueline and no fake Jac. She was getting used to the solitary life and liking it when Cassidy showed up at her door unannounced, fresh off the plane from Los Angeles. She was just in time for Cleopatra to work her frustrations out on her, and laugh in her face when Cassidy said she wanted to be her girl and needed their relationship to be exclusive. "Are you serious? How does one have an exclusive relationship with a porn star?" Cleopatra asked sarcastically. That didn't go over well, and ended with Cassidy storming out of Cleopatra's house with her feelings hurt.

Late one evening after work as Cleopatra approached her house, she spotted someone sitting on her doorstep. In the dark she couldn't tell if it was Mandisa or Jacqueline. She hoped it was Jacqueline. The pain of missing her outweighed her anger now. It was Mandisa.

"You know I haven't been able to have a moment's peace since I met you."

"I'm sorry to hear that." Cleopatra put her key in the door.

"Cute keychain." Disa pointed to the worn Scooby Doo charm dangling from her keys.

"Thanks." Cleopatra fingered the small Scooby that Jacqueline had given her on their first date. Like the heart charm necklace, she never let go of that key chain.

"I heard you were engaged," Disa said. "I could tell you were hurting. I wish you would let me help ease the pain."

"I don't need your help with anything, especially not with that," Cleopatra said, standing in her doorway.

"I also found out why it's hard for you to look at me. And why you've never touched me."

"You talked to Racquel, didn't you? She has a big mouth."

"She cares about your happiness, as I do. Does it really bother you to look at me?"

"No, I'm fine."

"Then look at me." Disa stepped inside the house and got in Cleopatra's face. "I'm not her. I would never hurt you."

"What do you want from me?"

"Right this minute? You know what I want. We can talk about my being in love with you in the morning."

◉ ◉ ◉

"You fucked her?"

"No." Cleopatra laughed.

"Yes, you did! Stop lying," Shawn yelled.

"Seriously, I didn't. We were going strong, it was getting serious. We were both naked on the living room floor, but I couldn't get the room dark enough. It was like being with Jacqueline. I'd rather be with the real one. Disa was cool, she said she would wait."

"You got issues, dude. Do everyone a favor. Please get back with Jacqueline. You know she is still waiting for you. The world would be a better place, for real."

◉ ◉ ◉

Two of the cutest little kids Cleopatra had ever seen ran right smack into her legs as she walked into the East Village bakery. She was coming in behind Disa when they barreled into her.

"Sorry," they both said in unison.

"That's ok, sweethearts." Cleopatra smiled. She looked up and saw Jacqueline standing behind them. Cleopatra made eye contact with Mandisa who nodded her head as if to say "take your time," and walked up to the counter.

"Did you apologize?" Jacqueline looked down at her twins.

"Yes, Mommy, we were eating and trying to walk at the same time." said the little boy.

"This is Maya, and this is Amir. This is Mommy's very special friend Cleopatra."

"Hi Cleopatra!" they giggled.

"Hi Maya, hi Amir." Cleopatra kneeled down to them.

"You're pretty, you're Mommy's fiancé, right?" Maya asked, struggling with the word *fiancé*.

"Uh, I guess I am," Cleopatra mumbled, and looked up at Jacqueline who winked at her. "Enjoy your donuts," Cleopatra said to the kids. "They are so cute," she gushed to Jacqueline. "They look so much like you, it's crazy."

"Those are my babies. This is the first time I've seen you smile in a long time."

Cleopatra's smile widened even more as Amir played with the chain hanging from her jeans.

"Up. Up." Maya held her arms for Cleopatra to pick her up. Cleopatra looked at Jacqueline.

"Someone wants to be in those big, strong arms. Guess she got that from me. Go ahead," she said.

"I guess she did." Cleopatra laughed as she picked up Maya. The little girl enjoyed eating her donut high in the air above everyone else, and dropped crumbs onto Cleopatra's shoulder. "I'm proud of you for getting your family back together."

"It's the only good thing to come out of this. They are all I have. She likes you," Jacqueline said. "Almost as quickly as I did, almost."

While Maya rested her head on Cleopatra's shoulder, Cleopatra grabbed a napkin from a nearby table to wipe the sugar off of her face.

"I miss you." Jacqueline reached her hand inside Cleopatra's shirt collar, and a smiled crossed her lips when she found the necklace. "I have on mine." She pulled her shirt collar to the side.

Cleopatra took her left hand, and saw she was still wearing her engagement ring. "I need to go."

"Ok," Jacqueline said hesitantly. Cleopatra handed Maya back over to her mom. Maya waved a sleepy goodbye and Amir screamed, "Bye Cleopatra!" The sugary donuts had totally opposite effects on the twins.

Jacqueline walked the kids over to a table where they sat down. Cleopatra couldn't take her eyes off of them.

"So that's her?" Mandisa asked.

"Yeah."

"She is beautiful. And those kids are so adorable."

"They are, aren't they?"

"I can tell by the way she looks at you, and how she's looking at you right now that she wants you back. You're going to leave me to be with her?"

"Probably."

TASHA C. MILLER

STILL MINE

Cleopatra sat outside on her front steps as she often did on weekend mornings when she was alone and when the weather permitted. She usually people-watched and read the *New York Times,* but on this morning, unlike any other time before, she felt a strong need to connect with Jacqueline. She sat with the box full of her letters. The first note Cleopatra opened was dated just after their first breakup, and Jacqueline wrote about missing her touch and the way Cleopatra used to look at her with so much love in her eyes. The next one she opened she'd received just the day before. It was a picture that Jacqueline snapped on her cell phone of Cleopatra holding her daughter, and her son playing with Cleopatra's belt chain.

She attached a one-sentence note. "The loves of my life." She wanted to call Jacqueline. She wasn't sure what she was going to say, but she wanted to hear her voice.

She saw two people walking down the street, and it wasn't long before she realized it was Jacqueline with another woman. The woman was tall, dark and muscular, with a shaved head.

Cleopatra thought she was handsome despite her lack of style. Her white button-down shirt was tucked snug into her mom jeans and her Birkenstock sandals were not a good look. Cleopatra wanted to run up to them, but the butch lesbian was talking nonstop. Cleopatra recognized the "get the panties" small-talk hand motions and body language when she saw it. She put the paper down and stood up on her top step. As they passed, Jacqueline made eye contact with her, and neither let up on their gaze. They kept walking, and Cleopatra let them go even though it took everything in her body to watch them walk away. She bent down, scooped up the newspaper and the letters, and headed into the house. She didn't know what to do. She imagined this was how Jacqueline felt all those times she saw her with other women. She wanted to throw up. She flung the paper against the wall. She didn't know whether to cry or to punch something or both. She could run them down in the street like a madwoman, beat on her chest, and throw Jacqueline over her shoulder and run off, or she could let this go. As she tried to compose herself, there was a pounding on the front door. When she opened it, Jacqueline stood on her doorstep.

"That's it? You're not gonna do anything or say anything?"

"I'll say something. Why the hell are you walking down my block? What is that shit about? Is that what you want? Do you want her? That's the best you can do?"

"I'm sorry – the chick that looks exactly like you was busy. Hell no, I don't want her."

"It doesn't look that way. Are you trying to make me jealous?

"Is it working?" Jacqueline asked, her lips twisted and arms folded.

Cleopatra glared at her. She was mad at herself for being jealous. She knew she had run through a lot of women since she ended her relationship with Jacqueline but Cleopatra was the one trying to heal from a broken heart. She thought Jacqueline deserved to feel pain when she saw her with other women. "If you let her so much as hold your hand, or kiss you on the cheek, I'll know, and I will never forgive you. Does that sound familiar? This is still mine." She put her hand on Jacqueline's heart. She didn't care about being a hypocrite.

Jacqueline stepped back, and put her weight on the wall as Cleopatra moved her fingers between Jacqueline's breasts.

"If it's still yours, then prove it," she said breathlessly as Cleopatra cupped her breasts in her hands.

Cleopatra slid her arms down around Jacqueline's waist, then to her ass and pulled her body hard against hers, their hips touching. Cleopatra kissed her slowly before slipping her tongue inside her mouth. Jacqueline wilted in her arms as her legs buckled. Cleopatra tongued her earlobe down to her neck as Jacqueline whimpered and clawed at her clothes.

"I want you, Cleopatra."

Cleopatra stood back from Jacqueline. "Is that enough proof? It's mine. You may have lied to me before, but your body can't."

"What do you want me to do? Just tell me."

"Get rid of her. Apologize for wasting her time. Tell her your heart and your pussy are mine and she never had a chance at either. I'll wait here." Cleopatra opened the door.

Jacqueline went to the bottom of the steps where the woman stood waiting on the sidewalk. Cleopatra was shocked as she read Jacqueline's lips. She repeated her word for word. The woman stuck her middle finger up at both of them as she walked away.

Cleopatra backed Jacqueline up against the front door as soon as she returned to the house. She held her tight around her waist. "Did you do anything with her?"

"No. I was just trying to make you mad. Trying to get you to make a move."

"Don't ever let me see you with another woman again. Next time I won't be so calm. Especially not as long as you are wearing my ring. Did she not see that big-ass diamond?" Jacqueline had never seen the jealous or possessive side of Cleopatra, and it was turning her on and scaring her at the same time. "Where are the kids?"

273

"With my mom. Where's your girlfriend?" Jacqueline looked up at her and tugged on her shirt.

"She's not my girlfriend." Cleopatra tried walking away from her.

Jacqueline pulled her back. "She's the only one I see you with. She's like my doppelganger, you realize this, right?"

"You been watching me?"

"Yeah. I have."

"She's in love with me. But I'm still in love with you."

"I know that. What we have doesn't go away, ever. Are you done suffering because of what I did?"

"What are you talking about?"

"You don't have to hurt like this. Not anymore. You still love me. I never stopped loving you. These past six months apart have been hell. I can't do this anymore. Do you know what today is?" She turned Cleopatra's face toward hers.

Cleopatra hung her head. "Our wedding day," she said.

"You remembered."

"Of course I remembered. This was supposed to be the happiest day of my life." She looked at Jacqueline. "Is that why you picked today to pull this stunt? I don't know what you want me to do?"

"Kiss me."

◎ ◎ ◎

Cleopatra went to Mandisa's house to tell her about her night with Jacqueline and to break off their relationship. "It was something you needed to get out of your system," Mandisa said. "She just caught you at a weak moment, that's all. I'll let it slide."

"It's more than that and you know it. And I'm not asking you to let it slide," Cleopatra said.

"So, we don't have a chance anymore because of this woman that broke your heart twice?"

"Well, when you put it like that, it doesn't sound very smart."

"No, it doesn't. I'm just trying to be clear. It's really too bad that we never took it to the next level. We wouldn't be having this conversation if we had."

"I guess we'll never know now, will we?"

"I wouldn't go that far. I always get what I want eventually. You never found out what Mandisa Lerato means." She smiled.

"Are you going to tell me?" Cleopatra asked.

"I had no intention of telling you. I was going to show you." She wrapped her arms around Cleopatra's neck and whispered in her ear. "It means sweet love."

Cleopatra laughed. "You need to stop." She pulled away from Disa and headed toward the door. As she stepped outside Disa grabbed her arm.

"Should I let your woman know that I'm right across the street? And that I'm here day or night if you need anything? You can just come and take whatever you want."

"Please, don't do that. I'm getting out of here, sweet love. I'll see you around."

○ ○ ○

Cleopatra and Jacqueline got back together after endless conversations on how to ease Mommy's girlfriend into the children's lives. They spent time with the kids as a couple, and Cleopatra spent time with them alone. It wasn't long before the kids fell in love with her and she with them.

Cleopatra surprised Jacqueline and had an interior designer redo one of the bedrooms for the kids so they would feel at home whenever they spent the night. It was there that she started a tradition of creating bedtime stories for them off the top of her head.

"Can you be our daddy, Cleo?" Amir asked, after she read him and his sister their first story. "Please be our daddy," Maya

275

said, excited. Cleopatra looked at Jacqueline, who just shrugged her shoulders, and waited for her response.

"I'm just Cleo, sweetie."

"Goodnight Daddy Cleo." Amir jumped up and hugged her. She twirled him around and put him on her back pretending to fly him around the room. Maya giggled and asked to be taken for a ride too.

"Is this the effect you're going to have on them? It was so quiet just a few minutes ago," Jacqueline laughed.

"Look at Mommy!" Maya yelled. "She's smiling."

"She smiles all the time now," Amir said. "Cleo makes her smile."

Cleopatra looked at Jacqueline and saw tears filling her eyes. She shook her head at Jacqueline, signaling to her not to do that to her. She couldn't take it when she cried. Jacqueline pulled Amir off of Cleopatra's back so Maya could get her turn to soar around the room.

Cleopatra watched Jacqueline as she tucked the kids in to their beds. It warmed her heart to see them together, the way it should be. It was so obvious in the way that Jacqueline cared for them that she adored her babies, and if Cleopatra had ever doubted that before those thoughts had been destroyed.

"You're amazing," Jacqueline said.

"Yeah, I've been told that before."

"Be serious." Jacqueline wrapped her arms around Cleopatra. "This is the first time our family has been complete. This is how it's supposed to feel. They love their new room, it's perfect. You put so much love and thought into it. They never want to leave."

"They never have to." Cleopatra played with the engagement ring on her finger.

"Never?" Jacqueline asked.

"Well, no question they are going to college. But then I'm kicking them out."

"What are you saying?"

"Marry me on New Year's Eve?"

KENYA AND PUNISHMENT

"What's wrong with you?" Jacqueline asked Cleopatra, concerned.

"Nothing."

"You can't speak, or give me a hug and a kiss when you come in to the house?"

Jacqueline and the kids were spending the weekend at Cleopatra's and were already there when she got home from work late that evening.

"Sorry." She rolled her eyes and pecked Jacqueline on the cheek.

"Did you roll your eyes at me?"

"If I rolled my eyes at you, you would know it."

Jacqueline glared at Cleopatra and walked away. They sat quiet through dinner with the kids only speaking to them without speaking a word to each other.

"Do you want an ice cream cone? I'm making some for the kids," Cleopatra said.

"If it's not too much trouble."

"If it was that much trouble, I wouldn't have offered."
Jacqueline sucked her teeth at Cleopatra.

"I got something you can suck on," Cleopatra said.

"What?"

"Nothing." Cleopatra went back into the kitchen. She set the kids up with their ice cream and brought Jacqueline her cone out to the garden.

"Thank you."

"You're welcome," Cleopatra said as she sat down next to her and began eating her cone. Out of the corner of her eye she watched Jacqueline lick the ice cream. She licked it slow as she held the cone tight in her hand.

"What are you staring at?"

"Nothing." Cleopatra continued to eat her ice cream. She caught Jacqueline staring at her. "What are you staring at?"

"Nothing." *Damn, she is sexy when she is mad at me.*

That night they lay in bed in total darkness and silence. Cleopatra couldn't take it anymore and she rolled on top of Jacqueline and pinned her arms down to the bed.

"You are so sexy when you're mad at me," she said.

"You are so sexy when you're being mean. Lick me like you were licking that ice cream. I was getting jealous."

"Why should I?" Cleopatra asked. "You been rolling your eyes and sucking your teeth at me all night."

"I know you're stressed, baby, your life is changing drastically and so quickly but you are taking it out on me. You been putting in long hours at work and not spending much time with me and the kids. I wish you would talk to me about your feelings, tell me what you are going through."

Cleopatra rolled back onto the bed. "I know I shut you out. That's how I am, and you know this. I don't want to burden people with my problems. The few times I've opened up it's only been used to hurt me in the end. I work it out myself."

"I'm not 'people.' I'm going to be your wife. How can you think you're burdening me? You give the kids and me so much, yet you won't let me be there for you. It's not fair. Do you know how much that hurts me?"

"I'm sorry, baby. I didn't know." Cleopatra confided in Jacqueline that she was scared of marriage. Jacqueline knew she grew up not knowing one happily married couple or what that even looked like. Her father cheated on her mother. Her uncles beat their wives, and had kids outside of their marriages. Her estranged older brother that Cleopatra rarely spoke of was a womanizing sex addict who repeatedly cheated on his wife and disappeared for weeks at a time, leaving his wife and kids to fend for themselves.

"Baby, I understand where you are coming from, but what about Racquel and her husband? What about my parents?"

"Your parents are freaks of nature." Cleopatra said. "They can't keep their hands off of each other. The pantry on Thanksgiving? And I've never been around them and they not vanish for a half hour or more. It's incredible."

"I know! I grew up knowing that type of passion in a marriage was possible." She paused. "So, I have to ask you. Do you still want to get married? Are you changing your mind?"

"I'm not changing my mind baby. There is no question that I want to spend the rest of my life with you."

Cleopatra made an effort to be more open and Jacqueline didn't push her. Things were good, but never stayed that way for long.

◙ ◙ ◙

"Cleopatra, a Detective Humphrey from the NYPD is here for you," Racquel said over the intercom.

"Detective who? Did they say what it was regarding?"

"It's a she. A personal matter. What did you do?" Racquel scolded her.

"Nothing! What does she look like?"

"She's pretty. Big chest though."

"Send her in." Cleopatra laughed. Recognizing one of New York's finest, Cleopatra smiled. "Hey, Nia, how are you?"

"I'm good." She came in and kissed Cleopatra on the cheek.

"It's been a long time." The short dark chocolate woman smiled.

"Have a seat. What brings you by?"

"Didn't think you'd ever see me again after you broke up with me, huh?" She took off her dark gray suit jacket and revealed a tight baby blue button down shirt. She slicked back her bun as she sat down in front of Cleopatra's desk.

"Can't say I did, actually. But that was a lifetime ago. What can I do for you?"

"I'm a detective now." She proudly flashed her badge that hung low around her neck. She got up from the chair and leaned against the front of Cleopatra's desk. "And I'm here on a police matter. I need you to come down to the station, so we can talk."

"What's going on?" Cleopatra asked, confused. "Why can't we talk here?"

"I need to ask you a few questions. Trust me on this, you need to come with me."

"You can reach me on my cell if you need me," Cleopatra told Racquel as she walked out and went with Nia to the Midtown South precinct.

"This is my partner, Detective Martinez." Nia introduced her to an older Latino gentleman with gray streaks running through his sideburns and beard, as they entered an interrogation room.

"Hello Cleopatra. We have some questions for you." He shook her hand. "Please have a seat."

Cleopatra looked around the small, dark, windowless room, lit only by a lone ceiling light fixture that was missing two of its five bulbs. The gray walls blended into the cement floor and brushed metal furniture, and the smell of stale cigarettes and old coffee was stifling.

"Do you know this woman?" He slid a mug shot photo across the large metal table.

"Kenya. She looks terrible. But that's Kenya Rampersad. What did she do?" Cleopatra asked concerned.

"How do you know her?"

"We used to date, but that was over a while ago."

"She's been arrested." Nia folded her arms across her chest.

"For what? And what does it have to do with me?"

"I have some more questions for you first. Tell me about you and Kenya and start from the beginning."

Cleopatra told Nia and Detective Martinez the sordid tale of their relationship from the house party in East New York up until the last time she saw her when she taped that incriminating conversation about Jacqueline and the assault charges on her cell phone.

Cleopatra's patience had worn out. "Can you please tell me what's going on? What did she do? What are the charges?"

"Conspiracy to commit kidnapping, and murder," Detective Martinez said.

Cleopatra's mouth fell open, though she was only a little surprised. "She was going to kill me?"

"No, your fiancé," Nia said.

"What?" Cleopatra rose out of her seat.

"Cleopatra, sit, please." Nia stepped toward Cleopatra before she had a chance to get too excited and placed her hands on both of her shoulders.

Cleopatra sat back down. "How did you find out?"

"We got an anonymous tip three days ago, but the sting went down this morning. We have her on video and everything." Detective Martinez said.

"So, who turned her in?" Cleopatra asked.

"Cleopatra, the tipster was anonymous," Nia answered.

"Are you just telling me that, or do you really not know?"

"All we know is that it was a woman who turned her in."

"How much was she willing to pay?"

"Twenty-five thousand dollars," Nia said.

"No way. Not when people in her neighborhood would do some shit like that for five hundred." Cleopatra shook her head. "She doesn't even have that type of money. She stripped her way through law school."

"She's a first-year associate at a big firm downtown. I think she can afford it. She wanted Jacqueline dead, and she talked to the wrong people about it."

"I have to call Jac." Cleopatra searched for her cell phone.

"Our detectives are with her right now. She should be here soon," Detective Martinez said.

"Kenya is going away for a long time, trust me," Nia said.

"You knew about this for three days and didn't tell me?" Cleopatra scowled at Nia.

"Can you excuse us, Martinez?" Nia said. He nodded his head and ducked out of the room.

"You and I have known each other for a long time." She touched Cleopatra's hand. "I was never going to let anything happen to you or your family. You were never in danger. As soon as I found out, I had you all put under twenty-four-hour protection. I handled this myself, because it was you. Honestly, it was best that you didn't know about this until now."

"How do you figure that?"

"It takes a lot to get you angry, but when you do it's hard to control you and talk you down. I know you well enough to know you would have gone after her, and you'd be in jail right now instead of her. Am I lying?"

Cleopatra didn't answer, only rocked back and forth in her chair, holding her head in her hands and rubbing her temples. Thinking Jacqueline could have been taken away from her and the kids because of Kenya. "I want to see the video. Was there anyone else involved?"

"We don't have any evidence of anyone else being in on this, and she hasn't implicated anyone."

"I don't see her coming up with this on her own. She just wasn't that evil. Yeah, a little crazy, but I don't really buy it."

Nia sat down at the table. "Cleopatra, she wanted you to suffer. She blamed Jacqueline for your breakup, that's what this was about. She's pathetic. I wanted to shoot the bitch myself. But if there is someone else that you think may be involved in this, you need to let me know."

Cleopatra hesitated and thought for a moment. "I have no idea." She shook her head. "I want to see the video."

"It's just going to make you mad."

"I'm already there. Please."

Nia flipped open her laptop and for the next twenty minutes Cleopatra watched Kenya sitting in a car with Nia on a dimly lit street in the Tremont section of the Bronx, setting up Jacqueline's hit. Kenya was nuts, just as Nia said. She blamed Jacqueline for ruining her life and for every other little thing wrong in the world. Offing her was the only option Kenya could think of.

When Nia asked her outright what she wanted, she said, "I want that bitch dead. I want to be there when you do her. I want her to know it was me." Her eyes were glassy and black. "I'm going to tell her Cleopatra will be my wife and I'm going to raise those cute ass kids of hers." Then she laughed.

"That bitch is really crazy. I've seen enough. Turn it off." Cleopatra said.

"I'm glad she's off the streets." Nia closed the laptop. "I looked in her eyes the whole time, and there was nothing in them. She is just all gone."

"I've never seen her like that before. I don't think we should show this tape to Jacqueline."

"You're probably right. She's here now." Nia peeked through the blinds and into the squad room.

"Baby, what's going on? They wouldn't tell me anything. Are you ok?" She grabbed Cleopatra and held her tight.

"I'm ok."

"What is it?" She took her hand as Cleopatra pulled a chair out for her.

"They arrested Kenya." Cleopatra looked down at the floor.

"What does that have to do with us?" Jacqueline touched her face in order to make Cleopatra look at her.

Cleopatra hesitated at first. There was no easy way to say it, so she just blurted it out. "She was trying to put a hit out on you. She was trying to have you killed." Cleopatra shut her eyes and waited for hell to break loose. Jacqueline squeezed her hand and Cleopatra opened her eyes. She just sat there and stared at her for what seemed like forever, then Cleopatra saw her eyes widen and she turned deep purple. She watched her chest heave up and down.

"Where is she?! We can do this right now." Jacqueline exploded and knocked over a chair. "She can step to me now. She has to get somebody do me? Where is her bitch ass at? I'll kill her myself." Nia moved forward to restrain Jacqueline.

"Leave her alone," Cleopatra said to Nia. Cleopatra cornered Jacqueline and held her so she couldn't move. Jacqueline hugged Cleopatra tight, shaking uncontrollably.

"Baby, we are in a police station, ok? You're safe. She's in jail." Cleopatra said as she held her. "She's going to pay for this, I promise you."

◉ ◉ ◉

Cleopatra was worried Jacqueline would blame the Kenya plot on her and she asked her straight out one night as they lay in bed.

"Do you blame me? If you do, if you feel like this is my fault, I want you to say it. I would understand if you did."

Jacqueline rolled over and turned on the lamp. She looked at Cleopatra whose eyes were filled with sadness. "Don't be ridiculous. I don't. You aren't responsible for her actions." Jacqueline caressed her face and kissed her. "I love you so much, baby. This is not your fault."

"Are you sure?"

"I'm sure." She laid her head on Cleopatra's chest. "We were destined to be together no matter what. We've been through so much already and still made it through. No one is ever going to keep us apart. I won't let them."

FRIENDS IN LOW PLACES

"You have a call," Racquel said as Cleopatra headed out the door.

"Take a message for me please," she yelled from the elevator.

Racquel shook her head and used her finger to motion Cleopatra to the phone.

"Who is it?"

"She wouldn't give her name. She only said she's the friend of an ex. Doesn't narrow it down for you, does it?" She winked at Cleopatra.

Cleopatra didn't have the energy to deal with another ex. Kenya was at Riker's Island awaiting her trial, so everything was on hold for the moment, and quiet.

"I'll take it in my office." She closed the door behind her.

"Is this Cleopatra Giovanni?"

"Who's speaking?"

"Natalie. I'm Kenya's cousin. I'm calling for her."

"For what? I know she's not going to try to harass me from jail."

"Listen. She said she's been trying to call you for a while. But you blocked her calls. She has been after me to contact you. She wants you to visit her."

"She must be out of her mind. Why?" Cleopatra asked.

"She just said that it's important that you go and see her right away. She wouldn't tell me anymore, but I promised to call you."

"Tell her to hold her breath and wait for me to come. She's got plenty of time." Cleopatra hung up.

Damn…what did she want? A few days passed. The phone call with Kenya's cousin began to bother Cleopatra more and more. Then she got a letter in the mail at work.

Cleopatra,
You were always fucking hardheaded.
That's part of what made you so damn sexy.
But I'm not bullshitting.
You need to come and see me now.
I still love you bitch,
Kenya

Cleopatra ignored that letter. A week later, she got another one.

Dear Cleopatra,
Come see me right now!
Your life and possibly that of your family depends on it.
I still love you bitch,
Kenya

Was she threatening her from inside? How the letter made it out of jail, Cleopatra couldn't figure out. It was obviously a threat.

"Shit." Cleopatra banged her hand down on her desk. *Get yourself together.* She thought of calling Shawn but changed her mind when she remembered her reaction to Kenya's arrest. She had never seen Shawn so angry. She had to plead with her not to have her associates at Rikers pay Kenya a visit. *Maybe I should call Nia. Definitely not telling Jacqueline. I will handle this myself.*

Cleopatra took the bus out to Rikers Island and with the Rose M. Singer Center's long lines, multiple metal detectors and numerous pat-downs, she had to dedicate the whole day to the trip. When Kenya sat down in front of her in a dreadful gray sweat suit two sizes too large, Cleopatra was stunned by the rapid aging on her face, and what looked like at least a thirty-pound weight loss.

"Cleopatra. It's so good to see you. I'm glad you came."

"How are you?" Cleopatra asked over a screaming baby's cries.

"Some days are better than others."

"How are they treating you?" Cleopatra scanned the other visitors in the large room.

"The inmates treat me ok, they know I'm a lawyer, or that I used to be, so they think I can help them. No one fucks with me, not yet, anyway. A lot of the staff is shady, though." She touched Cleopatra's hand. "God. I want to kiss you so bad right now."

Cleopatra snatched her hand away and stared at her with a blank expression on her face. "You are joking, right? So, you want to tell me why I'm here?"

"This woman, her name is Alexis ... or at least I think it's Alexis..." Kenya said. "I don't even know her last name or anything."

A chill went down Cleopatra's spine at the mention of the name. She fidgeted in her chair.

"How do you know Alexis? What about her?" Cleopatra asked.

"How do you know her, Cleopatra?" she asked, stunned.

"Never mind, Kenya. What does she have to do with anything?"

"She's the reason I'm in this bitch."

"What? Start from the beginning?"

"I was outside of your job one day, and she came up to me on the street. She befriended me just like that, out of the blue. She was nice and really pretty you know? She reeked of money. You ever smell money on someone?"

"Yeah. On Alexis. What were you doing outside of my job?"

"I wanted to see you even if I couldn't talk to you. I missed you."

"You were stalking me?"

Kenya looked down at the dingy cement floor. "I don't like that word."

"But that's what the fuck you were doing?"

"That's not the point. Damn!" She raised her voice. The guard shook his head and ordered Kenya to lower her volume, but said nothing to the girl a few feet from them who was fingering her girlfriend under the table.

"I was wandering around, and she approached me, and struck up a conversation. We hit it off, started hanging out and spending a lot of time together – "

Cleopatra interrupted her. "Get to the point." She was distracted for a moment when she noticed a girl walk in to the visitors' area wearing an oversized green muumuu and flip flops.

"They make the girls put those on when they try to come up in here half naked," Kenya explained.

"Sorry, go ahead." Cleopatra turned her attention back to Kenya.

"Alexis and I became best friends practically overnight. I confided in her about you, and she concocted a plan so I could get you back. She was going to get a hit man to get rid of your girl. It shocked me at first. I didn't think she was serious. But she had it all figured out, and she had me convinced the shit would work. This bitch has money, like it doesn't end. I started thinking she could actually make this happen. I wasn't concerned about getting into trouble, because I hadn't done anything or talked to anyone. There was nothing to incriminate me, at least nothing that would hold up in court if it came to that, or so I thought. But that bitch set me up and she went to the police and helped them bust me. She arranged the meeting with the hit woman but bailed at the last minute, so I went to the Bronx to meet her. You know the rest of the story. I'm telling you the truth, I swear."

"I believe you. You have never lied to me. That I can say for certain." Cleopatra nodded her head. "Why are you telling me this? Why didn't you just tell the police about her?"

"I don't have any proof she even exists. What would I tell them? Some phantom rich Jamaican woman set me up? I don't know her last name; no address, no phone number, nothing. And I don't have pictures of her which wouldn't even matter because every time I saw her she had in different colored contacts and a different wig on."

"Jamaican? Alexis isn't Jamaican."

"She spoke with a really thick Jamaican accent." Kenya replied.

"Yeah, she may have but she's not Jamaican. What wig?" Cleopatra repeated with her eyebrows raised. "Alexis doesn't wear wigs, and contacts?" Cleopatra laughed. "Wow. And yet you didn't think any of this was suspicious at all?"

"I thought that's just how she changed up her looks. Rich people do that all the time. But you know her. You can lead the police to her."

"I want to get this straight. You met Alexis on the street, in front of my job. You befriend her, because she pretended to be nice, she was beautiful, and let's not forget rich." Cleopatra rolled her eyes annoyed. "You become BFFs, and because of the pain over our breakup, she offered to hook you up with a hit woman to kill my fiancé?"

"Yeah. Basically." She nodded her head in shame.

"You thought that was a good idea? You thought you would get away with murder? You thought you would get me back, and we'd raise Jacqueline's kids together?" Cleopatra folded her arms across her chest and chewed on her bottom lip. "At no point did Alexis ever tell you that I fucked her for like four years?"

Kenya's face dropped.

"That's what I thought." It was clear to Cleopatra then. "Kenya, sweetheart, she obviously set you up. She had no intentions of contracting a hit. Do you realize that now? Do you understand this was all about you? She was getting rid of *you*." Cleopatra pointed to Kenya. "You simple bitch."

Kenya had that same glassy-eyed expression Cleopatra had seen on the video, struggling to connect the dots in her head. But it was too late.

Cleopatra stared at Kenya in disbelief. She stared hard, hoping a reason for her being so stupid would make itself apparent.

"You shouldn't be in here, Kenya. You should be somewhere with a padded cell in a fucking straitjacket like Diana Ross in *Lady Sings the Blues*. How the hell did you get into anybody's law school?" Cleopatra yelled at her. "This is the dumbest shit I've ever heard. Look around, look where you are – you got played so hard." Cleopatra clapped her hands together. "Do you realize that Alexis must have really liked you, because this right here," Cleopatra patted her hand on the table, "this was your best case scenario. Do you even know who Alexis really is? Do you know where she lives, have a phone number for her?" Cleopatra already knew the answer.

"No, we always met somewhere or else we were at my apartment. I found out later the phone number she gave me was to a throw-away prepaid cell that couldn't be traced."

Cleopatra stared at Kenya in silence again.

"You know her, you can tell the police who she is and what she did."

"Don't even try it. Maybe it wasn't your idea from the start, but you were involved. You wanted to watch my woman, the mother of my future stepchildren, die. It's on the video. You wanted her to know it was you. You wanted to be there when she got done. Twelve people will convict your ass based on that video. And I will be in the courtroom eating popcorn and sucking on a Slurpee when they do. It's a wrap." Cleopatra got up and put on her coat.

"What are you going to do?" Kenya asked, concerned.

"Get married."

Shawn called Cleopatra on her cell as she rode the bus back into Manhattan.

"They dropped the criminal case against me. They aren't pressing charges. So I won't be going to prison." Shawn sighed. "They decided to take me to civil court and rob my ass instead. They got a hold of my financials, all of my accounts, they want to take all of my shit."

"They want you to pay for your freedom. So, hand over your dough." Cleopatra had her own problems to worry about. Alexis had come back to town. The city was plenty big enough for both of them, so she wasn't too freaked out. She hadn't made herself visible, so she must not have wanted anything from Cleopatra, at least not yet, and that was fine with her. Cleopatra would keep her secrets as long as Alexis kept hers.

TASHA C. MILLER

WILL YOU MARRY ME?

"What do you mean exactly by *slow down*?" Cleopatra asked.

Jacqueline decided they should slow down on sex the last month before the wedding.

"Uhm... stop having it," she mumbled.

"As in *none*? Until the wedding night?" Cleopatra asked, surprised. "You're funny. Whatever you say, sweetheart."

Cleopatra knew they wouldn't be able to do it.

◻ ◻ ◻

Three sexless, clit-throbbing weeks later, Cleopatra got a call on her cell phone as she exited the jewelry store. She'd just picked up their wedding bands.

A sultry female voice whispered, "So, you're getting married in a week, huh?"

"Who is this?" Cleopatra couldn't place the voice. She walked away from the crowds of holiday shoppers going up

293

and down Fifth Avenue.

"You don't recognize my voice? Probably because I'm not screaming your name. We broke a lot of headboards together."

"Is that supposed to narrow it down for me?" Cleopatra laughed.

"You don't remember my telling you nobody has ever fucked me or eaten my pussy the way you did?"

"I used to hear that a lot, actually."

"I'm sure you did."

"So, are you going to tell me who you are?" Cleopatra tried to warm her hands in the cold December air.

"I won't tell you, but I'll show you. Come to the Tribeca Grand right now. There is a key waiting for you at the front desk."

"I'm getting married in like a week. You must be crazy. I love my woman."

The caller started to moan. "Just talking to you is making me wet."

Cleopatra stood on the sidewalk listening to this woman moan in between the sounds of Christmas carolers, Salvation Army bells, and taxi horns.

"I don't think your girl is a freak like me. You need to come, and take this one last time."

"You talk a lot of shit. You have no idea how freaky my girl is."

"You got soft, didn't you? Maybe you can't handle this anymore. That must be it." Cleopatra looked up in the sky as snowflakes the size of nickels began to fall.

"I'm on my way." She hung up the phone.

The room was black when she opened the door. She stepped inside, and immediately stripped naked. Cleopatra saw Jacqueline lying on the bed.

"You ready for me?" Cleopatra stood over her. Snippets of the city lights peeked through the curtains and illuminated her body.

"I don't want to waste any time...I haven't been able to get you off of my mind. It's been much too long." Jacqueline pulled her down to the bed, crawled on top of her, and fell into Cleopatra's embrace.

Cleopatra couldn't wait to taste her. She pushed Jacqueline down on the bed, and buried her face in between her legs. Her tongue glided in and out of her. This was her thing. There was nothing like the taste of her woman. Cleopatra wanted to make her come, drink all she had to offer, and then make her come some more.

"Don't stop." Jacqueline moaned and pulled Cleopatra's locs.

Cleopatra sucked on her swollen clit, bobbed her head, all the while drinking the sweetness that gushed from her. When her body couldn't convulse anymore, she released her, and licked a trail up her body, over her breasts, lingering at her nipples, then to her lips.

Cleopatra's body was hot; she got strapped quickly. Jacqueline lay back down on the bed, legs parted, inviting Cleopatra in. She slid into her; wrapped her legs around her waist. Her breath was heavy, as she nibbled on her ear. Jacqueline whispered to Cleopatra. "You feel so good...harder. Is this how you fuck your girl? I won't break, fuck me."

"You want it harder?"

"Please." She moaned.

Cleopatra slid out of her, and flipped her over. Jacqueline arched her back as Cleopatra slid into her from behind, and she placed her hands on her hips to steady herself as she thrust inside of her. Her crotch slammed into her hard, making a smacking sound. Their bodies pounded into each other, and the bedsprings began to squeak. Cleopatra's body was tense. Her pussy was wet, and her clit thumped.

"Do you always respond to booty calls from women at hotels?" Jacqueline laughed. "You could never resist me."

"Only booty calls from my fiancé." Cleopatra kissed Jacqueline on her nose, and lay on her chest. She enjoyed the feel of Jacqueline's silky skin on hers. This was her woman, her love, and her soul mate.

"So much for waiting until our wedding night."

"I admit it. I can't resist you either. But I wanted to spend some time alone with you tonight." Jacqueline said. "There is something I want to give you." She opened the drawer from the nightstand and pulled out a small box.

"What are you doing?" Cleopatra looked at her suspiciously as Jacqueline got out of the bed and down on both knees.

"On the first day I saw you from afar, and before we ever met I made the decision to follow my heart with you. Right or incredibly wrong, everything I've done since then goes back to that first moment I saw you. I loved you long before we ever met. I've been waiting my whole life for you. You know already that I love you more than anything in this world. Will you marry me?"

She opened the box and presented Cleopatra with a pave diamond eternity band.

"You shouldn't have." Cleopatra pulled Jacqueline to her feet and kissed her.

"I wanted you to have an engagement ring too, baby. I want everyone to know from a mile away that you are all mine." She kissed her and slid the ring on her finger.

"I'm asking you to give yourself to me completely. Be mine forever. Will you marry me?"

"Yes, I'll marry you, baby."

◎ ◎ ◎

The day after Christmas Jacqueline and Cleopatra boarded a plane for Maui. They spent nearly a week alone at a five-star resort and spa on a former pineapple plantation, perched on the golden sands at the edge of the Pacific Ocean. Jacqueline's fairy tale was finally coming true. They spent the days sightseeing in historic Lahaina and had romantic dinners on the beach at night. Jacqueline's parents arrived with the kids. Shawn and Robin made it, and other family and friends trickled in over the final days. The big day was fast approaching.

◉ ◉ ◉

Close family and friends gathered with Cleopatra and Jacqueline the night before the wedding at the rehearsal luau. Guests were greeted with leis and cocktails. They participated in hula lessons and marveled at master fire dancers before they watched the roasted pig emerge from the underground oven. They feasted on pork, beef, chicken, mahi mahi and poi washed down with Hawaiian rum punch.

Cleopatra saw Racquel and Jacqueline talking and for the first time in a long while Racquel's head wasn't spinning. She took that as a good sign.

"What's up, sweets?" Robin had just constructed a massive pile of meat on her plate when Cleopatra asked to speak to her alone.

"I know Shawn told you about her giving me permission to go after you."

"Uhm hmm." Robin nodded.

"Your sister and I talked about this at length already, and I've apologized to her, but I never apologized to you. And since we are about to be family, I want to say I'm sorry, it was wrong, that's why I couldn't actually go through with it. I was hurt when I thought of it, but that's no excuse. I shouldn't have tried to involve you, and I apologize, I'm sorry."

A puff of smoke enveloped them as the fire dancers relit their torches.

"I understand more every day why my sister loves you so much." Robin had to yell over the beat of the drums. "It's really good you didn't call me, because I would have fucked you and loved every minute of it and this would just be a really awkward situation right now. But I understand now what you must have been going through. I love Shawn so much, that I'm not sure I wouldn't have tried to do the same thing."

"So we're cool?"

"Look at my big sister, and my niece, and nephew. How happy they are. I've never seen her like this, you take such good care of them. So we're more than cool. We're family." They embraced as Jacqueline walked over.

"Uh...hello, break it up over here." She slid her arm around Cleopatra.

Robin laughed. "Don't nobody want your girl, but you!"

She put a piece of fish in to her mouth and went over and sat on Shawn's lap.

Cleopatra kissed Jacqueline on the lips. "I was apologizing to her for things in the past."

"You're such a sweetheart. Racquel and I were actually doing some making up of our own. That is, if you want to consider her telling me to behave or she'd cut my head off with a rusty machete making up."

"For Racquel? Yes. That's making up. Perfect."

◉ ◉ ◉

By the end of the night, Jacqueline and Cleopatra had found a quiet spot away from everyone at a small table in the corner. Cleopatra was trying to convince Jacqueline to let her sleep in the suite with her instead of banishing her to her own room down the hall. She was making progress by kissing Jacqueline's neck and rubbing her thigh when Pop's voice caught their attention.

"If I can have everyone listen up for a minute. To the guests of honor, Jacqueline and Cleopatra." Cleopatra pulled her hand from under Jacqueline's dress and leaned back in her chair and Jacqueline closed her legs and fixed her hair as everyone's eyes turned to them. "First to my oldest baby, my first born. We've watched you grow into a beautiful woman and mother. But most importantly, you have the most beautiful and loyal heart of anyone I know. You are such a sensitive and caring soul. You know your mother and I love you and your sister deeply. We've always tried to give you the best of everything, but something was always missing, and no matter what, a cloud of unhappiness always surrounded you. I don't see that cloud over my child anymore, and it's because of Cleopatra."

"Now, Cleo, you are amazing. You are one of the most unselfish, loving and forgiving people I have ever met. I don't know if anyone here can understand what a man goes through when his daughter is in pain, and there is nothing he can do to help her. I was taught a man is supposed to protect his family, he is supposed to fix whatever is wrong, he is supposed to make everything all better. But there was absolutely nothing I could do to help Jacqueline. I don't think you have any idea, Cleopatra, of how many lives you have affected, how many you have saved. Just my grandchildren alone think you walk on water." He laughed. "I personally and for all of Jacqueline's family want to thank you for loving her, for loving Maya, for loving Amir. Welcome to the family. We love you back." He raised his glass.

Tears welled up in Cleopatra's eyes. "Are you crying?" Shawn asked Cleopatra, as she sniffled.

"Not if you aren't." Cleopatra wiped her face with her hand. She looked at Jacqueline who was wiping tears from her eyes. "You ok?" Cleopatra asked her.

"Yeah." She wiped her eyes with a napkin. "I think that's the sweetest thing he's ever said."

"Cleo." Racquel grabbed her. She had been dodging her all night.

"Yes, Racquel?" Cleopatra stared at the ground knowing what was coming. The same type of speech Racquel had given her for every accomplishment since her mother had passed away. "So, why didn't you bring my godchildren again?" Cleopatra asked her.

"I needed a break from all those kids and that man." She joked. "Seriously, I just wanted to say congratulations to you. Tomorrow is the big day. She is a good woman. And she does love the hell out of you, unconditionally. And I know she is going to take such good care of you. That's all that matters to me." Cleopatra smiled. "Your mother is looking down on you,

you know this." Cleopatra nodded her head. "She's proud of you. She was always so proud of you."

"You really have to do this to me tonight, Racquel?" Cleopatra's eyes were getting misty again, and her head started to hurt as she tried not to cry.

"Ok. Ok. I'll stop, but I have something for you." She waved Jacqueline and Shawn over, motioning them to bring the garment bag Shawn was holding.

"What are you doing with my tux? If you got my tux dirty, I'll kill you," Cleopatra said.

Shawn unzipped the bag half way. "Look inside at the lining."

Cleopatra unbuttoned the jacket and opened it and sewn inside and over the pocket was her favorite picture of her mother. Tears flowed from her eyes. She stepped back from the jacket and told Shawn to close it up. She covered her face with both hands and wiped the tears away. "Thank you, thank you, Racquel. I love it."

◉ ◉ ◉

"So, I guess I will see you later." Cleopatra kissed Jacqueline in the hallway outside of their suite.

"Definitely." Jacqueline tugged on Cleopatra's shirt.

"And there is no chance of your letting me sleep with you tonight?"

"No. We wouldn't be sleeping, that's why you have your own room tonight." She handed Cleopatra her key card. "The next time we meet, I'll be walking down the aisle to you, about to become your wife." Jacqueline kissed her goodnight.

She watched Cleopatra walk to her door at the opposite end of the hall. "Call me before you go to sleep."

"I will."

"I love you." She watched Cleopatra go into her room.

"Love you too, baby."

WEDDING DAY: I'M ALL YOURS

Shawn whispered to Cleopatra. "You know what you're doing, right?"

"Yeah. I want this more than anything."

"All right, that's what I wanted to hear." Shawn slapped her on the back.

The start of the sunset ceremony was moments away. Cleopatra paced back and forth in one of the chapel's small back rooms. The intimate sanctuary with views of the Pacific Ocean was filled to capacity with sixty of their closest friends and family.

"Mama, what if we fall?" Amir and Maya asked Cleopatra.

"I don't think you will, baby. But if you do just get up and keep walking."

Cleopatra prayed they didn't fall. She straightened Amir's violet ascot and fixed Maya's curls that were starting to fly all over her head as she twirled around in order to make her poufy

301

dress fly up. "Don't show everyone your stuff, sweetie," Cleopatra said to her as she combed her hair and put every curl back into place.

"We can't wait for you to marry Mommy," Maya said. "We are going to be a family." She gave Cleopatra a big hug.

"I can't wait either sweetie."

"Jacqueline's limousine just pulled up." Robin ran in and grabbed the kids and Shawn.

"Look at the hotness." Shawn kissed Robin. They all stopped and looked at Robin, who wore a violet strapless chiffon gown with a beaded bodice. The soft flowing chiffon created a long and lean silhouette as it gracefully draped from her waist to the floor. Her hair flowed freely over her shoulders and was adorned with a purple rose pinned next to her left ear.

"You two look amazing," Robin said to Cleopatra and Shawn.

"Yeah, we do, don't we?" Shawn said, posing back-to-back with Cleopatra in their white Armani tuxedos.

While Shawn wore violet accessories to match Robin, Cleopatra was decked out in nothing but white, except for the single purple rose boutonniere pinned to the satin peak lapel of her two-button single breasted tux. Underneath she wore all white satin, a slim fit Victorian Edwardian dress shirt, a four-button vest, an ascot, with a pocket square to top it all off.

"What are those?" Robin pointed to Cleopatra's shoes.

"They are hot, right?" Cleopatra pulled up her pants legs to display her purple and white alligator wing tips shoes.

"Hot is one word for them," Robin laughed.

The wedding march started, and Cleopatra and Shawn hugged for a moment. "Let's do this, Cleo." Shawn punched Cleopatra in the arm.

"I'm all over it." Cleopatra smiled. She went to get Moms from her dressing room next door.

"You look gorgeous, Moms," Cleopatra said when Jacqueline's mother answered the door. She looked stunning in her violet wrapped chiffon gown. Crisp pleats shaped the bodice and clung to her small waist. The gown's off-centered wrapping led to a floaty ruffle, partially concealing an off-center slit. "Watch out now!" Cleopatra teased her when Moms modeled the dress and stuck her leg out from the split. "Pops will be all over that later, I'm sure." Cleopatra joked.

"Ah, sweetheart. You have so much to learn. He's already been all over it." She dabbed the corners of her mouth with her index finger.

"Ewww…uhm…ok." Cleopatra face flushed with embarrassment.

Moms straightened out Cleopatra's ascot and checked to make sure the bun that she had put her locs up in was secure.

"You, my dear, look fabulously handsome."

She pinched Cleopatra's cheeks. "You are truly a beautiful human being. You take such good care of my baby and her babies. I wish you all the joy and happiness in the world. You come to me or her father if you ever need anything. We are your family now. I love you." She hugged Cleopatra.

"I love you too, Moms. Don't make me cry." Cleopatra hugged her back.

"Let's go." Robin waved them down the hall.

All of their friends and Jacqueline's family rose and applauded when Cleopatra and Moms walked down the aisle arm and arm. After kissing her on the cheek, Cleopatra escorted her to her seat.

Cleopatra greeted the minister as she took her place on the right side of the altar. Minister Kalani was the only African American lesbian minister in Maui. She took joy in the opportunity to preside over Cleopatra and Jacqueline's nuptials as she didn't come in contact with many black lesbians on the island. The lanky minister looked like a stretched-out version of Shawn, Cleopatra thought, with her strong masculine features, and her freshly lined caesar haircut. Minister Kalani took a moment to speak with Cleopatra.

"I just spoke to Jacqueline briefly outside. She is such a beautiful bride. She's loves you so much. You are truly blessed."

"I definitely am. I have an angel watching over me." Cleopatra patted her breast pocket where the picture of her mother lay snug in the lining over her heart.

Moments later the chapel doors opened. Robin eased down the aisle on Shawn's arm. She stood on the other side of the alter as Shawn took her position behind Cleopatra. Then Amir ran toward them in his little white tux, holding on to the ring pillow for dear life. Maya followed close behind in her purple ruffled flower girl dress. Instead of sprinkling the flowers delicately on the ground behind Amir, she thought it was much more fun to ping the guests in the head with orchid petals. Everyone thought it was adorable as Maya made her way down the aisle bestowing the flowers on any given person's free and willing lap. There was a pause and the doors closed shut again. A moment later, which felt like a lifetime to Cleopatra, they reopened. The guests rose to their feet and turned around. Jacqueline appeared alongside her father.

Cleopatra took a long exhale and moved backward to lean on Shawn. The entire chapel gasped at the sight of her gorgeous bride-to-be.

"Wow, Cleo. That's your wife right there," Shawn whispered in her ear, and pushed her back on her feet. Jacqueline had always been more beautiful than Cleopatra's words could express but this day, her beauty, Cleopatra thought, was far beyond indescribable.

She smiled wide knowing Jacqueline was wearing her dream wedding dress, the Vera Wang ball gown that she wouldn't let her see until this very moment. The strapless fit and flare gown with its draped bodice and hand-cut bias flange skirt spiraled down to the floor. It hugged Jacqueline's curves and followed the motion of her hips. The dress's architecture was dramatic yet feminine. It was made of a delicate white sheer fabric layered over satin, and the cathedral-length train flowed effortlessly from her waist. The asymmetrically beaded bodice that pushed Jacqueline's glistening breasts up and out provided a balanced, streamlined contrast to the bottom of the gown that looked like a calla lily in full bloom.

Cleopatra could only pull her eyes off her cleavage to look at the split that went up her right leg exposing her thigh. She was as mesmerized by Jacqueline as she was on the first day they met.

Her hair was in an elegant half updo. The front was pinned up with Swarovski crystal embellished floral hair combs that matched the beading on her dress. The back of her hair flowed down naturally over her bare shoulders. Jacqueline's right arm held tight to her father, who looked striking in his own white tuxedo as he escorted his firstborn down the aisle. In her other arm she cradled her bouquet, a stunning arrangement of eggplant calla lilies and purple fringed tulips.

Jacqueline smiled as she walked toward Cleopatra and their eyes met. Once they came to the altar, Jacqueline handed her bouquet to Robin, and Pops turned, kissed her and ceremonially handed her over to Cleopatra.

Jacqueline's skin was dewy and glowing. Her makeup was flawless, her lips soft and natural with a subtle currant-colored gloss. Cleopatra saw a light in her eyes, a happiness like she'd never seen before.

"You are so beautiful," Cleopatra said softly.

"You are so fine, baby. Those gators are hot." Jacqueline winked at her.

"Ooh. All of your back is out too? I'm going to tear that up." Cleopatra got excited as she brushed her back with her fingers and Jacqueline shivered at her touch.

"You may all be seated," Minister Kalani said. "Jacqueline, Cleopatra. Please face each other." They turned and looked into each other's eyes as they held hands. "Friends and family, we are gathered this evening in celebration of an extraordinarily special love, the love between Jacqueline and Cleopatra. We have been invited to share in this most momentous time in their lives because they have decided to live their lives together forever. Cleopatra and Jacqueline, the vows you are about to take are not to be taken without careful thought. In them you are committing yourselves exclusively to one another for as long as you both shall live. This love is not to ever be diminished and it is only to be dissolved by death." Jacqueline squeezed Cleopatra's hand and winked at her.

"They've written their own vows of love that they wish to express to one another. Cleopatra." The minister motioned to her. Cleopatra paused briefly and cleared her throat.

Jacqueline shook her head. "You forgot to write your vows, didn't you?" Jacqueline whispered to her. Cleopatra shrugged her shoulders.

"Jacqueline, sweetheart." Cleopatra paused again. She cleared her throat and gazed into her eyes.

"I'm going to cut you," Jacqueline mouthed to Cleopatra.

Cleopatra cleared her throat again. "I used to be afraid of falling in love, of giving my heart away. But from the first time I laid eyes on you, I loved you. You've been my entire world ever since. My air. You have renewed my life, and today I join my life with yours. I, Cleopatra, choose you, Jacqueline, and Maya and Amir, to be my family." Cleopatra waved to them sitting in the first pew. "I promise to love, honor and respect you, and to provide for you to the best of my ability. I promise to make our home a haven, where trust, love, and laughter are always abundant. I pledge to grow in my love for you. I pledge to nurture our love, for loving you nurtures my soul. To know you is to know love. You are the one who completes me. I see your love for me in your eyes, and I see what true love is. I promise to support your growth and share the fullness of myself." She winked at Jacqueline. "I promise to honor you by being open to all the expressions of your inner self. Above all, I promise to be true to you and true to myself so that we may grow in our love. I can't wait to start our lives together, as one lifetime with you could never be enough. I will always support you and our family and our relationship, through the good times and the bad. I promise to love you all the days of my life. I love you." Cleopatra blew a kiss at Jacqueline. "Gotcha."

Tears flowed down Jacqueline's face. She fanned her eyes in an attempt to stop crying.

"Jacqueline?" The minister said softly. Jacqueline paused to get her composure.

"I'm going to get you for that." She whispered to Cleopatra. She cleared her throat and took a deep breath. "I could live a thousand years, tell you every day I love you, and I could still never express just how much. You were once a dream, then you became a desire that I prayed for before I ever knew you, and now you, the woman I never thought existed, holds my heart in the palms of your hands. As my best friend, my lover, my soul mate. I give myself in whole to you as your wife. I vow to listen to you and to keep an open mind, sacrificing my pride to be your strength, your joy, and your air. Whatever lies ahead, good or bad, great or horrible, we will face together. But if we look to each other first, we will always see a friend. Look to me for all the days to come; today I take my place as your wife. You are the one who gives me breath. While I stand here I find myself thinking of a thousand different things that make me the luckiest person to have ever walked the face of this earth. You are in my every thought. You have taken your unconditional love and added trust, respect, compassion, desire and so much more. The result of our endeavors and the intensity of our passion is what fairy tales are made of. You have touched my heart. You've given me the power, I am now the light. I give you my love, my protection, my support, my children, my life…Unconditionally and forever. I love you." Jacqueline was surprised when a tear streamed down Cleopatra's cheek.

"Cleopatra, please hold Jacqueline's hands, palms up, in yours where you may see the gift that they are to you." The minister said. "These are the hands of your best friend, holding yours on your wedding day, as you pledge your love and commitment to each other for all the days of your life. These are the hands that will massage tension from your neck and back in the evenings after you've both had a long hard day."

Jacqueline smiled and said, "Oh yeah." And everyone laughed, including the minister. "Sorry, inside thought," Jacqueline apologized. But she was smiling.

The minister continued. "These are the hands that will hold you tight as you struggle through difficult times. These hands will comfort you when you are sick, and console you when you are grieving. These are the hands that will passionately love you and cherish you through the years and for a lifetime. These are the hands that will give you support as you are encouraged to follow your dreams. Together, everything you wish for can be realized."

"The exchange of rings, please." The minister gestured to Amir. He ran over and held up the pillow with their rings high over his head.

Cleopatra took the ring from Amir, and held it tight in her hand.

"Jacqueline, I give you this ring as a symbol of our vows, and with all that I am, and all that I have, I honor you."

"Jacqueline, do you take Cleopatra as your lawfully wedded wife?"

"I do." She smiled and stuck out her finger.

"With this ring, I thee wed." Cleopatra slid on her wedding band.

Jacqueline took Cleopatra's ring from Amir. "Cleopatra, I give you this ring as a symbol of our vows, and with all that I am, and all that I have, I honor you."

"Cleopatra, do you take Jacqueline as your lawfully wedded wife?"

"I do." Cleopatra grinned from ear to ear.

"With this ring, I thee wed." Jacqueline slid the ring on her finger.

"Inasmuch as you have each pledged to the other your lifelong commitment, love and devotion, I now pronounce you wife and wife. Jacqueline, Cleopatra, you may kiss your bride!"

They kissed long and hard as the chapel burst into applause.

"Ladies and gentlemen, I present to you Cleopatra and Jacqueline Tripp-Giovanni."

◉ ◉ ◉

They had eaten and partied at the reception for a few hours. Jacqueline was feeding her wife red velvet wedding cake with her fingers. "So are you ready to get out of here, or what?" Jacqueline whispered in Cleopatra's ear.

"And you call me antisocial?" Cleopatra teased. "We're supposed to stay at least until midnight when the ball drops. Did you forget it's New Year's Eve?"

"Actually, I kind of did." She laughed. "But how long do you expect me to last, with you sucking cake off of my fingers?" Jacqueline kissed her.

Maya and Amir had fallen asleep in the middle of the reception and Jacqueline's mom and dad decided to turn in, and take the kids with them. They all needed to get some rest before their flight home the next morning. Jacqueline, Cleopatra, Robin and Shawn stayed with the rest of the guests until the ball dropped and watched the fireworks on the beach. About ten minutes into the New Year, Jacqueline grabbed Cleopatra's hand and they disappeared from the party.

Jacqueline required her new wife's presence in their honeymoon suite. Cleopatra lit candles around their bedroom as she watched her. "You are so fucking sexy in that tuxedo. I almost hate for you to take it off."

Cleopatra smiled at her. "I can leave it on if you want."

"Oh no. I want you butt ass naked and wet just like the day you were born." She licked her lips.

Cleopatra scrunched her face in surprise. "Ooh, you so nasty."

"I miss your body." Cleopatra came over to Jacqueline and wrapped her arms around her. "Are you tired?" Jacqueline asked her as she is massaged her neck.

"Not really. You?"

"Not on my wedding night, I'm not." She took off Cleopatra's tuxedo jacket and pressed her fingers into her satin shirt and pulled her toward the bed.

"I want you to do everything to me tonight. I'm your wife now, nothing is off limits. I want to experience *everything* with you."

"What are you talking about?"

"Taking it to the next level." She kissed Cleopatra.

Cleopatra ran her hand up and down her dress and inside the slit exposing her thigh.

"Are you ready to come out of this dress?"

"I am so ready." Jacqueline turned around.

Cleopatra stood behind her and unzipped her gown, kissing her back along the way.

"Your lips feel so good." She moaned as the dress fell to the floor. Jacqueline stepped out the gown and Cleopatra carried it over to the chaise longue where she carefully laid it out flat. She turned around and saw her bride waiting for her at the end of the bed, wearing a white lace bra and garter belt with matching thigh highs and a g-string.

"Damn baby." Cleopatra nodded her head. "Now that is sexy."

"And it's all yours." Jacqueline grabbed Cleopatra and pulled her to the bed. She laid her down and stripped Cleopatra naked. Starting with her lips, Jacqueline kissed her way down Cleopatra's body. She lowered herself between Cleopatra's legs and spread her thighs.

"Ooh my God." Jacqueline's exclamation broke the trance Cleopatra was in.

"Do you like it?"

"When did you get this?" She lifted her head for a closer inspection of the tattoo on the inside of Cleopatra's right thigh.

Cleopatra rose up on her elbows to look at Jacqueline. "I got it two weeks ago. I've been trying to hide it all this time."

This and my heart belong to Jacqueline.

"I love it, it's beautiful," Jacqueline said, kissing it.

"That's one of my wedding presents to you." Cleopatra caressed her face as Jacqueline kissed the tattoo again, fascinated by it.

"You just never stop showing me how much you love me."

"And I never will." Cleopatra pulled her close. "So, there is something else I want to give you." She caressed the side of Jacqueline's cheek as she continued to study the tattoo. "I know how important it is to you, so, if you will let me, I want to send you back to grad school. You can quit work. I can pay your tuition and take care of the family."

Jacqueline was silent.

"Did you hear me?" Cleopatra waved her hand in front of her face.

"I don't know what to say." Jacqueline pressed her fingertips to her eyes.

"How about *yes*? Baby, are you about to cry?"

"How about you are incredible? You are so good to me. Yes baby, I want to go back to school!"

"But this is all on one condition." Cleopatra said. "School *can not*, I repeat, *can not* cut into my sex."

"Very funny. Nothing is going to cut into our sex, ever."

Jacqueline kissed her. She wanted Cleopatra to fill her up, and watched with an animalistic look in her eyes as Cleopatra put on her strap. Cleopatra crawled on top of her and placed light kisses all over her body. Jacqueline whispered in her ear.

"Every time we make love it feels like the first time. And every single time I want you just as bad as that first night." She yearned to be fucked by her new wife and in an instant Cleopatra was inside of her, sucking her tongue into her mouth while she pumped her pussy slow, moving her ass the way Jacqueline loved it. Their bodies fell into a rhythm as Cleopatra stroked Jacqueline deep and gently. Her back arched, and her body trembled under Cleopatra's thrusts as she clawed at her ass. Cleopatra flipped over and watched Jacqueline ride her as her body went into convulsions.

"Remember, I said I want you to do *everything* to me," Jacqueline reminded Cleopatra as she lay across her chest.

"Uh hmm…."

"There is something we've never done before. Something no one else has had. I want to give that to you tonight." She stroked Cleopatra's dick in her hand.

"You're not talking about….are you sure?" Cleopatra asked, excited. "You said never, ever."

"That was a long time ago. Every part of my body is yours now. I can't deny my wife, now can I?" Jacqueline rolled onto her back and pulled Cleopatra on top of her. She spread her legs wide inviting her in.

"Do it, baby. You know you want to. You want to take it as much as I want to give it to you." She took Cleopatra's hand. "My ass wants to try new things." She rubbed Cleopatra's fingers along her hole. Isn't that tight?" she gasped. "You don't want to get inside of that?" Jacqueline moaned and bucked her hips upward. Cleopatra rimmed her ass as she struggled to contain the excitement that had quickly welled up between her legs. She buried her face in Jacqueline's pussy, licking her clit slow before making a trail back down to her hole. She jabbed her tongue into her ass and sent Jacqueline over the edge.

Jacqueline spread her ass wide so Cleopatra could tongue-fuck her some more. Cleopatra rammed her tongue in as deep as it would go. Jacqueline came hard as Cleopatra's tongue invaded her tight hole.

Jacqueline squirted a blob of lube into Cleopatra's hand. Cleopatra took her middle finger and played with her hole as Jacqueline grinded against the bed. She eased her slick finger inside of her. Jacqueline screamed and banged her hand on the bed. Her ass tensed up around Cleopatra's finger.

"Relax." Cleopatra teased her clit with her other hand.

Slowly and gently Cleopatra worked her finger deeper, and Jacqueline opened up for her. She pounded on the bed and cursed into the pillow. Cleopatra felt her insides throb as her ass locked in on her finger.

"Don't stop," she moaned as Cleopatra slid her finger in and out of her. "That's so good." Her ass had loosened up. The pain had turned into pleasure and her body jerked.

"I want it." Jacqueline popped the top off of the lube and poured it on her pussy, letting it run down into her ass. She poured the rest of the bottle on Cleopatra's dick; it dripped down her legs and drenched the bed. She jacked Cleopatra's cock hard.

"You really do want it, don't you?" Cleopatra smiled.

"No matter what I say, don't stop." Jacqueline kissed her before rolling over on her stomach. She got up on her hands and knees.

"Take it." Jacqueline arched her back and closed her eyes. Cleopatra rubbed the head of her cock against Jacqueline's hole. She was excited but was planning to take her time and move as slow as her body would allow. But Jacqueline pushed back on her and Cleopatra's dick popped into her ass. Jacqueline screamed as Cleopatra's thickness spread her open and filled her up.

"Don't move," Jacqueline managed to whisper. "It's like fire." She gasped.

"Breathe, baby. Relax." Cleopatra caressed Jacqueline's ass and rubbed her back. Cleopatra was gentle as she stroked her slow and slid deeper until she got all of her dick inside of her. Jacqueline pushed back, surprising Cleopatra, grunting with each thrust.

"Damn!" Cleopatra swore softly, letting Jacqueline control the movements. Cleopatra's clit thumped harder each time Jacqueline slid back taking in all of her dick.

"I can feel every inch," Jacqueline moaned. "That's all yours baby. You need to take it." Jacqueline threw her head back.

"That's so tight." Cleopatra pushed into Jacqueline as she popped her hips. Watching Jacqueline's tight ass swallow her thickness threatened her control. She yanked Jacqueline by her hair and sped up her strokes, as she watched her dick disappearing into Jacqueline's taut hole. Cleopatra had never seen Jacqueline cum so hard and for so long.......her pussy thumped as their strokes grew slower. Both of their bodies convulsed and exploded. Still inside of her, Cleopatra lay on Jacqueline's back.

"You ok, baby?" Cleopatra asked her bride.

"I'm all yours."

NO MORE DRAMA

"Damn." Cleopatra fumbled to pick up her cell phone. "Hello."

"What's up?" Shawn yelled.

"What newlyweds do," she said, as she watched Jacqueline pull off her top.

"Y'all didn't get enough on the honeymoon?" The clock had struck midnight, the kids were sound asleep, and Cleopatra sat on the couch while the fireplace crackled with orange and blue flames. She watched Jacqueline unbutton her shirt, and kiss her stomach.

"Oooh."

"What was that?" Shawn asked.

"Sorry," Cleopatra said, as Jacqueline straddled her and undid her belt buckle.

"So how was the honeymoon?" Shawn asked.

"So good," Cleopatra said real soft into the phone, as Jacqueline trailed her lips across Cleopatra's neck.

"Uh…y'all fucking!" Shawn screamed. "Get the hell off the

phone."

Cleopatra hung up without a word to Shawn.

"You are so bad." Cleopatra looked up at Jacqueline.

"You want me to stop?" Jacqueline took off her bra and tossed it to the floor. She pulled Cleopatra into her breasts.

"Don't stop."

They had been back from their honeymoon almost a week and hadn't seen anyone or been anywhere. Jacqueline and the kids moved into the house, and Jacqueline and Cleopatra failed to keep their hands off of each other for any considerable amount of time. They stayed in and on each other constantly. Marriage had changed Jacqueline. She was totally uninhibited, even more than before. Marriage had secured her, and Cleopatra loved it. Every day they spent quality time with the kids and at night made love to the point of exhaustion. The next day they did it all over again. Perfection.

◉ ◉ ◉

"Y'all nasty, you know that, right?" Shawn grabbed Cleopatra and gave her a hug.

"We just got married." Cleopatra tried to defend herself and Jacqueline.

"Sex is supposed to stop after you get married." Robin laughed as she kissed her sister.

"That's not what your mama thinks," Jacqueline teased her sister.

"You two need a room," Shawn teased the newlyweds. Shawn and Robin had invited themselves over to Cleopatra's for dinner. They'd moved in together while Jacqueline and Cleopatra were on their honeymoon. They were officially committed, or on lockdown, as Shawn eloquently put it.

"Let me talk to you for a second." Shawn pulled Cleopatra away from their ladies and into the kitchen. "So how is married life?"

Cleopatra sat down at the island. "Beautiful, everything is

good, we are settling in."

"About time, you've been through some shit. Kenya too? I still wish you had told me everything she was up to." Shawn sat down next to her. "Wait – you fucked on this counter, didn't you?"

Cleopatra laughed. "Come on now. There is no flat surface in this house that hasn't been utilized. What are you going to do, stand outside?" She chuckled. "Anyway, I didn't tell you about Kenya because of your temper. The fewer people involved the better. That foolishness is all over with, anyway. Life is good now," Cleopatra said. "What about you? Got a spring in your step now that you're waking up next to your girl every morning, I see."

"Yeah, it's been good since Robin moved in."

"You'll be getting married before you know it."

"Slow down. I'm still trying to get used to this monogamous shit."

"Yeah. I seem to recall your version of settling down being two girls, not one. Don't mess this up, Shawn. Please don't mess up."

"So, I didn't want to bother you with this on your honeymoon. There have been some developments with my civil case." Shawn leaned back to make sure the coast was clear before she continued.

Cleopatra sighed. "What happened now?"

"I paid them off. Catherine is an amazing attorney. We have an iron-clad agreement. I won't have to deal with them again."

"How much?"

"You don't need that number in your head, no one does. But I got nothing now. Less than when my apartment burnt up. When was the last time we lived paycheck to paycheck? I don't even have money to pay our rent."

"Email me your landlord's info. I'll cover your rent until you get back on your feet. Do you have food in the house? You have cash on you?" Cleopatra felt her pants and pulled a wad from her front pocket.

"I can't let you do that," Shawn said, as Cleopatra put the

money in her hand.

"Oh yes you can, cause you ain't staying with me," Cleopatra said. "Just take it." She put the money in Shawn's hand.

"I'll pay you back for this, and my bail and attorney's fees, everything."

"I didn't ask for it back. It's not a loan."

"I'm giving you all your money even if I have to go back…"

"Even if what? Go back to what?" Cleopatra lowered her voice to a whisper. "We are done with bullshit." Cleopatra glared at Shawn. "Don't worry about the money. You want to repay me, for real? Stop doing stupid shit. That's just something we used to do because we didn't have a choice at the time. Money grew on trees then, but all of that isn't necessary anymore."

"It's not necessary for you anymore. But it's still what we do best. Why not get paid for it again?"

"That's not who I am anymore, or who I want to be. I have a family now, and you have Robin. Are you really trying to fuck that up?"

"Mama, look." The kids ran in to the kitchen to show Cleopatra a drawing they made. Amir jumped into Cleopatra's lap. They had been calling her Mama for a while, but it still shocked her each time. She really was their mama now, and partly responsible for their lives.

"Beautiful, baby, I'm going to put it on the refrigerator, so everyone can see it." She picked Amir up in one arm and stuck the drawing on the fridge with the other.

"That's nice! Thank you" Maya said. Amir was excited. "Love you, Mama." He wrapped his arms tight around Cleopatra's neck. Cleopatra adjusted the Scooby Doo slipper that was falling off of his foot.

"Love you too, baby."

Cleopatra looked at Shawn. "You ok?" Cleopatra asked her, as she put Amir down.

"Yeah. Yeah. I'm all right." She batted her eyes quickly.

"Are you about to cry?" Cleopatra teased her.

"Don't cry, Auntie Shawn." Amir tugged on her pants leg.

"I'm here." He put his hands on his hips and stood in his Superman stance. He whipped around his pajama cape in dramatic fashion.

"I'm ok, sweetie," she told Amir as she sniffled. "It's just hitting me, you do have a family now, and it's beautiful to see," she said to Cleopatra. "But I ain't about to cry about it or nothing. You know?"

"Uh huh." Cleopatra mocked her as she picked Maya up. "I know what you mean. It didn't hit me the first night we were together in this house. I didn't go into the ugly cry or nothing. So, I know what you mean." Cleopatra winked at her.

◻ ◻ ◻

A few days later Cleopatra ran into her next-door neighbor walking his dog.

"I was going to leave you a note," the wiry old gay man said as he cradled a shivering Chihuahua in his arms. "You had visitors earlier today. They stayed around for a while. They left not too long ago."

"Who was it?" Cleopatra asked, as she threw her hood over her head.

"I don't know. They drove up in a black Mercedes truck with tinted windows and only the chauffeur got out. He asked if I knew a Taylor Du Bois."

Cleopatra's heart dropped into her stomach. "Really?" She leaned against the wrought iron fence after nearly losing her balance.

"Yeah. I said I didn't know any Taylor. Then he showed me your picture. Is that some kind of nickname or something?"

"Or something." Cleopatra could see her breath in the frigid winter air.

"He asked when you would be back and your comings and goings. You know, personal shit."

"Thanks a lot." Cleopatra walked off down the street.

It just got real. Alexis was looking for her now. She had

failed to make an appearance after Kenya told her how Alexis had set her up, so why had she chosen now to contact her after all of this time? Cleopatra's awareness was heightened over the next few days but nothing happened. Every call, text and email she got, she expected to be from Alexis, but Cleopatra knew that wasn't really Alexis' style. Alexis liked to make memorable grand entrances. Cleopatra braced herself for the spectacle to come. Another week passed and still nothing. She forgot about Alexis, and got comfortable again. That all changed when Cleopatra came home alone one night and found Alexis sprawled across her bed, wearing a chinchilla fur coat with only a bra and panties on underneath.

"You scared the shit out of me!" Cleopatra yelled.

"I didn't mean to. I just wanted to surprise you." Alexis hopped up off of the bed. "Taylor, darling. I've missed you. I'm sorry, Cleopatra Taylor Du Bois Giovanni, I've missed you." She smirked at Cleopatra as she threw her arms around her and pressed her full breasts into her. "I love what you've done with the place. It's almost unrecognizable. The kids' room is precious." She inhaled the side of Cleopatra's neck. "You smell so good. And still fine as hell I see."

Alexis looked appetizing, Cleopatra thought. The years and all that money had been exceedingly kind to her. At any other time, Cleopatra would have had her way with the voluptuous, hazel eyed beauty.

"What are you doing here?" Cleopatra peeled out of Alexis's embrace.

"The bra and panties haven't clued you in?" She dropped the fur coat to the floor.

"You know that's never going to happen again, right? How did you get in my house without setting the alarm off?"

"My little secret." She winked at her and lay back down on the bed.

"I thought you moved to the West Coast for good?" Cleopatra stood over her.

"I miss New York and all the Taylors and Cleopatra's it has to offer." She looked at her watch. "My pilot is waiting on me, but I thought you'd want to thank me in person before I went back home."

"Thank you for what?"

"For getting rid of that pathetic Kenya. I mean, the bitch was really crazy. You do realize that? She wasn't going to leave you alone, she really wasn't. But now she's out of the picture, thanks to me." Alexis stood up and took a ceremonial bow.

"Don't lose those." Cleopatra pointed to her breasts that were threatening to emerge from her red lace bra.

"They must know you're in the building. Other parts of me know. Want to feel how wet I am?"

"No thanks." Cleopatra brushed off her offer. "You are proud of yourself. What you did to Kenya?"

"Ooh my dear, you have no idea. It was one of my better performances. Flawless, actually." She clapped her hands in the air. "Irie. How a Trinidadian can't tell a fake island accent is beyond me."

Cleopatra tried not to laugh. "What you did was wrong. It was cruel and manipulative and if Kenya hadn't been such a vengeful dumb ass I would probably feel sorry for her and be upset with you."

"But you aren't, are you?" Alexis smiled. "I left you out of it, didn't I? I operated on a need-to-know basis. All you needed to know was that she was no longer going to be a problem."

"So what do you want in return, Alexis?"

"The same as always, your happiness." She touched her heart. "I'm not here to make you do anything you don't want to do. Consider Kenya's extended hiatus a wedding present," she said, as she circled Cleopatra.

"Thanks. You are so generous."

"I still love you, Taylor. Sorry, *Cleopatra*. I'll wait until you come to your senses – or until I can't wait anymore. Whichever comes first." She caressed the side of Cleopatra's face and kissed her softly on the cheek, before attempting to kiss her on the mouth. Cleopatra pushed her away.

"What's with the cold reception? Don't tell me you're still mad at me? The last time I saw you, you slammed the door in my face. I should be upset with *you*," she said. "You remember that night?"

"Of course I do. That was a long time ago."

"I was about to leave my husband for you, give up everything, and I do mean millions and millions, and come out to the world… and I find out that you were fucking my best friend."

"I never asked you to leave your husband, Alexis. You created a fantasy relationship in your head. All we ever had was a business arrangement. You paid for companionship, and I supplied it. And I wasn't just fucking Woo – she was my girlfriend, we were in a relationship, and a serious one. By the way, any idea what happened to her? She vanished into thin air." Cleopatra looked at Alexis accusingly.

"Did she really? And if I did know anything, would it matter to you now, Mrs. Newlywed?"

"I guess not." Cleopatra laughed.

"Tell me one thing." Alexis started to put on her coat. "Do you still do that slow circular motion thing when you make love? That used to drive me crazy. So good. I've tried teaching my husband but, well, he's not you. Never will be, that's for sure."

"That's too bad. And yeah, I do."

"Does she make you happy?" Alexis asked.

"Extremely."

"Good. She better keep it up. She's lucky I didn't hurt her for breaking your heart twice."

Cleopatra learned long ago never to question how Alexis knew everything. They hadn't spoken or seen each other in years, and yet she knew about Kenya, too. No question her wealth came with tremendous power. But Cleopatra stopped worrying about her omnipotence a long time ago.

"If she hurts you again I won't be responsible for what happens to her."

"Really, Alexis? Let's not go there. You are not hurting anyone. I can take care of myself. I'm a big girl."

"Uh hmm... you sure are big." Alexis smiled. "On that note I have a car waiting. I'm going back to L.A. tonight." She buttoned up her fur.

"I have an idea. How about you stay there?" Cleopatra suggested.

"Your wish is my command." Alexis nodded her head.

"Thank you Alexis. You should probably use the back way." Cleopatra pointed toward the door.

"I remember. After all, this did used to be my house."

"Do me a favor. However you got in, can you not do that again? I have a family now, which you are well aware of."

"Cleopatra." Jacqueline called from downstairs.

"Out, now." Cleopatra shooed Alexis out the back stairway and wiped the sweat from her forehead.

Jacqueline found Cleopatra in the bedroom. "You didn't hear me calling you, baby?"

"Sorry baby." She hugged Jacqueline tight.

"I've missed you. I don't like being away from you all day," Jacqueline said.

"Me either. You dropped the kids off at Grandma's ok?"

"They're good." Jacqueline kissed her hard as she pulled Cleopatra's sweater off over her head.

"What's gotten into you?" Cleopatra asked. "I'm not complaining, but *damn*."

"This is the first night we've been alone with no kids since the honeymoon. I want to make love in every room. I get to scream at the top of my lungs again." She unbuckled Cleopatra's belt.

"I kind of like it when you have to bite the pillow." Cleopatra laughed. "Damn. I almost feel dirty," Cleopatra said. "Almost." She watched Jacqueline yank her pants off.

Cleopatra peeked out of the window as she closed the blinds. She saw Alexis walk out the front of the house, but she didn't get into any waiting car. She crossed the street and went into Mandisa's house.

Fuck.

Jacqueline had stripped naked and slid in to bed. "Baby. Come." She reached out for her. Cleopatra pulled the curtains closed and exhaled deeply as she slipped into bed and on top of Jacqueline.

"Baby, listen to me." Cleopatra looked down at Jacqueline. "I love you more than anything in this world. Nothing and no one will ever come between us."

"I love you baby. I'm yours forever." Jacqueline said. "No more drama?"

"No more." Cleopatra trailed her tongue across Jacqueline's bottom lip and kissed her neck as she pressed her body hard against Jacqueline's.

"Baby, you hear that?" Jacqueline whispered.

"What?" Cleopatra strained her ears.

"Nothing. Just you and me. Finally."

ABOUT THE AUTHOR
MEET TASHA C. MILLER

TASHA C. MILLER'S FICTION

has appeared in *Longing, Lust, and Love: Black Lesbian Stories* and *Saints & Sinners 2011: New Fiction From the Festival*. Miller currently splits her time between Cambridge, MA and Brooklyn, NY. This is her first novel. Visit her at www.tashacmiller.com.

tashacmiller.com   **email Tasha**   **send a tweet**